PRAISE FOR JOHN MCF...

DIRTY SWEET

"McFetridge is an author to watch. He has a great eye for detail, and Toronto has never looked seedier." — *Globe and Mail*

"McFetridge combines a tough and gritty story populated by engagingly seedy characters . . . with an effective use of a setting, Toronto." —*Booklist*

"The dubious fun is in the dialogue and details of a very entertaining and libidinous local debut." — *Toronto Star*

"A sexy, fast-paced story about ambition, greed, and motorcycle gangs." — *Hour*

"If more people wrote the kind of clean-as-a-whistle, no-fat prose McFetridge does, this reviewer would finish a lot more of their books." — *National Post*

"McFetridge describes a Toronto of opportunists, seedy deals, and double-crosses not unlike Elmore Leonard's Detroit or James Ellroy's Los Angeles, but his books are distinctly rooted in his home city's rhythms and flavours." — *Quill & Quire*

EVERYBODY KNOWS THIS IS NOWHERE

"Amid the busy plot, McFetridge does a good job depicting a crime-ridden Toronto (a.k.a. the Big Smoke) that resembles the wide-open Chicago of Prohibition days with corrupt cops, gang warfare, and flourishing prostitution." — *Publishers Weekly*

"This is McFetridge's second novel, and once again, Toronto is a leading character in a fine crime novel. The city's sprawling growth, its ethnic diversity, and its 'almost American' focus on money are all ongoing motifs that enrich a novel already rich in on-the-make immigrants, edgy cops, and charming, devious women. Sex. Dope. Immigration. Gang war. Filmmaking. In McFetridge's hands, Toronto might as well be the new L.A. of crime fiction." — *Booklist*

"An absorbingly complex tale that combines the concerns of troubled cops with accounts from an underworld of bikers, the Mafia, sex-trade workers and ethnic-based gangs." — *London Free Press*

SWAP

"[*Swap*] grabs you by the throat and squeezes until you agree to read just one page, just one more page." — *Quill & Quire*

"In just three novels . . . McFetridge has demonstrated gifts that put him in Elmore Leonard territory as a writer, and make Toronto as gritty and fascinating as Leonard's Detroit. . . . [McFetridge] is a class act, and he's creating fictional classics — maybe even that great urban literature of Toronto the critics now and then long for." — *London Free Press*

TUMBLIN' DICE

"He's the guy with just the right balance of grit, humour, and rock'n'roll knowledge to do the job." — *Toronto Star*

"Dialogue that sizzles and sparks through the pages, providing its own music, naturally of the hard-rocking kind." — *Toronto Sun*

"McFetridge is Canada's best kept crime fiction secret, and we think it's a good time for the rest of the world to take notice."
— *Crime Fiction Lover*

"Each of John McFetridge's . . . novels has a rhythm to them, mixing taut dialogue, spare description, and a dark sensibility with the cool calm of a master bass player." — *National Post*

"John McFetridge is — or should be — a star in the world of crime fiction." — *London Free Press*

"Like [Elmore] Leonard, McFetridge is able to convincingly portray flawed figures on both sides of the law." — *Publishers Weekly*

BLACK ROCK

BLACK ROCK

AN EDDIE DOUGHERTY MYSTERY

JOHN McFETRIDGE

ECW PRESS

Published by ECW Press
2120 Queen Street East, Suite 200, Toronto, Ontario, Canada, M4E 1E2
416-694-3348, info@ecwpress.com

LIBRARY AND ARCHIVES CANADA CATALOGUING IN PUBLICATION

McFetridge, John, 1959-, author
Black rock : an Eddie Dougherty mystery / John McFetridge.

Issued in print and electronic formats.
ISBN 978-1-55022-975-2 (pbk)
ISBN 978-1-77090-299-2 (PDF)
ISBN 978-1-77090-489-7 (epub)

I. Title.

PS8575.F48B53 2014   C813'.6   C2013-907773-1
C2013-907774-X

Cover design: Cyanotype
Cover images: two armed soldiers, Dec 3, 1970
    © *Montreal Gazette*/CP Images
    Dead girl on floor © Stokkete/Shutterstock

Back cover image: Gangster in car © sint/
    Shutterstock
Type: Rachel Ironstone
Printing: Friesens 1 2 3 4 5
Printed and bound in Canada

The publication of *Black Rock* has been generously supported by the Canada Council for the Arts
which last year invested $157 million to bring the arts to Canadians throughout the country, and by
the Ontario Arts Council (OAC), an agency of the Government of Ontario, which last year funded
1,681 individual artists and 1,125 organizations in 216 communities across Ontario for a total of
$52.8 million. We also acknowledge the financial support of the Government of Canada through the
Canada Book Fund for our publishing activities, and the contribution of the Government of Ontario
through the Ontario Book Publishing Tax Credit and the Ontario Media Development Corporation.

For my sister Susan
who was there

&

For Laurie, always

PART ONE

CHAPTER
ONE

Constable Eddie Dougherty climbed up the ironwork of the Victoria Bridge and said to his partner standing by the radio car, "Yeah, *c'est une bombe.*"

They were halfway between the island of Montreal and the South Shore, cars slowing down but still managing to get past in the single lane, and Gauthier said, "*Vachon arrive,*" as the unmarked black station wagon pulled up behind the radio car and Gilles Vachon and Robert Meloche got out.

The bomb squad.

Dougherty walked over the railway tracks in the middle of the bridge and showed Vachon the blue Expo 67 flight bag wedged between one of the stone piers and an iron truss.

"*Tabarnak,*" Meloche said, and Vachon nodded and looked from the flight bag to Dougherty's badge and name tag and then, in English, said, "Did you hear anything?"

"Just the river."

Vachon said, "Of course." Twenty feet below the bridge the St. Lawrence flowed by. "This bridge is over a hundred years old," Vachon said. "It would be a shame to lose it."

Dougherty didn't know what to say: he'd only been a cop two years, practically still a rookie, and Vachon was already a legend, he'd dismantled so many bombs.

"It was the longest bridge in the world when it was built, almost two miles. Just for trains then, of course," Vachon said. "These lanes were added later." He stomped on the metal grated surface the cars drove on.

Meloche said, "Come on," and started climbing down the ironwork.

Vachon nodded, looked down at the bag and then back to Dougherty and said, "You didn't get too close, did you?"

Dougherty said no, but now he was feeling too close. A bag stuffed with dynamite and the bomb squad turns out to be two guys in overalls.

Vachon reached down and took something out of a leather pouch on his belt. Dougherty figured it must be some kind of fancy bomb squad tool, then saw it was a pair of nail clippers.

"Snips the wires," Vachon said and followed Meloche until they were standing on the concrete pier, face-to-face with the blue bag.

Dougherty followed as far as he could, holding onto

a truss and watching as the two-man squad who'd dismantled almost a hundred of these dynamite bombs in the last year talked over what to do. The flight bag was zipper-down, wedged in fairly tight.

From up top Gauthier yelled, "What are you doing, come up here," speaking English, but Dougherty didn't say anything. He watched Vachon and Meloche waving their hands and talking but couldn't hear what they were saying over the rushing water below.

After a few minutes Meloche shrugged and pushed one end of the bag until it came loose and fell into the river. It disappeared in the fast-moving current. And then the two bomb squad guys climbed back up the ironwork to the railway tracks.

Dougherty said, "What the hell?" and Vachon said, "It's gone now."

"Yeah, but now there's a bomb in the river."

"You don't know that," Meloche said, "could be a bag of doughnuts," and he climbed up past Dougherty.

Vachon said, "The dynamite is ruined. In any case, it's safe now."

"What are you going to say in your report?"

"What report?" Vachon walked to the unmarked station wagon, stood by the passenger door and said, "If we report it, it gets in the press. Why give these bastards what they want?"

Dougherty said, "Yeah, I guess," and Vachon smiled and got into the passenger seat and Meloche drove towards the South Shore to turn around and head back onto the island of Montreal.

Dougherty watched them go and then Gauthier, who'd been a cop longer than Dougherty'd been alive, said, "Come on, that's enough action for me, I need a drink," and got into the squad car.

The action was why Dougherty had joined the police.

It was 1967, the Summer of Love. Montreal had thrown a party and invited the world. Dougherty'd been out of high school a couple of years with no plan and no direction, kicking around construction sites and fighting with his father, who had never finished high school himself. He'd finally given up on Dougherty going to McGill but was still trying to talk him into night classes at Sir George Williams, still bent on him getting that all-important piece of paper that would set him up for life.

But there was no way Dougherty could sit in another classroom, listen to more boring crap just so he could sit in an office, watch the world through a window. He said to his father, "When you were my age you'd already been in the navy fighting the war for years, in the north Atlantic. You'd dropped depth charges on U-boats and had corvettes torpedoed out from under you. You were already a Chief Petty Officer."

"You want to join the navy?" his father said, and Dougherty said, "No, I don't want to join the navy."

"So what do you want to do?"

Dougherty joined the police force.

He told his father he wanted to help people and make a difference, do something productive with his life. His father, sitting at the kitchen table, smoking a Player's Plain and drinking a rum and Pepsi, said, "Great, just what the world needs, another Irish cop," and closed the *Gazette* he was reading. There was no way Dougherty could tell him he really joined because when he was working construction on the American pavilion, the big geodesic dome everybody said the Yanks were just going to roll back home when Expo was over, he saw a bunch of cops race through traffic on the Jacques Cartier bridge and he wanted to drive fast like that.

He wanted to get in on the action.

Picked up an application form at police headquarters on Bonsecours Street and carried it around in his pocket for a week, not saying anything to anyone. When he finally handed it in the desk sergeant said, "We don't get many English anymore."

Dougherty said, "My mother's French," and the desk sergeant looked at the form and said, "Dog-eh-dee?"

"Doe-er-dee."

The Summer of Love ended and the year of the revolution started. It was all over the world; Paris was shut down, tanks rolled into Prague, riots in Mexico and New York and Washington, Martin Luther King and Robert Kennedy assassinated.

Dougherty was on the front lines in Montreal, hit in the head with a bottle in the Saint-Jean-Baptiste parade riot and it just got worse when every dignitary left the reviewing stand, diving for cover, except Pierre Trudeau, who stood there giving the rioters the finger. Dougherty was in the middle of it with the rest of the cops, swinging his nightstick and wishing the prime minister would just get the hell out of there, but the next day the guy won the federal election.

7

More than fifty bombs were planted in Montreal in 1968 and they were different than the first wave of bombs in '63, the ones in mailboxes, and the ones in

'66 that were mostly in the offices of businesses where the workers were on strike. In '68 the bombs were a lot more powerful — five, ten sticks of dynamite wired to cheap alarm clocks and put in public buildings: post offices, shopping centres, army recruiting offices, banks. Someone always called in the location a few minutes before the bomb was set to go off. Dougherty got his wish to drive fast through city streets.

It was always a little tense clearing all the people out of the building and waiting for the bomb squad. Dougherty's partner, Gauthier, was counting the days to retirement and had no problem saying, "You want action, it's all yours," and staying out of the way. Afterwards there were always a few beers and a lot of cops not admitting it was actually kind of fun.

Then on January 1, 1969, two bombs exploded: one at city hall and one at a federal Manpower office downtown. Middle of the night, no one was hurt, but no warning calls were made. It was a new year and a new era. A half dozen more bombs went off around the city in January. In February, Dougherty got to work another riot, this one at Sir George Williams University, de Maisonneuve Street covered in a million computer punch cards and the four hundred students who'd been occupying the Henry F. Hall Building for a week driven out when the place caught fire.

8   Two days later a bomb went off in the Montreal Stock Exchange in Place Victoria and blew out the southwest wall. Dougherty and Gauthier were among the first radio cars on the scene, Dougherty driving right up onto Victoria Square in time to see a huge slab of concrete fall off the fourth or fifth floor of the

almost fifty-storey building, catch a ledge and smash through the window of the bank in the lobby.

The bomb squad was right behind them, Sergeant Vachon in his black, unmarked station wagon. Gauthier said, *"Trop tard,"* and Vachon said, *"On a reçu l'appel juste cinq minutes avant l'explosion."*

Dougherty ran to the building, thinking, At least this time there was a call, and saw about a dozen women stepping out through the busted plate glass wall of the bank.

"Is everybody okay?" he said.

One of the women said, "So far. We heard there was another bomb."

More cops had arrived, Dougherty thinking probably every car on shift was coming, and people were pouring out of the building, almost every one of them stopping to look back up at the hole blown out of the side.

In the lobby Dougherty saw a guy had taken charge and was directing people from the smoke-filled stairwell out of the building, and he figured he wasn't a banker, more likely from building security, so he asked, *"Quel étage?"* and the guy said, *"Quatrième."*

The fourth floor was a mess. The main trading floor — a huge open room — was filled with smoke and there was debris everywhere. The ceiling had collapsed, the viewing gallery railing was in the middle of the trading floor, smashed desks were blown across the room, and there were still people everywhere but there was no panic or yelling.

A man came up to Dougherty and said, "It was in the visitor's gallery — blew out the wall and the ceiling is caving in," and headed to the stairwell.

"Over here," another man yelled, and Dougherty rushed over to where the guy was pulling pieces of rubble off a pile and saying, "There's a girl under here."

Dougherty started tossing pieces of wall and desks and ceiling tiles until they saw a woman's face covered in blood and they dug faster. They had her out from under the rubble in less than a minute and saw right away she was still breathing. Dougherty stood up and saw the St. John's Ambulance guys wheeling in stretchers and called them over. The ambulance guy started to tell the man who'd been digging in the rubble to sit down, but the guy said, "Not me, her," and then Dougherty saw the blood dripping down off the guy's mostly bald head and said to him, "Yeah, but you, too."

The guy had a handkerchief in his hand and was pressing it against his head. "I'm fine, this is nothing."

Dougherty looked around at the trading floor and said, "Nothing? It looks like a war zone."

"Son, I was at Normandy."

Dougherty said, "Okay, you want some help getting down the stairs?"

"What I want is a gun so I can shoot back at these bastards."

Dougherty was thinking that sounded like something his father would say — another guy who was at Normandy but never talked about it. Then Dougherty saw the ambulance guys had the young woman up on the stretcher and were starting to look for a way out through the rubble and he said, "Maybe you can help these guys find their way out."

The man had the blood mostly wiped off his face

and the top of his head and he nodded. "Yes, come around this way, we'll use the members' stairs," and led the stretcher through the smoke and debris.

They walked a few feet and almost bumped into a man standing still and staring blankly, not really looking at anything, and Dougherty said, "Are you okay?"

The man turned and Dougherty realized he was young, in his twenties, shaking his head and saying, "They would have all been killed." Dougherty said, "Who?" and the young guy said, "The phone boys. If the New York exchange hadn't closed early — they've been closing at two since the beginning of the year, catching up on the backlog, last year was so busy. If New York had been open they would all have been . . ." He motioned to where the gallery had collapsed, and Dougherty saw the row of small desks under the rubble.

"Well, we're lucky," Dougherty said, and the young guy said, "Yeah, lucky."

Dougherty got the young guy moving, got him to the main stairwell, where people were walking down in a steady stream. An hour later they had the whole trading floor and most of the rest of the building cleared, and Dougherty was out front directing traffic in the middle of Victoria Square, getting the ambulances and the cop cars back into the street for the trip to the hospitals.

The last of the injured were taken to the hospital: over two dozen it turned out, most of them women. Lots of head wounds and shock but it looked like everyone would survive. Dougherty leaned back against his squad car, lit a cigarette and looked up at the hole in the side of the building. The smoke had stopped pouring out and it didn't look like any more pieces of concrete were going to fall off. He was thinking they really had been lucky when he heard a woman's voice say, "You have another one of those?"

He said, "Sure," and got out his pack.

She was wearing a miniskirt and was holding a man's suit jacket around herself and managed to extend a hand and put the cigarette in her mouth. She leaned forward a little so Dougherty could light it.

"I left my purse, my coat, everything."

Dougherty said, "You should get inside, people are in the Métro station," motioning to the subway entrance, the art nouveau portico that looked like a Métro entrance in Paris — in fact, it was a gift from Paris — installed right beside the statue of Queen Victoria. The woman shook her head, exhaled a long stream of smoke, and said, "I don't want to be under-ground." Then she said, "I was looking for Barbara but I don't see her anywhere."

"Was she hurt?"

"A little, I think. We were all knocked over," she waved her hand. "The ceiling was falling, the walls. The whole members' lounge. I'm a hostess."

"Well," Dougherty said, "maybe she was taken to the hospital."

A man came up to them and said, "Helen, my girl, you could say the stocks went up today, eh?" and laughed at his own joke. He was in his fifties and his suit was covered in dust, his tie loosened around his neck, and Dougherty was pretty sure he'd had a few drinks. Must have had a bottle in his desk.

The woman, Helen, said, "Yes, Mr. Gillespie," and

smiled at him and he said, "We're going to Michael's. Come on, only doubles — we're only drinking doubles." She said she'd see him later and he walked away. She looked at Dougherty and said, "He's in shock," and Dougherty said, "He's something."

Helen took another drag on the smoke and said, "Maybe a drink isn't a bad idea," and Dougherty said, "Yeah, maybe, but not at Michael's," and they went to the St. James Pub, which was full of cops and firemen.

The cops were talking in French about who could have planted the bomb. There were really only a few guys who could have done it, guys who'd been picked up over the last couple of years for other bombings and bank robberies, mostly out on bail now, and everybody was confident there'd be some arrests in a few days.

Dougherty translated for Helen, and she said it was too bad the arrests couldn't have been a few days ago, and he nodded. Then she said his French was very good, and he told her about his mother being from Bathurst in northern New Brunswick and how she'd moved to Montreal to work in a munitions factory during the war and met his father, who was in the navy.

Helen said, "How romantic," and Dougherty shrugged and said, "Yeah, I guess." He'd never thought about it like that.

Helen said she had no idea how she was going to get home, and Dougherty said he could drive her. "In your police car?" she said, and he said, "Sure, this seems like an emergency." She lived in a new apartment building near the river in LaSalle. She invited him to come up but Dougherty said he did have to get the car back at some point and she said, "At some point," and ran her fingers lightly down his cheek.

It took more than a few days, but it was only a couple of weeks later that the Montreal police and the RCMP put together a task force and raided dozens of apartments in one night. Dougherty was with the first group of cops up the stairs to apartment number four on the third floor of a building on St. Dominique, a block off the Main. They banged on the door and it opened. A young guy, Dougherty's age but with long hair and a scraggly beard, stood there in his underwear. The cops pushed past him and right away saw the wooden crates of dynamite — must have been two hundred sticks, detonators and booby trap wires.

One of the cops told the guy to unhook the trap, and the guy said, in English, even though the cop spoke to him in French, "Fuck you." The cop slammed his nightstick into the guy's stomach, doubling him over, and then said, *"Vide les autres,"* and Dougherty and a couple of the other cops who were still in the hall started knocking on the other doors and waking people up.

Dougherty drove a man and his wife, Greek immigrants, and their kids, twins, to Station Seventeen, the guy talking the whole way, saying, "Noise, noise all the time from them. Many times I take broom, bang on walls, all drums, guitars, not music — noise."

Even from the hall, Dougherty had seen guitars in the apartment. And posters on the walls, the usual stuff: Che Guevara, Marx, Trotsky. Nothing very original. Nothing very original with the explosives, either, the bomb squad guy, Vachon, said, like he was complaining, "Always the same, an alarm clock, two wires, a detonator and the dynamite. Not like Ireland with the booby traps."

The long-haired guy in the apartment took the fall for all his buddies, refused to name any of them, said he did everything by himself, which was really crazy when the next day a couple of cops in St. Leonard found 141 sticks of dynamite wired into two bombs under the Metropolitan Expressway. But he still wouldn't talk.

Dougherty and Helen dated for a while and he managed to get her onto the floor of the Queen Elizabeth Hotel where John and Yoko were having their Bed-In for Peace. But it turned into a fight when Dougherty said the Beatle hadn't really chosen Montreal for the next stop after Amsterdam, he was only in town because the marijuana bust kept him out of New York.

Then when the Montreal cops went on a one-day strike and the city exploded into another riot — taxi drivers kicking it off this time, not students — and a man was killed, Helen went back to dating stockbrokers.

At the end of September, a bomb exploded at the back door of the mayor's house just before dawn. It blew a huge hole in the foundation, destroyed an office in the basement and the mayor's darkroom.

The rest of the world was still going crazy — riots, hijackings and kidnappings on every continent. Charles Manson and his hippie family were arrested for seven murders in Los Angeles and at the beginning of May 1970 four students at Kent State University were shot and killed by the Ohio National Guard.

Late on a Saturday night at the end of May, a car coming across the Champlain Bridge into Montreal exploded as it passed the Nuns' Island exit just past the tollbooths. There were already two squad cars on the scene when Dougherty got there, working alone because Gauthier was taking all his sick days before his retirement, and he ran up to a cop he recognized, Bergeron, who was dropping a road flare a good two hundred feet from the smouldering car.

"What's out here?"

Bergeron pointed and it took Dougherty a few seconds to make out the severed arm on the pavement. They closed the road, traffic backed up across the bridge and for miles past that, and walked around with flashlights showing the detectives and the tech guys as much of the debris as they could find. It looked like there was only one guy in the car, which looked like an Oldsmobile, a Cutlass, Dougherty figured, by what was left of the roof and the pieces of the front grille.

Dougherty watched the police photographer, Rozovsky, take a hundred pictures of the wreckage and dozens of every body part they could find and then stop and change lenses on the camera and then turn and aim it back towards the skyline of Montreal.

One of the detectives said, "What's that for?" and Rozovsky said, "It looks like a postcard."

"You can't sell a picture you take while you're on the clock."

Rozovsky snapped off a few more shots and said, "It's for my personal collection."

"Yeah, your personal collection on the rack in every drugstore in town," and Rozovsky said, "From your lips . . ."

Dougherty was thinking it did look like a postcard; the ships in the port, the big old Sun Life building, the shiny aluminum Place Ville-Marie, the black tower of Place Victoria, all of them under the big cross on Mount Royal.

The detectives finally arrived, and one of them asked Vachon if it was the FLQ, and the bomb squad guy said, *"Non, c'est la mob."*

"Certains?"

One of the other bomb squad guys handed Vachon a piece of debris, and Vachon explained to the detectives that it was a radio receiver and that probably the transmitter was in a car behind the Cutlass. "Or over there," he said, pointing to the row of tollbooths on the southbound lanes.

The detectives talked among themselves for a while, and Dougherty overheard a little of what they were saying, trying to figure out who would take the case as most of the organized crime squad was working terrorism cases and the homicide squad was also stretched pretty thin.

One of the detectives looked at Dougherty with that *what are you still doing here?* look on his face, and Dougherty walked back to the other uniformed cops, wondering if anyone was ever going to investigate this.

The bomb squad wrapped up about four in the morning. Dougherty was moving his car to open up the road and let them head back to their offices at police headquarters when Vachon rolled the window of his station wagon down and said, "Westmount, right away. Number five Lansdowne Ridge, let's go."

Dougherty turned on the flashing light on top of his car and peeled out, driving fast through the city. He took the next exit off the expressway, Atwater Street, and headed up the hill. He didn't know exactly where Lansdowne Ridge was. Westmount had its own police force right there in the middle of Montreal, no way all those Anglos, the richest of the rich, were going to let Montreal cops in their business. When he got to Sherbrooke, Dougherty turned left and saw the Westmount police car waiting to lead them up the winding streets on the southwest side of Mount Royal.

Number five Lansdowne Ridge was a big stone house over a hundred years old and it looked like the bomb had been placed in a basement window well. The explosion had blown into the house, destroyed some furniture and a big colour TV but didn't seem to have done much damage to the building itself.

An ambulance and a bunch of Westmount police cars were on the scene.

While Vachon and the rest of the bomb squad guys went to check it out Dougherty hung back with the Westmount cop, an older guy, looked to be in his fifties. Dougherty said, "Anybody hurt?"

"The wife's in shock, they're taking her to the hospital. The kids, too. If it had gone off a couple hours earlier," and he motioned to the smoking rubble in the basement, the rec room, and Dougherty said yeah.

A few more Montreal cop cars pulled up, and Dougherty said, "Since when did you start letting us in here?"

"Only for bombs," the Westmount cop said. "Back when they were in mailboxes we'd call in the army, they'd take them out to a field and blow them up — one guy had his hands blown off, you remember that?"

Dougherty said no, and the Westmount cop

shrugged and said, "Now they want to treat them like a crime scene, try and get evidence, fingerprints, that kind of thing."

Dougherty said, "Makes sense," and the Westmount cop said, "Yeah, like we don't know who's doing it."

Dougherty said yeah and started to get out his cigarettes when he heard a second blast. The Westmount cop said, "Shit, another one?" He got into his car and Dougherty got into his and followed.

They could see the smoke rising a few blocks away, but Dougherty didn't think he would have been able to find his way on these streets, all twists and turns and up and down.

Another old stone house. Smoke coming out through smashed windows, man and a woman, both in their sixties or seventies, coming out as Dougherty and the Westmount cop rushed up, the Westmount cop yelling, "Anybody else in the house?" and the old man shaking his head, saying, "No, it's just us."

Dougherty saw the blackened stones at the base of a retaining wall beside the house. The street had houses only on the south side, the north was a rock wall keeping back Mount Royal. Dougherty walked around the outside of the house, looking for another bomb or a package, something — he didn't even know what, really. Beyond the house to the south was a steep drop-off and a great view of the St. Lawrence river and the South Shore. When he was on the small patio behind the house Dougherty realized that the idea behind the bomb was probably to knock out the retaining wall and have the house collapse on the ones below it down the hill, but the wall had held. He walked back out front of the house, saw the Westmount cop had the old couple in the back seat of his car, and just then Vachon pulled up and got out of his car saying, *"Une autre."*

Dougherty said, "That makes three," and before Vachon could say anything there was another explosion.

This one was just down the street. It was set in the retaining wall on the north side and blew huge chunks of brick through windows in the house across the street. Again the wall held.

"They were trying for an avalanche," Vachon said.

The next bomb exploded twenty minutes later at the back of an office building on Sherbrooke a few blocks down the hill and blew out the windows of a couple of houses on Elm Avenue.

By the time the sun was coming up a few thousand people had been evacuated and every Westmount cop and half the Montreal cops were scouring the neighbourhood for more bombs. At ten o'clock a call came in that a man had found a suspicious package under his car, and when Vachon delicately pulled it out from under the Buick and opened it he saw fifteen sticks of dynamite wired to an alarm clock. Dougherty led the way — this driving fast through city streets starting to get old — to an open field off Côte-des-Neiges Road, where the bomb was dismantled.

At noon the mayor of Westmount announced it was safe for people to return to their homes and then he invited the Montreal cops to join him at the Westmount City Hall for lunch. A couple dozen cops still on the scene took him up on the offer, and when Vachon pointed out that the alarm clock they'd taken off the dismantled bomb was stamped *Made in China* instead of the usual *Made in Japan*, the mayor decided they should have Chinese food and had his assistant call Ruby Foo's.

There was a lot of talk about a blue sports car with four bearded men in it that a few people said they saw just before the first bomb went off. Most of the cops weren't too surprised. The usual suspects.

"They all want to be Che Guevara."

When they were finally packing up to leave after lunch, another call came in. A boy had found a package on the patio behind his house and when he opened it he saw, as he put it, "A whole lot of dynamite."

Dougherty was about to get going when he heard, "Hey Dog-eh-dee," and turned to see Delisle, the desk sergeant from Station Ten, walking up to him.

"You know a *taverne dans le Point, s'appelle Nap*?" he said in his Franglish and Dougherty said, "Yeah, Nap's — Napoleon's. I know it."

And Delisle said, in English, "Go down there and get Detective Carpentier." Being in Westmount must have thrown him off.

One of the bomb squad guys standing nearby packing up equipment said, "Is he drunk again?"

Delisle said, "Bring him *au dix*."

By then it was three o'clock Sunday afternoon. Dougherty had been on shift since he started the four to midnight on Saturday and he was wiped. But he got in his car and drove down the hill to Point St. Charles, his old neighbourhood. Only a few miles away but it felt like a million, the big stone houses replaced by three-storey walk-ups, wrought-iron staircases on the outside. No front lawns here.

Dougherty had lived in the Point until his last year of high school when his parents bought one side of a duplex across the river in Greenfield Park.

Nap's was on Hibernia Street, almost on the corner of Mullins, near the Grand Trunk yard. On a weekday most of the drinkers would be men who'd just got off a shift in the yard or one of the factories along the Lachine Canal, but Sunday afternoon the place had some women in it, too, and they were doing most of the shouting Dougherty heard as he walked in.

As soon as they saw him, one of the women said, "Jesus Christ, is that little Eddie Dougherty?"

There were maybe a dozen people in the place but the room wasn't very big so it looked tight. Detective Carpentier was standing at the far end of the bar and he wasn't hammered, but he'd had a few, no doubt. Some men were standing by the back door, blocking it, and Dougherty knew some of them, guys his father's age. There were younger guys in the bar, too, guys Dougherty's age, and he looked at one of them who was standing behind the others and said, "Buck-Buck."

The woman who'd recognized Dougherty said, "You know what this asshole is doing here?"

Dougherty kept staring at Danny Buckley for another couple of seconds, letting him know things were different now, Dougherty wasn't the little kid getting smacked around on his way home from École Jeanne-LeBer, the only kid on the street going to the French school. Then he looked at the woman and recognized her, Mrs. Malley.

She said, "He's looking for that Bill, the man killed those girls downtown." She kept looking at Dougherty as if he'd be as outraged as she was. When he didn't say anything she yelled, "Brenda Webber's not dead!"

One of the other women said, "He comes down here, as if Millie isn't going crazy enough."

Dougherty knew the Webbers: Arlene had been in his class and now he was thinking that Brenda was one of her sisters — there were six or seven Webber kids, mostly girls — and Millie was the mother.

A man's deep voice came from the back of the room. "You don't even know, do you?"

Dougherty couldn't see who said it, but he felt everyone turning on him, staring him down. It wasn't that different from being the scared kid cornered between the sheds in the back lane, Buck-Buck and his friends giving him a beating, telling him his father knocked up a French whore and nobody wants the stupid half-breed kid.

Silence, everybody staring at Dougherty, and he stared back, looking them over, trying to recognize as many faces as he could. He was sweating and starting to shake a little.

Mrs. Malley looked at him and said, "Brenda Webber is missing. She's been missing for three days."

Another woman said, "You should be looking for her."

Dougherty looked at Carpentier, and Mrs. Malley said, "*You* should be looking for Brenda, not him, not a guy looking for a murderer. Brenda's not dead."

One of the men said, "Useless pigs."

The place felt like it was about to explode.

Then Carpentier pushed away from the bar and started through the crowd, saying, "Come on,

Constable, let's go."

Mrs. Malley said, "Yeah, you get out of here," and then the others all had something to say: get out, pigs; run away; why don't you do your job; get the hell out of here.

Outside Nap's, Dougherty was still nervous and kept speaking English, saying, "Where'd you park?" and Carpentier answered in English, "I don't know." He looked around and said, "I was walking around. I don't know this neighbourhood."

They walked half a block to Dougherty's squad car, and Carpentier said, "They know you."

"Yeah."

"But you're not one of them?"

"English can be *pure laine*, too."

Carpentier laughed and Dougherty realized he was older than he'd thought, well into his fifties, wearing a dark suit and an overcoat, looking like Joe Friday playing detective.

"They don't want to believe," Carpentier said, "that the girl is dead."

"But you don't know that for sure."

Carpentier nodded but then he shrugged. "Not for sure, no, but . . ."

Dougherty said yeah.

Carpentier leaned against the squad car and got out his cigarettes. He lit one and took a deep drag then blew smoke at the sky. "You know her, Brenda Webber?"

"I knew her sister. How old is Brenda?"

"Fifteen."

"So maybe she ran away."

"Maybe. Lots of kids doing it."

"But you think that this Bill killed her?"

"He's killed three in the last six months."

"Three?"

Carpentier looked at Dougherty and said, "Don't you know?"

"I've heard something," Dougherty said. "They were downtown, weren't they? I've been chasing bombs."

"You and every other cop in the city," Carpentier said. "But we still have murders, you know."

Dougherty said, "Yeah, I know, I was at a murder scene last night," and Carpentier said, "The Westmount bombs, they kill somebody?"

"Not for lack of trying — seven bombs, but no. One girl, maybe ten years old, bomb went off in an office building on Sherbrooke and blew a hole in the apartment behind it; she was on the couch in the front room. She was hit with a lot of glass and bricks, but they got her to the Children's Hospital. It's just a few blocks away, looks like she'll be okay."

"Cocksuckers. Ten-year-old girl. Cowards."

Dougherty said yeah, then he said, "The murder was a car bomb, blew it up just as it came across the Champlain Bridge."

"Coming into Montreal?"

"Yeah, just past the tollbooths. Vachon said it was probably mobsters, used a radio transmitter."

Carpentier nodded, took a drag on his cigarette. "What kind of car?"

"Olds, it was in pieces when I got there. Could've been a Cutlass, maybe a '67 by the tail lights."

Carpentier said, "Johnny Vaccaro, probably. Coming back from New York — he runs the heroin."

Dougherty didn't say anything. He was surprised Carpentier was so sure.

"Comes in from Marseilles, gets unloaded here. Your friends, the Irish working the port, give it to the Italians, they take it to New York."

"That's a book," Dougherty said, "last year. *The French Connection*, they got those guys," and Carpentier said, "Yeah, that's right — so now there's no more drugs," and he threw his cigarette on the sidewalk. "Come on, drive me around. Let's find my car."

"Well, the Webbers live on Coleraine or Knox off Liverpool, did you start at their house?"

Carpentier opened the passenger door. "The first one, what you call it, Coleraine? They live there."

"It's just a couple blocks, just the other side of Charlevoix." Dougherty started the car, pulled a U and headed south.

Coleraine Street looked the same as Fortune Street, where Dougherty grew up, the same rows of three-storey houses with iron stairs and railings winding up to the second floor. The Doughertys had lived on the first floor and he thought the Webbers did, too, but as he turned onto Coleraine he wasn't sure.

Carpentier said, "This Bill, this guy killed the other women, you know what they call him?"

Dougherty drove slowly along Coleraine, looking at the parked cars but not seeing an unmarked, and said no.

"Vampire. You know why? He bite their breast. Michaelchuk say after they're dead, he can tell by the blood or something."

"I remember one," Dougherty said, "there was talk about it at Ten, it was just before the strike."

"Police action. We don't call it a strike."

"She had an apartment on Dorchester."

"Shirley Audette, she live with her boyfriend."

"He didn't do it?"

"He was at work. She was maybe on drug," Carpentier said. "She had been in the Douglas, you know, *l'hôpital psychiatrique*," and Dougherty said, "Yeah, I know it. In Verdun."

"The boyfriend say she have other boyfriends, too, that she like all kinds of crazy stuff, sex stuff. Hippies."

They were at the end of Coleraine then, at Liverpool Street, and Dougherty said, "Your car doesn't seem to be here."

"No."

Dougherty looked sideways at the detective and figured he'd had more to drink than just what he had at Nap's, probably had a mickey in his pocket. Dougherty said, "Where was the first place you looked in the Point?" and Carpentier said, "The last place she was seen."

"Where was that?"

Carpentier closed his eyes and leaned back, and Dougherty couldn't tell if he was trying to remember or trying to fall asleep.

They turned onto Liverpool and Dougherty headed south towards Wellington, the main street through the Point and Carpentier said, "The boss?" Then he opened his eyes and looked at Dougherty and said, "Something about the boss."

"Boss's, it's a store," Dougherty said, "I know it," and turned onto Wellington.

"He strangle them," Carpentier said. "Marielle

Archambeault, she was found in her apartment in the east end, Rue Ontario. She work in Place Ville-Marie, in a store, maybe he meet her there. That was November 23."

Dougherty turned onto Fortune Street.

Back on his old street it did look just like Coleraine or Ash or Dublin or Charon, three-storey row houses, iron stairs bolted to the front.

"He kill Jean Way in her apartment on Lincoln. That's Station Ten — you work that one?" Dougherty said no and Carpentier said, "January 26. She have a boyfriend, *aussi*. He find her but he didn't do it."

Dougherty was amazed how Carpentier could remember details, the names and dates and the circumstances, and he wasn't sure he could ever manage that. All the cops he knew wanted to become detectives — get into plainclothes, work homicides and big-time frauds — but Dougherty wasn't sure he could do it.

"There was a TV show," Carpentier said, "on the CBC, national network, everything we had on Bill, we showed them everything. You remember it?"

"Didn't see it."

"They saw it here, those people at Nap. And we got lot of calls, hundreds, thousands, everybody know Bill but no one know him."

Dougherty slowed down as they passed Boss's, looking at the kids hanging out front drinking Cokes and eating chips, probably the same age as Brenda Webber, the boys with hair as long as the girls'. Only a few years younger than the women Carpentier was talking about.

"Do you see your car?"

Carpentier still had his eyes closed. "Brenda

Webber did not come home on the night of May the twenty-eight."

"Last Thursday," Dougherty said.

"Were you working?"

"Two bombs that night," Dougherty said. "One at the Reddy Memorial Hospital and one in a warehouse on Van Horne. No phone calls, they both exploded."

"They were cover for the robbery," Carpentier said, "at the Université de Montréal Student Centre."

"What could they get at a student centre?"

Carpentier shook his head, still didn't want to believe it, and said, "Fifty-seven thousand dollars."

"What?"

"Must have been an inside job, the students helping out the FLQ."

"Not one of their forced donations?"

"Maybe, who knows. There's my car."

At the end of Fortune Street in the parking lot of École Jeanne-LeBer there was one car, a four-door Ford. Dougherty pulled into the lot and beside Carpentier's car.

"The mother call police Friday, file a missing person report. She say that Brenda stay out all night before but she call the friends and they don't see her."

Dougherty was thinking he should say something in French to get Carpentier speaking French, he might be easier to understand, but the detective was still talking: 29 "She left the house, she stop at Boss and no one see her after. The other kids, the friends, they don't want to say where they were, but probably right here in this park smoking dope."

There hadn't been much dope smoking when

Dougherty's family moved out of the Point a few years earlier, but he wasn't surprised to hear there was plenty of it now. Past the park were the CN rail yards and the garbage dump — Dougherty could still hear his mother warning him not to go near it because of the stray dogs. Rabid dogs, she'd said.

Carpentier opened the car door and started to get out, then stopped and looked at Dougherty and said, "Tell Delisle I went home," and got into his Ford and drove away.

Dougherty sat in the parking lot of Jeanne-LeBer for a few minutes. It was a nice Sunday afternoon — quiet, sunny — and even the Point was a pleasant place.

A few miles away from the terrorist bombs and the mobster bombs.

And maybe a few miles away from the strangled women.

Two days later a man working at a factory in LaSalle found the body of Brenda Webber.

CHAPTER TWO

Dougherty was checking in for his four-to-midnight at Station Ten when Sergeant Delisle called him over to the front desk and said, "You know where is the lift bridge on the Canal Lachine, in Ville St. Pierre?" and Dougherty said, "What is it with you, am I the only west-end guy you've got?" and Delisle said, "You know it?"

"Yeah, I know it."

"On Rue Dollard?"

Dougherty said, "Yes, right, that's it," losing patience, and Delisle said, "Go and see Detective Carpentier." Dougherty said, "Is he drunk again?" and Delisle said, "They find the body," and Dougherty knew right away. "Shit."

"Get going, don't say anything to the press."

Dougherty turned and walked out of the station, thinking that not talking to the press was about the first thing they taught him when he joined the force.

Rush hour was just about to start, and Dougherty drove down Guy and onto the 2-20 expressway heading west. Most of the west island traffic, the office guys heading out to suburban bungalows in Dorval and Beaconsfield and Baie-D'Urfé, hadn't really started, and in only a few minutes Dougherty got off the expressway in Ville St. Pierre. He could see a couple of guys leaning up against LaSalle cop cars in the parking lot of the Transfer Restaurant and pulled up beside them.

One of the guys said, *"C'est toi, Dog-eh-dee?"* and Dougherty said yeah.

The guy tossed his cigarette and got in his car, saying, *"Suis-moi,"* and pulled out of the lot, crossed the lift bridge and turned left onto St. Patrick Street. Dougherty followed him for about half a mile along the canal, the south side of St. Patrick lined with factories and a truck terminal, and then they turned off and drove around a huge, vacant building and into the empty lot behind it.

Dougherty could see cars in the tall weeds, a cop car with the red light turning, an ambulance without any lights on, the coroner's station wagon and Carpentier's Ford. A flash went off as Dougherty got out of his car and walked towards the half dozen or so men standing in a small semicircle. Rozovsky was taking pictures of something on the ground.

Someone on the ground.

Dougherty stepped up beside Carpentier and the

detective said in English, "It's her, isn't it?"

Even though Dougherty was expecting it, he was still stunned. At first he thought it was Arlene Webber and he said, "What?" but then he said, "Yeah, that's Brenda Webber. She looks older than I expected."

"As old as she'll ever be," Carpentier said. He looked at the coroner, Dr. Michaelchuk, leaning against the station wagon smoking a cigarette, and said, "We'll get the priest; go talk to the parents and meet you at the morgue," and Dougherty said, "No, she's not Catholic. They went to Grace Church — it's some kind of Protestant."

"The minister then."

"Reverend Barker."

Michaelchuk tossed his cigarette and nodded to his assistant, and the two men started pulling a stretcher out of their car.

Carpentier looked around and spoke in French to the LaSalle cops, saying, "Can you ask around, see if anybody saw anything last night, maybe the night before," and the cops looked at each other a little and shuffled their feet. There had been a lot of talk about merging all the police on the island of Montreal into a single force, but most of the suburban cities were against it and Dougherty had no idea how this kind of murder investigation would work.

After a minute one of the LaSalle cops said, "How do you know it was at night?"

A hundred feet in one direction were the back ends of the factories, St. Patrick Street, the canal and then the 2-20 expressway, and Dougherty knew someone could have dumped Brenda Webber here and been miles away in a few minutes. They could've taken the 2-20 west to the suburbs or all the way to Toronto; they could've taken it east into Montreal then north on the Décarie Expressway up to the Laurentians or south over the Champlain Bridge to the Eastern Townships or even to New York State thirty miles away.

Dougherty said, "Maybe someone in those houses saw something," pointing across the empty lot to a row of brand new, squat, two-storey houses — fourplexes with flat roofs that looked like cinderblock buildings, newer versions of the houses in the Point, but with the stairs to the second floor on the inside.

"Seems far away," Carpentier said, "but you might as well ask around."

There were stakes in the ground of the empty field, where new roads and probably more of the squat houses were going to go in, so it did seem unlikely anyone had seen anything.

Dougherty said, "Who found her?" and Carpentier motioned to a group of men standing by the back of one of the factories.

"Saw the birds circling and one came closer and saw the scarf."

Brenda Webber had been left face down, naked, with something tied around her neck that looked like a scarf, but Dougherty said, "It's a bedsheet."

"He wins the booby prize," Rozovsky said and stood up from taking a picture. "Torn into strips, it looks like." He started to raise his camera but stopped. No postcard shots here.

"All right," Carpentier said, "let's go get this Reverend Barker."

Dougherty stood for a moment and watched the coroner and his assistant move the stretcher closer and then start to pick up Brenda Webber's body. The torn bedsheet caught on a rock on the ground and slipped off easily as the girl's body was lifted, and Dougherty noticed she was still wearing her black running shoes.

Carpentier was in his car then, and Dougherty got into his squad car and led the way. Grace Church, corner of Wellington and Fortune, a big old red brick building. Reverend Barker was in his office and recognized Dougherty as soon as he walked in. "Édouard, young man, what brings you here?"

Dougherty said, "My mom's still making me go to mass, Reverend. This is business."

Reverend Barker had hold of Dougherty's hand, shaking it, and said, "Oh?"

"Brenda Webber."

Reverend Barker nodded and let go of Dougherty's hand. "I'll get my coat."

It was only a couple of blocks to the Webber house but Dougherty drove and Reverend Barker sat in the passenger seat and asked for anything Dougherty could tell him.

"It's as bad as you can imagine — she was naked, tied up, dumped in a field behind a factory off St. Patrick in LaSalle."

Reverend Barker nodded. That was all he needed and then they were in front of the Webbers'.

There was a small boy, maybe five years old, sitting on the front steps pushing a Matchbox car around and he looked excited to see the police car and to see Dougherty in his uniform getting out of it. At that moment a young woman emerged from the ground floor apartment, saw Dougherty, smiled and said, "Eddie," and then she saw Reverend Barker getting out of the car and Carpentier getting out of his own car he'd double-parked and said, "Oh no."

Reverend Barker took both her hands in his. "Arlene, is your mother home?" and the young woman nodded and Barker walked past her into the house.

Dougherty said, "Where's your father?" and she looked at him for moment and then said, "He's at work, he's working a double," and Dougherty said, "Domtar?" She shook her head and said, "Packers."

Then they heard the scream from inside the house, the wailing, the sobbing, and Arlene turned and went inside.

Carpentier said, "*Mon dieu*, it could be the same girl," and Dougherty said yeah.

A few people who had been sitting on their balconies or on their front stoops were starting to move closer to the Webbers'. Dougherty recognized a few faces, some parents of kids he'd known. Even after his family moved to the South Shore, Dougherty finished his last year of high school in Verdun and still hung out with his friends from the Point. He'd thought he'd stay friends with them forever but when he'd started working construction instead of going into one of the factories or the railroad or working the port unloading ships they'd started to drift and when he'd joined the police that was it. He knew going to the French elementary school made him different when he started at Verdun High in English and the Point didn't really like anyone different.

A woman's voice said, "It must be Brenda, it's gotta be," and then a man's voice said, "Dougherty, is it Brenda?"

It was becoming a crowd and Carpentier said, "It's like in Nap's," and Dougherty said yeah, feeling the tension and fear coming off the people in the street.

"Did you find her?"

"Where is she?"

"Who did it?"

Carpentier said, "Don't say anything," but Dougherty looked at the crowd standing in the street and said, "We have to take Mr. and Mrs. Webber to headquarters," and a woman said, "I knew it."

A man said, "Jesus Christ," and another man said, "Take that frog cop with you. Didn't do fuck all to find Brenda."

Then Reverend Barker was coming out of the house with Millie Webber and Carpentier said, "My car," and motioned to the Ford. Reverend Barker helped Millie into the back seat and Carpentier drove down Coleraine Street, the crowd not moving quite enough out of the way and the men brushing up against the car as it passed.

Arlene was out of the house then and picking up the little boy and looking at Dougherty. "I'll go get your father and take him to the station," he said, "then I'll bring them both back in a couple of hours."

The look on Arlene's face was blank — she was in shock — and Dougherty said, "Is he yours?" and Arlene said, "Yeah, Mickey. Michael. We live upstairs now, I married Bobby Buchanan."

Dougherty said, "That's good, he's a good guy,"

and Arlene nodded.

Then Dougherty got in his squad car and the men crowded around it and walked in front of it and beside it, only letting Dougherty crawl down the street. He recognized the men, a lot of them had been in Nap's, Carpentier was right about that — Danny Buckley; one of the Murphy kids and his father; Gordon Malley; Scotty Kendricks.

At the Canada Packers plant loading dock Joe Webber looked at Dougherty the way every guy in the Point looks at a cop, like he was going to take a swing at him, until Dougherty said, "It's Brenda," and Joe just stared at him. Dougherty got him in the car and drove to Old Montreal, to police headquarters, where he handed him over to Carpentier, who was waiting by the front desk with Reverend Barker and Millie Webber.

It was very quiet in the lobby then, the place empty except for the desk sergeant reading a newspaper. Dougherty had no idea how long Joe and Millie Webber would be in the morgue but didn't imagine it would be more than a few minutes. He lit a cigarette and leaned against the wall and was thinking about Brenda's body, something about the way it looked, and then he was startled by the bang of the front door of the building being pushed open hard and a man's voice saying, "They're not here yet," as a few reporters and photographers rushed into the building.

Dougherty looked at the desk sergeant, who was standing as the reporters crowded around the counter. Dougherty tried to get his attention, to motion to him that he'd get the squad car and drive it around back and the Webbers could come out that way, but just then Vachon and Meloche came into the station and the reporters turned on them, saying, "How much dynamite, Pierre?"

More than a dozen cops followed them in, some of the big-shot detectives from anti-terrorist and a few uniformed cops carrying wooden crates and a couple of green duffle bags. A camera flash went off and a reporter said, "Is that guns?"

The cop carrying one of the bags, an older cop Dougherty didn't know, hefted it and said, "Machine guns," and the flash went off again.

"The Mayor of Westmount says you have no leads at all on the bombs there, is that true?"

Vachon stopped and turned to face the reporters, and Dougherty saw Carpentier coming down the hall leading the Webbers, Joe with his arm around Millie, through the lobby.

No one else noticed them.

Dougherty got the Webbers into the back seat and was walking around the car when Carpentier said, "Tell them I'll be by tomorrow."

"You're not coming?" Dougherty said.

Reverend Barker was standing by the car then, and Carpentier motioned for him to get into the passenger seat. Then he looked back at the big front doors of police headquarters and said, "Did you hear? They found dynamite, detonators, machine guns and bulletproof vests. These fucking guys want a war."

Dougherty didn't know what to say, from the chatter he heard in the station houses a lot of the cops wanted a war, too, get it out in the open and be done with it, but it didn't look like that's what Carpentier wanted. The detective stood there for another moment and then said, "*Bon, c'est ça.* Take the Webbers home," and walked back into the station.

The crowd was gone on Coleraine Street but Arlene Webber was still sitting on the front stoop when Dougherty pulled up. She didn't get up when Reverend Barker led her parents into the house, just moved over a little to let them pass and then she said, "Did you see her?"

Dougherty said yeah, and he was thinking about saying "she looked just like you" but didn't.

Arlene nodded and took a drag on her cigarette then blew out a long stream of smoke and said, "Little bitch, never listened," and Dougherty saw the streaks of tears on her face and watched as she started to shake and sob.

He had no idea what to say, standing there in his uniform, feeling so useless. This sure wasn't the kind of action he'd signed up for.

Arlene looked up at him. "Who did it?"

"I don't know."

"Is anybody going to try and find out?"

"Yeah, of course."

"Really, Eddie?"

She was looking right at him, shaking a little, not angry or resentful, just wanting an honest answer.

And he didn't want to lie to her so he didn't say anything.

CHAPTER

THREE

The loud, clanging bell of the phone woke Dougherty from a deep sleep. He stumbled out of bed and took the three steps into his kitchenette, thinking he must have slept all day and was late for his four-to-midnight. He hadn't been able to fall asleep for hours when he'd got back from the Point, the sun was just coming up when he finally nodded off. When he picked up the receiver and said, "Hello," it was his mother's voice saying, "Is it true?"

"Ma, wha— is what true?"

"Brenda Webber," his mother's French accent drawing out the name and he said, "Yeah, it's true."

"You see her?"

Dougherty sat down on the only chair in the place,

a wooden kitchen chair that came with his furnished room. "Yeah, I saw her. How do you know?"

"It's in the *Gazette*. Tommy saw it."

"Front page?"

"No, the front page is the dynamite and the machine guns they find in the garage. Tommy, after he finish his route he read the paper."

Dougherty stood up and retrieved his smokes from the pocket coat, saying, "I thought he just read the sports."

"He read the whole paper." She didn't sound too happy about it. Tommy was her youngest — her baby, almost twelve — and Dougherty was getting ready for her usual speech about how the kid should be out playing in the fresh air but she said, "Poor Millie, *mon dieu*."

"I took her and Mr. Webber to the station to identify the body."

"*Mon dieu*."

Dougherty lit his cigarette and looked for his watch but couldn't find it.

"When will be the funeral?"

"I don't know, Ma. When I left last night Reverend Barker was still there. I guess he's going to take care of it." Dougherty wasn't sure what day it was and had to count back to Sunday and then forward to Wednesday and then he said, "Friday, I guess. Would that be right, three days?"

"Protestants," his mother said, "I don't know."

"What time is it?"

"Nine thirty. I'm on my coffee break — I have to go back to work. You coming Sunday?"

"If I'm not working."

He hung up and found his watch. Nine thirty-five; he'd had maybe two hours' sleep. He went back to bed but felt wide awake, blowing smoke at the ceiling. The single room was barely big enough for the bed, the dresser and an armchair but it had a private bathroom and for thirteen dollars a week it was in a three-storey walk-up on Pierce, half a block up from St. Catherine Street, only a couple of blocks from Station Ten.

And then he thought he knew what it was about Brenda's body that seemed odd. Not odd, familiar. He got up and looked for some clothes but everything he had was ready for the laundry, which he'd do if he made it to his parents' on Sunday, so he put on his uniform and headed out. He found his car, a five-year-old Mustang with just over eighty thousand miles on it, parked a block over and drove down to Bonsecours Street in Old Montreal.

On the third floor, Dougherty asked the desk sergeant at the *section de l'identification judiciaire* if Rozovsky was in, and the sergeant didn't even look up from the newspaper he was reading, just motioned towards the offices.

Rozovsky was standing in front of a desk, looking at a big leather-covered book and he said, "I'm looking at the requests now." He looked up and saw it was Dougherty. "Oh, it's you."

"You got a minute?"

Rozovsky looked like he was still in his twenties, barely, maybe a couple of years older than Dougherty, but he had a full beard and his hair was a little too long to be a cop, a uniform cop anyway. Maybe a detective could get away with his hair touching his collar like that, though Dougherty had no idea why anybody would want to.

"One minute." Rozovsky put a piece of paper in the front pocket of the book and looked at Dougherty, waiting.

"That girl last night, Brenda Webber — I've seen something like that before."

"Like what?"

"A girl tied up with a bedsheet. It was last year, I was working out of Eleven."

"The deepest, darkest east end and your name is Dougherty? Whose cereal did you piss in?"

"Found her in a lane behind that little restaurant on the corner of Craig and Wolfe."

Rozovsky said, "That's still there — it didn't get bulldozed for the expressway where the Ville-Marie Tunnel lets out," and Dougherty said, "Or where the tunnel starts if you're coming that way."

Rozovsky said, "The next street is Montcalm, right?" and Dougherty said yeah, and Rozovsky said, "That's funny, isn't it?" but he wasn't smiling like he found it funny, and Dougherty didn't say anything.

"This city named the streets next to each other Montcalm and Wolfe, the generals who fought each other on the Plains of Abraham. You went to school, didn't you?"

Dougherty said, "Yeah, it's funny." Then he said, "She was just the same, naked but with shoes on, boots I think, and a bedsheet around her neck."

"You know the date?"

"It was right around the first Expos game, the spring."

Rozovsky walked across the office to some filing cabinets. "Beginning of April, right? Who was the detective?"

Dougherty said, "Campagnolo," and Rozovsky stopped with his hand on a drawer handle and said, "Of course," shaking his head and opening the drawer.

"I was reassigned to Station Ten in May. I never heard anything else about it."

"Probably because there was nothing to hear." Rozovsky flipped through files and then pulled one out of the drawer and opened it as he walked back. "These were taken by Geoffrion — he retired in January." He dropped the file open on the desk. "Nice boots, probably a go-go dancer."

"That's what Campagnolo figured. That or a prostitute."

"No reason she couldn't be both," Rozovsky said. "Hard-working girl from the Gaspé, looks like. Sylvie Berubé. There's no bedsheet."

"No, it was just like with Brenda Webber, it wasn't really tied, it was just kind of wrapped around her neck."

"It's not in any of these pictures."

"I remember it, I saw it."

"Geoffrion would have taken a picture of it, it's evidence."

Now Dougherty wasn't sure. "But everything else, it's the same."

"Close enough," Rozovsky said.

"I guess we better tell Campagnolo."

"He's working mad bombers now."

"Who's working this?"

Rozovsky shrugged. "No one."

"I guess we better tell Carpentier."

"We?" He held out the file. "Around the corner and down the hall."

Dougherty walked down the hall, further than he'd expected, and stopped at the open door to the Homicide Office. He stood there for a moment, too nervous to just walk in but not wanting to knock on the door frame, not sure of the protocol or if there was any protocol. Usually as the uniform cop you didn't say anything to the detectives, just answered their questions.

But Dougherty didn't think any of the detectives were ever going to ask about this, so he cleared his throat and tapped the file against his thigh and walked into the office.

Carpentier was standing by the big window facing Rue St. Louis, the side street behind the police station, and he didn't turn around, he just said, "*Laisse-le sur mon bureau,*" and Dougherty said, "Excuse me?"

Carpentier turned around then and said, "I thought you spoke French?" and Dougherty said he did, and then he said, "I didn't want to just leave it on your desk."

"That's not coffee."

Dougherty really wished Rozovsky had come with him. Now he wasn't sure what to say, and just then a woman pushed past him into the office, carrying a coffee mug that she put down on Carpentier's desk. She looked at Dougherty.

Carpentier said, "Would you like a coffee?"

For a moment Dougherty thought, Yeah, I would like a coffee, but he was still nervous being in the homicide office and he didn't say anything. Carpentier nodded at the secretary, and she shrugged and rolled her eyes a little and walked out. Carpentier said, "What is it?"

Dougherty took a couple of quick steps closer to the detective's desk, they were the only two people in the office now and Dougherty said, "There was another murder last year."

"There were many murders last year."

"Yes, but this one . . ." He put the open file on Carpentier's desk and stood back a bit while the detective picked up his cup of coffee.

Carpentier sat down then and looked through all the pictures of the body of Sylvie Berubé and then looked up at Dougherty and said, "You remembered this from . . ." He looked at the date on the file, "The ninth of April last year?"

"I just remembered it was around the first Expos game; Rozovsky found the file."

Carpentier sipped his coffee and looked through the whole file and said, "There isn't much."

Dougherty didn't say anything, just stood there feeling like he was standing in front of the vice-principal.

"This was before Bill," Carpentier said, "so we didn't know."

Dougherty looked at the wall of the homicide office where the pictures of the victims were tacked up and he said, "They look like nice girls."

"I'm sure when Sylvie Berubé went home to her *maman* in Matane, she looked like a nice girl, too. You find out a lot about people in homicide. Too much."

Dougherty nodded and he was thinking how all the new recruits wanted to get promoted into plainclothes, how they all wanted to work robbery and fraud and homicide but it seemed like they never thought about what that really meant.

Then Carpentier stood up. "We'll have to show this to Detective-Lieutenant Desjardins — he's in charge of the investigation." He looked at Dougherty and said, "Good work, Constable."

"Thank you, sir."

"Well, now I have to go to Point St. Charles and talk to the family of Brenda Webber. Would you like to come?"

"Sir?"

"Maybe you could help."

"Yes sir, it's just . . . I'm working a four-to-midnight at Station Ten, sir."

Carpentier motioned to Dougherty's uniform. "You're not on duty now?"

"No, sir." He didn't know what else to say, so he just stood there and Carpentier shrugged a little and said, "We should be done by four, Constable."

In the car Carpentier told Dougherty the coroner's report on Brenda Webber would be ready in a few days, but it looked like she was strangled, though probably not with the bedsheet they found around her neck. "Michaelchuk says it was probably a rope."

"So why the bedsheet?"

"Don't know."

They drove through the Wellington Tunnel under the Lachine canal and came out the other side in the Point. Turning onto Coleraine Street, Carpentier said, *"Tout le monde est ici,"* and Dougherty said yeah, not surprised by the crowd in front of the Webbers'.

Carpentier parked a few houses down, and as they approached the Webbers' door in the row house, the crowd saw them and seemed to perk up a little. But really nobody moved.

A man said, "What do you want, Dougherty?" and that's when Dougherty realized there were a lot of men in the crowd, more than he expected in the middle of a weekday in June.

Carpentier just pushed his way through the crowd like he owned the place and Dougherty followed. The Webbers' place looked exactly the same as the first-floor house Dougherty grew up in — front room, long hallway, kitchen at the back.

And that's where Millie Webber was sitting, of course, at the kitchen table, smoking and drinking coffee in the middle of another crowd. They all looked up when Carpentier pushed his way into the kitchen, and Millie Webber said, "Oh, you."

Dougherty hung back in the hallway. He didn't see Arlene anywhere, but he did recognize a few of the faces in the kitchen, mostly women.

Carpentier said, "Perhaps we could speak alone, Mrs. Webber?"

The back door was open and Dougherty saw a couple more people standing outside in the lane, all men it looked like, and again he was surprised to see so many.

The bedroom door off the kitchen opened, and Joe Webber came out saying, "Whatever you've got to say, say it."

Dougherty watched Carpentier move a little further into the kitchen and speak quietly to Millie, drawing Joe in closer as he spoke, and Dougherty was impressed by the detective and thinking, How do you get good at something as hard as talking to parents whose child has been killed? He heard Millie Webber start to cry softly, and Dougherty felt if he stood there another second he was going to bust open himself, so he backed away down the hall and out onto the front stoop.

Arlene was there then, sitting on the stoop, smoking a cigarette and drinking a cup of coffee. Most of the crowd was gone, and Dougherty looked up and down the street but all he saw was Arlene's boy a few houses down in front of another house with a few other kids playing with Dinky cars.

Dougherty said, "They finally go to work?" and Arlene said, "No, they're on strike."

"Who is?"

"The port."

"Since when?"

"Last night, I guess. It's a wildcat."

"Longshoremen or checkers and coopers?"

Arlene looked up at Dougherty and said, "I don't know, Eddie — what fucking difference does it make?" and Dougherty said, "Yeah, I guess." He really had no idea what he was doing, what help he could be on a homicide investigation.

After a few minutes of silence, Carpentier came out of the house and nodded to Arlene and then to Dougherty and then started back to the car. Dougherty caught up to him and Carpentier said, "Why don't you drive?" and tossed him the keys.

"Where are we going?"

"That store, what did you call it, Boss?"

In the car Dougherty said, "Most of these guys

work at the port but they're on strike today, some kind of wildcat walkout."

"Not them," Carpentier said, "it's the locks, St. Lambert and Côte St. Catherine. The ships are not getting through."

It was only a few blocks and Dougherty stopped the car in front of Boss's on Fortune Street. Before he opened the door Carpentier said, "I forgot to ask which funeral home they'll be using,"

"It'll be McGillivray's," Dougherty said.

"Are you sure? Could you find out?"

Dougherty said he would and they both got out of the car.

Carpentier walked ahead into the store, and as Dougherty started to follow him Danny Buckley came out and stopped and said, "You back again, Eddie?"

Dougherty said yeah and stood in the way so Buckley would have to walk around him, thinking, Yeah, I'm back, but it's different now, not just the uniform and the gun — everything. Then he watched Buckley pretend he had nowhere to go and open up the pack of smokes he'd just bought and take one out and light it and then finally say, "It's a shame about Brenda Webber." Dougherty said yeah, and just kept staring.

Dougherty saw Buckley looking past him towards the street, and he glanced around and saw a car and looked back at Buckley and said, "Cadillac?"

Buckley shrugged, and Dougherty said, "You working for the Higginses now?" and Buckley didn't say anything.

"Okay," Dougherty said, "that's good, Buck-Buck,"

and he stepped forward so Buckley had to move to get out of the way.

Then Dougherty stopped by the door and watched Buckley rush to the Caddy and get into the back seat without looking back, and Dougherty had to admit he was enjoying himself.

In the store, Carpentier was standing by the cash, smoking a cigarette and talking to Herbie, saying, "Are you sure?" and Herbie, a guy who'd owned the store as long as anyone could remember and never seemed to change, was saying, "I guess."

"Don't guess," Carpentier said, "think. When she came in, what did she buy?"

Herbie shrugged.

Dougherty said, "I got Brenda mixed up with Arlene, you ever do that?" and the two men at the cash both turned and looked at Dougherty. "They look so much alike."

Herbie said no, he didn't get them mixed up, and Dougherty said, "Not even when they come in here and buy a case of beer?" and he motioned to the walk-in cooler at the back of the small, cramped store.

"No."

"Brenda Webber never bought any beer? What about cigarettes?"

"There's no age limit on smokes."

"But you do need to be eighteen to buy beer, right?"

Herbie looked at Carpentier and then back to Dougherty and said, "Okay, a six-pack, Eddie, big deal. You used to come in here for a two-four when you were twelve."

"Yeah, for my father."

"So," Carpentier said, "Brenda Webber bought six bottles of beer?"

Herbie said, "Yeah, Black Label."

Dougherty said, "And?"

Herbie shrugged and Dougherty said, "This is important. Stop fucking around and tell the man everything Brenda Webber bought."

Carpentier never took his eyes off Herbie, who shook his head a little. "They ram the nightstick up your ass when they give you the uniform, Eddie?"

Then Herbie jumped back and knocked over a rack of chips as Dougherty made a move like he was going to start swinging that nightstick.

"A pack of Export 'A' and rolling papers — you happy?"

"No one's happy," Dougherty said, "a girl's dead. But that wasn't too hard, was it?" and he turned and walked out.

Outside the store, Dougherty realized he was shaking. He walked to Carpentier's car and took a deep breath and tried to relax. He hadn't been taught anything about intimidating people in his training, now he was thinking maybe it came more naturally for most recruits. And then he was thinking maybe it would've come more naturally for him in some other neighbourhood, maybe a little further away from where he'd been terrorized as a kid.

Carpentier came out of the store then and said, "You would think they'd want to help us."

"Goes against everything around here, helping cops."

"So," Carpentier said, "what do we know now?"

53

"She had bad taste in beer?"

"Anything else?"

"She bought cigarettes and rolling papers," Dougherty said, "to smoke hashish with her friends, but she never made it to the park."

"So they said. We'll have to talk to her friends again."

"Do you have any names?"

Carpentier got out his notebook and said, "Donna Fergus and Gail Murphy; do you know them?"

"I know a couple of Gail Murphy's brothers."

"Do you know where the Murphys live?"

Dougherty pointed right across the street from where they were standing and said, "Second floor."

"It's like a small town," Carpentier said, "everybody know everybody."

"Is that good?"

"We'll find out."

He started across the street and Dougherty said, "But she'll be in school now," and Carpentier looked at his watch and said, "Yes." Then he said, "We might as well have lunch."

Dougherty said, "There's a steamie place on Wellington, Nick's."

"Hot dogs? You're in CIB now — let's go to Magnan's."

54   Patrolmen might go to Magnan's on payday or some special occasion, take over a couple of tables and order pitchers of beer and the roast beef, but Dougherty would never have just stopped in for lunch on a workday. It might be a Point St. Charles tavern, but it was on St. Patrick at Charlevoix by the bridge

and attracted businessmen from across the canal, as far into the Point as most of them had ever been.

Carpentier sat down at a corner table and ordered roast beef and a Labatt 50 from the waiter in the black vest, white shirt and bow tie, and Dougherty wasn't sure what to do. He wasn't on duty but he was working, so he didn't think he should have a beer but Carpentier was, so he just ordered the same thing.

When the beers came Carpentier lit a cigarette and said, "So, *un maudit anglais, une tête carrée*, why would you join the police force?"

Dougherty took a drink of Fifty while he thought about what to say to that, and Carpentier said, "Actually, you do have a square head."

"So, I've heard."

Carpentier laughed and Dougherty said, "It seemed like a good idea at the time."

"All your friends growing their hair long and marching in protests and it looked like a good idea to become a cop?"

"Not my friends."

"In the Point?"

"We moved out of the Point," Dougherty said. "My parents bought a house on the South Shore, Greenfield Park, but I didn't make many friends there. I only had one year of school left and I finished it at Verdun High and then I wasn't sure what to do."

"Where does your father work?"

Dougherty looked at Carpentier and thought the detective and his father were about the same age, close to fifty. "He works for the phone company, so does my mom. The Bell, they call it."

"You didn't want to do that?"

"My dad went to work there after the war. Well, a little before the war and then he went back after. It seemed like a good thing to do after the war, but now . . ."

"If we were in America you'd be in Vietnam."

"I guess."

He felt Carpentier looking at him and he didn't know what to say.

The waiter, a fussy little guy of course, arrived with two plates of roast beef and mashed potatoes covered in gravy and a pile of peas. He put the plates down without really stopping and was gone.

Then Carpentier said, "Well, that's a different war, isn't it, not the same at all."

"Were you in?"

"The air force," he said, taking a bite of roast beef. "But the war was almost over when I turned eighteen; I never went overseas."

Dougherty nodded and took a bite himself, surprised at how good it was. Then he said, "My dad joined the Legion but said it was full of guys who never got any further than Longueil, and he stopped going."

Carpentier nodded and said, "Your father went?"

"Served on corvettes, spent the whole war in the North Atlantic."

"Does he tell you much about it?"

Dougherty had a mouth full of mashed potatoes and he swallowed and said, "No, not really."

Carpentier picked up his beer. "You ever have a few of these with him?" He looked around the tavern and said, "In a place like this?"

"He might be here tomorrow," Dougherty said, "if he's working in the area."

Carpentier took a long drink, finished off the beer and said, "Okay, so Brenda Webber was probably meeting her friends to drink beer and smoke dope. Where do you think she got the dope?"

"If she bought the beer," Dougherty said, "maybe one of the other girls bought the dope."

"Yes, maybe." Carpentier motioned a little for the waiter. Dougherty barely noticed it and a minute later the little guy was at the table with two more beers and then gone again.

Carpentier said, "Maybe the man at the store knows who's selling the dope."

"Or maybe Buck-Buck knows."

"Who?"

"Danny Buckley. He was at Nap's the other day and he was coming out of Boss's when we went in. He got in a car with Frank Higgins."

"One of the Higgins brothers?"

"Yeah. I'm not surprised Buck-Buck's working for him, was just a matter of time."

"I remember the father, Michael Higgins," Carpentier said, setting down his almost-empty glass, "when he worked at the port. A lot of things fell off the backs of trucks."

"I'm sure a lot of things are still falling off. I think all five of the Higgins brothers work at the port, or did sometimes when they weren't in jail. We could talk to them."

Carpentier put a little horseradish on top of a piece of roast beef and ate it, chewing slowly, and then said,

57

"We'll start with the girls, see what they say." Then he looked at Dougherty and said, "You liked it in the store when he was afraid of you."

"I liked that he told us what we wanted to know."

"Be careful not to like that too much."

And then Carpentier waved at the waiter and ordered one more round.

When they got back to Boss's there were a lot of kids on the street and Dougherty asked around until one of the younger kids, maybe ten years old, pointed out Gail Murphy walking by herself towards the store.

Carpentier stepped in front of her. "Gail?"

She said yeah and looked at Carpentier and then at Dougherty. "Are you Eddie Dougherty?"

"Yeah."

Gail Murphy nodded, crossed her arms under her breasts, showing a fair amount of cleavage in her plaid shirt. She kept staring at Dougherty until he said, "You know we want to talk about Brenda."

"Now you do."

"She stopped here to buy the beer and the rolling papers for the dope and then you were going to meet in the park, is that right?"

"What dope?"

"She bought cigarettes and rolling papers, you must have had some hash."

"No, we didn't."

Dougherty looked around at the crowd of kids who were gathering just out of earshot, in front of the store and in front of the houses on either side of it, and he leaned in a little closer. "We don't care about the dope, Gail, or the beer, We're just trying to find out where

Brenda was going when she left here. Were you going to meet at the park, at the bandshell in Marguerite Bourgeoys?"

Gail shrugged a little, barely moving her shoulders, and looked up at Dougherty. She didn't say anything for a moment but he was sure she would. He waited.

"Okay, not the park, we were going to meet behind Jeanne-LeBer first."

Dougherty nodded, recognizing his old elementary school. "To smoke dope?"

"I told you, we weren't smoking up."

Carpentier spoke then. "What about Brenda?"

Gail shrugged and Dougherty looked from her to Carpentier, surprised he'd asked the question but also surprised by the answer. He'd figured teenage girls did everything together, the way his sister did with her friends, but now Gail looked like she was telling the truth. The other girls hadn't smoked dope, but she didn't know about Brenda.

Carpentier said, "How long did you wait for Brenda?"

"I don't know, half an hour? Some guys came by and we went with them."

"Who?"

"Just guys from school."

"Not older guys?"

"No, what do you think? Just . . . guys we know."   59

"And when did you go home?"

Gail shrugged, said, "I don't know," and then thought about it some more, "Maybe eleven thirty?"

Dougherty said, "You didn't find it strange, that Brenda just didn't show up?"

"Lately, no."

"She did that a lot?"

"Not a lot, but sometimes."

Dougherty said okay, and Carpentier said, "Who did Brenda buy the hash from?"

Gail said, "I don't know," and Dougherty said, "Did she buy it from your brother?"

"Timmy?"

"Did she?

"No."

Dougherty said, "What about Mike?"

Gail shook her head and said, "Mike's in Parthenais — in jail."

"I know what it is. He in for dope?"

"He didn't do anything, got in some stupid fight — he didn't even start it."

Dougherty said, "No, of course not," and then he said, "You were never with Brenda when she bought it?"

"No. She just started . . ."

"Started what?"

Gail looked at him the way his sister did when she was about to ask him how dumb he was. "Playing with Barbies?"

Carpentier said, "Okay, that's enough."

They stood there for a moment, no one saying anything, and then Gail said, "Can I go now?" and Dougherty looked at Carpentier, who nodded.

"Yeah, sure."

She went into the store, and Carpentier started walking down Fortune Street towards Jeanne-LeBer school.

Dougherty followed, saying, "Do you want to talk to her friend, Donna Fergus?"

Carpentier looked at his watch and said, "I don't think we need to today."

"Does that seem odd, that Brenda would be smoking dope but not her friends?"

"Not necessarily. They're at the age where they start to try new things and make new friends, drift apart."

"Maybe not so much here."

"But they're leaving here more," Carpentier said, "going to high school in Verdun, going downtown to clubs, concerts."

Dougherty said, "Yeah, maybe," and looked around and said, "Usually people in the Point stay in the Point." .

"You didn't."

"No."

"And things are different now," Carpentier said. He pointed to a couple of teenage boys coming out of Boss's. "From behind they look like girls, the long hair and the jeans. The whole world is upside down."

Dougherty didn't say anything but he was thinking, That's for sure, the whole world is upside down. He was only a few years older than those boys, but he felt like he was from another generation.

Carpentier said, "I wonder who she buy the hash from?"

"If someone's selling it around here," Dougherty said, "then one of the Higgins will be in on it."

"We better find out."

"I can ask Buck-Buck."

Carpentier looked at him and Dougherty said,

"Danny Buckley, that's what we call him," and Carpentier said, "Oh, Buckley, Buck-Buck, yes," and Dougherty said, "Yeah, but really it's because of his buck teeth, that's why he hates it so much."

"And why you use it."

"Yeah."

Carpentier said, "Before you talk to him you should probably talk to Ste. Marie, see what he says."

"Who?"

"Detective Ste. Marie, the Social Security Squad."

"Oh right, narcotics."

"And the mob stuff," Carpentier said, "and the undercover operations."

Dougherty nodded and didn't say anything, and Carpentier said, "Tell him I sent you." Dougherty said okay, but he still wasn't sure how it would work.

Then Carpentier said, *"Bon,"* and started walking half a block until they were at the corner of Favard, and he stopped and looked up and down the street. "This street goes back to Wellington?"

Dougherty said, "Yeah, that way back to Marguerite Bourgeoys Park and up by the park or you can go along here the other way and then up one of the other streets, Ash or Charon or all the way to Sepastapol."

"So, if Brenda Webber left that store and was going to meet her friends behind the school there, she would have walked along here and presumably . . ." Carpentier held his hands out and turned around a little, looking up and down the streets. "If she got into a car here someone might have seen."

The school was on one side of Favard but the other side was lined with three-storey row houses like every other street in the Point, and Dougherty said, "Yeah, like Mrs. Wilburn, who's looking at us right now," and he pointed to the window of a house on Favard, the drapes moving a little.

"Would she tell us?"

"Maybe if we ask nice."

"All right," Carpentier said, "then maybe I better do the talking."

Dougherty looked at him and Carpentier smiled a little and said, "I'm kidding, *l'anglais*, relax."

He did do most of the talking, especially after Mrs. Wilburn called Dougherty "Little Eddie," and asked him if he wanted a piece of toffee.

Once Carpentier mentioned Brenda Webber, though, Mrs. Wilburn had very little to say. No, she hadn't seen her that night; yes, she knew her, of course, from church. Although Brenda wasn't there very much these days.

"What about strange cars," Dougherty said, "driving around?"

"Like Jackie Murphy's? So loud."

"Someone you don't know," Dougherty said.

"Maybe." Mrs. Wilburn shrugged. "I don't know everyone who drives by."

Carpentier said, "No, of course not," and then he thanked her and he and Dougherty left.

Outside on the street, Carpentier said, "You think the guy who picked up Brenda live in the Point?"

"I was just thinking that all these streets are one way and dead end here, or on the other side of Wellington at the Grand Trunk line. You have to know your way around."

"And people here notice strangers."

"Yeah."

Carpentier nodded. "This Bill, the other women, he knew them before he killed them. It makes sense."

"But where would Brenda have met him?"

"Maybe he sell her the hash, the other women they all use drugs."

"Yeah, I'll talk to Buck-Buck."

Carpentier nodded. "*Bon*. We should go and talk to Detective-Lieutenant Desjardins, fill him in on this and the other one, Sylvie Berubé."

Dougherty almost said, "Who's that?" before he remembered the reason he was out with Carpentier in the first place — the murder of the other woman, the one who also had a bedsheet around her neck. He'd been feeling pretty good about the way this was going, but now he was thinking again how the detectives seemed to remember everything, every detail, and he was feeling out his depth.

They walked back to the car and Dougherty drove them to Bonsecours Street, Carpentier going over everything again: the last time Brenda Webber was seen alive at Boss's store, the girls she was supposed to meet behind the school, the route she would have taken. Then he talked about the other murders, the three women downtown and now another one further into the east end. By the time they got to the station, Dougherty was even more confused by the details than he had been before, and Carpentier could tell. "Don't worry," he said "You take it one thing at a time. When we get back to the homicide office, you read all the files."

When they got there the homicide office was empty, and Carpentier told Dougherty half the squad was working on the terrorists, chasing down leads about stolen dynamite and machine guns. Then he said, "That's why you're working this."

Dougherty called Sgt. Delisle at Station Ten and he was told to get back right away.

"Another bomb," Dougherty told Carpentier when he hung up. "On the McGill campus."

Carpentier said, "Duty calls," and Dougherty said, "But I have to talk to Detective Ste. Marie about Danny Buckley and the hash, who sold it to Brenda?"

Carpentier shrugged a little, looking like he'd heard all this many times before. "Go and work your shift, find the bomb."

Dougherty said okay and walked out, leaving Carpentier alone in the homicide office.

CHAPTER
FOUR

The call had said the bomb was on campus but didn't say which building. Dougherty drove his Mustang back up the hill and turned off Sherbrooke and stopped at the Roddick Gates, the security guard waving him to back up. Dougherty leaned out the window showing his uniform saying, "I'm on duty."

The security guard said, "So what, turn around and go up McTavish to the Physical Plant on Dr. Penfield. That's where all the cops are."

Dougherty said, "Can I cut through campus?" and motioned to the road circling the big lawn spreading out ahead of him, and the guard said, "Okay, park in front of Dawson Hall. You can cut through the arts building."

"I know the way," Dougherty said.

As he drove through campus he saw a few people standing at the doors to a new concrete slab building that looked to be over ten storeys, taller than the chemistry building beside it, Dougherty couldn't remember the name. He parked by Dawson Hall and walked up the steps of the arts building, looking back over the big lawn and Sherbrooke Street beyond and realized he'd wanted to come in this way because it was coming in the front door. He hadn't wanted to go in through the Physical Plant — there wasn't a sign that said *tradesman's entrance*, but that's what it was. He'd been to the arts building once before, looking for admissions back when he thought he might fill out the form. But he'd ended up leaving the campus, too intimidated to even ask anyone where admissions was.

This time he walked up the steps and into the Arts Building and found the place pretty much empty. He walked past rows of offices and through the halls that connected the building with the Physical Plant and came up on the dispatcher's office from behind.

The Physical Plant he knew from when he was a kid, working Saturday mornings with his father, running phone lines on campus. They'd start and end in the Plant, a building it was unlikely any student had ever been in.

Dougherty stopped at the dispatcher's office and realized his hands had been balled into fists and his jaw was clenched. He took a breath and relaxed when he saw the other uniformed cops standing around smoking cigarettes and drinking coffee in the break room.

One of the cops said, "Hey Dog-eh-dee, nice of

you to join us," and some of the others laughed and Dougherty said, "Yeah, you're having trouble holding up that wall by yourself."

A young cop said, "I was hoping there'd be more students here, hippie chicks looking for free love," and the dispatcher said, "It's June, idiot, school's over."

"No summer school?"

Dougherty stepped up to the window to the dispatcher's office and said, "Where's Vachon?"

"He was in Otto Maass and then Burnside Hall, and now I think he's in the library — most of the buildings are closed."

Dougherty remembered the chemistry building was called Otto Maas and the new concrete slab was Burnside Hall, some kind of science building. Then he said, "We're just waiting?"

The dispatcher shrugged.

Dougherty motioned to the alarm board beside him and said, "What's going on?"

The board was covered with square buttons: all of the bigger buildings on campus were listed and beside each name the buttons were marked *intrusion*, *fire* and *flood*. A few of the buttons were lit up and paper clips were stuck into them. The dispatcher said, "The alarm goes off, usually when some student is late handing something in and shakes the door. You stick the paper clip in to stop the buzzer but the light stays on."

Dougherty saw that all the lit-up buttons were *intrusion*, and he said, "So what do you do?"

"Send the foot patrol; he resets the alarm."

"But some buildings are unlocked?"

"Yeah, there are some summer classes." He shrugged

again and said, "There are some chicks here."

"But what if it's in one of the locked buildings?"

The dispatcher said they'd have to check them all, and Dougherty said, "How many is that?" Before the dispatcher could answer, one of the cops in the break room said, *"Delisle arrive,"* and everybody straightened up as the Sergeant came up the stairs, saying, *"Mettez vos patins, les boys."*

The first one he saw was Dougherty standing by the dispatcher's desk and he said, "Okay, Dougherty, you and . . ." he looked around and waved a couple of cops out of the break room saying, ". . . Champoux and Deslauriers, go to the Redpath Building — the museum not the library," speaking English as he looked back at the dispatcher, saying, "A lot of the buildings are Redpath."

"The library and the museum," the dispatcher said. "Redpath Hall, too, I guess, but that's sort of the same as the library."

Delisle said, "Sort of," and looked at Dougherty. "You know where is the museum? Meet the foot patrol, he has the keys." Then Delisle went into the break room and started speaking French to the other cops, handing out assignments.

Dougherty looked at the dispatcher. "Where is it?"

"Go out to Dr. Penfield," he said, pointing down the stairs to the front door of the Physical Plant, "turn left and turn left again. It faces in towards the campus, the big lawn. You can't miss it, it looks just like a museum."

Walking downhill along Dr. Penfield Avenue, Dougherty said, "If we have to check all the locked buildings, too, we could be here all day."

"All week," Champoux said. "How many buildings they got?"

Deslauriers said, "If only the school was open," and Dougherty realized he'd been the guy looking for hippie chicks and free love.

When they got to the Redpath Museum, a building that did look like a museum, there was a security guard waiting by the door. Dougherty said, "Okay, we're here, unlock the door." The guard, sixty or seventy years old, a *commissaire*, retired military, turned to the door and started going through the many keys on his big key ring.

Deslauriers said, "No rush," and laughed and then he said hello to the half dozen or so students who had suddenly appeared at the bottom of the museum's steps.

One of the students, a male voice, said, "No pigs on campus."

Deslauriers said, "What?"

More students had walked up now and another male voice repeated, "No pigs on campus," and the others started saying it, too.

Dougherty turned and looked at the students, then back to the security guard and said, "Come on, let's go. We better find it before it finds us."

The guard finally got the door open and Dougherty led the cops into the building while the students chanted, "No pigs, no pigs!"

Inside Deslauriers said, "You'd think they'd want us to find the bomb," and Champoux said, "And maybe stay away from the buildings."

Dougherty said, "They can't help it. They see the uniform, it's moths to a flame. Okay, let's spread out and work our way up, it's probably in an Expo 67 flight bag, a blue one, but look for anything, any bag or package. And check all the garbage cans."

The middle of the building was open all the way to the top, at least three floors, and a huge dinosaur skeleton stared down at the front doors, where the cops were standing.

Champoux said, "Have you ever seen one?" and Dougherty said, "I think it's a T. Rex."

Champoux said, "No, a bomb?"

"Of course, haven't you?"

"Not close up."

"Well, don't touch it. You'll hear the ticking from the alarm clock. They take the minute hand off and put a bolt through the face of the clock with a wire on it. When the hour hand hits it that completes the circuit and it blows."

"So," Champoux said, "we hear the ticking, we get out."

"You hear the ticking, you call me."

Then Dougherty made his way to the row of exhibit tables on his left while Champoux and Deslauriers walked to their right. They covered the whole first floor and found nothing and then went up the stairs to the second storey, the balconies that overlooked the main floor. Still nothing.

When they got back to the front doors, the security guard was still standing there and Dougherty said, "Is that it?"

"There are offices in the back."

Dougherty said okay, and then looked at Champoux and Deslauriers and said, "You might as well go back to the Physical Plant, see where we're going next. I'll check the offices." The two cops said that was a good idea and were out the door before Dougherty could say anything else.

The security guard led him through the building, saying, "This place isn't open as much as it used to be. There used to be a lot of high school classes through here, but now they say that costs too much so this place is going back to more scientific research." He unlocked the door to the offices. "Here you go."

Dougherty nodded and walked into the hallway. There were a few doors on each side, all unlocked, and he searched each office, in the garbage cans and the desk drawers but didn't find anything and didn't hear any ticking.

Outside it was starting to get dark, and as the guard locked the front door to the museum Dougherty surveyed the campus and saw a couple of cop cars parked in front of buildings but not much activity.

The guard said, "I'm supposed to be doing my rounds now."

"Okay, well, I guess we're done here."

Dougherty walked back along Dr. Penfield Avenue, now lined with cop cars, and he recognized Vachon's unmarked station wagon. The Physical Plant was crowded with cops. Dougherty found a spot by the dispatcher's desk and leaned against the wall and lit a cigarette.

In the break room, Vachon was telling a story about a bomb in a post office, how they found it because the ticking woke up the night watchman.

Then Sergeant Delisle came down the hall from the security captain's office, saying he'd just got off the phone with the Chief and that was it for the search. "We're done here, let's get back to work."

The dispatcher said, "You checked everywhere?"

Already cops were streaming out of the building as Delisle told him, "As much as we can. The call said the bomb would go off at five o'clock. It's almost nine now — it was probably a hoax."

"Probably? But there could still be a bomb?"

"It's doubtful," Delisle said.

Vachon came up behind Delisle and said, "Still, if anyone sees something, call us."

"What do you mean, anything?"

Vachon shrugged. "A package, a bag, anything. Sometimes it's a flight bag, a little suitcase, sometimes it's wrapped in a garbage bag and taped."

Delisle said, "You'll hear the ticking," but Vachon said, "No, maybe not. Maybe the clock broke and that's why the bomb didn't go off. Could have been overwound."

"But the bomb," the dispatcher said, "it could still be live?"

"Oh the dynamite, sure," Vachon said, "so don't touch it, call us."

"Great."

"There probably never was a bomb," Delisle said. "We get these calls all the time."

Vachon said, *"Bon, c'est tout,"* and turned and left. Delisle followed, then stopped and turned back and looked at Dougherty. "Constable, I almost forgot."

"Yeah?"

"Detective Carpentier called, he wants you to go with him to the funeral tomorrow."

"What funeral?"

"In the Point. He says don't wear your uniform, wear a suit."

"A suit?"

"You still have your confirmation suit?"

Dougherty said he didn't think it would fit, and Delisle started down the stairs to the front door, saying, "But you're still starting your shift at four, so don't be late."

"So, is the funeral overtime?" Dougherty said, but Delisle was gone. The dispatcher, looking at his still-lit alarm board, said, "I don't think he heard you."

———

Dougherty wore black pants and a dark blue sports coat, a white shirt and a tie — the same outfit he had worn to the banquet at the Expo 67 opening ceremonies for the construction workers who'd built the pavilions.

But there were a lot of confirmation suits and dresses at the funeral — every teenager in the Point was there, and pretty much every adult, too.

Dougherty and Carpentier stood at the back of Grace Church and listened to Reverend Barker say a lot of nice things about Brenda Webber. He even made a couple of jokes about how she was "taking full advantage of her teenaged opportunities," and Dougherty thought that was pretty gutsy, to not whitewash everything in the face of such a tragedy.

Carpentier watched the people in the church, and

Dougherty noticed him looking closely at Danny Buckley, who was sitting next to his mother. Then he realized Carpentier was actually looking at a couple of the Higgins brothers sitting behind Buckley, and Dougherty whispered that it didn't look like they were buying their suits in Verdun.

Carpentier said, "No, they look Italian. Must have new friends."

After the funeral most of the adults went downstairs to a reception while the teenagers left the church and went to the Boys & Girls Club for their own memorial.

Dougherty and Carpentier stood on Wellington just down from the doors and watched people leaving. Carpentier said it was a good service and Dougherty agreed. "Different from mass," Carpentier said.

"Yeah," Dougherty said, "they're not the frozen chosen like we are. They get right in there and sing; they don't leave that up to the choir."

"You're Catholic?"

"My mother is, so . . ." He shrugged. Then he saw Buckley and the Higgins brothers get into a Cadillac that had been idling by the curb, and he said to Carpentier, "Getting right back to work."

"The wildcat is over, the ships are coming into the port."

"I don't think they unload ships."

"No," Carpentier said, "but the older Higgins still runs the Coopers and Checkers union. They'll be getting something off the boats."

"How do you know all this?"

Carpentier shrugged. "You work homicide, you work mob. It's a lot of drug, a lot of extortion, a lot of homicide." He motioned towards the doors of the church, Mr. and Mrs. Webber coming out now with Reverend Barker and behind them a couple guys in nice suits. "There, that's Detective-Lieutenant Desjardins and the Chief."

"Should we talk to the family?"

"No, we just needed to be here. Anybody look out of place?"

"Not that I can tell but I don't know everybody."

"There should have been more of us," Carpentier said.

"More cops?"

"More from homicide, but we don't have a full squad, less than half, really, so many working the anti-terrorist squad."

"There's been a lot of bombs."

"Assholes with bombs," Carpentier said, "*Bon*, look around a little, maybe take a walk, you never know."

"I haven't had a chance to talk to Detective Ste. Marie yet, about the hash. Do you want me to talk to Buck-Buck anyway?"

"Not yet, just look around."

Dougherty said okay and walked back up Fortune Street, watching people come out through the side door of the church, mostly older people, women, used to being in the church, used to funerals.

Dougherty crossed the street and watched from the other side for a few minutes but it didn't take long for the people who were leaving to be gone. Dougherty figured the ones who were in the church basement would be there for hours. Protestants, his mother would say, eating bologna sandwiches and squares.

He crossed Wellington and walked a block west towards St. Gabriel's, the English Catholic school Dougherty had begged his mother to let him go to with no success, and then turned around to walk back and stopped suddenly, staring at Gail Murphy walking towards him. "Are you looking for me?"

She was wearing a white dress and had her hair in braids, looking a lot younger than she had when he and Carpentier questioned her outside Boss's store, but she still crossed her arms and cocked her hip a little and said, "Maybe."

"What is it?"

"I don't know. I don't know if it's anything."

"Why don't you tell me and I'll find out?"

Gail looked back towards the church and then to Dougherty and said, "You were asking about a car?"

"Yeah, that's right."

"I think I saw one."

"Picking up Brenda?"

"I didn't see Brenda near the car."

"You saw the car the night Brenda disappeared?"

"Yeah."

"What kind of car was it?"

"I don't know, a big one."

"What colour?"

"You have a cigarette?"

Dougherty looked past Gail towards the church and saw that pretty much everyone was gone. He got out his smokes and held open the pack for Gail. He went to light it for her at the same time she was reaching for the lighter. She pulled back, looking worried, until she figured out was he was doing and leaned back in towards his hand with the lighter.

Straightening up and exhaling a stream of smoke, she said, "It was white, a big white car with a black roof."

"A convertible?"

She took another drag and shook her head. "No, I don't think so."

"New or old? Did it have any rust?"

"Jesus, I barely saw it."

"But there was something about it you wanted to tell me?"

She shrugged, looked around, flicked ash off her smoke, folded her arms over her chest and said, "Maybe I've seen it before."

"Did you see the driver?"

"It's just not someone from around here, you know, but it's been here sometimes."

"Creep you out?"

She shrugged, took another drag, blew smoke. "I don't know."

"Did you talk to Brenda about it?"

"No," Gail said, dragging out the word like it was the stupidest question she'd ever heard. "Nobody noticed it."

"Except for you."

"Yeah, I guess."

"Well this is good," Dougherty said. "Thanks for telling me."

For a second he thought he saw the hint of a smile from Gail, a little bit of being pleased with herself, but it disappeared as fast as it came and she said, "Well, I gotta go." Dougherty said, "Yeah, I guess," and watched her walk away, tossing the smoke to the sidewalk and turning down Fortune Street.

A car drove by then, a big one, a Cadillac, the same one that had picked up Danny Buckley and the Higgins brothers in front of the church, and Dougherty thought that a couple of years ago that car would have been out of place here. It would have been the one all the kids noticed but not now. Not driven by a Higgins.

He spent another hour walking around the Point but he didn't talk to anyone else, and then it was time to get home and change into his uniform and get to work.

CHAPTER
FIVE

The minute Dougherty walked into Station Ten at four he got sent on a call. It was almost seven when he got back, stomping into the ground floor lobby of the old building and saying he was going to take a shower.

The desk sergeant, Delisle, said, "Was it bad?"

Dougherty stopped and looked at him sitting behind the desk. "That call came in at three, you could've sent the day shift."

"Look, you're just back now, that would have been at least three hours of overtime."

"Maybe they wouldn't have had to wait so long for the ident guys."

Delisle stood up, trying to make nice now, saying, "It was really bad?"

"The landlord called because of the smell."

"Sometimes it's just garbage."

"This wasn't garbage," Dougherty said, "this was a dead body. Probably been there for days."

"Suicide?"

"Yeah, shot himself. Boisjoli thinks it was some kind of service revolver the British used. Looks like the guy's from England."

"He have any ID?"

Dougherty had calmed down, losing the tension and starting to feel the sadness of the situation, and he said, "Yeah, all kinds of ID: immigration papers, discharge papers, everything. Very neat, organized. He even left a note."

"*Câlisse*, what it say?"

"Boisjoli's bringing it in, you'll see. The guy's wife went back to England, he lost his job, having nightmares, drinking."

"The usual."

Dougherty said yeah, and went downstairs to the change room. He took a hot shower and then brushed his teeth but couldn't get rid of the taste. He figured there probably wasn't really a taste — it was just in his head. Still, he wished he'd known Rozovsky's trick of putting the entire roll of spearmint Life Savers in his mouth before he went into the apartment. Well, like Rozovsky said, he'd know for next time.

Next time.

Back upstairs, in a fresh blue shirt and underwear but the same pants, Dougherty said to Delisle, "Boisjoli back yet?" Delisle shook his head, saying, "Someone here to see you," and pointed to a woman standing at the end of the counter nearest the door, as if she didn't want to come too far into the station.

Dougherty glanced back at Delisle and stepped towards the woman. "Can I help you?"

"Are you Constable Dougherty?" speaking English with no accent and pronouncing it correctly.

"Yeah."

Just as Dougherty was saying it, Detective Boisjoli and his partner arrived along with a few constables, and the station filled with noise and activity as they started to tell Delisle all about the suicide, the note and how much blood had been on the walls of the apartment.

The woman said to Dougherty, "Can we talk somewhere quiet?" and he looked around and saw Delisle going into the detective's offices with the rest of them. He turned back to the woman. "What's this about?"

"Detective Carpentier said I should talk to you. It's about Brenda Webber and . . ." She checked a small notebook but didn't see what she was looking for, so Dougherty said, "Sylvie Berubé?"

"Yes, that's it."

More cops came into the station then and Dougherty said, "You want to get a cup of coffee?"

She said okay, so Dougherty led the way and they went around the corner and half a block down St. Matthew to the lunch counter across the street from the fire station. The place was empty so they sat on stools at the counter. From the kitchen a man called, "We close."

Dougherty said, "Hey Pete, you going to be here for ten minutes? We just need coffee."

From the kitchen they heard Pete say, "Take a piece a pie, too."

Dougherty was already up and pouring the last of the coffee from the glass pot into a couple of mugs, and he motioned at the pies in their stacked display case, but the woman shook her head and said, "Just the coffee's fine."

"Well, I don't know if it's fine," Dougherty said, "but it's all we've got. What's your name?"

"Oh, I'm sorry, Ruth Garber," and she held out her hand, and Dougherty shook it.

"You were talking to Detective Carpentier?"

"Yes. We've been working with the CIB task force, what's left of it."

"Yeah, everybody's gone to anti-terrorist, but who's 'we'? What are you working on?"

"Oh, Dr. Pendleton and myself, we're working on the Bill murders. Some people call them the Vampire murders because of the . . . mutilations."

Dougherty said, "Sure, but I don't understand. What exactly are you doing?"

"Oh right, I should start from the beginning. I've been dealing with this for a while, since February anyway, and I forget not everyone's up to speed."

She stopped for a moment, took a sip of coffee and got right back into it. "I'm a graduate student at McGill. I'm doing my M.A. and I'm Dr. Pendleton's research assistant . . . well, he has a couple but I'm the main one at the moment. We're collecting information about the murders committed by Bill."

Dougherty said, "Okay, sure. But why?"

Ruth Garber looked at him, and Dougherty realized

that even though she said she was a student they were about the same age. He wondered how long she'd been at McGill but he didn't say anything, he just listened as she told him about Dr. Pendleton being a sociology professor and how he was working on a theory about murder. "About murderers, really, multiple murderers."

"I hope he's against it."

She looked right at Dougherty but she didn't smile. He said, "A joke?" and she said, "Oh, okay, I see," and Dougherty could hear his grandmother's voice adding, "said the blind man, but he didn't see at all."

"Why do you want to talk to me?"

"You were first on the scene when the bodies were discovered, weren't you?"

"Carpentier called me to identify Brenda Webber. I knew the family when I was growing up in the Point — well, I guess I still do, her older sister Arlene, couple of brothers."

Ruth had her notebook out again and was writing something down, and then she looked up at Dougherty and said, "You mean Pointe St-Charles?"

"That's right."

She nodded and wrote that down and then said, "So you weren't the first on the scene?"

"No."

84   She looked disappointed. "What about Sylvie Berubé?"

"I was the first cop on that one. Some kids found her body, told one of their mothers and she called it in."

"This was last year, April 9, 1969, is that right?"

"April, yeah, the ninth, I guess."

She read something from her notebook and said, "Detective Carpentier said you had some information about similarities?"

"He did?"

"Something not in the file?"

"Oh," Dougherty said, "the bedsheet."

"What about it?"

"Brenda Webber had a bedsheet around her neck. So did Sylvie Berubé, but it's not in any of the pictures and there's no mention of it in the report."

"And you're sure it was there?"

"You don't see a dead body very often," Dougherty said, "you remember a lot of the details."

"Why isn't it in the pictures or the report?"

"I don't know, I guess that's my fault. When you're the first on the scene you're supposed to secure the area, make sure nothing gets touched, hold it till the detectives get there."

"But you didn't do that?"

Dougherty leaned back on the stool and looked at this Ruth Garber and really didn't know what to think. She had long dark hair and wore glasses and from what he could tell no make-up, not even lipstick, and she looked very serious, nothing like the girls he knew. But then he figured he didn't know any McGill students, though she also seemed different from the ones who were calling him pig the day before when he was looking for a bomb on campus.

"No, I guess I didn't secure the scene well enough."

She wrote something down and said, "But the bedsheet wasn't what was used to strangle either victim?"

"I don't know," Dougherty said, "I don't think so but you'll have to ask the coroner about that."

She nodded. "And both women were nude, or partially nude?"

"Yeah, but they were both wearing shoes. Well, Sylvie Berubé was wearing boots."

"She was the one . . ." she flipped a page in her notebook, "in the east end, April 9, 1969?"

"Yeah."

"She was a go-go dancer and possibly a prostitute, is that right?"

Dougherty looked at her and was thinking, How can she talk about this stuff, these naked, strangled women dumped in fields, so easily? "I don't really know anything about her."

Ruth nodded. "And Brenda Webber was wearing shoes, tennis shoes, right?"

"Runners, yeah."

"Nothing else?"

Dougherty didn't say anything for a moment, and Ruth looked up at him, waiting. "Just the sheet around her neck. It wasn't tied tight, so at first we thought it was a scarf. I guess it was the same for Sylvie Berubé — the sheet wasn't tied tight and it blew away or came off and got misplaced or something. It's a tough thing to see a dead body, especially a young person. The sheets covered their faces so they didn't look dead. They could have been sleeping."

"There were no marks on their bodies, no blood?"

"Not on their bodies," Dougherty said, "but the nose . . ."

"Yes?"

"Well," Dougherty said, "they'd been strangled, you know, so there was blood coming out of their noses. Not much, just spots really, but even before you see that, when you get close you feel it, you know."

"Feel what?"

"That they aren't sleeping, that they aren't breathing. It's like . . . it's cold, you know. You get close and even before you touch them and try to wake them up you can tell."

"How?"

"You can feel it. I don't know if I can explain it," Dougherty said, and Ruth was looking at him, no expression, so he said, "The first time I was close to a dead person was when Gauthier and I — he was my first partner, he was training me but he retired. I was supposed to get another partner but we're always so short. Anyway, we got a call about some rummies fighting and when we got there one of them had stabbed another one, slit his throat — guy was dead before he hit the ground. The other guy, the one who did it, he was already crying, moaning about how he killed his best friend and we all knew the guy was dead. Not because of the blood, it was still pumping, but you could just feel it."

"Feel what?"

"Death."

Ruth nodded a little and started writing in her notebook. Dougherty waited till she stopped writing and then said, "Is this helping?"

She shrugged a little and said, "I don't know yet," and he could tell she knew he didn't understand. He watched her think about it for a few seconds and then she said, "I know most sociology departments are theoretical and speculative — armchair social science, they say, right? At McGill we're a smaller department but we're different, we put a lot more emphasis on empirical observation, much more intensive interviewing and field work."

"Like this?"

"Yes, Dr. Pendleton has done a lot of research with multiple murderers — he's interviewed Peter Woodcock and Léopold Dion and Richard Speck. He may interview Manson."

"Charlie Manson?"

"Maybe. And he's worked with Dr. MacDonald."

"At McGill?"

Ruth said, "No, Dr. MacDonald is from New Zealand," but she didn't act like it was a dumb question or anything like that, so Dougherty nodded, and then she said, "He wrote *The Murderer and His Victim* and developed the MacDonald Triad."

Before Dougherty could think of anything to say, Pete came out of the kitchen. "So, what you have planned for Friday night? A little dining, a little dancing?"

Dressed in a dark suit with a crisp white shirt, his hair slicked back and a fresh shave, Pete was ready for a night on the town, and he stopped short when he saw Dougherty in his uniform. "Eddie, you can't take this lovely lady out dressed like that. All the good discos, you need a jacket and a tie."

"I'm working tonight."

Pete said, "Oh," and looked at Ruth, "too bad."

"Ruth Garber, this is Pete Spirodakis. His father

owns this place." Pete was about the same age as Dougherty, but in his suit, with his European looks, he could pass for early thirties.

"Come on, we'll go to Le Crash."

"I've seen enough car accidents, Pete."

Ruth looked like she didn't get it, so Dougherty said, "It's the disco on Dorchester and Mackay — you've seen it, there's half a car on the wall outside," and she said oh, not looking too pleased, and Dougherty said, "Yeah, and inside there's another half a car over the bar and pieces of cars all over."

"But the best part," Pete said, "is the dance floor is steel and they've got strobe lights."

Ruth said, "No thanks," and Pete said, "Okay, I can get you into George's."

"Sorry."

Pete looked at Ruth and said, "Anywhere you like, I can get you in."

"I don't go to *discothèques*."

"You've never been?"

"No, I wouldn't like it."

"How do you know if you've never been?"

Dougherty said, "Why don't you offer to take her to the Marquis de Sade," and Pete said, " Hey, if I want to hear Charles Aznavour I can stay home and listen to my mom's records." Then he winked at Ruth. "But Le Vieux Rafiot's just around the corner. You can have a great time on the old boat."

"No, thank you, I have to get back to work myself."

"Working on a Friday night, it's not healthy."

Dougherty stood up and started to get some money out of his pocket, but Pete put a hand on his arm.

"Since when you pay for coffee?"

They walked out of the diner, and while Pete was locking the door he looked over his shoulder at Ruth and said, "Come back some time for lunch. You ever have souvlaki?"

Ruth smiled and said, "Okay, thanks, that I'll do," and Pete said to Dougherty, "You better show her a good time before someone else does." He laughed and walked away towards St. Catherine Street.

"Next month he'll probably be a hippie," Dougherty said, and Ruth said yes and they started walking towards de Maisonneuve.

"Why are you working on Friday night?"

"Dr. Pendleton wanted me to get your impressions as soon as I could, while they were still fresh."

"In case the beat cop forgets the details?"

She started to say, "Oh no, it's not," but Dougherty said, "It's okay." And then they were in front of Station Ten and he said, "Some things you don't forget."

She smiled and held out her hand. "Well, there are lots of things I forget, so if I remember something I should have asked would it be okay if I come back and we talk again?"

"Anytime," Dougherty said, shaking her hand. "Anytime."

She squeezed a little harder on his hand, then let go and walked away.

After a minute Dougherty walked into the precinct and saw Delisle at the desk. "Hey, what's the MacDonald Triad?"

Delisle said, "I don't know, sounds like a bridge, where is it?"

Dougherty said he wasn't sure, and then Delisle said, "*Bon*, we have a call, the girls are going at it."

"Where?"

"Baby Face."

"The night hasn't even started. It's still light out."

"Crazy dykes. Get down there before it gets into the street."

Dougherty started out of the station, then said, "Who else is coming?"

"You think you need help?"

"Last time it was six of them."

Delisle said, "Call if you need backup," and Dougherty waved him off, knowing if he called it would take half an hour for anyone to show up anyway.

Friday night, going to be a long one.

CHAPTER
SIX

Sunday dinner in Greenfield Park. The Park, as everybody called it, a little English town surrounded by Ville LeMoyne and Laflèche and Longueil and the rest of the French South Shore.

When Dougherty's parents bought the house in the Park he had one year left in high school and thought it was the worst thing they could've done, but now, driving over the Champlain Bridge, he could understand the move to the South Shore a little better. A two-storey semi, three bedrooms, a front yard, a backyard. Dougherty helped his dad finish the basement, putting down black-and-white tiles on the cement floor and knotty pine up on the walls. It was *Leave It to Beaver*, or it would've been if Dougherty and his father hadn't been fighting the whole time about what Eddie was going to with his life.

Just off the bridge and past the sign pointing to the Eastern Townships and New York State, Dougherty took the Taschereau Boulevard exit and drove past the motels and bars, the Canadian Tire and the Burger Ranch, and turned left at the Fina station into the Park. It felt a little like the Point, a tight-knit community surrounded by what the people felt were outsiders, people they never really associated with, separated by language. The two solitudes, like that book Dougherty was supposed to read in school but never finished.

But unlike the Point, this part of the Park was almost new, red brick duplexes and triplexes barely ten years old, skinny little maple trees on the front lawns. It could be a thousand miles away, not just across a bridge.

Dougherty's mother was working in the garden, kneeling in front of a flower bed that bordered the driveway, his father's old Pontiac backed in and ready to leave for work Monday morning. She looked up when she saw Dougherty parking on the street and then went right back to work, and he was thinking, Shit, are they fighting already?

The house was on the corner of Patricia and Margaret — the developer who had bought the property from the city had smoothed things over with the councillors by naming the streets after their wives: Margaret, Patricia, Dorothy, Gail, Vivian, Doris. Dougherty opened the gate in the white picket fence and walked into the side yard. His father was bent over an aluminum folding chair, weaving new vinyl strapping onto it, and when he looked up he looked happy.

"Son, grab this, will you," he said, and Dougherty took an end of the vinyl while his father got the bolt into the hole in the frame and looked around on the ground.

Dougherty found the nut and handed it to his father, who tightened it in place and then turned the deck chair over and sat it on the patio. "There you go."

Dougherty started to sit down but his father said, "Would you like a drink, a beer?"

"It's kind of early."

"Can't be that early, your sister's up."

Dougherty laughed and said, "Yeah, okay, I'll have a beer," and followed him up the stairs and into the kitchen, where his father rolled his eyes at the ceiling and said, "It's not Benny Goodman," and Dougherty listened to the music coming from Cheryl's room and said, "No, I think it's The Doors."

They went back outside and sat on deck chairs, Dougherty's the newly repaired one and his father's looking like it would be next to go through the process, and Dougherty said, "Is Mom fighting with Cheryl again?"

"Again? You mean 'still'?"

Dougherty shook his head and looked at the newspaper. "The posties going on strike?"

"Everybody's going on strike."

Another thing they fought about. Dougherty couldn't understand his father, one minute defending all these guys going out on strike, going out on strike himself with the lineman's union at the Bell, talking about building the country from the ground up, the solid foundation, and the next minute going on about how Eddie needed to get a university degree and not be part of it.

"Well," Dougherty said, thinking he should leave it alone even as the words were coming out, "maybe we'll be next. Marcil is trying to get us the right to strike."

"After what happened last time?"

The Murray Hill riot during the one-day police strike the year before. A million dollars in damage and one off-duty cop from out of town killed. The army was called in, but by the time they got there it was all over.

Dougherty said, "Springate says, 'Why ask for the right to strike if you're not going to use it?'"

"I knew Hanley couldn't hold his seat in the Point forever," his father said, "but I never thought he'd lose it to a guy from Westmount."

Dougherty thought about rising to that one but there was no way he was going to talk politics, and for once his father didn't press it. But then his father said, "Did you hear Mayor Drapeau talking about the bombs?"

"He's against them, right?"

"He says we have to admit there are no more freelancers — those responsible are well-paid professionals."

"Yeah, he's been saying that," Dougherty said. "Says they've been brought in from somewhere — Algeria or Cuba or something."

"And Americans. He wants to crack down on draft dodgers again — says they're behind the bombs."

"He keeps saying that, but we've never run into any yet."

"Then he said that last year when Saulnier said there were groups out to destroy the city and the country, the whole thing, that people laughed at him."

Dougherty said, "It was funny."

"Oh, but now he says he's been proven right."

"Is he finally going to get his royal commission?"

"He said they only aim at destroying for the sake of destroying — they have no new ideas, no better ideas."

"Well," Dougherty said, "they're getting us a lot of overtime."

"Your mother's worried."

Dougherty followed his father's look to the back-yard and watched his mother work in the garden, pulling up weeds only she could see, and after a moment he said, "Did she talk to Cheryl about Brenda Webber?"

His father was lighting a cigarette, a Player's Plain, and before he could say anything the back door to the house opened and Cheryl came out onto the wooden balcony with another girl Dougherty didn't recognize. Cheryl's friends all looked the same to him these days, long straight hair, jeans, t-shirts, dazed expressions. Cheryl was saying, "Will it happen, do you know? It'll happen, won't it?" and Dougherty said, "What?"

"The Festival Express, it's coming, right?"

"I don't know."

Cheryl and the other girl came down the stairs to the patio, and Cheryl said, "There's a rumour the cops are trying to stop it."

"At least you didn't say pigs."

She shook her head at him. "Are you going to stop it?"

"What, me?"

"The cops."

"I have no idea, that's not my department."

Cheryl said, "Typical, don't take any responsibility," and Dougherty said, "Wow, I didn't think you knew that word."

She ignored that. "They're saying because it's going to be on Saint-Jean-Baptiste Day there won't be enough cops for security."

"Well, that's possible, Saint-Jean-Baptiste always takes a lot of us."

"But why do they need so many cops? It's just a concert."

Dougherty shrugged. "After what happened at the Autostade last month."

"They called in the riot squad for no reason."

"Seemed like a good reason at the time," Dougherty said.

"Do you know who's on the Festival Express? Janis and The Grateful Dead and Mashmakhan and Robert Charlebois."

"He's not going to be at a Saint-Jean-Baptiste party? Then there is going to be a riot."

"We already bought our tickets — they were ten dollars."

"Cheryl, I have no idea if they're going to let the concert go on or not."

"It's going on in Toronto."

"Good for them. They don't have bombs going off all the time. They won't have a parade and a riot on the same day as the concert."

"I can't wait to get out of this stupid city."

"So, you're eighteen — who's stopping you?"

"Screw you," and she walked back up the stairs and into the house.

The friend stood there for a minute, smiling her dopey smile at Dougherty till he recognized her. "Frances Massey?"

She said, "Hi Eddie," but then Cheryl said, "Franny, come on." Franny kept smiling at him as she slowly walked back up the stairs and into the house.

Dougherty drank some beer. "Franny's sure changed; she's looking grown up."

"How long till she's knocked up?"

Dougherty said, "Well, at least Cheryl's too crabby, you don't have to worry about that," and his father shook his head and smiled a little.

Eddie lit a cigarette. "Is she going to CEGEP this year?"

"She's still upset about it."

Dougherty said, "Well, what else is she going to do?" but he was thinking how he couldn't really blame her — imagine being a year away from finishing high school and the government brings in a whole new college system, CEGEP, which was a French acronym and Dougherty could never remember what the letters stood for other than college. Two more years before you can go to university and it pretty much makes your high school diploma worthless on its own.

"She's always talking about moving out," his father said, "but I don't see any signs of it."

"You don't want her to."

"Not until she has some idea where she wants to go, what she wants to do."

Dougherty left that alone and drank a little more

beer and watched his mother finish up in the garden and walk towards the patio, looking like she could go either way, acting happy to see him or complaining right away.

"How was it, the funeral?" she said, and Dougherty said oh, realizing he should have expected that. "Good, you know, Protestant, looking for the good side."

His mother scowled a little, then sat down on a deck chair and shook her head. Dougherty knew she just didn't really understand the Protestants and their Good News Bible and guitars in church. She still wasn't happy that mass wasn't in Latin anymore.

"*Mon dieu*, Millie must be going crazy."

Dougherty didn't say anything and neither did his father. After a moment his mother said, "*Bon*, you have laundry?" and Dougherty said, "You think that's the only reason I visit." She just stared at him and made a face until he said, "It's in my car, I'll get it."

When he handed her the bag, he said, "I think you'll have to bleach the uniform shirts." "You telling me how to do laundry?" she said, but she was mostly joking.

A minute later, though, as she was going downstairs to the basement, Dougherty could hear her yelling at Cheryl to turn the music down and Cheryl yelling back about it being the middle of the day and no one's trying to sleep. Then some more yelling and then the needle scraping across the record and a minute later Cheryl and Franny stomping out the back door with records under their arms, Cheryl saying, "We're going to Franny's," and Franny saying, "I told you, my sister's there, we can't play records," and they were out the gate and gone.

Dougherty and his father didn't say anything for a few minutes, enjoying the quiet on a summer day, and then Dougherty said, "Hey, I heard something on the radio — isn't it the D-Day anniversary today?"

"Yesterday, the sixth," his father said.

Dougherty said, "Right, twenty-five years ago,"

"Twenty-six."

"Yeah." And Dougherty realized he didn't know very much about it, just what he'd seen in the movies. He said, "Where were you on D-Day?" realizing he didn't even know that.

"On a corvette in the English Channel."

"Carrying troops?"

"Not on a corvette, too small. We were with the sweepers, looking for U-boats and mines."

"Must have been something."

"Yeah, something."

Dougherty wanted to ask more questions but he didn't know where to start, and then Tommy came through the gate saying, "Hey Eddie," and throwing a baseball that Dougherty managed to catch without spilling any beer.

Tommy was still on his bike, with its banana seat and high handlebars. "You staying for supper?"

Dougherty said, "Yeah, of course," and then he said, "You playing ball?"

Tommy's baseball glove was hanging from the handlebar and he said, "Just throwing it around in the schoolyard." He dropped his bike in the middle of the patio and ran into the house, the door slamming behind him.

Dougherty was thinking of something to ask his

father, something about D-Day that might get him to open up and talk about it a little, but before he could come up with anything his father said, "It must have been hard to see Brenda Webber."

Dougherty almost sighed with relief and said, "I thought it was Arlene. The last time I saw Brenda she was probably younger than Tommy is now."

"She looked like Arlene?"

"Her face was bloated and purple, she'd been strangled and left in the field for a couple of days but I guess because I knew it would be her . . ." His voice trailed off and it was quiet for a moment. Then his father said, "It's a shocking thing to see a dead body."

"Have you ever seen one?"

"Sometimes we'd hit a U-boat with a depth charge, bodies would come up to the surface."

Dougherty finished off his beer and said, "What about guys you knew?"

"A few."

Dougherty wanted to ask but he really had no idea what to say. He was starting to think he understood why there were no mementos of his father's service in the house, no pictures or medals — he was pretty sure his father must've had at least service medals — and why his father never really talked about it. But now he was thinking maybe his father never talked about to him because he wouldn't understand.

"I remember little Georgie Stein; he wanted maple syrup."

"What?"

"We had a two-day leave; we were docked in Liverpool and we took the train to London. There was a place there, Canada House — you could get pancakes for breakfast with real maple syrup."

"A restaurant?"

"No, it was part of the Canadian High Commission, right there on Trafalgar Square."

"And it served pancakes?"

"You could get mail there, find out where guys were stationed, that kind of thing. They tried to make it like a little piece of home."

"And pancakes were a big deal?"

"After Spam three times a day for two weeks all the way across the Atlantic? Yeah, it was a big deal. And the real maple syrup, we all wanted it, not just George, so we went there and got ourselves beds in a rooming house around the corner, dropped our stuff and then we went out on the town."

"Even in a war you have to get out."

"Especially. But George didn't want to, said he was going to go to bed early so the rest of us went out. And," his father paused and lit another cigarette, "got into a fight with some Americans."

"A fist fight?" Dougherty said, having a tough time picturing his father in a bar brawl.

"Yeah. There were Americans all over England then, building up for . . . well, for what yesterday's the anniversary of. Overpaid, over-sexed and over here."

"What?"

"What we said about the Americans. They had that song, 'Over There.' For us the war'd been going on for years by then and then they came in like . . . well, like they were going to save the day, like we'd been waiting around for them."

Dougherty was looking sideways at his father, hearing this for the first time, worried that if he said anything his father would stop talking. So he didn't and his father smiled a little and said, "The streets were dark, no lights, the whole city was completely dark so the bombers coming in couldn't target anything. The bars all had these plywood entrances built in front of the doors, little vestibules so you could go in there and then open the door and not let the light out. We were walking down one of these dark streets and all of a sudden there was all this light, a couple of guys holding open both sets of doors and then a body came flying out."

"A dead body?"

"No, an Irishman from Belfast, Royal Navy. He got up and said there were a bunch of Yanks making a lot of noise in the bar, the pub, I guess he said, so we went in to straighten them out."

"Straighten them out?"

"Of course we all ended up in the drunk tank at the police station."

"I don't get it," Dougherty said. "What's this got to do with George Stein?"

His father nodded, the smile fading. "The next morning we had to get our things and get back to Liverpool, get back on our ship, and when we got to the rooming house it was rubble."

103

"Rubble?"

"Everybody in it killed. Canada House was hit, too, and a big hotel next door."

Dougherty waited a moment and then he said, "What did you do?"

"We got on the train back to Liverpool."

After a moment his father said, "You want another beer?" and Dougherty said sure, and watched his dad go into the house.

Then Dougherty's mother came out and sat down and said, "So, you gonna catch this guy?"

"What guy?"

Dougherty's father came out and handed Dougherty a beer and sat down.

"The guy, Bill, whatever his name, the guy killing these girls. You gonna catch him?"

"We're trying, Ma."

"Yeah?"

Dougherty said, "Yeah, of course," and then he was going to tell them how he was helping, how he was part of it, how maybe the information he got from Gail Murphy about the big white car might be really important and Detective Carpentier was bringing him into the investigation, but he didn't want to say too much, make himself sound important because he figured he was probably finished now, been all the use he could be to a murder investigation, so he just let it go.

A couple of hours later his father lit the barbecue and they had hamburgers and potato salad and steamed fiddleheads. Cheryl missed it but came back a little while after they'd finished and stomped off to her room and slammed the door. Tommy made a face and Dougherty laughed, but his mother didn't see anything funny about it.

When it got dark, Dougherty and his father were sitting on the patio by themselves, and Dougherty told him about helping Carpentier and talking to people in the Point and even a little about how good it felt to intimidate Danny Buckley. His father didn't tell him to be careful about that or not to let it go to his head or anything, he just nodded and said, "I guess it would."

By the time Dougherty was driving home over the Champlain Bridge, he was feeling pretty good, felt he was doing a good job and was part of something.

CHAPTER
SEVEN

Dougherty had called the homicide office Sunday morning before he went to the Park but was told that Detective Carpentier was unavailable. Same thing on Monday, so when he got to work Tuesday morning to start a couple weeks of day shifts the first thing he did was call the homicide office again and this time, instead of being told he was unavailable he was told Carpentier had been reassigned.

"What?"

The receptionist repeated very slowly in English, "Detective Carpentier has been reassigned," and Dougherty said, "What are you talking about? I need to talk to him."

"Is there a message you would like to leave for him?"

It didn't seem like something that could be left in a message, that he'd talked to a girl in Pointe St-Charles who didn't want her name coming out and said she saw a car that looked suspicious but she wasn't exactly sure what kind or what the licence plate was or even that it was actually suspicious in any way. This was really something he wanted to tell Carpentier face-to-face, so he just said, "No thanks," and hung up.

Then he asked Delisle what the hell was going on.

"What?"

"Detective Carpentier in homicide has been reassigned?"

"Probably going to CATS."

"What's CATS?"

"Didn't you hear about the new task force?"

"No, I didn't hear anything; I was off for two days."

"Some of our guys, some QPP and some Mounties, they're calling it the CAT Squad, Combined Anti-Terrorist."

"Why now?"

Delisle shrugged and said it was all for show, "for politics. They had a press conference, said eleven bombs have exploded in Montreal in the last five weeks."

"Bombs have been going off for months."

"In Westmount?"

"Oh right," Dougherty said.

"So they have to look like they're doing more."

"More about the bombs, but what about everything else?"

"We also got a memo," Delisle said. "Police on routine patrols are asked to use extreme caution."

"Does it really say that, extreme caution?"

Delisle held up the memo and waved it. "You want to read it yourself?"

"Carpentier was working on these murders. What am I supposed to do?"

"What do you mean? You work your shift."

"But I have information for Carpentier."

"So give it to Desjardins — he's still in charge at homicide — and then get to work."

Dougherty checked out a patrol car and drove down the hill to Bonsecours Street, but before he went to the homicide office he went to ident, where he found Rozovsky dividing a pile of photos into three stacks.

"You find another body?"

"What?"

"Did you find another body that fits with the case?"

"Oh, no, I'm looking for Carpentier."

"He's on the new task force."

"I heard, but is he around?"

Rozovsky said, "What are you asking me for?" and Dougherty said, "Do you know?"

"They're upstairs, fourth floor, but they can't decide if the offices will be here or in the RCMP building on Dorchester."

"How many are on the task force?"

"They don't know that, either, yet."

"This is bullshit," Dougherty said. "A few kids with bombs and we're making it sound like such a big deal, Drapeau going on the radio saying it's professionals from Algeria. You ever heard of that?"

"Or Cubans or draft dodgers — anybody but us, right?" Rozovsky held up one of the pictures. "What kind of car is this?"

"A Comet GT, looks like a '64."

"Is that a Ford?"

"Mercury."

Rozovsky wrote that down and said, "Desjardins is in the homicide office, I think," and Dougherty said yeah, but didn't move. Rozovsky said, "He's probably lonely, you could talk to him," and Dougherty said okay and headed back down the hall.

He stood there for a moment looking at the closed door of the homicide office and imagined how the meeting would go. He'd introduce himself to Detective-Lieutenant Desjardins, who wouldn't know anything about him, so he'd explain about working with Carpentier, leaving out the part about picking him up drunk in Nap's, and then tell him about talking to people in the Point and about the white car and Desjardins would say, that's it? Then Dougherty would say yeah and the detective-lieutenant would stare at him like he was an idiot and then he'd leave and spend the rest of his life working night shifts out of Station Ten.

So he went upstairs, looking for Carpentier, didn't find him, and then walked out of the building and found him getting out of a car on Bonsecours.

"Detective, hey, I was looking for you." He thought for a second that Carpentier was trying to remember where he knew him from and wasn't sure what to say.

"Yes, Constable Dougherty?"

109

Dougherty said he had some information, so Carpentier waved at the other detectives going into the greasy spoon across the street and said, "Yes, so, what is it?"

"I talked to Gail Murphy after the funeral."

He waited a moment, making sure Carpentier remembered what he was talking about, but now the detective looked impatient so he said, "She said she saw a suspicious car the night Brenda Webber went missing."

"What made it suspicious?"

"She just didn't think it belonged in the Point. It was a big white car with a black roof."

"A convertible?"

"She didn't think so."

"Has she seen it before?"

"She thinks so, yeah. A man driving, by himself."

Carpentier nodded. "Okay, sounds interesting. Can you ask around some more?"

"In the Point?"

"She didn't think the car was local?"

"No, she'd only seen it a couple of times. She couldn't really say why she noticed, it just kind of creeped her out."

Carpentier said, "A hunch?" and Dougherty said, "Yeah, I guess."

"Okay, that's not much. We need more than that for Desjardins."

Dougherty said yeah, thinking this was exactly why he hadn't wanted to take it to Desjardins himself and then Carpentier said, "*Bon*, why don't you take a drive out where Brenda Webber's body was found, see if you get anything there."

"That's not our jurisdiction. Should I talk to the LaSalle cops?"

"Just ask around a little, unofficial for now — you probably won't get anything."

Dougherty said, "Right, probably not," and then, "But if I do, I bring it to you?"

Carpentier nodded and said, "If you find anything? Sure, bring it to me. Officially I'm not working this, either, I've been assigned to this new task force, but if you find something, or you think you find something, yes, bring it to me. It's probably nothing, a guy got a new car, that's all, so let's not send the homicide detectives on a wild goose chase now that there's hardly anybody left."

Dougherty said okay and got in the patrol car thinking, Sure, a wild goose chase, that would be my job. He thought for a minute about just going back to Station Ten but then he got on the Ville-Marie Expressway and headed west.

———

The old guy said, "It's HMCS *Hochelaga*, or it was," and Dougherty said, "Oh yeah," thinking he could barely see the canal across the street and past the train tracks.

"It was a naval repair station, very busy during the war, and after for a while, too. It only closed last year."

Dougherty said he'd thought it was a factory, like the rest of the buildings along St. Patrick and the old guy said no. Then he looked around at the weeds and the brush and the pieces of old cars and washing machines. "This is where she was left?"

Dougherty nodded, thinking that was the first time he'd heard it described as anything but "dumped," and he said, "Yeah, right here."

"Well," the old guy said, "a lot of guys worked at

the shipyard, thousands over the years, and the other factories here."

"You thinking about how many people know about this place?"

"I guess, yeah, still thinking like a cop."

"You were a cop?"

"Oh, not Montreal," the guy said, "not the big city, just here in LaSalle. Made it to sergeant," and he held out his hand. "Denison."

Dougherty shook his hand. "Well, Sergeant Denison, it looks like it's all going to be one city soon, the whole island of Montreal."

"We'll see."

"At least one police force, that's the talk."

Dougherty had driven to LaSalle and parked on Cordner Street, where the new houses were going in, and looked for someone to talk to. People were living in some of the finished houses but the whole area just felt empty. Then as Dougherty walked into the field, coming at it from the opposite side as he had when he'd come from St. Patrick Street, the old guy, Denison, had come up behind him and asked what a Montreal police car was doing in LaSalle. Dougherty asked him if he'd heard about the girl's body that was found, and the old guy'd said, "Yes, a tragedy."

Now Denison was looking past the closed-down HMCS *Hochelaga* building to the raised expressway on the other side of the canal. "Well, it sounds like there's a little more cooperation now, that's good."

"There wasn't always?"

"One of the last things I did before I retired was the explosion we had here."

"Oh yeah," Dougherty said, "at the Monsanto plant?" and he pointed along the canal towards Verdun, but Denison said, "No, that was '66, after I retired, I mean the apartment building in the Heights in '65. Place went up just after eight in the morning — we didn't get any help from Montreal until the afternoon, four, five hours later."

"I remember that explosion," Dougherty said, "some kids were killed."

"Twenty-eight. Not all kids, fifteen were kids. They hadn't left for school yet."

Dougherty said, "Wow," and Denison said, "Oh yes. Monsanto was bad, too, eleven men killed." Then he looked at Dougherty and said, "You know, there was another gas explosion in LaSalle in 1956, just around the corner from the other one, seven people were killed."

"I didn't know that," Dougherty said. "But I'm just trying to find out about one death now."

Denison said, "No less important," and Dougherty said, "Yeah, that's right."

"So, you said you think she was brought here in a white car?"

"With a black roof."

"On Thursday night?"

"Sometime between Thursday night and Tuesday morning."

"Jesus," Denison said. "That's all you've got?"

Dougherty said, "He could have driven in here off Cordner," and Denison said, "Or Elmslie or Lapierre."

"Yeah, and left by a different way."

"There are some kids in some of those houses, you

could ask," Dension said. "Come on, my granddaughter's one of them."

They walked back to Cordner Street and Denison explained how his daughter and her husband had bought two units in a fourplex on Thierry Street and were renting out one unit and he was living in the bachelor apartment in the basement. "Not really the basement," he said. "It's a walkout, has a door to the backyard."

The granddaughter was maybe ten years old, playing with a couple of friends, and didn't know anything about a big white car with a black roof. Denison asked if any older kids were around, and one of the friends said her brother was in the house, so Denison asked her to go get him.

The kid was maybe fourteen or fifteen and Dougherty was a little surprised to see he was clean cut and seemed respectful. He figured it was because the kid was Italian, probably still translating for his parents.

Denison asked the kid if he'd seen a white car and the kid said yes, and Dougherty said, "With a black roof?"

The kid said, "Yes,"

"A big car?"

"Yes, a big white car with a black roof."

"When was this?"

"In the morning, I was delivering my papers."

Dougherty said, "The *Gazette*?" and the kid said yeah.

"My little brother has a *Gazette* route, too."

"Around here?"

"No, on the South Shore, Greenfield Park."

The kid nodded but didn't say anything, and then

Dougherty said, "But you remember the car?"

"Yeah, there's not many cars around when I deliver."

"You have to be finished by seven, right?"

"Yeah, but I'm usually finished before that. I have to help my mom make lunches."

"So what time do you think you saw the car?"

The kid thought about it. "Well, I was just starting, and I was right here, so it must have been before six, maybe quarter to."

"And what day was this?"

"I'm not sure."

"But not Sunday, there's no *Gazette* on Sunday."

"And not Saturday, my little brother helps me then — we have all the flyers to deliver."

Dougherty said, "Maybe Friday?" and Denison looked sideways at him, seemed to be trying to get him to realize something, but Dougherty didn't know what. The kid said, "Yes, that's right."

Dougherty said, "But not this past Friday, it was the Friday before, right?"

"Yes, that's right."

"That's quite a while ago," Denison said, and the kid said yeah and thought about it for a moment. "I think there was a story on the front page about a hijacking."

Dougherty said, "Okay, so this was Friday morning and you saw the white car on Cordner. Which way was it going?"

The kid looked up the street and thought about it for a bit and then said, "That way," pointing past the field towards Montreal.

"Okay, that's good, thanks very much."

The kid shrugged and started to turn away, and Denison said, "You better write down his name."

Both the kid and Dougherty were looking at Denison and he said, "The boy's name and address, you better write it down for your report." Dougherty said, "Right, yeah," and then asked the kid his name and had to make him spell it, "Masaracchia," one letter at a time.

Denison walked back to Cordner with Dougherty and said, "That could be some good information," and Dougherty said, "It sure could."

"If it's right."

They were at Dougherty's car then and he said, "What do you mean?"

"Just that he was trying very hard to be helpful."

"That's good, isn't it? We're not getting a lot of help on this."

Denison said, "Yes, of course it's good, it's just . . . maybe he was trying too hard."

"I can check on the hijacking, see what day it was."

"Of course, it's just . . ."

"What?"

"Maybe a detective, maybe someone a little more experienced in this kind of interrogation should talk to him."

"If I can find one who's not chasing bombs," Dougherty said, "I'll drive him out here myself."

Denison nodded, understanding, and shook his hand goodbye.

Dougherty got in his car, pulled a U on Cordner, drove in the direction the kid said the big white car went for a few blocks and came to Lapierre. From there he could go north to St. Patrick and along the canal, either into Montreal or out to the West Island suburbs or south into more of LaSalle and Ville-Émard and Verdun. He could even keep going on Cordner to more factories and warehouses.

Anywhere.

Dougherty turned left and headed up to St. Patrick, anxious to get back to Station Ten.

Inside the station, the first thing Dougherty saw was Delisle hanging up the phone and saying, "There goes your overtime."

"What?"

"Saint-Jean-Baptiste, it's all getting covered out of Station Four and Six, and that concert at the Autostade is canceled."

"The Festival Express?"

"The train, yeah."

"No overtime downtown at all?"

"Regular shifts."

Dougherty said okay, then Delisle said, "Detective Carpentier wants to see you."

"Now?"

"After your shift, across from Bonsecours, the restaurant, there's a room in the back. Be there after seven."

Dougherty said okay, and started towards the break room looking for some coffee. "Where you going?" Delisle said. "We have a call."

"Bomb?"

"Drunk and disorderly. We still do police work, you know."

Dougherty took the address and left the station thinking, Yeah, fighting with drunks, real police work.

CHAPTER
EIGHT

It was almost ten by the time Dougherty got to the restaurant on Bonsecours Street, across from police HQ. The front room was filled with empty booths but the back room was packed with detectives and thick with smoke. He looked around for a minute and spotted Carpentier at a table in the corner with four other men, all looking like they owned they place, and made his way over.

He didn't know what to say so he just stood there waiting for Carpentier to notice him. When he finally did the detective said, *"Qu'est-ce qui t'es arrivé?"* and Dougherty touched the side of his face and said, *"Oh, seulement les drunks."*

Carpentier switched to English: "Are you on shift

now?" And Dougherty said, "No, I'm on days. The fight started after lunch and kept going, all the way to the hospital."

Carpentier was leaning back in his chair, looking him up and down, and Dougherty felt like he was standing in front of his old football coach after fumbling the kickoff, but then Carpentier said, "Sit down, you want a drink?"

"Sure."

The detective waved across the crowded room, and Dougherty saw the waitress, who didn't look old enough to be in the bar, nod.

"So, do you have anything?"

"I might, yeah."

"Don't tell me someone saw the car?"

"Maybe." Dougherty put his constable's hat on the table, but then, looking at the number of empty beer bottles and highball glasses, he thought better of it and held it in his lap. "A kid, a boy, maybe fourteen, delivering newspapers in the morning thinks he saw the car."

"Where?"

"Where you said to look, in LaSalle, near where the body was found."

"What do you think?"

The waitress was at the table then, putting a Molson Export and a shot glass in front of Dougherty, and he reached for his wallet but Carpentier stopped him. "We're letting homicide pay for one last night." He motioned for him to continue, and Dougherty said, "I can't really tell, the kid was trying very hard to be helpful." He decided he wasn't going to say anything about the retired LaSalle cop helping him out.

"It's possible," Carpentier said. "Maybe he was younger than fourteen — not many kids want to help the police anymore."

"I think the kid's family hasn't been in the country very long."

"Have you shown the girl pictures of cars, figured out what kind it was?" Before Dougherty could say anything, Carpentier looked past him and waved across the room, saying, "Hold on, here's Ste. Marie," and then calling, "Robert," pronouncing it the French way, *Ro-bair*.

Dougherty turned and saw a middle-aged guy in a wrinkled suit push his way through the crowd to the table and hold his hand over Dougherty's head to shake with Carpentier.

The other three guys at the table were involved in a heated discussion in French, one of them doing most of the talking but the other two jumping in and disagreeing every few words. Ste. Marie patted one of the guys on the back and the guy held up his hand to wait, but Ste. Marie looked back at Carpentier.

"Robert, j'te présente le constable Doe-er-dee."

It was too crowded for Dougherty to stand up, so he just held up his hand. Ste. Marie shook it and said, "Call me Bob," with almost no accent at all.

Carpentier yelled at the other detectives at the table to clear some room, and Ste. Marie squeezed in beside Dougherty as Carpentier was saying, "Bob has also been assigned to the anti-terrorist squad."

"Like everybody else," Ste. Marie said, not looking too happy about it.

Carpentier said, "You coming from Cleo's?"

"Fuck you."

Carpentier laughed and Dougherty had no idea what they were talking about and didn't want to ask. They'd already slipped into English, probably an old habit from back when they were rookies and there were still Scotsmen in senior positions.

Carpentier lit a cigarette. "The apartments upstairs are rented by hookers — Cleo is the madam. Sometimes from homicide you see them in the windows."

"Sometimes," Ste. Marie said, "you see a lot," and Carpentier laughed.

Ste. Marie looked at Dougherty then and said, *"Mais t'es un vrai anglais, vraiment?"*

"My mother's French," Dougherty explained.

"Québécois, or did your father bring her back from France after the war?"

"From New Brunswick."

Ste. Marie said, "Almost Québécois," and Dougherty thought, Well, yeah, a lot closer than I'll ever be, even though I was born here, but he didn't say anything, the difference between *Québécois* and Quebecker getting further apart every day.

Carpentier said, "He's working my murder investigation," and Ste. Marie said, *"Tabarnak*, a murder he's working?"

"The girl from last week."

"That's one of Bill's, isn't it?"

"Yes," Carpentier said, "and the kid has something."

Ste. Marie was looking at Dougherty then.

"A car. One of the girl's friends told me she saw a car in the neighbourhood she thought was suspicious."

"Why suspicious? She ever see it before?"

"A couple of times, maybe, but doesn't think it's local."

Ste. Marie said, "What do you mean, local?" and Carpentier said, "Point St. Charles," and then nodded at Dougherty. "He's from there."

Dougherty saw Ste. Marie nod like that meant something, maybe explained why an English guy joined the police instead of going to McGill, but he let it go and said, "I know her brother."

Ste. Marie said, "The victim or the witness?"

"Both."

Then Carpentier said, "But that's not all," and motioned to Dougherty to continue.

"Right. The body was . . . left in LaSalle, behind an old naval repair yard on St. Patrick."

"HMCS *Hochelaga*."

"That's right."

"Where I learned English," Ste. Marie said.

Dougherty didn't know what to say to that so he just went on. "I talked to a kid who lives nearby and he saw a car that could be the same one in the morning when he was delivering the *Gazette*."

"That's not bad," Ste. Marie said. "That could actually be something." He looked at Carpentier and said, "You training this kid?" and Carpentier said, "Yeah, in all my spare time."

"What kind of car?"

Dougherty said he wasn't sure yet, "Both kids said a big white one with a black roof."

"Convertible?"

Dougherty said, "Not sure."

Ste. Marie said, "Okay. In the Point these days the new cars usually have some connection to the Point Boys — they're bringing in a lot more dope now, making some real money."

Carpentier said, "They're bringing it in themselves?"

Ste. Marie a cigarette and exhaled, adding to the thick cloud hanging over the room. "It's still the Italians but some of us, too," he said, motioning to himself and Carpentier, meaning French guys. "Bringing in hashish. The Higgins brothers still have the port so everybody has to deal with them, but now there are more drugs and more players."

Carpentier said, "Hash users are not the same as heroin users," and Ste. Marie nodded, "The same jazz musicians and the boys down around Rockheads, but now also students. And the dealers are different, too. We got a guy last month bringing in thirteen pounds of hashish from Beirut he said was for personal use. We got a guy last week — an American student nineteen years old — coming in from Tel Aviv with hashish claiming he was 'terrorized' into doing it."

"Maybe he was," Carpentier said.

"Maybe."

Dougherty said, "Are the Higgins brothers the Point Boys?" and Ste. Marie said, "Yes. And there are others, they come and go. The Point Boys aren't like the Italians — they're not so structured, not so *famiglia*. It's not like guys have to join and work their way up, become made or anything like that."

Dougherty didn't say anything but he was pretty sure the Higgins brothers and the rest of the guys in the Point were only working with guys they knew, guys they'd known all their lives like Danny Buckley and the Murphys.

"The Italians have been bringing drugs through Montreal for years, the Corsicans in Marseilles to Montreal and then it goes to New York. The Irish have always had the port in Montreal and took their piece to pass it through. But now that it's hashish and marijuana and there's so much more, they want a bigger piece."

"Is this why Johnny Vaccaro was killed on the Champlain Bridge?" said Dougherty. Ste. Marie looked at Dougherty over the rising smoke of his cigarette and said, "How do you know that?"

"I was on the scene. He was driving a Cutlass, blown all over the road by the tollbooths."

"That's right, he was coming back from New York."

"Did the Point Boys kill him?"

Ste. Marie shrugged. "Who knows? Nobody's talking. Could have been internal. The Italians don't always get along — there's some from Sicily some from Calabria. It could have even come from New York."

"You'd think they'd be too busy counting their money," Carpentier said. He knocked back his shot and then looked at Dougherty and said, "They've had a piece of every construction in this city for the last ten years: look what they had — Expo, the Métro, the Champlain Bridge."

"The expressways," Ste. Marie added, "Décarie, Metropolitan, Bonaventure."

"The office towers: Place Ville-Marie, Place Bonaventure, Place Victoria."

"All that construction."

Dougherty said, "I worked construction at Expo,

the American pavilion."

"Oh yeah, you pay union dues?"

Dougherty shrugged. "Or you don't work." Another fight he'd had with his father a few times before their unspoken truce.

"And now," Carpentier said, "we get the Olympics — more construction."

"Yes, but the Olympics," Ste. Marie said, "can no more lose money than —" and Carpentier joined in with "a man can have a baby," and they both laughed.

Then Carpentier said, "*Bon*, about the hashish." He drank some of his beer and looked at Ste. Marie. "The victim from the Point was buying hashish."

"In the Point?"

"We think so, yes. The last place she was seen was the *dépanneur*. She bought cigarettes and rolling papers."

"Did she already have the hash?"

"We don't know. There was none in her system when she died."

"How do you know that?" Dougherty said, and Carpentier said, "It's in the coroner's report, haven't you read it?"

"No, I didn't see it, I mean, I'm at Station Ten, I couldn't . . ." and Carpentier said, "Of course, yeah, you're not actually in homicide, I forget." Then he turned back to Ste. Marie. "Her clothes were not with the body, so we don't know."

"But the drug connection is good," Ste. Marie said. "Some of the other victims were also taking drugs, weren't they?"

"Yes."

"Just hashish?"

"And other drugs."

"So," Ste. Marie said, "Bill is a dealer?"

"Maybe."

"Well," Ste. Marie said, "that's something."

"Can you ask some of your informants, see if they know any dealers driving big white cars?"

Ste. Marie shrugged. "It's a homicide investigation, can't they do it?"

Carpentier looked around the bar. "When they get to it."

"It's the same for us," Ste. Marie said. "I can ask the guys who are still left. You know how many we have working the mob?"

Carpentier nodded, what could he say, and Ste. Marie said, "And then there's the Mounties, did you hear?"

"What?"

"Complete shakeup, they're shipping out almost every guy they have in Montreal."

Carpentier said, "Why?"

"Officially? Because they don't speak French, but really, it's because of their guy, what's his name, arrested last year with the heroin."

"Oh yeah," Carpentier said, "Kozlik."

Dougherty remembered something about an RCMP officer being charged with drug smuggling, something about a girlfriend in New York who maybe had mob connections but he didn't know the details.

"So now they have guys on the street who've been behind desks for years."

"They should stay behind the desks," Carpentier

said. "They can do less damage there."

"So," Ste. Marie said, "that's where we are now."

They all drank and it was quiet for a moment, and then Dougherty wanted to contribute something so he said, "One of the guys I know in the Point, a guy named Danny Buckley, I saw him getting into a brand new Cadillac with one of the Higgins brothers. The youngest, I think, Danny."

Ste. Marie and Carpentier were both nodding then and Carpentier said, "The one you ran into at the *dépanneur*," and Dougherty said, "Yeah. Maybe we could talk to him."

Carpentier said, "Maybe," and looked at Ste. Marie, who said, "He's a young guy, your age?" Dougherty nodded and Ste. Marie said, "Okay, so he might be a good contact for you."

"For me?"

Ste. Marie said, "Sure, until they bring all the constables onto the CATS, too, everybody is chasing terrorists and we just hand the city over to the mobs."

Someone in the crowd yelled, *"Eille Gilles, c'est le public qui fait ta job asteure?"* and a bunch of guys laughed, and Dougherty turned to see the bomb squad guys coming into the bar, Gilles Vachon saying, *"Il a travaillé avec des explosifs dans l'armée,"* the other guys all nodding and shrugging as if that explained nothing.

Dougherty looked at Carpentier, who said, "There was a bomb at the post office on Queen Mary Road last night. The janitor dismantled it before he called it in."

"It's true," Ste. Marie said. "He did work with explosives in the war. There were four sticks of dynamite."

"It wasn't called in?" Dougherty asked.

"Looks like they aren't calling them all in anymore," Carpentier said, and then Ste. Marie looked at Dougherty and said, "So you be careful."

Dougherty said, "Yeah, they sent us a memo," and the two detectives looked very serious, both nodding in understanding.

Carpentier said, "Oh, well, a memo." Then he looked at Dougherty, "Have you done your time with the night patrol?"

Dougherty said, "Not yet," and noticed Ste. Marie smirking a little.

Carpentier noticed, too, and shrugged and Ste. Marie said, "He must know how to punch people, look at him."

"A few months," Carpentier said, "it's good for the constables."

Dougherty didn't say anything but this was the first he'd ever heard of a cop in Montreal not being positive about the night patrol. Being honest with himself, Dougherty would've had to admit he'd been suspicious, all those stories about these legendary cops, a dozen detectives not connected to any particular station, working the whole city from midnight until they decided the night was over, taking on the bad guys all by themselves. But Dougherty'd worked enough night shifts to know that it was mostly fighting with drunks and grabbing kids breaking into *dépanneurs* for cigarettes or chasing low-level drug dealers. Most constables rotated through the night patrol, working three months with the detectives. Dougherty hadn't been asked, but he figured it was just another case of his last

128

name pushing him to the bottom of the list.

Now Ste. Marie was saying, sure, "For a few months it's okay, but we have other things to do right now," and Carpentier said, "Yeah, sure, of course." Ste. Marie looked at Dougherty and said, "Look, you're only as good a cop as your information. You need good informants."

"Yeah, sure," Dougherty said, seeing right away this could be good, this could really help him get noticed in the department.

"Just be quiet about it," Ste. Marie said. "Maybe you can just run into some old friends, not on duty, not in uniform. Maybe you could buy some hash yourself."

"But this isn't an official assignment?"

Neither Ste. Marie nor Carpentier said anything, and Dougherty nodded. "Okay, I get it."

And he was thinking too bad there wasn't a memo for buying hash in the Point.

But he was looking forward to talking to Buck-Buck again.

CHAPTER
NINE

The call came in, as they usually did, to a French radio station, CKAC. It was just after one in the morning, and CKAC did what they always did and called the police.

The call said the bomb was in the north side of the IBM building at 150 Montée de Liesse Boulevard, out by the airport, so the St. Laurent cops were also called and a member of the Montreal bomb squad who lived nearby was woken up and sent over. When he got there and found the bomb was much bigger than he expected, at least fifty pounds of dynamite, he immediately called for the evacuation of the motel next door.

Dougherty was working days all week but he'd pulled a double shift and was sitting in Station Ten half-listening to the radio and filling out an arrest report — some big spenders at the Playboy Club got into a fight during one of the acts, a guy billing himself as a "super pickpocket," and one of the belligerent drunks wouldn't calm down and finally had to be brought back to the station.

The night sergeant said, "Motel by the airport? Might be full of stewardesses, you want in on that evac?"

Dougherty said, "Yeah, maybe I do."

Before the sergeant realized he wasn't joking, there was a loud explosion. The ground beneath their feet shook, and Dougherty was up walking towards the desk, saying, "That can't be the airport."

"It's got to be closer," the sergeant said, and then the call came in from dispatch saying a bomb had gone off on the McGill University campus. Dougherty was out the door before the sergeant had a chance to say a word.

Up Guy and east on Sherbrooke, it was about ten blocks to the Roddick Gates entrance to the campus and Dougherty was there in about three minutes with the light flashing and the siren blaring. He could see the smoke pouring out of one of the newer buildings on the east side of the campus. He drove another block to University Street, turned up and saw the lights of two other cop cars flashing red on the sides of the buildings.

Less than a week since Dougherty and the other cops had been all over the campus looking for a bomb that turned out to be a false alarm, and now no call for one that did explode — with the bomb squad way out by the airport.

One of the other cops already on the scene was an older guy Dougherty didn't recognize, but when he yelled, *"Fermez la rue,"* Dougherty jumped back into his car and drove the half block back towards Sherbrooke and parked across University Street, blocking it. As he got out he saw another cop car doing the same on the corner of Milton, a little further ahead of the building with the smoke pouring out of it, which Dougherty could now see was the McConnell Engineering Building, about ten storeys of concrete and glass.

There was an apartment building across the street and people were starting to look out the windows, but Dougherty didn't think they'd have to evacuate.

The fire engines started showing up then, so Dougherty had to move his car to let them through and then move it back to keep the street blocked. After that there wasn't much for him to do, but he was used to this kind of uniformed police work now, closing a street, leaning against his car and having a smoke, and that's exactly what he was doing a few hours later when the sun came up and the city started to come to life. He had to keep some reporters and photographers back and CFCF even sent a camera team, but there wasn't much for them to see.

One man tried to push his way through, and when Dougherty held him back the guy said, "I am the vice-principal. I have to get through." And Dougherty was thinking he looked more like a businessman than his high school vice-principal, but then he figured at McGill the vice-principal probably wasn't giving boys the strap and expelling girls for smoking on school property.

Once he'd said who he was, some reporters started asking him questions, and the vice-principal said, "I forecasted this." That was when Dougherty knew he could go back and lean against his car. Now that this guy had an audience he wasn't going to stop talking, and that's what happened. "I said it only stands to reason after Westmount," he said and looked meaningfully at Dougherty.

"And what's going to be next? These terrorists get bolder every day — the next time a bomb goes off it will be in the middle of the day, the building full of people." Dougherty was thinking, Yeah, like the stock exchange that this guy forgot all about because it didn't affect him personally and they were just lucky no one was killed, but he didn't say anything. "Or they'll start assassinations like Robert Kennedy and Dr. King or hijackings or anything they want because no one's stopping them. Look at this," he continued, waving the *Gazette* in his hand, "West German envoy kidnapped in Brazil and now 40 criminals are being let out of jail. This giving in to terrorists just can't continue."

The reporters all agreed with the vice-principal and Dougherty heard a few things about nothing being done and what are all the cops doing and that kind of thing, and he lit up another cigarette and waited. He didn't know anything about the West German guy kidnapped in Brazil but now he was figuring he'd pick up a paper and have a look.

Around seven Sergeant Delisle came by and Dougherty asked him when he was going to be relieved. Delisle said, "You want to go for a coffee, go, but come back — we have no more men."

"I've been on since yesterday afternoon."

"I know but there's nothing I can do. Did you hear about the other bombs?"

"One out by the airport?"

"Two at the IBM building," Delisle said, "and one more at Domtar."

"In the Point?"

"No, in Senneville. Did you know there was a Domtar plant in Senneville?"

Dougherty said, "I'm not even sure where Senneville is," and Delisle said, "No one is. The DJ from the radio said it was on Kenneville Street, so we spent twenty minutes looking for that until Vachon said maybe he meant Senneville."

"Did it go off?"

"No, all three of those bombs were defused and brought in." The sergeant looked up at the McConnell building and said, "This is the only one that went off."

"And it wasn't called in."

"These cocksuckers are getting too bold."

"There's a man over there," Dougherty said, "who agrees with you."

Delisle said, "Go get your coffee," and then as Dougherty walked into the crowd yelled after him, "And come back!"

Dougherty decided if he was going to be on the scene for a few more hours he was going to have a proper breakfast, so he walked the few blocks to Park Avenue and sat in a padded booth in the Hollywood Restaurant and ate bacon and eggs and toast and drank two cups of coffee while reading the *Gazette*. He'd never been much of a newspaper reader — he thought it was kind of funny his little brother was reading it cover to cover now and not just the sports — but when he did pick one up it was usually the evening paper, the *Star*, or one of the French papers, usually the *Journal de Montréal*.

The article about the West German guy kidnapped in Brazil didn't have much more information than what the vice-principal complained about. The envoy, a guy named Ehrenfried von Holleben was, as the article said, "snatched from his car by urban guerrillas after a street gun battle," and had been held for a few days by a group calling themselves the "Popular Revolutionary Vanguard," which sounded to Dougherty like something out of a movie. But then every country in the world seemed to have these "popular front" groups setting off bombs and robbing banks and hijacking planes and kidnapping people. And then asking for asylum in Cuba or, since that movie came out, Algeria.

Dougherty was thinking how the McGill vice-principal had no idea how right he was. Back in the winter, February or March, a tip had come in from an informant and a couple of cops pulled over a rented truck. The cops said the truck was driving erratically, but the two guys they arrested knew better. In the truck with them were a couple of sawed-off shotguns, a basket big enough to put a man inside and, in one of the guy's pockets, a press release saying that the Israeli trade consul in Montreal, Moshe Golan, had been kidnapped. Both the guys arrested were out on bail. The story had been in the papers, but Dougherty couldn't remember many people talking about it.

Another article was more interesting for Dougherty, a city column called "On and Off the Record," that said things were very quiet in the Montreal underworld, a nice break from the past two years, and although there were still a lot of armed hold-ups and thefts, these were criminals on a completely different level. The column said the "smoother, more professional criminals prefer to operate in a less obvious manner," and Dougherty realized this was what Detective Carpentier and Ste. Marie were talking about when they said the Night Patrol wasn't going to be much help. The criminal world was becoming a lot more organized and the police had to keep up if they ever wanted to get beyond street dealers and low-level thugs.

Then Dougherty was thinking, Low-level thugs like Danny Buckley, working for the Higgins brothers, who were getting smoother and more professional every day. Now he wanted to get to the Point and talk to Buck-Buck about hash dealers and what kind of cars they drive, but first there was a bomb scene to clear.

When he got back to his car, still parked in the middle of University Street, he saw someone he knew walking by.

"Ruth. Hey Miss Garber."

It took her a second to recognize him. "Constable Dougherty, right?"

"That's right, we talked about the Bill murders."

She said she remembered and kept looking at him. He wasn't sure if she was waiting for him to elaborate or not. "You said you were at McGill."

"Yes, but my office is on the other side of the campus. It's open, isn't it?"

Dougherty lit a cigarette and nodded. "Yeah, there wasn't that much damage — it's mostly broken glass and some kind of heating pipes, steam pipes, nothing structural. This is the only building that's closed."

She walked right up to the cop car and stood beside Dougherty and said, "I heard there were some more bombs last night?" and he said, "Yeah, but not around here. A couple at the airport and one in Senneville."

"They're trying to blow up planes now?"

"It was in an office building near the airport, IBM. The one in Senneville was at a Domtar office, some kind of research facility."

Ruth was pulling a cigarette out of a pack of Peter Jacksons. "So, engineering, IBM and Domtar research; not exactly the oppressive government." She was digging around in her purse so Dougherty flipped open his Zippo, and she looked up at him as she bent forward a little and got her smoke lit.

"No," he said, "just English."

"At least it's just English business. I guess we're safe in sociology." She tilted her head back and blew out smoke, and Dougherty said, "For now."

Then she said, "There hasn't been anything more on the Bill murders?"

"Not that I know, just . . ."

"What?"

"I think I'm supposed to say it's ongoing."

Ruth frowned a little. "I'm not a reporter. I'm working on it, too."

Dougherty said, "Yeah, of course," and then she said, "I've been working on it for months," and Dougherty realized she probably knew more about it than he did. "Maybe we could talk about this some more."

"I guess, if you want."

"Do you want to go to dinner?"

She was just getting the cigarette to her mouth and took it away without taking a drag. "I haven't even had breakfast yet."

"I was thinking maybe tonight."

"That's a little short notice," she said.

"You eat dinner every day, though, right?"

"Straight to dinner. No meeting for coffee, not lunch, not even just drinks after work?"

"With all these bombs going off," Dougherty said, "anything can happen — we've got to act fast."

He'd fallen into flirting without even thinking about it, and she seemed to be going with it. But there was a fire engine and the bomb squad truck just up the street.

"Can we wait until Wednesday?"

"We'll be taking a big chance."

"We take a chance just going to work."

Dougherty said yeah, but he was thinking the flirting was starting to lose its charm.

Then it looked like Ruth was thinking the same thing because she looked a little more serious when she said, "So, dinner on Wednesday."

"Yeah."

"At the greasy spoon by the police station?"

"Pete would like that, but no. What would be your second choice?"

A cop was yelling at Dougherty now to move his car out of the way so the fire engine could get past, and Dougherty looked at Ruth.

"Do you know the Mazurka?" she said.

He had the door to the squad car opened and said, "On Prince Arthur, sure," and as he was getting in Ruth was moving away but she was nodding. "It'll be seven before I can get there," and Dougherty said, "Okay, see you then."

He moved the car out of the way and watched Ruth cut between the buildings on campus. Then he tried to remember in all this running around if he was working days or nights.

CHAPTER
TEN

Dougherty finished his eight-to-four at seven thirty, the earliest he'd finished in a long time, and went straight home and changed out of his uniform into a pair of jeans and a short-sleeved shirt with a collar. He thought he looked like one of the Beach Boys. Well, one of the Beach Boys five years ago, even they've got long hair now. But it was the best he could do.

It's not like he was ready for undercover work.

The radio came on when he started his car, Chantal Renaud singing "Plattsburgh Drive-In Blues," and he realized he'd left it on a French station and went to change it, but he liked the song, the way she sang the line about taking Canadian money in English but the rest in French and then all the doobie-doobie-dos at the end. But the next song was too go-go, so he pushed the clunky button and the needle jumped to 1050 CKGM, where "American Woman" was playing. That took him all the way down the hill on Atwater, through the tunnel under the Lachine Canal and into the Point on St. Patrick.

He ate at the Capri, skipped the pig knuckles and splurged on a steak. He was in a good mood, anxious but excited.

The only other customers were sitting at the bar, older guys in their forties or fifties he didn't recognize but was pretty sure were from the Point. They were talking about working at the port or, really, they were talking about an article that had been in the *Gazette* that morning, one of the guys throwing the rolled-up paper on the bar and saying, "Fucking reporters," his buddies agreeing with him.

Dougherty ate his steak and mashed potatoes and peas and drank his beer, a quart bottle of Fifty, and tried to listen to as much of the conversation as he could without being noticed. He heard the words, "pilfering and theft," and figured that was a direct quote from the article and a lot of complaints about more shipments coming in steel containers instead of loose bags. One of the guys said something about the problem being that they didn't need as many guys to unload that way, while another guy said something like, "Oh, so that's the problem," and Dougherty smiled to himself, thinking, Yeah, that's right, it's not that the real problem was stuff was harder to steal that way. Harder to pilfer.

Then he realized the place was quiet, and Dougherty

looked up to see the men at the bar looking at him and he knew he'd been caught. Shit. Only one thing to do. He had a knife in one hand and a fork in the other and squeezed them tight, hoping no one would notice his hands shaking, and said, "What the fuck are you looking at?"

One of the guys at the bar said, "That's Hughie Dougherty's boy, went and joined the cops," and another guy said, "Fucken hell."

"What the fuck you do that for boy?"

Dougherty stood up then and dropped the fork on the plate. He picked up his glass and downed the rest of his Fifty and then took out his wallet and dropped a five and two on the table. He still had the steak knife in his hand so it was awkward, and it was also a bigger tip than he'd wanted to leave, but there was no way he was waiting around for change. Then he dropped the knife and started towards the door, saying, "Because I wanted to," and walked out.

On St. Patrick he turned quickly down Laprairie Street, got into his car and drove off without looking back.

By the time he got to Hibernia and took the underpass at Grand Trunk, Dougherty was laughing. Still shaking and still scared, but laughing. Nervous.

He drove a few blocks on Wellington and parked near Sébastopol Street and then walked down to Westlake's bar, wondering how he was ever going to buy hash with everybody knowing he was a cop, and sure enough, as soon as he walked into the bar he could feel it tense up a little.

There were a few guys at the bar who could have

been brothers of the guys in the Capri — but Westlake's also had a table full of kids, maybe eight or ten of them, all wearing t-shirts and torn jeans and all of them with long hair. Dougherty figured the boys were probably all over eighteen and old enough to be in the bar, but a couple of the girls looked underage. Not that anyone in Westlake's cared, and it wasn't like any cops had nothing better to do than roust bars in the Point.

Dougherty was pretty sure he'd be the only cop who'd been in the place for a long time, and as he was standing at the bar ordering a beer, he was thinking everybody would probably agree with that. He looked at the table of kids and a couple of the boys tried to stare him down. They were only a couple of years younger than him, but a few years working as a beat cop in Montreal made a big difference.

And everybody in Westlake's knew it.

None of these kids would sell Dougherty any dope — they'd all pegged him for a cop the minute he walked in — so he paid for his beer and left. As he cleared the door he could feel the place relax a little and that felt good.

Outside on the sidewalk he thought about trying another one of the bars within walking distance but figured it would be the same thing in all of them, so he got in his car and drove around a little, looking at cars.

The streets were lined with them, mostly old sedans and station wagons. On Fortune Street he saw a fairly new Volkswagen Beetle and a Renault sedan, looked like the R10, same as the poor bastards on the youth squad drove, and Dougherty couldn't imagine who was driving those in the Point.

But no big white car with a black roof.

On Wellington, going east towards downtown, across the tracks but before heading into the tunnel under the canal, Dougherty turned right onto Bridge Street towards the Victoria Bridge and the South Shore and pulled into the parking lot by the Autostade, probably the ugliest building left over from Expo 67.

It was supposed to have become the home of the Expos, the new baseball team, but they moved into Jarry Park instead. Now only the football team, the Alouettes, were playing in the big, concrete bowl — not even a bowl really, just a bunch of concrete slabs rising out of the ground in a large oval.

Getting out of his car, Dougherty looked around at the empty parking lot, built for the crowds of Expo and now, like the Autostade, almost never used, the Canada Packers plant and the rail yards across Bridge Street. He remembered all the talk when Goose Village was bulldozed, almost ten years ago now, and he heard his father's voice saying it was because Drapeau couldn't stand the idea that the first thing American tourists would see when they got onto the island of Montreal was an Irish slum.

Whatever, Goose Village was gone and the people moved into the Point, giving the old-timers there at least a few people they could look down on.

144   Dougherty walked up to Wellington and went into the Arawana. The crowd was older here, serious drinkers getting off shift at Packers and the port and Northern Electric, and the place was quiet.

It was only when he was inside and at the bar that it occurred to Dougherty he might run into Joe Webber, but he didn't see him.

He did see a couple of the Higgins brothers, though, sitting at a table in the corner with a few other guys. No one noticed Dougherty, or more likely, no one would admit to noticing him. He ordered a beer, wondering for a moment how many he'd had in the last hour, but when the bartender put the glass down Dougherty tried to make it look like his first of the night.

The night was starting to feel like a complete waste of time, and Dougherty was ready to give up. After talking to the detectives, getting encouragement from Carpentier and Ste. Marie, and with more and more cops getting assigned to the terrorist squad every day, Dougherty was thinking this was a real chance for him to get noticed. Maybe he wouldn't have to spend the rest of his life working night shifts at Station Ten.

Then he was thinking he'd just finish his beer and go home.

A man's voice said, "Shit, it's Norbert the Narc," and there was Buck-Buck, standing at the bar with a beer in his hand and a smile on his face. "What the fuck are you doing here?"

Dougherty straightened up and Buck-Buck pulled back a bit. That felt good so he moved forward a little and saw Buck-Buck glance over to the Higginses' table. That felt good, too. Dougherty said, "Relax," and then said, "Danny."

Buck-Buck didn't relax but moved a little closer to Dougherty, looking like he was up for a private conversation.

"I'm not a narc, I'm not even working now."

"So what are you doing here?"

Now it was Dougherty looking nervous, hoping he wasn't laying it on too thick, trying to be natural but wondering if there was a difference between the real nervousness he felt and the way he was trying to look nervous for a different reason.

"I've got a date," he said, and Buck-Buck said, "So? Even ugly chicks need to get laid."

Dougherty let that go. "McGill student."

Buck-Buck smiled, almost laughed, and said, "You kill me, narc," and then his smile disappeared as he realized that hadn't come out the way he'd wanted it to.

"So I was looking for a little something, you know," Dougherty said, and Buck-Buck nodded like oh yeah, he knew. "And you think you can find that here?"

Dougherty shrugged.

"Sorry, man, I don't know anyone who can help you."

Dougherty said, "Yeah, okay, I didn't figure you did," and Buck-Buck looked for a second like he wanted to challenge that but then it passed and he walked — as slowly as he could — back to the table in the corner.

A few minutes later, Dougherty paid for his beer and left. On Wellington he looked across the street at the CN rail sheds and the long row of loading docks. He thought about walking for a while, further into the Point and trying his luck at a few other bars — the one thing the Point had plenty of — but now he figured he might as well get home and get some sleep, be ready for his day shift tomorrow.

Then, just before he got to the parking lot on Bridge

Street a brand new Camaro slowed down beside him, the passenger window down and Buck-Buck behind the wheel, saying, "Hey Norbert, get in." Dougherty opened the door and sunk into the bucket seat.

Buck-Buck drove and said, "Look, maybe I can help you out."

Dougherty said, "Oh yeah?" and Buck-Buck said, "Yeah, but this is just between you and me, right? Nobody can know I'm talking to you."

"Sure, yeah." Dougherty nodded and tried to look really grateful but he knew there was no way Buck-Buck was doing this on his own, he knew that the minute he walked out of the Arawana and Buck-Buck told Ritchie Higgins what they'd talked about the brothers had sent him to sell to the cop. If Dougherty really was undercover, then Buck-Buck would take the fall on his own, the price of working for the Higginses. But if Dougherty really was just a guy trying to score some dope to impress a chick, well then, the Higginses would have something.

So when Buck-Buck pulled over to the curb, stopping with his headlights shining on the Black Rock, and said, "I'm taking a big chance here, so you know, if I need something . . ." and let that hang there. Dougherty just said, "Yeah, sure, you know it, man," hoping that sounded genuine enough.

"Okay, you want grass or hash?"

"Hash."

"You want Morrocan or Kasmiri?"

Dougherty didn't know what to say so he shrugged. "This is my first date with this chick."

"I can let you have two grams of Green Morrocan

for a fin."

"Sounds good."

Dougherty got a five dollar bill out of his wallet and handed it to Buck-Buck, who held up a small ball of tinfoil.

"You need anything else, you come to me, right?"

"Sure, Danny, of course."

Buck-Buck dropped the tinfoil into Dougherty's hand and said, "Okay, good," and nodded.

Dougherty opened the door and got out, standing on the sidewalk and looking back into the Camaro. "Thanks, Danny."

Buck-Buck said, "Don't mention it. And I really mean that," and he laughed and pulled a U and took off in a cloud of dust.

Dougherty stood there for a minute, trying to figure out which one of them had been the more scared and decided it was a tie. Then he smiled, thinking, It's early in the season, nowhere near the playoffs, so they can leave it a tie, don't need overtime yet. He looked at the little tinfoil ball he'd just paid five bucks for and thought no wonder all these guys want to sell drugs, nowhere else could they get so much for so little.

He waited for a few cars to pass and he was trying not jump up and down but, shit, his first drug buy, his first connection. And it was somebody working directly for the Higgins brothers, the top of the Point Boys. This was good.

He was thinking about how he was going to tell Detective Carpentier, how he was going to try to make sure Detective Ste. Marie was there, how he was going to be casual about it, say something like, oh yeah, you know that idea you had about how I should ask around some old friends in the Point? One of them is selling me dope.

He was looking around, glad he was alone so no one could see how much he was smiling and then he looked at the Black Rock.

He read the inscription:

To
preserve from desecration
the remains of 6,000 immigrants
who died of ship fever
A.D. 1847–8.
This stone
is erected by the workmen
of
Messrs. Peto, Brassey & Betts
employed in the construction
of the
Victoria Bridge
A.D. 1859

He'd passed the rock hundreds of times but never stopped to read the words. It wasn't in much of a location for stopping, by the time you noticed it you were just about going down into the little tunnel under the railway tracks and coming up on the bridge. A few times when he was inching along in traffic, Dougherty could remember thinking it wasn't much of a memorial — it really was just a big black rock some workmen pulled out of the ground when they were digging out the piers for the bridge.

But now, for the first time, the number hit him — six thousand immigrants. Dead.

He'd heard the story from his father, how during the famine in Ireland the ships were coming over steady, and by the time they got here the people were sick. Ship fever they called it. Typhus. Two huge sheds were built down here by the river and people coming off the ships were quarantined. If they didn't have typhoid when they got to Montreal, they did after a few hours in the sheds.

Six thousand immigrants died of ship fever and were buried right here. And forgotten.

Then, only a dozen years later, new Irish immigrants showed up and didn't know anything about the ones who'd come before. The new immigrants went to work digging and found the bodies.

Dougherty stood there on Bridge Street, practically in the shadow of the Autostade, cars coming and going from the city, and tried to imagine what it was like for those Irish workmen — men and probably boys, who probably looked like he did and like his father and his little brother Tommy and every other man in his family — when their shovels hit the first bones.

Then more bones and more, until they realized there were thousands of skeletons.

How could they have not known? How could no one have told them, oh yeah, when you start digging there you're going to hit a mass grave? The bodies hadn't been buried for a hundred years or a thousand, they'd only been there twelve. If it was today, Dougherty thought, it would mean that the bodies had been buried in 1958. He would have been in Mademoiselle

Gratton's class, grade six at Jeanne-LeBer school, less than two miles from the Black Rock.

Six thousand bodies in an unmarked grave. Well, it was marked now. Good thing the railway decided to build the bridge and good thing the workmen for Messrs. Peto., Brassy & Betts dug up the rock.

And, Dougherty figured, good thing those workmen put up enough of a fuss to have the rock inscribed and stood up here. They probably got docked a day's pay to get it done.

He crossed the street then and got into his car and started it. The radio was playing a new one from The Beatles, "Let It Be," and it was the right mood for the way Dougherty was feeling as he drove back through the Point, thinking about Brenda Webber.

Not six thousand bodies, just one.

One he wasn't going to let be forgotten.

PART TWO

"Is it true cops get all the best dope?" Ruth said, and
Dougherty took out the little tinfoil ball he still had in
his pocket and dropped it on the coffee table. "Oh my
god, I was kidding."

He said, "Well, if you don't want it," and started
to pick it up but she got to it first saying, "I didn't say
that," and kind of danced away to the kitchenette at
the end of the living room in her small apartment.

When they'd got to the Mazurka a few hours earlier, Ruth didn't want to talk about the Bill case, she
wanted to talk about the Manson murders. The trial
had just started in California, nothing was happening,
really, still in jury selection, but she said she'd been following the case since the arrests last year and said, "Dr.

Pendleton may be called as an expert witness."

"Expert in what?"

"Multiple murders, but maybe also brainwashing — he worked a little with Dr. Cameron."

"Brainwashing?" Dougherty said, and Ruth nodded, quite seriously. "But it looks like Dr. Singer will be the expert on that," and before Dougherty could say anything she explained, "Dr. Margaret Singer. She's at Berkeley and she's done some amazing research on coercive persuasion and brainwashing."

"That's what they're going to claim, these kids?" Dougherty said. "That they were brainwashed by Charlie Manson?"

"If that's what happened."

At that moment in the date, which neither was really treating like a date, Dougherty felt it could have gone completely off the rails, but Ruth didn't seem to notice. She'd started talking about Dr. Pendleton and she talked about him for a long time, explaining his theories about multiple murderers and Dougherty remembered something she'd said the first time they talked, so he asked her about the MacDonald Triad. Without skipping a beat she told him all about John Marshall MacDonald, a psychiatrist from New Zealand and his theory — not a theory, she'd said, "a finding" — MacDonald first proposed in a 1963 paper that showed, she said, "Three behavioural characteristics that, if presented together, will be associated with later violent tendencies."

Dougherty nodded and was finding himself paying a lot more attention. He'd never heard anyone talking about this kind of thing before.

"The three behavioural characteristics are bed-wetting, setting fires and cruelty to animals."

"Bed-wetting?" Dougherty said and imagined what the detectives and inspectors in the homicide office would say if someone told them to look for bed-wetters.

"Persistent bed-wetting, past the age of five."

Dougherty said, "Oh well, then." Ruth ignored that and said, "And obsessive fire-setting and extreme cruelty to animals, killing animals." Dougherty asked if any of the kids in the Manson trial had any of those traits, and Ruth said that Dr. Pendleton was hoping to talk to them. "Maybe I'll get to go along."

That was about the most excited she'd looked in the restaurant and now, back at her apartment, Dougherty was thinking how he couldn't figure this Ruth Garber at all. She wasn't anything like his sister and the other kids at the pop festivals where he worked security. She also wasn't anything like the secretaries in the offices they cleared out during bomb scares and got together with later in the bars. Ruth was serious and straightforward, even now as she was sitting back down on the couch and unwrapping the tinfoil ball. She set it down on the coffee table, squeezed some tobacco out of a cigarette onto a rolling paper and then picked up a penknife that was already blackened at the tip and started to slice off a piece of the hash. But she had to really put some pressure on it and the hash went flying off the table in two directions.

"Shit," Ruth said, and Dougherty laughed.

"It's a little brittle," she said, getting down on her knees on the orange shag carpet and digging around. "What is it?"

Dougherty saw the other half of the hash sitting on top of a carpet shag and picked it up. "He said Green Morrocan but I'm not sure he's reliable," and put it on the tinfoil.

Ruth sat back on the couch, holding the penknife stuck into the other piece of hash, and picked up a book of matches. Before it got awkward, with her trying to light one with one hand while holding the penknife in the other, Dougherty fired up his Zippo and she met his eyes as she held the hash over the flame.

Once she had it warmed up she crumpled it over top of the tobacco and Dougherty watched her tongue slip out between her lips and lick the glue on the rolling paper. The only other person he'd ever seen roll a spliff was a construction worker at Expo and that certainly wasn't sexy.

Ruth was, raising her eyebrows at him over the rising smoke as she inhaled and held it while she passed the joint. Dougherty took a deep drag and held it himself, waiting until Ruth slowly exhaled, her lips in a crinkled O.

"It is pretty good," she said, and Dougherty exhaled and said, "It is?"

"You can't tell?"

"I've never done this before."

"Really?"

"Really."

Ruth took another hit, held it, and then let it out. "But there's probably a lot of other stuff you have done."

"A few things, yeah." He took the joint from her, looking into her dark eyes, still so serious.

Later, in the bedroom, she whispered in his ear, "It's okay, I'm on the pill," and Dougherty didn't say anything. It was the first time he'd heard that since the hostess from the stock exchange, but he figured it was being said a lot these days.

They kissed and Ruth pulled away and started to unbutton her blouse. Dougherty took hold of her hands and moved them away, but she said, "I can undo my own buttons," and Dougherty was kissing her neck then and said, "But what's the fun in that?" and kissed his way to her breasts.

She stayed serious for a long time and only really let go near the end, digging her fingers into his back and pulling him down on her as hard as she could.

Then, almost as soon as Dougherty flopped back on the bed, she got up and walked into the living room.

Dougherty thought about getting up to see what she was doing but instead he lay there listening to her, thinking about her walking around naked. He could hear ashtrays being moved and his lighter being flicked, and a minute later Ruth came back with a pack of Peter Jacksons in one hand and a joint in the other. She climbed back onto the bed, inhaling deep, and handed the joint to Dougherty. "I didn't see your cigarettes; you'll have to smoke mine."

He said, "Sure," and took the joint. Ruth sat cross-legged on the bed and took back the joint when he handed it to her, and Dougherty was thinking how he really couldn't figure her at all.

When the joint was done she picked up her smokes and waved the pack at him but he shook his head. "Not right now."

"Okay, fine," she said and put the pack on the bed-side table.

It had been awkward like this after sex for Dougherty before, but usually that was when all he could think about was getting out of there. He didn't want to get away from Ruth, and then he thought maybe it was because he wasn't feeling all that close to her.

And maybe he wanted to.

So he said, "Where are you from?"

"How do you know I'm not from here?"

"Well, you're not living at home, you're paying rent, and you're not living in the McGill ghetto and you're not living up on St. Urbain — you're way out here in the east end."

"It's not way out."

He looked at her sideways and said, "Does anybody else in this building speak English?"

"I'm not sure."

"Are there any other McGill students around here?"

"I'm not some undergrad," she said. "I'm finishing my Master's."

"English Montrealers don't move into the east end," Dougherty said. "It's that two solitudes thing, remember?"

"What about a guy like you who's both?"

"I think my name's a bit of a giveaway."

"You think you have to choose to be one or the other?"

Dougherty shrugged. It wasn't something he'd thought about and not something he wanted to be thinking about at that moment. He really wanted to know more about Ruth and then it hit him. "You're

American."

"So, what's that supposed to mean?"

"It's not supposed to mean anything, it's just most of the Americans I meet these days are men. You know, draft dodgers."

"Would you go to Vietnam?"

Dougherty shook his head a little and said, "To tell you the truth, I don't know. My dad joined the navy in 1938 but when I said something about joining the army he wasn't too keen on it."

Ruth was still sitting cross-legged and looking at him. "Why was it okay for him but not you?"

"I asked him that and he just said, 'Nazis.'"

"Not much you can say to that."

They were quiet for a minute and then Dougherty said, "Marielle Archambeault was killed a few blocks from here."

"I know," Ruth said.

"Is that what got you interested in this neighbourhood?"

"No, I was already working for Dr. Pendleton."

"Studying murderers?"

"Yes. I started here last September. I came here to work with him. I'd read all his papers and I saw a talk he gave at Columbia."

"Is that where you went?"

He thought he saw the beginning of a smile and she said, "NYU."

It was quiet then, but Dougherty wanted to keep listening to Ruth talk.

"Why do you want study murderers?"

She looked at him and for a moment he thought she

wasn't going to answer but then she turned sideways and picked up her pack of smokes from the bedside table and said, "Kitty Genovese."

Dougherty shrugged and Ruth lit her cigarette and blew out the match, then said, " 'Thirty-Seven Who Saw Murder Didn't Call the Police.' That was the headline."

"Oh yeah, I remember now. New York, right?"

"Yeah, Queens."

"Is that where you're from?"

"No, the Bronx, Christopher Columbus High. I was a junior — we talked about Kitty Genovese a lot."

"That no one called?" Dougherty shrugged. "People get scared."

"No, it wasn't that no one called the police, that's what all the newspapers were talking about, that's what all my friends were talking about. What I remember is that when they caught the guy, when he went to trial, the only reason he had for doing it, the only motive he said he had was that he wanted to kill a woman. That's all he had to say. He drove around for hours that night looking for a woman to kill and found Kitty Genovese."

She took a drag on her cigarette, and Dougherty held up his hand and she handed it to him and he said, "That's strange."

162 "What's strange?" She held out her hand for the cigarette.

"The driving around all night."

"What do you mean, did you find something?"

"Maybe, I don't know."

"What is it?"

"Maybe a car, we don't know if it's anything."

"What do you think it is?"

"It was just when you said driving around all night. I've been looking for a car because a girl in the Point said she saw one and then a kid in LaSalle said he saw one that could be the same one, but it was when you said driving around looking for a woman I realized Sylvie Berubé was found right by the entrance to the Ville-Marie Tunnel and where Brenda Webber was found you can see the expressway, the 2-20, and that's actually the same road."

"So he was driving back and forth?"

"It's probably nothing. The reason the car stood out a little in the Point is the place isn't really somewhere you pass through, you know? Even if you're taking the Victoria Bridge you don't really go into the Point."

"And the other three women were all killed downtown."

"Shirley Audette was killed on Dorchester. There's an on-ramp to the expressway right there and Jean Way's apartment was on Lincoln — you can take Guy or Atwater."

"Well sure," Ruth said, "you can drive anywhere."

"Yeah, I guess that's what he did."

"What he's *doing*."

Dougherty said yeah, thinking, Right, this guy has killed five women, why would he stop now? "They were all downtown, right? Even Marielle Archambeault, who lived around the corner here, he met her at Place Ville-Marie, didn't he?"

"She worked in a jewellery store," Ruth said. "He picked her up there. That's how we know his name is

Bill — she mentioned it to one of the other women at the store."

"So he killed those three in their own apartments but Sylvie Berubé and Brenda Webber he didn't."

"Brenda Webber lived at home, didn't she?"

"Yeah, and she was a lot younger than the other girls."

Ruth slid off the bed then and picked up her glasses as she walked back into the living room. "I'm just going to write some of this down." She came back with a notebook and a pen. Still naked.

Dougherty was going to say something about how good she looked under the jeans and loose blouses she wore, like a *Playboy* centrefold, but it didn't seem like the time. And it didn't seem like the kind of thing Ruth Garber cared about.

She wrote a few things down in the notebook and then said, "Also there were no mutilations on Brenda Webber's body, were there? He didn't bite her breasts?"

"No, he didn't."

She nodded, wrote a few words on the notepad and then flipped it shut like a stenographer.

Then she took off her glasses and looked at Dougherty. "Are you going to stay the night?"

He couldn't tell if she wanted him to or not, if it made a difference to her one way or the other but then without really thinking about it he said, "Of course," and thought he saw her start to smile.

Or maybe that's just what he wanted to see.

CHAPTER
TWELVE

Rozovsky said, "You're banging a member of the tribe?"

"What?"

"Ruth Garber — she's Jewish, right?"

"I don't know, we didn't talk religion."

Dougherty didn't want to tell Rozovsky that what they did talk about was murderers — multiple murderers — and that Ruth Garber knew a lot more about them than Dougherty did. Probably more than any of the cops on the force.

Rozovsky was pulling pictures out of the stack of files on the desk. "Trust me, it'll come up. So how far back are we going?"

"I don't know, five years?"

"Five years, you know how many cars that is?"

"We don't have to get every one. We can probably start with a few, narrow it down."

"Why don't you go to some lots, get some brochures?"

"Yeah, I can do that, too," Dougherty said, "but it could be a couple years old and these kids didn't see it in a showroom."

Rozovsky sighed. "I've got a lot of work to do, you know. Don't you?"

"Here," Dougherty said, holding up a picture, "anything that looks like this."

"What's that?"

"Buick Skylark. No wait, Wildcat."

"Oh yeah, that was used in a bank robbery at the Rockland Shopping Centre. See the scrape along the side? There was a chase on the Metropolitan Expressway, remember?"

"Vaguely. If it was white it would be a big white car with a black roof, wouldn't it?"

"Like this." Rozovsky held up another picture, and Dougherty said, "What is it?"

"Chevy. Impala, I think."

"Was it in a bank robbery, too?"

"No, it was broken into. It could take days to find pictures of all the possible cars."

"Five or six will do. I just need to show the kids and see if they pick the same one."

"Here," Rozovsky said, "this one's even white."

Dougherty took the picture. "Nice car, Galaxy." He put the picture with the others they'd pulled from the files and said, "Two or three more should do it. Have you got any Pontiacs? Maybe a Grand Prix or a Ventura?"

"I told you," Rozovsky said, "they're not in here by car. These are evidence photos."

"But you can remember."

"They're all over the place, they're not filed by car, they're filed by case."

"So?"

"So, some of them are victim's cars like that one, cars that were broken into or vandalized, and some were used in crimes and some were stolen vehicles."

Dougherty said, "Okay, but we don't need everything. I can start with a few and eliminate some, narrow it down. Have you got a Buick?"

"Somewhere."

"That mobster on the Champlain bridge, he was driving a Cutlass, right?"

"I've got plenty of pictures of that one," Rozovsky said, "but it was in about a hundred pieces."

"But mobster cars, they're big. There must be plenty of pictures of them."

Rozovsky said, "Not as many as you'd think," but he was walking back to the row of filing cabinets. Dougherty started out of the office, saying, "Okay, this is a good start, thanks. I'll be back in a couple of hours."

Dougherty could hear Rozovsky complaining about not having time for this, but he knew he'd get the pictures together.

Down the hall the homicide office was empty except for Carpentier sitting at his desk, going through notebooks. Dougherty stood at the door, watching as the detective flipped the pages and dropped notebook after notebook into a growing pile. The longer

Dougherty stood there, the more awkward it got, but he didn't want to barge in on the detective. Then he saw Carpentier stop and reread a page of a notebook, nod and then write something down.

Carpentier looked up. "Constable Dougherty."

Dougherty started into the office. "You find something?"

"Maybe, don't know yet." Carpentier shrugged and leaned back, the wooden chair creaking as it tilted and rolled a few inches. He rubbed his eyes, then looked up at Dougherty. "Something some guy said three months ago, didn't seem like anything at the time, now maybe there's something to connect it to."

"Working the informants."

Carpentier nodded. "Now that we have the task force and a lot of money to spend everybody is selling something."

"Some of it could be good."

"Oh yes, some of it. A lot to go through." Carpentier started to pick up another notebook but stopped and looked back at Dougherty. "What about your inform-ant, the drug dealer in the Point, how is that going?"

"Pretty good, I think. I bought some hash off him."

"That's good. What did you do with it?"

Dougherty hadn't expected that. "I flushed it," he said, and Carpentier said, "Good."

"That's all I did, I didn't ask him about anything else."

"No, you don't want to do that yet," Carpentier said. "Buy a little more from him, get him to think he has a cop in his pocket. You may need to give him something."

"Like what?"

That shrug again. "Maybe the next time we raid the bars you can tip him off, something like that."

"Okay, yeah, sounds good."

"This could be good for you," Carpentier said, "if this guy is close to the Higginses. Does he seem close?"

Dougherty thought about it a little. "He seems close. I think he's a little brighter than the younger Higgins brothers."

"If he can tie his own shoes that puts him ahead of those two. So, become his friend."

"Okay."

"Anything else?"

"I'm getting pictures of different kinds of cars to show the kids, see if they can recognize the make."

"Why?"

Dougherty shrugged and was feeling out of his depth again.

Then Carpentier said, "Can't hurt, I suppose," and Dougherty said yeah. He didn't want to leave the office on that so he said, "Hey, I was talking to Dr. Pendleton's assistant."

"The girl with the glasses?"

Dougherty said yeah, and Carpentier said, "And the big tits under those sweaters she wears?"

"Yeah, right. Anyway, she asked me a lot of questions. That's okay, right?"

Carpentier nodded, "Dr. Pendleton has some con-nections." He raised his eyebrows and motioned slightly upwards with his chin. "High up, you know?"

"It was just the usual stuff."

"What else could it be?"

Dougherty said, "I don't know," but he was thinking

about the bed-wetting and wondered if Dr. Pendleton had told his connections about that.

Just then another detective came in, saying, *"Henri, viens ici, faut que tu entendes ça,"* and Carpentier said, "Okay, *j'arrive*," and stood up to leave. He turned at the doorway, looked back and said, "Don't wait too long to buy more dope from your friend. Be a good customer."

"Yeah, for sure," Dougherty said and watched the two detectives leave.

Something was up. He could tell, he could feel it.

But as his father would say, that was above his pay grade, so Dougherty went to the big filing cabinet against the east wall of the office.

The first file Dougherty read was Shirley Audette's. She'd been murdered on October 3, 1969. Eight months ago, six months after Dougherty had been called to the scene and discovered the body of Sylvie Berubé on the other side of the city.

Looking at the picture of Shirley Audette, Dougherty saw the similarities to Sylvie Berubé right away: white women, early twenties, attractive. And strangled.

Shirley Audette's body was also found in a lane, this one right behind her apartment building on Dorchester, between St. Mark and St. Matthew, about four blocks from Station Ten. She was wearing red pants and a turtleneck sweater and a brown leather vest. She was twenty years old.

She was also five weeks pregnant. Dougherty was surprised to see that. He couldn't remember it from any of the press, although there had been very little press when Shirley Audette had been killed. There was also a note that said she had been treated at the Douglas, a psychiatric hospital in Verdun Dougherty only knew from all the jokes about the place he had heard growing up.

The file also included the transcript of an interview with Shirley Audette's boyfriend that said the two lived together in the apartment but the boyfriend was at work all night. He said she had called him at three in the morning and they spoke for a few minutes — she was scared being alone — and then he called her back at five and there was no answer. In the interview the boyfriend said Shirley sometimes took part in what he called "rough sex" with a man he didn't know. The detective interviewing him asked if she did it for money, but the boyfriend said no. In the margin someone had written, *drugs?*

Dougherty looked at the pictures of Shirley Audette taken at the morgue, and other than the mark around her neck the only other mark on her body was where her breasts had been bitten. One of the pictures was a close-up and Dougherty could see distinct teeth marks around the nipple that went almost completely through the skin.

And that was pretty much it. The boyfriend's story about being at work checked out and there wasn't anything else.

The Marielle Archambeault file was just as thin, and 171 the little information in it was starting to look familiar. Also twenty years old, she worked in a jewellery store in the mall under Place Ville-Marie and she was strangled on November 23, barely two months after Shirley Audette. The next day when Marielle didn't show up for work, her boss went to her apartment and got the landlady to let him in. The apartment was neat; there was a typewriter on a small desk and a novel by Françoise Sagan on an end table. Marielle was found on the couch and she was wearing brown pants and a green blouse with three buttons missing. Her bra had been ripped apart but put back on her body. There were no signs of a struggle or forced entry.

She'd also been strangled. And her breast had been bitten.

This time there was no boyfriend to talk to and the other women at the jewellery store didn't seem to know much about Marielle's personal life. Like Sylvie Berubé, she had only moved to Montreal a few months earlier. The only thing coming out of the interviews was that one of the women thought she'd heard Marielle say she was meeting a man named Bill after work.

The first detective on the scene had recognized the similarities to Shirley Audette — right away they knew they were dealing with the same murderer.

But they didn't go public with that information until after another woman was killed.

Dougherty couldn't figure out why he hadn't heard about these murders, right downtown, last October and November, six months ago.

Then he remembered that was during the massive police prep for the Grey Cup game, everybody so worried it would be such a great target for bombs, the city full of English from across Canada. People were worried; it was all they talked about. Trudeau was at the game, there were lots of threats against him and the more threats there were the more he insisted on going and not being surrounded by security, so there were hundreds of cops in plainclothes in attendance.

The prep had gone on for weeks, Dougherty'd logged lots of overtime then — around-the-clock watches on the Autostade, guarding the parade floats after the bomb squad cleared them, sweeping the hotels, escorting the Miss Grey Cup contestants. Anything that should normally have taken two cops had six.

The Grey Cup being the national championship, the only really Canadian championship, not like hockey with American teams in it, did seem like it could be a real target. The game hadn't been held in Montreal since before the war, more than thirty years ago. There'd been talk of cancelling it, or at least some of the events. Dougherty remembered the Santa Claus Parade was cancelled.

But the game was played. And all the events went on as usual, just with massive security. People did come from all over the country, the Calgary fans set up their pancake breakfasts on the sidewalks and took their horse into the hotel like they did at every Grey Cup, the Ottawa fans were everywhere, the Saskatchewan fans in green were out in force.

And nothing happened.

It was only after the game when everybody started to relax that they found a bomb, a big one, ten sticks of dynamite, in Eaton's department store. Dougherty remembered the Christmas decorations were up and they emptied the place, thousands of people spilling out onto St. Catherine Street, and when Vachon came out with the device — still in the shoebox he'd found it in under a counter in the jewellery department on the fourth floor — the Sally Ann Santa rang his bell and everybody — French and English — cheered. Dougherty remembered Vachon telling people it was the first time he'd ever had a crowd cheer for him.

The next murder came in January 1970.

Dougherty picked up the Jean Way file and read it, and as he did the sadness passed and he started to get angry. He read the same details again. Jean Way was twenty-four years old and had been strangled, but her breasts had not been mutilated. Dougherty read on and found out that Jean Way had a boyfriend who had come to her apartment on Lincoln, also a few blocks from Station Ten, to pick her up for a date but there was no answer. The boyfriend left, but when he came back a couple of hours later, he found the apartment door slightly open. He went in and found Jean naked on her bed.

The detective's theory was that the first time the boyfriend came to the apartment the killer, Bill, was still inside. When the boyfriend left, Bill took off and didn't bite her breasts and put Jean's clothes back on as he had the other victims.

Other than the boyfriend's claim about rough sex and the question about drugs in Shirley Audette's file, there wasn't any mention of "crazy sex stuff" anywhere else, but now Dougherty was starting to understand what Ruth was talking about when she'd said Dr. Pendleton might be called as an expert about brainwashing in the Manson trial. The detectives believed the women had been charmed by Bill and were willing participants right up till the end.

Dougherty couldn't imagine Brenda Webber getting

charmed by a guy like Bill, and looking at the pictures of the other victims, if it wasn't for that one mention of the Douglas Hospital he couldn't imagine any of these women being involved in the kind of hippie stuff the detectives were talking about.

Dougherty put the files back in the cabinet, feeling like he hadn't really learned much, except that now he really wanted to find this Bill and wrap his fingers around the prick's neck and squeeze until his head came right off.

And then kick it like he was going for a fifty-yard field goal.

Back in the ident office, Rozovsky said, "What's wrong?"

"What?"

"You look like you're going to kill someone."

"I am."

"Well, don't do it here — this place is crawling with cops."

Dougherty didn't get it at first, and then realized Rozovsky was joking and that snapped him out of it a little.

"Where? I don't see any."

Rozovsky held out a manila envelope. "That's true, they're all running around out there, something's happening."

"Oh yeah?"

"They're getting tips about something — every cop in the place is working on it."

Dougherty said, "Good," and then he took the envelope. "That's why I'm doing this."

CHAPTER
THIRTEEN

It happened Sunday.

Dougherty had the day off after a late night Saturday, breaking up fights outside discos and directing traffic around an accident on the corner of St. Catherine and Atwater, in front of the Forum. It was near the end of June and it was finally starting to get hot, high sixties and even into the seventies. Dougherty was glad for that but not looking forward to the stinking heat and humidity he knew was coming. The fights and fender-benders took on a sharper edge when that stifling heat came down like it did every August.

But Sunday morning was beautiful and Dougherty drove out to LaSalle with his envelope of pictures and waited around on Thierry Street for Giovani

Masaracchia. As expected, the kid and his family came home from church just after noon, and even though Dougherty was wearing jeans and a t-shirt Giovani recognized him right away. The kid said something to his parents in Italian and the mom and the little sister went into the house, but the dad stayed by the car.

"I'm Constable Dougherty," he said, and the dad said, "Yes?"

"I just want to show your son some pictures."

The kid said something in Italian and his father said something back and then they went back and forth a few times until the kid waved him off. "I didn't tell them you were here before. He's not happy about that."

Dougherty looked at the father and nodded and the father nodded back. Then Dougherty slid the eight-by-ten pictures out of the envelope and handed them to the kid. "Can you tell me if one of these looks like the car you saw?"

Giovani flipped through the pictures. "I don't know, I don't think so."

"It didn't look like any of them?"

"It looked like all of them. Well, not this one," and he eliminated the Galaxy. He flipped through the rest and said, "Sorry."

"I know they're not the right colours, can you picture them white with a black roof?"

"Sure, but it's not any of these."

The father said something in Italian and the kid said something back and then said to Dougherty, "It was more square at the back."

"Not a fastback?"

"No."

Dougherty took the pictures and slid them back into the envelope. He thanked the kid, shook the father's hand and asked if it would be okay if he brought back some more pictures.

"Sure."

"You want to let your father know I'll be back?"

But the father was already nodding, and Dougherty realized he understood English pretty well.

"That's a good son you have there," he said, and the father said yes.

Then Dougherty drove to the Point and looked around for Gail Murphy. There was no one at her house when he knocked, so he returned to Bonsecours Street and the ident office.

Sunday afternoon the place was quiet, but Rozovsky was there and when he saw Dougherty he said, "What are you doing here?"

"I need more pictures of cars. What are you doing here?"

"Working."

"Okay," Dougherty said, "let's work."

"You're on your own this time. I've been told to clear up all the outstanding jobs and be ready."

"Ready for what?"

"I don't know, but I told you something was up."

Dougherty said okay and got to work.

Throughout the afternoon the building filled up with people, and Dougherty kept going out into the hall to find out what was going on. Around four o'clock a couple of desk sergeants checked in and started calling people in for overtime, but neither would tell Dougherty what was happening.

At six o'clock Rozovsky said his shift was over, but he made no move to leave. Dougherty told him he had only a couple more pictures that could be the car, so Rozovsky said he'd help, and by eight they had a dozen possibilities and the place was really buzzing. A few of the detectives on the CAT Squad were in the building, and Vachon and Meloche from the bomb squad stopped in but left a few minutes later with four constables on motorcycles leading the bomb truck.

Dougherty grabbed a couple of smoked meat sandwiches from the place across the street, and when he got back he told Rozovsky there were people on the fourth floor.

"Big shots on Sunday night? I told you."

A little after nine, word had spread through the building that the CAT Squad and a couple dozen cops from the Quebec Provincial Police Force had raided a cottage in Prévost, north of the city, and they were bringing in four people. And a lot of dynamite.

Dougherty went down to the lobby to watch them bring the suspects in — three men and a woman, all in their early twenties, all with the same long, stringy hair and the same pissed-off look — and move them into separate interrogation rooms.

By then, the lobby was full of reporters and cops, and Dougherty managed to push through the crowd to Detective Carpentier and say, "Congratulations."

"We got some good tips," Carpentier said.

"No trouble at the scene?"

"It was under surveillance for a while," Carpentier said.

"Lot of dynamite?"

Carpentier laughed. "Three hundred pounds —
Vachon almost shit himself. He's like a kid at Christmas."

Then more detectives came into the lobby carrying
sawed-off shotguns and holding up bags they told the
reporters were full of revolvers.

Carpentier leaned a little closer to Dougherty and
said, "And cash, almost thirty grand."

"Bank robberies?" Dougherty said.

"Looks like it was from the Université de Montréal.
Remember, the student centre was robbed a few weeks
ago?"

"That was over fifty grand, wasn't it?" Dougherty
said, "I remember that night, two bombs went off."

"That's right."

"Shit. So why was the raid now?"

Carpentier motioned towards the crowd by the
front desk, the reporters trying to get at Marcel St.
Aubin, the chief. "Because of what he's not going to
tell them now. There was going to be a kidnapping.
The press release was at the chalet."

"That's old, isn't it?" Dougherty said. "Last winter,
they were after that guy from Israel."

"This was a new one," Carpentier said. "It was to
be the American consul general, a guy named Harrison
Burgess."

"Shit."

"It's much the same. Same demands, same manifesto."

"Are these the same guys? They're out on bail,
aren't they?"

"Yes, those ones are, but these are different."

"But local," Dougherty said, "not foreigners like
the mayor said."

Carpentier lit a cigarette, inhaled, blew smoke at the ceiling and shook his head. "I still think there are no more than twenty or thirty assholes doing all this. You know how many cops we have on the task force now?"

"But even twenty guys can do a lot of damage."

Carpentier nodded, but Dougherty could see he wasn't convinced, maybe remembering that in the old days they would've just rounded up as many of them as they could find and beat the shit out of them: hang them off the Jacques Cartier Bridge by their ankles and scare them silly.

"Well," Dougherty said, "it's still a surprise they were going after an American."

"Why not?" Carpentier said, "Americans are getting kidnapped in South America."

"Yeah, but we're not South America."

Now the reporters had turned and moved towards the front doors to watch Vachon and Meloche coming in with wooden boxes of dynamite. Vachon waved the questions and pushed his way through the crowd.

"We're not?" Carpentier said.

The front page of the *Gazette* Monday morning was a picture of a cottage under the headline "Bombers' cache found."

After he'd checked in for his eight-to-four, Dougherty walked down St. Matthew and sat in the greasy spoon, reading the paper while he ate poached eggs on toast. He wasn't surprised to see that Carpentier was right. There was no mention of the planned kidnapping or any connection to the arrest four months earlier of different people with the same manifesto and the same ransom note.

Pete emerged from the kitchen. "You think they'll do it?"

Dougherty said, "Yeah, I do."

"Legalize pot, really? The hippies will go crazy."

Dougherty looked up, quizzical, from the paper and Pete pointed to another headline, the one right beside the lead story that read, "Policy on pot' due for house battle today," and said, "Oh, I don't know about that."

"That Le Dain Commission really blew it up," Pete said. He filled Dougherty's mug with coffee and poured himself a cup. It was just after nine and the place was empty.

"Yeah."

"Hey, how's it going with that girl you were in here with, the one with the glasses."

"Okay, I guess."

A couple of firemen from across the street came in and Pete moved down the counter, saying, "You fellas ready for a long shift? You bring your pillows?"

Dougherty drank the coffee and read the article about the pot battle. The Le Dain Commission had filed its interim report on the non-medical use of drugs and now the NDP and Conservatives were asking Trudeau and the Liberals if they were going to move marijuana out of the Narcotics Control Act and into the Food and Drugs Act, in effect making it legal. Dougherty liked the quote from the Minister of Health, John Munro, who said that the question of legalizing marijuana was "the symbolic battleground for a fight between the generations."

Not like the actual battleground of bombs and bank robberies and riots and kidnapping plans.

Dougherty read another story on the front page about a battleground that wasn't just symbolic: "Devlin party turns into stone fight." The article stated that "police wielding clubs and nightsticks charged a crowd after a celebration of Miss Bernadette Devlin's election turned to stone-throwing." Northern Ireland.

Pete came back then. "You have to love the quiet ones."

"What?"

"You know the type — when she finally looks up from the books and takes off the glasses she goes wild."

"Yeah, I guess." Dougherty wouldn't exactly call what Ruth had done *wild*, but he had liked it.

"You play your cards right, you'll find out."

"I'm not very good at cards."

"You better learn."

Dougherty said, "Yeah, I'll see what I can do," and dropped a two-dollar bill on the counter.

Walking back to Station Ten, Dougherty thought about Ruth Garber and how Pete was sort of right — she did change when she took off her glasses, at least a little. But she was also so different from the girls Dougherty had known, he wasn't sure what to do next. When he'd left the morning after their date, they hadn't made any plans to see each other again. He really had no idea if she wanted to, and he didn't even have her phone number.

The station was quiet when Dougherty arrived. Delisle looked up from the newspaper he was reading, and Dougherty expected to be sent out on a call right away. But the sergeant just nodded and went back to the paper, the same one Dougherty had been reading at Pete's. Beside it on the desk was the French paper, *Le Devoir*, so Dougherty picked it up and looked at the front page. No scare headline about the bombers' cache, no picture of the cottage, no mention of the raid at all. And nothing about the Le Dain Commission and marijuana. The top stories were about the federal government considering wage and price controls, and a hijacking in Iran.

"Is there anything in there about a hijacking?" Dougherty said, and Delisle said, "Yeah, I think so," and flipped back a couple of pages. He turned the paper so Dougherty could see the headline on page 10: "Teens skyjack Iranian plane." Above it, in smaller letters, it said, "Shah's nephew aboard."

"Think we'll get hijackings next?"

"If we do," Delisle said, "it'll be the Mounties' problem."

"Yeah, I guess."

Delisle continued to read the paper. "Choquette is having a press conference this afternoon." The Quebec Minister of Justice, Jérôme Choquette.

Dougherty said, "Another task force?"

"Commission of Inquiry. He's getting some lawyer from Quebec City to run it. Says under the Fire Investigation Act they can find out from the ones arrested at the chalet yesterday who set off all the other bombs."

"We don't need a lawyer from Quebec City for that," Dougherty said. "We just have to take them down into the cells and ask them nice."

"You got that right, but he can't say that to the

press, can he? How many riots do you want?"

"Will you give me any overtime?"

"You want to work the parade?"

Dougherty said sure, and Delisle said, "Too bad, it's all in the east end."

The last time Dougherty worked a Saint-Jean-Baptiste Day parade was in '68 with the riot. Last year's had violence, too. A huge crowd, five, maybe ten thousand people followed the parade along Sherbrooke and finally rushed a float and flipped it over right in front of the Ritz-Carlton Hotel. Twenty people arrested, four cops ended up in the hospital, but Dougherty wasn't working. And now this year the parade was only going to be in the east end. Dougherty figured that might help or it might make it worse.

The phone rang then and Delisle picked it up, listened for a minute, then said, "Okay, okay," and hung up. "Go over to Ogilvy's — they picked up a shoplifter and he started a fight."

"At least it's not a bomb."

Dougherty drove the squad car a few blocks to the big department store and parked in a no parking zone on St. Catherine.

Inside Ogilvy's, Dougherty found a salesgirl and asked her where the manager's office was, and she said, "Just past the elevators, way over there." He thanked her and she said, "I know where the cafeteria is, too, if you're looking for lunch," and giggled.

He recognized her Nova Scotian accent and wondered how long she'd been in the big city. "We'll see how long this takes."

In the manager's office, Dougherty was surprised to

see the shoplifter was a well-dressed man in his fifties. Looked just like the manager. They were sitting across the desk from each other.

"About time," the manager said, and it looked to Dougherty like the shoplifter was about to say exactly the same thing.

There was a third man in the office, a little younger, a little more round in the middle, standing beside the manager's desk with the same indignant look on his face as the other two.

Dougherty said, "All right, what happened?" and the manager said, "What do you mean, what happened? I told the officer everything on the phone."

"Could you tell me again?"

The manager gave an exasperated sigh, and it seemed to Dougherty the shoplifter did, too. This was nothing like the usual shoplifting call he went on, where he'd be met with a sobbing housewife begging the manager not to tell her husband.

"As I explained to the officer on the phone," the manager said, "he stole something."

The shoplifter said, "I did not."

"You put the watch strap in your pocket and you walked out of the store."

"I told you, I was looking at watch straps and hadn't decided, and I got distracted and I forget I had it in my hand."

186

"It was in your pocket."

"It was not."

Dougherty looked at the guy standing beside the desk and figured he was the floorwalker who'd grabbed the shoplifter. "Was it in his hand or in his pocket?"

Before the guy could say anything, the manager said, "What difference does it make? He took it out of the store without paying for it."

"I offered to pay."

"Oh sure, once you got caught."

Now Dougherty was trying not to laugh, these two guys both trying as hard as they could to be the more dignified outraged party and both of them looking pathetic. Dougherty said, "So, it was a watch strap?"

The manager picked it up off his desk and waved it around saying, "Leather."

"Two dollars," the shoplifter said.

The manager turned on the guy. "It doesn't matter how much it costs, two dollars or two thousand."

"It's only two dollars."

"Only, only, only. It doesn't matter what it only costs — you didn't pay for it!"

"I'll pay for it now."

"It's too late now."

Dougherty said, "Is it?"

The manager looked up at him and said, "What do you mean? Of course it is."

"Well, as much as I'd love to spend the afternoon down at Station Ten writing up this report," Dougherty said, "and as much as we'd all love to take a day off work and go down to the courthouse and pay some lawyers, I'm wondering if we really have to."

The shoplifter looked like he was almost amused, but the manager wasn't cracking. "Are you being sarcastic?"

"I really thought you'd be able to tell."

"Well, I never . . ."

"Yeah, sure you have. So why not now?" Dougherty looked at the shoplifter. "What do you say, Mr. . . . ?"

"Barrett."

"What do you say Mr. Barrett here pays you for the watch strap. And the next time he wants to spend twenty-five dollars on a watch he'll come here and not Eaton's."

"I don't want him here."

"I guess that's up to you."

"If I want him charged, you'll have to charge him."

"Yeah, I will, sure."

That seemed to make the manager happy, or at least less angry, to know that it was still his decision. Dougherty knew then how it would go, how the manager would make a big deal about letting the guy go and the guy would refuse to admit that he'd done anything wrong and they'd both think they were the one who made the big concession and took the high road and that's exactly how it went.

Walking back out through the main floor of the store Dougherty didn't see the Nova Scotian salesgirl and he figured it was just as well. After taking down such big-time criminals he needed to get his bearings back.

Then he realized what he actually needed to do was something important, so he stopped off at his apartment, got his envelope full of pictures of big square cars and drove down the hill to the Point to find Gail Murphy.

CHAPTER
FOURTEEN

Gail Murphy pulled out one of the pictures. "This one."

"You're sure?"

"Yeah, I saw it again."

The Lincoln. The picture Dougherty had was from an accident at the St. Laurent Boulevard exit from the Ville-Marie Tunnel. The Lincoln was hit by a delivery truck turning onto Berri, but there wasn't much damage to either vehicle.

"When did you see it?"

Gail shrugged and took a drag on the cigarette Dougherty had given her, then exhaled a long stream of smoke, chewed her bottom lip and said, "On the weekend. Sunday?"

While Dougherty was at the ident office with Rozovsky getting the pictures. While the task force was up in Prévost raiding the cottage.

"Where was it? Did you see who was driving?"

Dougherty was leaning against his squad car, parked by the CN rail yard around the corner from the Boys & Girls Club, where he'd seen Gail and waved to her. They weren't really out of sight, but they were far enough away that she'd talk to a cop.

"No, I didn't see anybody in the car, it just drove by."

"What street was it on?"

She thought for a moment. "Wellington."

"Where on Wellington?"

"By Bridge Street."

"Was it turning onto Wellington like it just came from the Victoria Bridge, or was it coming straight down Wellington from downtown?"

"I don't know, it might have been coming down Bridge the other way."

Right away Dougherty thought of the Arawana, the tavern on the corner. "What time was this?"

"Eleven?"

Dougherty looked at her, raising his eyebrows, and Gail added, "Maybe midnight."

"You're out late."

"Who cares?"

He let that go. "But you didn't see the driver?"

"No."

"Was there anybody else in the car?"

"I don't think so."

"Okay, now was it just like this," he held up the

picture, "but different colours, or were they any other differences?"

"No, it was just like that, but white with a black roof."

The Lincoln in the picture was red with a black roof, a '66, in pretty good shape. Dougherty said, "No rust? No scrapes or dents?"

"It just drove by — it might not even be the same car."

Yeah, but Dougherty could tell she knew it was the same car. Maybe she wouldn't want that in an official statement, maybe it was dark and the car just drove by and she didn't know any of the details, but she knew. He said, "Okay, that's good. This car probably has nothing to do with this, but you be careful, okay?"

Gail took a last drag and flicked the cigarette onto the street, then said, "Sure, of course," and moved away.

She got all the way around the car and looked back at Dougherty and said, "See you around," and he said, "Oh yeah, you'll be seeing plenty of me."

He watched her walk back up to the Boys & Girls Club and then he got into the squad car and started it up. He drove slowly through the Point, not expecting to see the Lincoln, or really having any idea what he was looking for.

After going up and down a few streets, Dougherty finally headed up the hill and punched out for the day.

Instead of walking the couple of blocks to his apartment he hopped on the Métro at Guy, took it to the Champ-de-Mars station and walked to police HQ on Bonsecours.

Rozovsky was in the ident office, and he looked up and said, "More cars?"

"Just narrowing it down now. Looks like a Lincoln."

"You use the one from the accident in the Ville-Marie Tunnel?"

Dougherty said yeah, and then saw the photos spread out on the desk in front of Rozovsky. "This from the raid at the cottage?"

"Evidence photos. Such big plans they had: a press release, a manifesto, a list of demands."

"Jesus Christ," Dougherty said, "'By the kidnapping of Consul Burgess the FLQ wishes to emphasize its revolutionary solidarity with all of the countries which struggle against the economic, cultural and social domination of the Americans in the world.' Are they serious?"

"They're going to save us all."

"'Harrison W. Burgess is in the hands of the Front de Libération du Québec. Here are the terms on which his life depends.' They must be going crazy upstairs."

"It's exactly the same as the ones from last February," Rozovsky said. "Here, look what's written in the margin: *Operation Marcil-Lanctôt*."

"Who wrote that?"

"One of the terrorists, I guess. It was on the press release when they found it in the cottage."

"Lanctôt, he was one of the ones from last winter?"

"Yeah, just change the name Harrison Burgess to Moshe Golan and the rest is the same. Well, except for the part about their revolutionary solidarity with the world against America."

Dougherty said, "Lanctôt's out on bail, isn't he?"

"Yeah, him and a few others. Every cop in the city is looking for them."

"Tell me about it."

"Now they think he'll grab someone else and add the names of the ones we just picked up to this list of political prisoners they want freed."

Dougherty looked at the list of names and said, "There's Geoffroy. Guy blew up the stock exchange — they expect him to be let out?"

"Maybe that's a negotiating point," Rozovsky said. "Maybe they'll give up on him if they can get their five hundred grand in gold."

Dougherty laughed and said, "Yeah. A half a million dollars in gold — a voluntary tax they call it. Not like they're going to spend it here — they want a flight to Cuba or Algeria. Shit, they don't even know where they're going."

"But they know they're not staying here," Rozovsky said.

"Well, who'd want to? There's bombs going off and people getting kidnapped — this place isn't safe," Dougherty said. Then he read the rest of the press release. "There's really nothing here about what they want for Quebec."

"They want the Lapalme drivers rehired."

Dougherty said, "Yeah, the drivers don't get any of the gold? Seems like an afterthought, the guys who were fired for being on strike."

Rozovsky said, "They shouldn't have lost their jobs," and Dougherty said, "You sound like my dad. But you're right, they shouldn't've lost their jobs. But that's it?"

"That's it. Oh, and the one-hour broadcast on the CBC."

Dougherty looked at the other pictures scattered over the desk. "What else did they find?"

"The money from the university robbery, or some of it, and you know about the guns?"

"The sawed-off shotguns and the revolvers?"

"And dynamite."

"The usual."

Rozovsky said, "Yeah, the usual."

Dougherty didn't say anything then. What was there to say? And then Rozovsky said, "So you want more pictures of cars?"

"One of the witnesses is pretty sure it's a Lincoln."

"Pretty sure?"

"She's sure. If the other witness is also sure then I can start looking at Lincoln drivers."

"That's your plan?"

Dougherty shrugged and looked around the empty room. "Gotta do something."

"How many Lincolns are there in town?"

"No idea, but first I'm going to try and narrow down the year. Have you got any pictures of a '65, and a '67 or '68?"

"Are they that different?"

"I don't know."

Rozovsky said, "Why don't you go to a dealer? They'll have old brochures or they'll be able to tell you what the differences are."

"Good idea. Where is there a Lincoln dealer?"

Rozovsky said, "I don't know — Latimer's on St. Catherine?"

"That's Ford."

"Mid-Town Motors."

"Oh yeah, on Dorchester," Dougherty said. "And Bishop, between Bishop and Crescent. No, wait, that's a Chrysler dealer."

"What about a used lot?"

Dougherty said, "Yeah, maybe," and then, "Hang on, there's one in Verdun. Cooke-something."

"There's got to be others."

"Cooke-Toledo Mercury-Lincoln, up where the avenues start. First Avenue, Second Avenue, near there, what's the street on the east side?"

"I'm from Côte Saint-Luc — what do I know about Verdun?"

"I think it's on Verdun Avenue."

"If you say so."

"All right, I'm going to try that."

Dougherty started out and Rozovsky said, "Hey, have you seen that girl again, what was her name?"

"Ruth Garber?"

"Yeah, you still seeing her?"

"I don't know."

"What do you mean, you don't know?"

"Well, I don't think I will."

"Maybe you'll get lucky, maybe there'll be another murder."

"I hope not."

"I'm joking."

Dougherty said, "Oh, right," and then, "You working nights all week?"

"Till Friday."

"Okay. I'll probably be back."

Riding the Métro back downtown, Dougherty was thinking about Ruth Garber, how he wanted to see her, go on another date and then back to her place again. So when the train pulled into the McGill station he got off and walked out through the 2020 Mall to de Maisonneuve Boulevard and then a couple blocks up University to the McGill campus. It was just after seven and the place was almost empty, near the end of June, not much going on. Dougherty walked through the Roddick Gates and looked around. He didn't expect to see Ruth; he didn't know what to expect. The big lawn spread out like a couple of football fields, but it was empty, no groups of students protesting anything.

Dougherty stood by the gates and could hear his father's voice, the old man talking about that "piece of paper" and how important it was. Dougherty had no doubt that that was true but it didn't make it right for him.

Over the past couple of years McGill had had a few protests but nothing like on an American campus. Dougherty figured with no draft to protest, no troops going to Vietnam, it just wasn't the same. There was the McGill Français protests, but now with the construction of UQAM starting and Université du Québec campuses going up all over the province — Chicoutimi, Trois Rivières, Rimouski — it looked like making McGill more French wouldn't be as big a deal.

But Dougherty had no idea anymore why some things became a big deal and others didn't. He watched a couple of girls cross the campus towards him and he realized he was still wearing his uniform. He thought for a moment they'd call him a pig and tell him to get off the campus, but by the time they got to him they were giggling and smiling and one of them was poking the other, and when they passed Dougherty one of them said, "Officer," and then they rushed out through the gates to Sherbrooke Street.

Flirting.

Dougherty waited a few minutes, then walked along Sherbrooke himself. He walked all the way to Guy, passing people out on dates and store windows filled with mannequins wearing colourful summer clothes. Maybe it had something to do with the long, cold winter but to Dougherty it felt like summer in Montreal was appreciated, maybe even savoured, a little more than in other cities.

None of these people out having a good time looked at all worried a bomb might blow up a building or guys with sawed-off shotguns might rob the bank next door or kidnap someone going to dinner at the Ritz-Carlton.

Or that someone driving a Lincoln Continental might grab a girl off the street and rape and strangle her.

CHAPTER
FIFTEEN

Dougherty got to Station Ten at seven thirty for his day shift and the place was already buzzing.

Delisle hung up the phone as Dougherty walked in. "Another bomb."

"Where?"

"Ottawa. Defence Department. Looks like two people killed."

"Holy shit."

"You missed ours last night."

"Where was it?" Dougherty said.

"Post office in the east end, on Crémazie."

"Anybody hurt?"

"No," Delisle said, "it went off at one thirty, nobody there."

"What time did the bomb go off in Ottawa?"

"About an hour ago."

"It's going to be a good parade today," Dougherty said.

"Fuck, I almost forgot about that, Saint-Jean-Baptiste."

"We going over?"

Delisle shook his head. "Nobody ask for extra men yet."

The phone rang and Delisle answered, listened for a minute then said thanks, and hung up and said, "Only one killed."

A detective came out of the office and said, "Who was killed?"

"A civilian, a woman working in the communications centre, some kind of relay office."

"Tabarnak."

Delisle said, "Yeah, she was fifty years old — they're checking to see if she has any kids."

"God dammit," Dougherty said.

"The Ottawa police have assigned all twenty-five detectives to it."

"And our task force, probably," the detective said.

Delisle said to Dougherty, "They want you driving around all day — they want to see the cars on the streets, show the flag."

"Driving around aimlessly?"

"Like a regular shift for you."

Some of the other cops in the station laughed, though no one really saw any humour in the situation.

Dougherty spent the morning driving around the Golden Mile, Sherbrooke to University, up to Pine and back down Guy. The mansions that had been built by Englishmen and Scots — the Molsons and Merediths and McIntyres and McConnells — were mostly demolished to make way for office buildings or became part of McGill University after World War I or during the Depression. But the neighbourhood was still old Anglo money all the way and as Dougherty drove around he did get waved at and nodded at by people who looked used to being protected.

Station Ten's territory also reached down the hill into St. Henri so Dougherty drove around there a little, too, but he didn't get waved at quite so much — well, sometimes, usually with just one finger.

By noon Dougherty had just about had enough and he was heading back to the station house when he saw a beat cop in uniform on Sherbrooke motion for him to pull over.

"*C'est un bon job, ça,*" Dougherty said, "walk around all day." The cop, Dougherty recognized now was Turcotte, a guy almost twenty years older than Dougherty but still a beat cop. Turcotte said, "Screw you," opened the passenger door and got into the car. "Let's get some lunch."

"Pete's?"

"*Criss*, no, let's get away from here."

Dougherty said, "Magnan's?" and Turcotte said, "No, not down the hill," so Dougherty headed up Atwater to Côte-des-Neiges Road, which ringed the base of Mount Royal, and drove all the way to Jean Talon. "*Okay, bon, là, la brasserie,*" Turcotte said, and Dougherty pulled up behind the other cop car already parked in front.

By twelve thirty there were seven cops at a table covered with empty plates and about the fourth round of draughts. They were all complaining about bullshit assignments, waving the flag, and talking about what they'd rather be doing.

Dougherty found a *Gazette* with the headline "Ulster on brink of civil war" and skimmed the article that said British troops were evacuating women and children from West Belfast which was "besieged by Protestant and Roman Catholic mobs hurling stones and gasoline bombs." He thought, well, sounds like everybody's getting their hits in. Dougherty knew his father's family came from some place in Ireland called Larne, but that was about all he knew. He was a Montrealer and he never felt particularly Irish. Even reading the article he felt mostly for the cops, probably getting it from both sides, caught in the middle trying to keep the casualties to a minimum.

Deeper in, past the sports section and the section with the headline "Abortions compete for time in operating rooms" was an article headlined "Mafia: no. 1 threat to city government."

Dougherty leaned further back from the table, the cops now complaining about not getting enough overtime, and read the article. It was written by a guy named Brian Stewart in a pretty sarcastic tone that usually Dougherty would have appreciated, but he was having a tough time with now.

"This week city officials graciously let us in on a secret most of us have known for some time — the Mafia is alive, well and apparently thriving in Montreal. After years of silence, the legal department suddenly issued a 'shock' report which suggests up to 400 of our 1,200 bars and restaurants have been taken over by the Mafia."

Looking around the brasserie, Dougherty figured this one was probably one of the other 800, perhaps only because of the number of cops who stopped in every day.

The article went on to say, "Amazing! All this time, it seems, the administration has watched helplessly while the province allowed the Cosa Nostra to infiltrate the city and suck off millions of our dollars to boost North America's largest business: organized crime."

Dougherty liked the exclamation point, though, that was a nice touch, and then the next part of the article tried to get serious talking about the implications and how "all the demonstrations and bomb-throwers are puny in comparison."

Well, that was tough timing, the article written before the latest bomb in Ottawa killed that woman, but Dougherty agreed, there was a lot more going on in the city than demonstrations and bombs.

Going for the big picture the article said, "There are unmistakable signs that some sectors of government are now in the hands of the Mafia. They have ceased to work for us. They are working for two New York 'families' now warring over the fruits of Montreal crime."

Dougherty finished off his beer and thought, Don't leave out the locals. The Higgins brothers don't work for anybody but the Higgins brothers as the New York families would find out soon enough.

One of the older beat cops stood up and said, "*Bon,*

d'la bière asteure," and there was a lot of grumbling and complaining but everybody stood up and each man dropped a few bucks on the table.

As they were walking out, the waitress was standing by the door and she smiled at Dougherty, the youngest guy in the group, and said, *"Reviens, eh."* Dougherty said, "Do you ever work evenings?" to see how she'd react to English. She kept on smiling and said, "Some time," with a heavy accent for even two words.

Dougherty wasn't sure if she was old enough to work in a bar, but he said, "Okay, some time."

Driving back down the hill, Dougherty asked Turcotte about the Mafia article and the older cop said, "They know the rule." Dougherty was about to ask which rule, then realized it was Turcotte's French accent and he meant rules. Yeah, they did know the rules. When that bomb went off in the car coming off the Champlain Bridge, the bomb squad knew right away it was mobsters, because they were following it and they used a remote control to set it off. Mobsters didn't just plant a bomb and run away, let it kill some secretary who just happened to be there.

When they got to Sherbrooke, Turcotte said, "Let me off here. I know a girl works out of an apartment on St. Mark — I'm going to take a nap," and he looked sideways at Dougherty. "You have a nest on your beat?"

"No."

Turcotte opened the car door. "You should get one."

"With a girl?"

Turcotte leaned back through the open passenger window. "You arrest her for prostitution and then you let her go, make a deal."

Dougherty said thanks, and Turcotte banged the roof the car as it drove away.

He couldn't stand the idea of driving around for the whole afternoon so rich Anglos could wave at him and feel a little safer. He felt like he had to do something worthwhile.

———

Cooke-Toledo Mercury-Lincoln was on the corner of Bannantyne and Willibrord, a block down from the aqueduct, across the street from a park in the middle of a neighbourhood of two-storey brick houses, a dozen blocks from where Dougherty went to school.

The lot was small, so Dougherty parked the squad car on the street. There was one Lincoln that he could see and as he walked towards it a young guy with a moustache and hair touching his collar intercepted him. "Hey there, Constable, you looking for a car?"

"You could be a detective," Dougherty said, but the guy didn't get it, so he said, "I want to talk to you about the Lincoln," and the salesman said, "No man, young guy like you, you want to look at the Comet."

"When I'm not working, I drive a Mustang."

"Then you should look at the Cougar."

"I'm not looking to buy a car," Dougherty said. "It's for an investigation."

"An investigation into Lincolns?"

Dougherty slid the picture out of the envelope and said, "This doesn't look much like it."

The salesman looked at the picture and said, "No, the Lincoln got a complete redesign for 1970, that's a '66."

"How different is it from the '65 or the '67?"

"A two-door hardtop? Well, it couldn't be older than '66 — that's the first two-door in years. Sixty-six was also the first year for the tilt steering wheel. It have one of those?"

Dougherty said, "I don't know," and the salesman said, "Okay, well, the '67 is almost exactly the same. It doesn't have the logos on the front fenders, but otherwise it looks the same. The thing about Lincoln drivers is that they don't change cars as often as other people, so the design doesn't need to change so much. The '68 has seatbelts."

"Don't know about that."

The salesman walked around the car. "The '68 has different tail lights, too, wraparound. Sixty-nine was the last year for suicide doors, but you're looking for the two-door, right?"

"Yeah."

"Well, if you can find out about the tail lights you can narrow it down to either '66 and '67 or '68 and '69. Gets you two years instead of four."

Dougherty said, "Do you have the old brochures? Any pictures of those years?"

"I don't know."

"Could you check?"

The salesman didn't want to but Dougherty kept staring at him, and he finally said, "Okay, come on," and Dougherty followed him into the small office. There were two desks in the room, and the salesman opened drawers and went through piles of papers and found a couple of brochures.

"Hey, you got lucky, here's the '68. See the tail lights?"

"Yeah, they wrap right around, they're different."

"That's pretty much what the '69 looks like, too. Then the '70 is like that," and he pointed to a calendar on the wall that showed a blue Lincoln all by itself on a highway that looked to be in the mountains somewhere. "And you've got that picture of the '66."

Dougherty said, "Do you sell a lot of these?"

"A few."

"Did you ever sell a white one with a black roof?"

"Going back to '66?"

"Yeah."

"I'm sure we have, but I'd have to go through every sale for years."

Dougherty said, "How many Lincoln dealers are there in Montreal?"

"Just Montreal or the West Island, too? And Laval and the South Shore?"

"Well," Dougherty said, "how many cars like this are on the road now?"

The salesman shrugged. "I don't know, couple thousand."

"Yeah?"

"At least."

Dougherty said, "Okay, thanks," and walked out of the office.

The salesman followed, saying, "Always like to help the police. I'd really like to help you into a Cougar. Why don't you bring your Mustang by — I can get you a good trade-in and get you into a real good car."

"Maybe next year."

"Next year? Why wait, we can finance it right here."

"I'll think about it, thanks."

Then instead of driving back downtown he headed further west to LaSalle and found Giovani Masaracchia playing baseball with some other kids in the schoolyard. As soon as he parked the squad car the kids stopped playing and stared. When Dougherty got out Giovani recognized him and jogged over. "You're back."

Dougherty said, "I'm back," and handed him the evidence photo of the Lincoln as well as the 1968 brochure. "Is either one of these the car you saw?"

The other kids had come up behind Giovani and were looking over his shoulder at the picture and the brochure. One of them said, "Man, what an ugly car," and one of the other kids said, "It's for old men."

Giovani held up the evidence picture and said, "This one."

"You're sure?"

"The tail lights are different, see?"

"And you're sure they look like this one? It can be hard to tell, in the picture in the brochure the car is brand new."

"This one, for sure. But the car was white. I mostly saw it driving away so I saw the tail lights. It was this one."

Dougherty took the picture of the 1966 Lincoln that had been in a minor accident coming out of the Ville-Marie Tunnel and said, "Thanks, Giovani, that's good work."

The kid's friends started making fun of him, one kid said something in Italian and Giovani laughed, so Dougherty put on a serious look and said, "Hey, I know where you live," then smiled when the kids all looked scared. Dougherty thanked Giovani again and watched as they returned to the schoolyard and their game.

———

For the first time in three years there was no violence at the Saint-Jean-Baptiste Day parade. There were just six floats, nothing like the elaborate parades of previous years. The route went through the east end only, from Laurier Park down St. Denis and into Old Montreal, no more going along Sherbrooke Street or St. Catherine, but there was a huge party all the way, thousands lining the streets and having a good time.

Dougherty finished his shift just after dinner and went down to Old Montreal in time to see the parade arrive, followed by a crowd of people calling themselves Chevaliers de l'Indépendence chanting the usual separatist slogans and one that went, *"Québec dans les rues,"* but it didn't really catch on. There were half a dozen motorcycle cops between the parade and the crowd following and at first Dougherty didn't think that would be nearly enough. But the end of the parade was a bunch of kids with Quebec flags and as people filled up Place Jacques-Cartier just down the street from City Hall and police HQ, it was just a party. There were no riot cops anywhere and the cops who were on duty looked pretty relaxed.

There was rock music and fiddle music and Dougherty was pretty sure he heard country music in some of the bars, and he saw women going in and out of the taverns that were supposed to be for men-only but no one complained. It was like Mardi Gras.

So Dougherty walked back to Bonsecours and

looked around police HQ, but he didn't see anyone — Rozovsky wasn't there and the homicide office was empty. But across the street the backroom of the restaurant was full of cops, detectives mostly, and Dougherty found Carpentier in a party mood, knocking back shots and beers and saying, *"Maudits Anglais,"* with a big smile when he saw Dougherty squeezing his way through the crowd.

"It's a party."

"It is," Carpentier said, "and just a party," and he held up his shot glass for a toast.

Dougherty held up his empty hand and Carpentier drank the shot and said, *"Bon, bière,"* and waved until the waitress saw him. He held up two fingers and then shook his head and held up four fingers.

"So, you don't work the parade?"

Dougherty said, "No, there was no overtime, no riot squad, nothing. Looks like it worked."

"Yes, looks like it."

Just before midnight, it started to rain and Old Montreal went from overflowing with people to pretty much emptied out in a few minutes. Even from the backroom of the restaurant across the street from police HQ the cops could sense that the party had broken up peacefully, and not too long after that the restaurant pretty much emptied out, too.

When it was quiet Dougherty said to Carpentier, "I think I have the car."

"What car?"

Dougherty pulled the evidence picture out of his pocket and unfolded it. "The Lincoln the kids saw, the one on the Point and one in LaSalle."

"That's good, whose is it?"

Dougherty shook his head. "I don't know who it belongs to, I just know that it's either a 1966 or 1967 Lincoln Continental."

"That's it?"

"It's white with a black roof. The girl in the Point, Gail Murphy, she saw it again on the weekend."

"Saw it where?"

"On Wellington Street in the Point."

Carpentier shrugged, and Dougherty said, "It could have been coming from the Arawana Tavern."

"Oh yeah," Carpentier said, "by the Canada Packers and the CN yard." He frowned. "So, maybe it's just a guy has a beer after work."

"That's the tavern where the Higgins Brothers hang out, where I saw my contact for the hash."

"So?"

"So, there's a drug connection here. Brenda Webber was going to buy hash and one of the women killed downtown was known to use drugs."

"Shirley Audette," Carpentier said. "But I think it was pills, that's not the same."

"But it's something. It's possible this guy driving the Lincoln gets his drugs from one of the Higgins brothers. They may know him."

Carpentier said, "But this guy with the Lincoln, he may not be Bill. He may not have anything to do with the murders."

Dougherty agreed. "Maybe not, but we should talk to him," and Carpentier nodded and said, "Yeah, sure, but Desjardins and the homicide guys, they think it's about the sex, not the drugs. None of the other women were on drugs."

"We should still talk to him."

"Get one of these Higgins brothers to tell us who he is?"

"A few of us go down to the Arawana, we ask nice," Dougherty said.

Carpentier nodded and looked at the nightstick on Dougherty's gun belt. "Use a little convincing if you have to?"

"That's right."

"It's not enough."

"What?"

"Look," Carpentier said, "the mob guys, they're just starting to get past the Italians and to these Point Boys — you heard Ste. Marie. Now he's on the anti-terrorist squad and so are the homicide guys. Nobody has time to chase this wild goose."

"But this could be Bill."

"Yeah," Carpentier said, "but probably not. You go busting in there now with nothing, you screw up some narcotics investigation."

"Is there one going on now?"

Carpentier shrugged. "I don't know."

"Is there even a homicide investigation going on?"

"Watch it, kid."

"I'm sorry, I'm just . . ."

"We all are," Carpentier said, looking right at Dougherty. "But we do what we have to do."

"Okay," Dougherty said, "so what are we doing?"

Carpentier drank some beer. "We followed everything, we interviewed more than a hundred people, we talk to every informant, we ran over a thousand tips that got phoned in."

"So now we have this car."

"Sure, yeah, but so far the only connection is to Brenda Webber."

Dougherty nodded.

"So," Carpentier said, "see if you can find a connection to the others."

"How?"

Carpentier shrugged. "Ask around, same as you did in the Point and Ville LaSalle." He motioned to the picture Dougherty was still holding.

"So," Dougherty said, "it's not worth the homicide detective's time but my time is okay?"

"Yes, exactly."

Dougherty leaned back in his chair and picked up his beer. Carpentier looked a little apologetic and said, "If things were normal, if we weren't all on this task force, if we had more guys."

"But we don't."

"So we have to do what we can."

"What's my sergeant going to say if I spend all my time working on this?"

"Delisle?" Carpentier laughed a little. "You'll be the smallest problem he has."

"I'm serious," Dougherty said. "Today during my shift I drove out to LaSalle. If I get caught doing that what do I say? Do I tell them you sent me?"

"I'm not your boss."

"Exactly."

"What do you want me to say, Dog-eh-dee, don't do it? You'll do it anyway. Look, if you do get disciplined that's good."

"It's good to get disciplined?"

"Yeah, sure it is. How's the brass going to know your name otherwise?"

"That's not how I want them to know me."

"It doesn't matter how, trust me."

Dougherty looked at the detective closely and saw there was a story there, but he knew this wasn't the time.

"Look, ask around, see if anyone saw the car near any of the apartments of the other murder victims, that's all. Just keep the picture with you and ask around when you get a chance."

Dougherty said, "Okay, when I get a chance."

The next day Dougherty started his day shift with the picture of the 1966 Lincoln Continental in his pocket, but before he got a chance to show it to anyone, there was an "all cars" call on the radio, and he raced to St. Denis, where a bank was robbed and shots had been fired.

By the time Dougherty got to the Banque Canadienne Nationale branch on the corner of St. Denis and Roy there were already half a dozen squad cars and at least a dozen uniformed cops on the scene.

And two cops had been shot.

The ambulance arrived behind Dougherty, and he started telling people to move out of the way and led the two guys with the stretcher through.

There was a body on the sidewalk with a huge pool of blood flowing into the street and a few feet away a uniformed cop sat leaning against the brick wall of the bank with blood streaming from his leg.

Dougherty recognized him. "Hey Jacques, you okay?"

Looking up the cop said, "Fuck, Dog-eh-dee, it fucken hurts."

"Yeah, I bet it does. What happened?"

The ambulance guys were on him then, and Dougherty turned and saw the other uniformed cop. "Holy shit, Maurice, you, too?" Maurice Brisbois, Jacques LeBlanc and Dougherty had all gone through police training together. They were all twenty-four years old and had all worked out of Station Four as rookies.

Now Brisbois was holding his handkerchief on his arm just below the short sleeve of his uniform shirt, but blood was dripping down his forearm. He shook his head and said, "We got a call, a teller managed to push the alarm. These two fucks came in with guns. They punched the manager — she's over there."

Dougherty said, "You went in?"

"We got here, we parked around the corner so they wouldn't see us and we came up to the door, but we couldn't see inside. Jacques went to the other side and they came out at that moment."

"He didn't see them?"

"You know how the witness, they all say it happen so fast?" Brisbois said, "Well, it fucking does happen fast."

Dougherty looked at the dead man on the sidewalk and said, "Nice shot," and Brisbois said, "They ran out and started shooting before we even saw them, bastards."

"You got them both?"

Brisbois motioned further down the sidewalk, in front of a deli, where the other bank robber was still face down with his hands cuffed behind his back. "I didn't even see Jacques was hit until I had the cuffs on this one."

The ambulance guys had LeBlanc loaded on the stretcher and started to lift it. *"Quel hôpital?"* Dougherty said, and one of the ambulance guys said, "St. Luc."

Dougherty looked at Brisbois and said, "You better go, too."

"I'm okay."

"You better go."

Brisbois said okay and got into the back of the ambulance with LeBlanc and one of the paramedics.

Dougherty worked the scene for a few hours. They found a car in the lane behind the bank with a blanket, a change of clothes for both men and a plastic bag of surgical gloves. They later found out that both robbers had been in prison until a few months before, the dead one for armed robbery, and their parole was scheduled to last well into the 1980s.

One of the older cops on the scene said, "It's good to have some normal fucking crime in this city."

"Bank robbery capital of North America," Dougherty said, and the older cop said, "You got that right," and laughed.

Dougherty drove the squad car Brisbois and LeBlanc had been driving back to Station Four and waited around for a while before getting a ride back to the scene. It was late afternoon by then, almost time for Dougherty to punch out, and except for the bank still being closed, the street now looked like nothing had happened.

A few of the cops were planning to go to the hospital and take Brisbois and LeBlanc out for a beer. They invited Dougherty along, so he drove his squad car back to Station Ten and took the Métro back to St. Denis Street.

It was two in the morning when Dougherty stumbled back to his apartment, and he was still a little drunk and a lot hungover when he checked in for his shift at eight.

In the afternoon he managed to show the picture of the Lincoln to a few people who lived in the same apartment building as Jean Way but no one recognized the car, so after work Dougherty checked on LeBlanc in the St. Luc hospital — they'd taken the bullet out of his thigh and told him he'd never play for the Canadiens, not even goalie, but he'd be back at work in a week. Then Dougherty showed the picture around Marielle Archambeault's apartment and no one recognized it there, either.

But he did run into Ruth Garber.

CHAPTER
SIXTEEN

She said, "Are you working here now?"

"No," Dougherty said, "I'm off-duty."

Ruth looked him up and down and Dougherty said, "I haven't changed yet, I was visiting someone in the hospital — a cop was shot during a bank hold-up, did you hear?"

They were standing on the sidewalk on Ontario Street, Ruth coming out of a *dépanneur* with a small bag of groceries and she said, "I heard something about it. One of the robbers was killed?"

Dougherty said, "Yeah, but not before he got off quite a few shots. Both cops were hit, actually, but LeBlanc took one right in the thigh, lost a lot of blood."

"You know him?"

"Both of them, yeah. We went through training together and we all worked out of Station Four before I got transferred. He's going to be okay."

"That's good."

Dougherty said yeah, and then didn't know what to say. Ruth was looking at him the way she always did, open, expectant, waiting for something, but he had no idea what. He couldn't believe this was a woman he'd been intimate with and then just walked away from, and now they'd run into each other and were chatting as if they were acquaintances from work or something.

But he felt something, for sure.

He motioned to the groceries. "Looks like you haven't eaten yet, you want to have dinner?"

"Now?"

"Sure." He looked around and saw a little Italian restaurant across the street and said, "That looks okay."

"I've never eaten there."

"So let's try it."

"I have to put some of these things in the fridge." And that was it, they walked around the corner and Dougherty waited on the street while Ruth went up the wrought-iron stairs to the second floor and disappeared inside. A moment later she was back and they walked over to the restaurant.

Dougherty ordered the rigatoni with meat sauce and Ruth had lasagna, and they were both a little surprised how good it was.

Over coffee Dougherty showed Ruth the picture of the Lincoln and asked her if she'd seen it around.

"This is about the Bill murders?"

Dougherty said, "Yes, I'm showing it to people around all the victims' apartments."

Ruth said, "Why didn't you tell me about this?"

"Tell you?"

"This is the car the murderer is driving?"

Dougherty said, "No, well, we don't know. I think it might be."

"Dr. Pendleton is supposed to be kept up to date with this investigation."

"This isn't officially the investigation."

"What do you mean?"

"You know that Detective Carpentier is on the anti-terrorism squad now?"

"No, I didn't know that. Who's taken over the investigation?"

Dougherty drank some coffee. "The rest of the homicide squad, I guess, but Carpentier still has me running around. I found a kid near where Brenda was last seen and another kid near where the body was found who both think they saw this kind of car around the right time."

"This is important."

"Maybe, but probably not. Carpentier didn't think it was enough to get a homicide detective chasing it all over town."

"But you're doing it."

"Yeah." Dougherty looked at the picture for a moment and then he looked at Ruth and said, "Have you seen a car like this around here?"

"No, like I said, I didn't live here when Marielle Archambeault was killed."

At the sound of the name Dougherty glanced around

the restaurant but there was only one other couple and they were deep in conversation. Their waiter was now sitting in a booth by the cash, reading the paper, and Dougherty didn't see anyone else in the place.

"I was thinking about what you said about that guy who killed the woman in New York." He couldn't remember the name and he was looking at Ruth for help, but she was just looking back at him. "The one where everyone just watched."

"Kitty Genovese."

"Right. I was thinking about what you said about the guy who killed her just driving around all night, driving for hours."

"That's what he said, that he just drove for hours."

"Well, I thought maybe this guy could have done that, too. Brenda Webber's body was found near an exit off the 2-20, the expressway through town. Some of it used to be the old highway 2, that's what the name means, it's highway 2 and the number 20 expressway. The Décarie is the number 15, the Bonaventure Expressway is the number 10, like that."

Ruth said, "Oh, I see. I don't drive."

"And Sylvie Berubé's body was found in the east end, near the exit for the Ville-Marie Tunnel."

"So?"

"Well, it's the same road, really — it's the 2-20."

"And you think Bill may have been driving around."

Dougherty said, "Maybe," but now that he was hearing it out loud it didn't seem important or unusual enough to mention.

But Ruth said, "This could really be something."

"Really?"

"I think Leslie Irvin also drove around a lot." She looked at Dougherty and said, "He killed six people in Indiana. And I think Starkweather drove a lot, too."

Dougherty recognized the name Starkweather, pretty sure he was the guy with the teenage girlfriend, wanted to be James Dean, killed a few people, also in Indiana or someplace like that.

Then Ruth said, "We've been looking at the strangulation and the breast mutilations, but maybe the driving is something, too."

Dougherty was amazed at the way she could talk about the murders so calmly, but then he figured that's what people meant by "scientifically" — that kind of detached analysis. It was certainly more detached than what he'd seen from the homicide detectives. Some of those guys could really tear up, though they always tried to hide it, and then some of them got pretty colourful when they were talking about what they wanted to do to the murderers.

Ruth was standing up then and saying, "This is interesting — I should make some notes."

Dougherty got out his wallet and motioned to the waiter, who was still reading the paper. He got up and came over and made a face as he was glancing at Ruth on her way out the door. "The lady is in a hurry."

"She's a scientist," Dougherty said and handed over ten bucks. The waiter put it in his pocket and said, "Like a Bunsen burner," and Dougherty shook his head and walked out.

Back at Ruth's she pulled out a cardboard box full of papers. "This is just what I have at home, you should see what's at the office."

"We believe the murderer is a young man, probably under thirty, good-looking, charming."

"Driving a Lincoln?"

"Is that odd?"

"One of the kids who saw it called it an old man's car."

Ruth was sitting at her small kitchen table, writing all this down, and Dougherty said, "It's not what I'd expect a young, good-looking, charming guy to be driving."

"What *would* he be driving?"

"A sports car. A Camaro, Cougar, maybe a Corvette if he has the money." Dougherty thought of his own car, the Mustang, but didn't add it to the list. Then he said, "What makes you think the guy is young and good-looking?"

"And charming." Ruth stopped writing and looked at Dougherty, who was sitting on the edge of the couch in the living room a few feet from the kitchen table. "Well, for a few reasons. The most obvious is what the other women at the jewellery store had to say about him when he came to pick up Marielle Archambeault, that's the way they described him. And then the way he was able to get into the other women's apartments without breaking in."

"The files said something about sex, rough sex, or something."

Ruth said, "Yes, sexually deviant behaviour. We feel this fits with the triad."

"Oh yeah, the bed-wetting," Dougherty said.

"And the fire-starting and the cruelty to animals. The murderers with this kind of background often engage in sexually deviant murders."

Dougherty said, "Often?"

"Well, yes. There isn't a very big sample group, thank god, but the evidence is growing. This is another reason Dr. Pendleton hopes to be able to interview Charles Manson."

Dougherty said, "I saw that little twerp's picture in the paper again — you're not saying that guy's charming?"

"Not in a way you or I would call charming, but there's certainly some evidence that the women in his so-called family find him attractive in some way."

"I thought that was the brainwashing?"

"In order for the coercive persuasion to be effective there must be some emotional connection," Ruth said, and then she looked at Dougherty and said, "Oh, you're joking."

"Not completely, but a little, yeah." And looking at Ruth, Dougherty could tell this was nowhere near the first time she'd taken a joke seriously. Then he said, "And some of the women were into this kind of crazy sex?"

"Yes, it was consensual. "

"You're sure about that?"

"The boyfriend of one of the victims said she was involved in rough sex with another man."

"So he says."

"And there were no struggles — they must have gone along with it."

"You sure?"

Ruth said, "You saw the bodies, there were no marks."

"The bite marks on the breasts."

"They were post-mortem. And they didn't all have them."

Dougherty said, "I think there was something else in the coroner's report."

"I have a copy here."

"You do?" Dougherty watched Ruth go through the files in the cardboard box.

"Here it is," Ruth said, "the *rapport médico-légal* from the *Institut de médecine legale et de police scientifique.*" She flipped through some pages, read a little and frowned and then she said, "You're right. It says here there were fibres found under Jean Way's fingernails."

"What about the others?"

Ruth looked through the files and said, "I don't have them all, but here's Brenda Webber's."

"What does it say?"

"Not much, but there was more bruising, could have been a struggle."

"What about drugs?"

"What do you mean?"

"Well, Brenda was probably buying drugs the night she went missing, so maybe she was buying them from Bill, maybe all the women were buying drugs."

"Maybe Shirley Audette — she was the one who'd been in the psychiatric hospital."

"The Douglas."

Then Ruth said, "There was also a longer gap between Brenda Webber and the other victims, quite a few months. That might be something."

"Like what?"

"I don't know. We're looking at everything."

"There were a few months between Sylvie Berubé and the next one, too," Dougherty said.

Ruth was writing it all down and nodding. "Could you check to see if there were many missing persons reports about other young women in these gaps?"

Dougherty said, "That won't work."

"Why not?"

"We get people in the station all the time wanting to file missing persons reports on their kids but if they're over eighteen, or even sixteen sometimes, we're told to tell them to wait a few days."

"A few days?"

"They always come back. They've been to Woodstock or whatever festival is going on and they met up with some other kids. We got a memo that said this year there are at least ten thousand kids hitch-hiking in this country on any day. And that doesn't even count Americans coming here."

"But if they're young, like Brenda Webber?"

"Sure, I can check on that," Dougherty said.

Ruth said, "This is very interesting; we have some work to do now," and Dougherty felt like he was being dismissed, so he stood up.

Ruth walked him to the door. "If I need to talk to you, what would be a good time?"

"Anytime, I guess. Just call Station Ten." Then he had an idea. "Or you can call me at home."

Ruth said, "That's a good idea, and look, you call me if there's anything else. Anything."

Ruth wrote Dougherty's phone number on one of the pieces of paper on her kitchen table and then tore off a small piece and wrote her own number on it and handed it to Dougherty.

He left thinking this wasn't really the way he wanted to see her again but feeling like he did really want to see her again.

When he got home the phone was ringing. He picked it up thinking it might be Ruth already but it was his mother.

"Cheryl is gone. She run away."

CHAPTER
SEVENTEEN

Dougherty managed to get his mother calmed down by asking her if Cheryl left a note or took her things, but his mother said she hadn't.

"But she never come home last night and she never come home today."

Dougherty said okay, trying to remember what day it was and coming up with Friday. "She's eighteen, Mom. She's not a runaway. She can leave if she wants," and that started his mother off again, crying and saying he sounded just like his father. Dougherty said, "Wow, bet you never thought you'd say that."

"He say to just wait, she be back."

"He's right. She's probably at some friend's house."

"But can't you do something."

"Me? What can I do?"

"The police, can't you find her?"

Dougherty said, "Ma, look, she's going to come back today or tomorrow. Or she'll be gone for the weekend, maybe, but there's nothing we can do."

"But those girls. They were all kill." Her French accent coming on a lot stronger than usual now.

"That was different, Ma. They were killed in their apartments — they all had apartments."

"Not Brenda."

Dougherty said, "No, not Brenda. But she was younger, not as old as Cheryl," and he was back in his conversation with Ruth, seeing all the differences.

"So you can look for her."

"There's nothing we can do."

"I don't believe that."

His mother was calm now, moving past her fear and anger and heading straight to helplessness, which Dougherty always found funny coming from her. She was about the last person he'd ever see as helpless, but she could play the card when she thought it would help.

So he said, "Okay, I'll go into the station and see what I can do. Have you called Franny's mother?"

"No, I don't want them to know."

"To know what?"

"That I don't know where is Cheryl."

He wanted to laugh. "Okay, well you wait, I bet you Franny's mother calls you."

"I'm worried."

"I know, I understand. Look, I'm off on Sunday. I'll come out for dinner and if she's not back by then I'll ask around."

"Ask who?"

"Her friends."

There was a pause and then a meek, "Okay," and then Dougherty said, "It'll be fine, Ma, you'll see. She'll be back as soon as she gets hungry."

"She's not so helpless you know." Dougherty knew that if his mother was defending Cheryl it meant she'd stopped worrying, or at least was less worried, and he could get off the phone.

"Okay, I'll see you Sunday."

"Okay."

———

Late Saturday night Cheryl called Dougherty crying and hysterical.

He'd spent the day and most of the early evening hanging around in front of Jean Way's apartment building, showing people the Lincoln pictures and getting a few maybes but mostly just shrugs. One guy said that in January there was a lot of snow and not much parking on the street and that gave Dougherty the idea to talk to the attendants working on the nearby parking lots. They looked at him like he was crazy, and one of them said, "It would be easier to tell you what kind of cars I haven't seen."

So Dougherty had a late dinner at Mr. Steer on St. Catherine Street and walked home, feeling strangely anonymous in the crowd without his uniform.

229

Now Cheryl was calming down and saying that she was at the police station. "Which one?"

"I don't know, it's in Toronto."

"What are you doing in Toronto?"

"We came to see the Festival Express. They got us buses, everybody who had a ticket. And we came here but there was a riot."

Dougherty tried to imagine what they'd call a riot in Toronto — a few hippies trying to cut in line? "Are you hurt?"

"What? No."

"Okay, so what do you want?"

Cheryl said, "Can you talk to them?"

"Pig to pig, like we have a secret code?"

She said, "Fu—," but caught herself and Dougherty felt a little bad. Then she said, "Come on, Eddie, please," so he said, "Okay. Put him on."

The Toronto cop said, "So, your sister's name is Cheryl Dougherty?"

"She's got long hair, she's wearing jeans and a jean jacket with patches all over them. She looks like all the rest. What did she do?"

"Maybe she incited a riot or maybe she was in the wrong place at the wrong time."

"If there's a wrong place," Dougherty said, "Cheryl will find it. Have you processed her?"

"No, we're just getting started."

"They crashed the gate?"

"The place is a mess — we're bringing some in so they don't get hurt."

230   Dougherty said, "Well, if it helps, Cheryl's harmless. She won't shut up sometimes but she's not real trouble."

"That's what I thought," the Toronto cop said. "She looks more scared than anything. And her friend, too. Look, if you can vouch for them, I'll put them on a bus to Montreal."

"All right, man, thanks."

"Hey, I'd rather she be your problem. We've got plenty more."

Then Dougherty spoke to Cheryl, told her to be nice to the cop, he didn't have to let her go, and for her and Franny to get on the midnight bus. They'd be in Montreal at six in the morning. Cheryl surprised him by speaking very softly and asking very nicely if he could meet them at the bus station in Montreal because the Métro wouldn't be running that early, and he said, "Yeah, all right."

And after he hung up he realized Cheryl sounded just like their mother, putting on the helpless act when it helped her. He thought about telling her that when he picked her up, but when he saw her getting off the bus in the brand new terminal at Berri-de-Montigny she looked too pathetic.

Still, he couldn't help smiling and saying, "So, did you have a good time?"

Cheryl didn't say anything, she just walked past him towards the doors, but Franny smiled and said, "Thank you." Dougherty looked them in the eye to see if they were still stoned or if they'd slept it off on the bus ride, but he couldn't tell.

Both girls sat in the cramped back seat of Dougherty's Mustang and no one said anything until they pulled up in front of the Doughertys' and Franny said thanks again.

The girls got out of the car and both of them went in via the side door and, Dougherty figured, right into the basement.

He was about to drive off when his little brother,

Tommy, rode up on his bike. "There's no *Gazette* on Sunday," Dougherty said, and Tommy said, "*Sunday Express.*"

"You going back to bed?"

"No, I'm up now."

Dougherty looked at the house and said, "Mom and Dad up yet?"

"Not yet."

"You want to get some breakfast, go to Pop's?"

Tommy said, "Yeah!" and Dougherty watched him put his bike in the backyard and jump excitedly into the passenger seat of the Mustang.

The sign on the front of the restaurant said *Pearl's Coffee Shoppe*, and Dougherty had no idea why everyone called it Pop's. It was in an old red brick building on Churchill, next to a barber shop and a dry cleaners in a row of storefronts. Inside it could have been the '50s — booths, a jukebox and a counter lined with stools.

Dougherty ordered coffee and bacon and eggs over easy, and Tommy said, "Me, too."

"Maybe you want milk instead of coffee?"

"Okay."

There were a few other people in the restaurant, a couple of guys at a booth who looked like they might have also been delivering the *Sunday Express* and a guy by himself who looked like he might have been up all night.

When the food came, Dougherty asked Tommy how things were at home and Tommy shrugged. Dougherty said, "Mom and Cheryl fighting a lot?"

"Just all the time."

"Well, it'll be okay."

Tommy poured ketchup on his plate and said, "Cheryl is such a bitch."

"What did you say?"

But Tommy could see that Dougherty was smiling a little and he smiled, too. Then he looked serious again and said, "She's just mad all the time."

"Yeah, lots of people are."

"Yeah."

Dougherty looked around the restaurant and out the window to Churchill Boulevard that cut through Greenfield Park. A block farther down was City Hall, the police station and the fire station and behind them Empire Park, where Tommy played football, and an indoor arena, where he'd play hockey in the winter. Dougherty was thinking now it was a nice little town. "Do Mom and Dad fight much?"

Tommy took a bite of some toast. "Not much."

Dougherty watched his little brother eat and thought, Yeah, tough times for everybody.

They'd been in the house six years and either his father or his mother had been on strike at least once almost every year. Both worked for the phone company, The Bell, but in different unions, his father a lineman, driving one of those green vans with ladders on the roof, and his mother an operator. Dougherty had lived there four years and been on his own for two, but sometimes he felt like he'd never really lived on the South Shore, like he'd gone straight from the Point to his apartment downtown. Now he was starting to see how Greenfield Park was Tommy's home. But what about Cheryl?

Dougherty was thinking his sister could be somewhere in between Brenda Webber and Shirley Audette, a kid maybe buying hash off some guy on the street and a woman living downtown inviting "good-looking, charming" guys into her apartment. But really, what did he know about Cheryl?

He looked at Tommy. "Hey, you want to go to an Expos game?"

"Yeah, when?"

"I'm working nights this week, and probably the next week, too, but I'll get some tickets and we'll go."

"Great."

Dougherty said, "Yeah, great," and was looking forward to it.

Getting anything positive done these days was starting to feel like a big deal.

———

After he dropped Tommy off, Dougherty headed back over the bridge into Montreal without stopping to see his parents. He knew the house would be tense, dishes dropped hard on the table, doors slamming and the only talking would be muttering. Not the way to spend his day off.

When he was coming off the bridge and "One Tin Soldier" finished ("Go ahead and hate your neighbour, go ahead and cheat your friend, do it in the name of heaven, you can justify it in the end"), the news guy came on CKGM instead of the DJ to say there had been a plane crash in Toronto. A flight from Montreal to Los Angeles was making a stop and crashed near Malton airport. Early reports were that all 109 people onboard were killed.

Then the news guy said that there wasn't much information yet but it was bright and sunny with excellent visibility in Toronto and they were checking into the possibility the plane had been hijacked or that a bomb was onboard.

Dougherty decided this would have been a good day to sleep through but there was no way he'd be able to do that now, so he parked near his apartment and walked to Station Ten.

The weekend desk sergeant, McKinney, putting in the last few months until retirement, was reading the sports section at the back of the *Sunday Express* tabloid when Dougherty walked in.

"You're not working today."

"No, but I've got things to do," Dougherty said. "What did you hear about the plane crash?"

"I heard everybody onboard died."

"They said on the radio it might have been hijacked or maybe there was a bomb?"

McKinney never looked up from the Expos box score, he just shook his head. "You really think these idiots could bring down a plane?"

"A bomb's a bomb — they figured out how to set those."

"Well, this is just plain old mechanical failure."

"They know that already?"

"Oh, there'll be a long investigation, don't worry," McKinney said, "but that's the way it looks."

Dougherty said, "Okay, thanks."

McKinney shrugged and said, "Don't mention it," clearly having no idea why Dougherty would come into the station on his day off.

Jean Way's apartment had been only two blocks from Station Ten, but instead of walking up to Lincoln Street, Dougherty walked east on de Maisonneuve to Guy.

It had been a year and a half since the riot at Sir George Williams University, and Dougherty looked at the Hall Building on de Maisonneuve between Bishop and Mountain and wondered if anything had changed. He couldn't remember why the students had taken over the new computer rooms on the top floor, something about racist professors or a racist institution. He remembered people saying at the time that it was just a lot of kids who wanted to be like the Americans and have a protest on campus, but the Hall Building wasn't anything like Dougherty imagined a campus would look like — it was just an office building, a modern-looking steel and glass building. Concrete and glass really, ten storeys high on a downtown intersection. The main floor lobby looked like the waiting room at the airport, with rows of plastic seats bolted to the floor and people sitting around waiting. Even on Sunday there were a few people sitting on the plastic chairs and reading books.

The campus of Sir George was spread over the neighbourhood a little, into the old three-storey brownstones on Mackay and Bishop. Dougherty wondered if Bill could be a student, showing up in his 1966 Lincoln and disappearing into the crowd.

He spent a few hours walking the neighbourhood, stopping people and showing them the picture of the Lincoln, but no one could say for sure if they'd seen the car. Dougherty was starting to wonder if it really was better to be doing something, *anything*, rather than nothing.

After the lunch crowds thinned out, Dougherty descended a couple of steps into the Café Prague, not the kind of place he'd ever go in uniform, so he was glad he wasn't wearing one. It was more of a student hangout, with overflowing ashtrays on every table and serving strong coffee and sandwiches on dark rye bread.

He wondered if this was the kind of place where Ruth Garber would be comfortable.

Then he thought he should call her and ask her out on another date but realized it would have to be tonight, before he started a couple of weeks working nights. Who would go out with a guy the same day he asked?

Maybe Ruth Garber.

So he called her and when she answered and recognized his voice she said, "Oh, did you find out about any more missing girls?"

"No, I'm still looking into that." He paused then, unsure about this, but then he said, "I was wondering if you'd want to get together tonight, maybe have dinner?"

"I have some leftovers."

"Oh. Maybe a movie?"

She said, "There's enough, why don't you come over?"

"Okay."

He hung up the payphone, thinking he couldn't tell if he'd just asked Ruth out on a date or not, but when he got to her apartment she'd set the table and, he thought, got dressed up a little.

After they ate the lasagna and the garlic bread (which now Dougherty was thinking she'd gone out and bought after he'd called), Ruth got a newspaper and opened it to the movie listings.

237

"*Il était une fois dans l'Ouest?*"

Dougherty said, "I saw it as *Once Upon a Time in the West*, but if you want to see it in French that'd be fine."

"*Hello, Dolly!?*"

They were sitting on the couch in the small living room, Ruth holdng the paper open so they could both see it and Dougherty said, "I'm surprised they're still showing *Airport* after the plane crash."

She said, "Oh look, a double bill, *I Am Curious (Yellow)* and *I Am Curious (Blue)*."

"Are you really that curious?"

Ruth was smiling then, moving a little closer to Dougherty, and she said, "*The Role of Sex in Society* — they're always trying to make them sound classy and scientific."

"Isn't that what you do in Sociology?"

"Yeah," she said, "we sit around all day watching skin flicks."

"I'm surprised we haven't busted you."

She turned to him then, sat up a little and said, "Oh, you'd like that, wouldn't you?" Then she swung a leg over and sat on his lap facing him, and he was thinking, Yeah, this is definitely a date.

He said, "Yeah, I would."

They never made it to a movie, just into the bedroom.

CHAPTER EIGHTEEN

Dougherty led the two bomb squad guys, Vachon and Meloche, down the lane, telling them, "It's still on the front seat."

Vachon was wearing his new bomb suit, thick arms and legs and chest protector that looked like an umpire's. He could barely walk, and the metal helmet looked like a welder's.

"I can't fucking see," he said.

Dougherty said, "Here," and stopped in front of a Volkswagen Beetle.

The lane was barely wide enough for the car, and Vachon said, "How the hell did you get in?"

"Squeezed in the driver's side. There's enough room."

Vachon said, "Yeah, for you," and took off the helmet

and looked back down the lane to Notre Dame Street and then started taking off the rest of the bomb suit. Meloche said, "What are you doing?"

"They can't see in here," Vachon said, motioning to the other cops and the reporters, all waiting on the street at the end of the lane. Then he looked at Dougherty and said, "Don't let them come down here."

"I don't think you have to worry about that," Dougherty said.

Meloche said, "What are you doing here, Dougherty? You don't work around here, do you?"

"No, but there was something at City Hall and something else somewhere, I don't know. Anyway they were short, so I got sent over here. Been here since Tuesday."

Meloche aimed his flashlight up the stone walls on either side of the lane, more like a tunnel as over the last hundred years the buildings on either side had put on additions that joined about ten feet up. "What is this, a bank?"

Dougherty said, "One on each side — Bank of Montreal and Royal Bank, I think. Maybe Bank of Nova Scotia."

"Why did you come in here?"

"I saw the car, I thought it was stolen and dumped here."

"It probably is stolen."

"So, you know, I got in it and looked in the glove box for the VIN and the registration and I heard the ticking."

Vachon was out of the bomb suit then and he said, "It must have been loud in this tunnel," and Dougherty said, "Yeah, once I was sitting still, it was loud."

He watched Vachon take out his nail clippers from the little leather pouch he always wore on his belt and squeeze through the driver's side door of the Beetle.

Once he'd heard the ticking, Dougherty had reached under the passenger seat, where the noise was coming from, and pulled out a rolled up green garbage bag covered in tape — the same set-up as the other hundred bombs planted in the last six months — and then he left it on the seat, squeezed out of the car and ran back to the street, where he found a call box.

Now Meloche was leaning up against the back of the car, looking through the small rear window watching, Vachon cut the garbage bag and revealed five sticks of dynamite and an alarm clock.

"The usual?"

Vachon said yes and cut the wires to the detonator. "Still just the wires, no booby trap." Then he held up his hand and said, "Wait."

In the quiet of the tunnel they could hear ticking.

Vachon reached under the seat and came up with another taped-up garbage bag.

"Holy shit," Dougherty said, "another one."

"They may not be any better at making the bombs," Meloche said, "but now it seems they know they aren't good at it." He smiled at his own joke but then he took on a serious look, *"Hey Gilles, le siège arrière."*

Dougherty leaned closer, looking past Meloche into the back seat of the Volkswagen and saw the wooden crate.

Vachon was cutting open the second garbage bag and he paused for a moment, reached into the back and gently pushed the crate. Then he said, "Fifty pounds."

Dougherty said, "It's full of dynamite?"

"The bombs under the seat must have been the trigger," Meloche said. "The crate probably doesn't have a detonator."

"Probably?"

And it didn't. When Vachon had cut the wires on the second five-stick bomb in the front seat he got a closer look at the crate and saw the nails on it had never been pried open.

The lane was too narrow to get the doors on the Beetle open far enough to get the crate out, so Vachon got Dougherty and a couple of other beat cops to push the car out of the lane while he sat in the driver's seat holding the steering wheel straight.

When they got to the street, Meloche said, "Good, you didn't wet your pants," and the other beat cops glanced at their own crotches.

Dougherty just looked at Meloche. "Did you?"

"Not this time. I'm not saying it never happens."

"The trunk is in the front, right?" Vachon said.

"Yeah."

He opened it and said, "I thought so."

Two more crates.

Vachon handed Meloche the garbage bags and said, "These two, all they would have done is blow up the car," and Meloche said. "But the 150 pounds, that would have been something."

And as he passed Dougherty, Vachon winked and said, "Something, for sure."

The reporters followed Vachon to his unmarked station wagon, and Dougherty went over to the bomb squad truck, where Meloche was putting the dynamite from the two small bombs into a steel safe box.

"How did he know?"

Meloche lit a cigarette and said, "There was a theft from a construction site in St. Joli last week — 250 pounds of dynamite."

"So there's still a hundred pounds out there?"

Meloche took a drag on the cigarette and then started for the Volkswagen to get the crates. "You be careful."

"You, too."

Meloche laughed and said, *"Toujours."*

Always.

———

Later that week Dougherty was pulled from a dream in which he was making out with a woman. They were kissing and groping each other, and there was a bell going off. They were in long grass in a field, and Dougherty's squad car was parked beside them, and he thought that was where the bell was coming from. Then he realized it was his phone ringing, and he woke up alone in his own bed and just as he did he realized the woman he was making out with in the dream was Arlene Webber.

He sat up and shook his head, and took the two steps to his kitchenette and picked up. "Hello?"

"Is this a bad time?" It was Ruth Garber.

Dougherty looked for his watch and asked, "What time is it?"

"Three thirty."

He'd finished his shift at eight that morning and been asleep since about ten o'clock when he'd finally gotten home. Not bad.

"No, this is fine, what's up?"

"I had a good meeting with Dr. Pendleton and I thought you'd want to know about it."

"Is there news?"

"Some very exciting refinements to our theory."

Dougherty said, "Oh, okay," and got a cigarette out of the pack on the kitchen table, where he'd dropped it earlier that morning.

Now Ruth was saying, "I have a couple more questions. Maybe we could get together?"

Dougherty said, "Sure, I don't have to be at work until later tonight."

"Could you come by my office?"

"Sure."

A few minutes later Dougherty got into the shower, wondering why he'd dreamt about Brenda Webber's older sister.

———

Ruth's office was on the sixth floor of the Leacock building, an almost-brand-new ten-storey concrete slab on the corner of MacTavish and Dr. Penfield, right beside a building Dougherty figured must be over a hundred years old.

He'd gone through the lobby and past a student lounge, where a couple of kids — well, as he passed them he realized they were about his own age but with their long hair and jeans and t-shirts they'd always be called "kids" by the newspapers — looked up and dismissed him as a cop, even though he was wearing jeans himself, and stuck their noses back in their books.

The sixth floor looked like pretty much every office

building Dougherty had ever been in. He found room 635 easily enough and knocked on the open door.

Ruth came out from behind a desk. "Come on in."

"Nice place you have here."

The office was small and crammed with boxes of files, every inch of the place covered with some kind of paper. Ruth lifted a stack of files off a chair. "Thanks for coming."

"Well, I'm dying to hear about this new theory." Dougherty was still being sarcastic.

"We're calling it 'progression.'"

"You are?" Dougherty took a step towards the chair but stopped when a man came into the doorway of the office, and Ruth said, "Oh, here's Dr. Pendleton now."

He was younger than Dougherty expected, and he wasn't wearing a tweed jacket with leather patches on the elbows or smoking a pipe — he had on a turtleneck and was smoking a cigarette. He was probably in his late thirties but seemed younger. Dougherty figured he was one of those cool profs he ran into at the demonstrations, the kind who stood with the students.

"You must be Constable Dougherty."

They shook hands and Dougherty said, "Nice to meet you."

Ruth said, "I was just telling the constable about our theory."

Dougherty thought he saw something from the professor, a tiny smile maybe, and the guy said, "Yes, our theory," and then he let go of Dougherty's hand and turned to look at Ruth.

"The progression."

She said, "Yes, the way the killer is progressing

from one type of victim to another."

Pendleton said, "Up until now we were just thinking of them as women."

Dougherty said, "Which they are."

"Yes," Pendleton said, "but remember the triad."

Dougherty said, "How could I forget the triad."

Pendleton looked at him and Dougherty thought for second he might call him on the sarcasm, but the professor let it go. Maybe there was a slightly superior dismissive look, but then Dougherty thought maybe he was just feeling out of his depth in the office and intimidated by the prof, like he was by the whole campus.

"Well," Pendleton said, looking from Dougherty to Ruth, "I have to get ready for my trip to Oregon. I'm sure you can fill in the constable on what we need?" A quick nod to Dougherty and the professor was gone.

"He's going to interview Jerry Brudos," Ruth said.

Dougherty got out his cigarettes and lit one. "Who's that?"

"A man who killed four women."

"Four?"

"That we know of."

It was quiet for a moment and then Dougherty said, "Okay, what do you need from me?"

"More information about the victims."

"What for?"

"To see if there's a progression. You see, the first violence is against animals. Usually dogs and cats but it can be any kind of animal, really."

"Usually?"

"Yes, but it's the violence that's the key. And the progression." Ruth got out her own cigarettes and lit one, dropping the match in a big glass ashtray on her desk. "With the cruelty to animals, it starts slowly with whatever animal he has access to; mice, squirrels, stray dogs or cats, and it usually starts with just a little violence, throwing stones, kicking."

Dougherty said, "Okay."

"But in many cases it progresses to more hands-on violence, stabbing, strangulation. And it often progresses from strays to a family pet."

Dougherty said, "More personal," and Ruth said, "Exactly."

Then she said, "So now I'm wondering if these men are making the same progression from women who are available, like prostitutes, to someone more personal."

"These men," Dougherty said. "How many are there?"

"More all the time."

"Wow," Dougherty said, "you really are doing some research here."

"Yes, we are," Ruth said. "What did you think we were doing?"

"I don't know, it just seems like a . . . tough way to spend the day." He motioned at the piles of files all over the office.

Ruth said, "It's important."

"Oh, for sure."

She paused a little but then got back to business. "In some cases where we have enough information we've seen that the first victims tend to be prostitutes."

Dougherty said, "Availability."

"They would be women who would get into cars with men they don't know."

"And hitchhikers."

"Yes," Ruth said, "we've seen that, too. But as we see more cases we see the progression."

Dougherty was getting the feeling that it was much more Ruth's theory than Dr. Pendleton's, but he didn't say anything.

"We've seen other men move from prostitutes to more personal victims and we think that's what's going on here."

Dougherty said, "We're not sure Sylvie Berubé was a prostitute."

"That's what I was hoping you could look into."

"Me? Shouldn't that be the detectives?"

Ruth tapped her cigarette on the edge of the ashtray, and Dougherty noticed for the first time she seemed a little nervous. He watched her wave her hand around a little, the smoke trailing behind, then she said, "The thing is, we've spoken to the detectives quite a bit."

"Yeah."

"And, well, they've answered a lot of our questions and given us access to a lot of the investigation."

"Yeah."

"And this theory is really at the early stages."

"So," Dougherty said, "this isn't between Dr. Pendleton and the detectives, this is between you and me? So if the theory doesn't pan out we look bad and not the higher-ups?"

248

"Theories don't look bad," Ruth said. "They have to be tested, if they don't pan out, as you say, that isn't wrong, it's part of the process."

"Sure," Dougherty said, "but I can imagine the conversation, talking about limited resources and where they would be better spent and how you can chase this theory but you're on your own."

Ruth took a drag on her cigarette and looked at Dougherty. "I don't care about that."

He believed her. "Okay, so you want me to find out if Sylvie Berubé was a prostitute?"

"Yes. At the time of the murder the detectives questioned the other people at her workplace, a club called Casa Loma. Do you know it?"

"It's on St. Catherine," Dougherty said, "near the St. Laurent, about a block east. It's actually a few bars in one: there's a disco, there's a bar called the Jacques Antonin and there's the strip club. I'm guessing she worked in the strip club."

"Yes. The detectives interviewed a couple of the other dancers as well as the manager, a Marcel Théroux. They said she'd only been there a few weeks."

"But none of the customers?"

Ruth looked in the file. "No, it just says she finished work and left and no one saw her until you."

Dougherty thought about the kids who'd actually found Sylvie Berubé's body and the woman they'd told, one of their mothers he'd thought. But now he wasn't sure.

"Yeah, until me. If she was a prostitute she likely used the club for hookups."

"You keep saying 'if.' What makes you think she wasn't?"

"She was working, she was making money, but she didn't seem to have a pimp. Maybe she worked the street a little before she got the job at Casa Loma, but we don't know. Anyway, they probably did talk to some customers but if they didn't get anything useful they wouldn't put any names into the file — good upstanding citizens and all that."

"But you think she met someone at the club?"

"Maybe somebody came to see her more than once, maybe one of the other girls or the bartenders noticed someone paying special attention to Sylvie." Maybe someone saw a white Lincoln with a black roof.

"It would be very interesting if she was working as a stripper when she met Bill," Ruth said.

"Why?"

"Now that we're working on the progression theory and looking at the victims, how they appeared to Bill is very important. If he's progressing from prostitutes, or maybe from go-go dancers, to women involved in sex and drugs and so on, until he gets to his idealized woman. How Bill sees the women is important."

"If he saw Sylvie first as a go-go dancer or prostitute?"

"Yes. We thought — the police thought — that Sylvie was a prostitute and Bill picked her up on the street, that was his first interaction with her."

Dougherty said, "It might have been like that."

"But he might have seen her first in the club. So you'll ask?"

"Yes," Dougherty said, standing up and heading for the door, "I'll ask."

"Eddie?"

"Yes?"

"You know that if I'm right it means there will be more murders."

If *I'm* right.

Dougherty knew it was her theory.

He said yes.

CHAPTER
NINETEEN

Dougherty found the hall in the Place Bonaventure Hotel and watched the waiters setting up for the closing banquet dinner for a few minutes until he heard a voice behind him say, "So, we finally get some overtime."

It was Maurice Brisbois, back in uniform and looking pretty good for a guy who'd been shot in the arm a couple of weeks ago.

Dougherty said, "For this, of course."

"What is it exactly?"

"The International Conference of Police Associations."

"So that's why they told us not to arrest any hookers this week."

"Yeah," Dougherty said, "they're getting overtime, too. Is it raining yet?"

Brisbois shook his head as he pulled a pack of cigarettes from his shirt pocket, took one out and held open the pack to Dougherty. "This goddamned summer; it's July and we haven't had one nice day." He lit his cigarette and handed the matchbook to Dougherty. "Not one day has it been over seventy degrees."

"You watch, though, August'll be stinking."

"And me with no more vacation this year."

Dougherty said yeah, and was thinking how he hadn't taken any vacation at all this year and didn't have any planned. Now he was thinking he might take a few days off and really work the Brenda Webber case, ask around Casa Loma about Sylvie Berubé and show the picture of the car. He could see Carpentier's point: he really didn't have anything much yet. It would be a waste of time for a homicide detective.

Brisbois said, "You working after this?" and Dougherty said, "Yeah, nights for two weeks, you?"

"I just finished a shift." He looked into the banquet room. "You think they'll give us dinner?"

"Maybe when it's over we can go into the kitchen."

"For the leftovers?"

"Do you want to go get something now?" Dougherty said, "I think I can keep an eye on the waiters myself."

"You sure? Some of them look like they're ready to snap."

"They do have all those butter knives."

"You want me to bring you something?"

"Don't worry about it if it's a hassle."

They had about a half hour before the big shots would start to arrive, and then they'd be standing by the doors, listening to speeches and watching guys eat, until close to midnight. After Dougherty would head out to finish his shift.

There was a newspaper on a bench a few feet down the hotel hallway so Dougherty sat down and read about a hijacking in Greece. Olympic Airways 747 flying from Beirut to Athens had been taken over by six people, including one woman, which Dougherty noticed the article mentioned was a blonde wearing a yellow blouse. The hijackers had machine guns, pistols and hand grenades, and when the plane landed in Athens they demanded the release of seven people in jail in Greece in exchange for the forty-five passengers.

Dougherty wondered if the seven people were like the prisoners in the ransom notes of the two kidnapping plans they'd found in Montreal — bank robbers and guys who'd set off bombs in stock exchanges and university buildings and people's houses.

What really surprised Dougherty, though, was that the prisoners had actually been released. Then the forty-five passengers were let go and the plane took off with the hijackers and a guy from the Red Cross who volunteered to be a hostage. They landed in Cairo and that was that.

"What is it?"

Dougherty looked up to see Delisle, looking uncomfortable in a suit and tie. "You look pissed off," he said.

Dougherty said, "They're letting sergeants in there?"

"By invitation only." Delisle headed for the banquet room and looked back, saying, "You go straight from here to your shift."

Dougherty waved him away and returned to the paper. A few minutes later Brisbois returned and handed him a smoked meat sandwich wrapped in green waxed paper. "Probably better than the rubber chicken they'll be serving in there?"

Dougherty said yeah, and it probably was.

By then cops were already filing into the banquet room and it wasn't long before the speeches started. The radio guy who served as host for the evening said there were cops from 133 different forces present, and he made jokes about the crime rate in Montreal being the lowest this week that it had ever been. He got heckled quite a bit, but he handled it well.

The highlight of the night was the speech by George Springate, former football player with the Alouettes, former cop, and now the Member of the National Assembly from, as Dougherty knew he insisted, Point St. Charles, even though he was really from Westmount.

Brisbois said, "He looks like a kid," and Dougherty agreed.

Springate gave a rousing speech, for sure, a real politician, and of course mentioned how he'd been a cop for ten years a couple of times. But he also talked about some real issues. Dougherty listened carefully when Springate said, "Stay on the job and face reality. Solutions will not be found with on-the-street justice."

It wasn't the first time Dougherty'd heard talk about a strike — hell, everybody else was going on strike, from the longshoremen to the posties to the city workers. Even the doctors were threatening to walk out if the government went ahead with Medicare — but this was the first time someone was talking about a police strike in public.

There was a lot of grumbling in the room, though

Dougherty noticed almost all of it was from the Montreal cops, or maybe the Canadian cops. He didn't think many of the American cops were going along with the strike talk, but when Springate said, again, that he knew what cops were up against, the grumbling did spread.

Brisbois leaned in close to Dougherty. "He was a cop? Did you know that?"

"I heard something about that, yeah." They were both shaking their heads.

Then Springate said, "The danger, sure, but also the lack of gratitude, the lack of co-operation and the apathy makes cops totally dissatisfied and frustrated. Society has backed you into a corner, and you, in turn, have built a wall around yourselves." That got the room quiet again. "But that has to change. No cop goes out looking to crack a skull. Walking off the job will only offer up a welcome mat for armed thugs, looters and rapists, child molesters and mobs. And don't say that won't happen . . . look at Montreal, October 7, 1969."

"*Câlisse*, they never forget that," Brisbois said.

"They'll never let us," Dougherty said. The one-day wildcat strike, the Murray Hill riot. A man killed.

Springate was wrapping up now: "You say you want the right to strike? I say, if you're not going to use it, then why the fuss? Do you want merely to hold the threat of terrorists over the heads of negotiators and the public? And if so, then you don't deserve to have it."

"*Tabarnak.*"

Dougherty was wondering now if they might have to do some actual work at this event. There was some polite applause, but mostly there were a few hundred pissed-off cops sitting there with their arms folded across their chests, dead eyes staring Springate off the stage.

The radio guy walked back onstage and pretended to have a heart attack, then leaned up to the mic. "I thought some of you guys were supposed to take Springate out and get him laid?" A few cops laughed and the emcee kept going, cracking more jokes and moving away from Springate as quick as he could.

Dougherty watched the room, feeling the tension let go, then he said, "I never saw him play football and I never worked with him on the force, but that guy sure seems like a natural politician."

"A long and glorious career ahead of him," Brisbois said.

The banquet finally broke up a little after eleven and representatives from 133 police forces in North America set out to test Montreal's hard-earned reputation as a party town.

For Dougherty it was a quiet night until about three thirty in the morning when he got the call about the dead body in Atwater Park.

———

It was a white male in his mid-twenties. He was on his back, looking up at the statue of Giovanni Caboto, or *John Cabot* as was carved in the stone, but his eyes were blank.

There was no one else around.

Dougherty looked at the streets circling the park: four lanes of Atwater with no traffic, the Forum across St. Catherine with its twin escalators lit up to look like hockey sticks behind the glass wall, the empty bus stops on Closse and the Children's Hospital to the south.

And no sounds.

Dougherty looked up at the statue and said, "So, did you see anything?" and the stone Cabot stood there with his long coat flowing and one hand held up to his eyes, looking off into the distance. "No, you're still looking for that shortcut to China, aren't you."

Then Dougherty looked at the dead guy and said, "Shit."

He jogged back to the squad car, which he'd left pulled up on the sidewalk on St. Catherine, and got on the radio to dispatch, telling them that, yes, there was a dead body in Atwater Park. He listened to the dispatcher telling him to secure the scene but cut her off with "Roger, over, yeah, I got it," and walked back to the statue.

The next person to walk into the park was a rookie beat cop, a kid named Mancini, who looked at the body and said, *"Tabarnak, y'en a du sang!"*

Dougherty said, " Yeah, a lot of blood."

It covered the dead guy, from his neck to his crotch, and spread out beyond the base of the statue.

Mancini said, *"La drogue?"* and Dougherty looked at him, about to say "what the hell kind of question is that," when he realized the kid meant a drug deal, not an overdose.

"Peut-être." Maybe.

Mancini said, *"Ou les tapettes?"*

Switching to English, Dougherty said, "Fags? It's possible, I guess."

Another squad car pulled up and a couple more uniformed cops got out. Then the detectives started arriving.

The first, of course, were the Night Patrol, four big men getting out of a sedan. "Eh, it's Humphrey Bogart," Mancini said.

They did look like they were from another era in their trench coats and fedoras, scowls and arrogance, from a time when people were afraid of cops and confessions could be beaten out of anybody. Before students had long hair and lawyers, and before everyone started talking about their rights.

The Night Patrol guys lit cigarettes and talked among themselves for a few minutes until it looked like they had it all figured out, then one of them asked Mancini what he found.

Mancini looked at Dougherty, who just shrugged and gave him a go-ahead motion. Mancini told them the body was exactly as they'd found it.

Dougherty took a few steps away from the statue and looked across St. Catherine Street towards the Forum at the white sign on the corner where the events were listed: a James Brown concert, boxing, wrestling, a Led Zeppelin — whatever that was. Summer in the city.

Another sedan pulled up on St. Catherine and two men got out. Dougherty walked towards them and met them by the edge of the park. "Homicide?"

The younger one nodded. "I'm Detective Laurier. This is Inspecteur Bouchard. What have we got here?"

"Young man, early twenties, throat slashed and stabbed in the chest."

Inspecteur Bouchard said, "Slashed and stabbed?"

"Looks like it."

"Did you see a woman in the park?" Laurier said.

"A woman called it in."

"No," Dougherty said, "but I was further down St. Catherine, past Guy, when the call came in. I pulled a U and came this way," he pointed to show how he came the wrong way on the one-way street, "and I passed a car with a man and a woman in it."

"Young woman?"

"Yeah, twenties, I think."

"What kind of woman?"

"What do you mean?"

Laurier shrugged a little. "Like a hippie or like a secretary?"

"Oh," Dougherty said, thinking about it, "like maybe she was going to a *discothèque*, kind of dressed up."

"And the man?"

"Older." Dougherty almost said, "Your age," but stopped himself.

"Also going to a *discothèque*?"

"I don't know, I guess so. They went by pretty quick."

"Okay. What kind of car?"

Dougherty said, "A Buick, I think."

"Can you be sure?"

"I didn't realize the car was important," Dougherty said, and Bouchard shrugged and said, "*Peut-être pas.*" But then he said, "But maybe it is, we don't know."

"Right, okay, well, let me think. It was dark but I'm pretty sure it was blue and not black and I'm pretty sure it was a Buick, new, not more than a year."

"Electra?"

"No," Dougherty said, "not so square — a Skylark."

"Okay, good. Now, what about the victim?"

Dougherty turned halfway around and motioned towards the statue, where the Night Patrol guys were still standing with Mancini and the other uniform cops, and he said, "He was right there, on the . . . I guess they're steps at the bottom of the statue."

"He was dead when you got here?"

"Oh yeah. Like I said, his throat's been slit."

Bouchard was looking past Dougherty. "The knife is in his chest?"

"Yes."

The two homicide detectives looked at one another and they both seemed to nod a little. Dougherty thought it was in recognition of something. "This happened before?"

"We don't know that. Thank you, Constable. We may need to talk later."

The homicide detectives pushed past Dougherty towards the statue. He watched them take over the scene, moving around with ease and confidence. Then he heard a man's voice say, "You're not getting any beauty sleep," and turned to see Rozovsky carrying his cameras into the park.

"Neither are you."

"I don't need it. Keep the crowds back while I work, will ya."

It was still dark and eerily quiet in the park and Dougherty said, "Yeah, sure."

Rozovsky's flashbulbs went off as the sun came up and the pigeons and the buses started to arrive, and a few people stopped to look. Dougherty and the other uniform cops moved everyone along, telling them there was nothing to see and that they didn't know what had happened.

After almost an hour Dr. Michaelchuk came and took the body away and the homicide detectives got back into their sedan and drove off.

Dougherty wanted to talk to them, but he settled for Rozovsky, who was packing up his cameras.

"Hey, has this happened before?"

Rozovsky didn't look up. "A murder? Gee, I don't know, this may be the first one in Montreal in two hundred years."

"The throat slashed and the knife stuck in his chest," Dougherty said. "The homicide guys looked liked they'd seen it before."

Rozovsky stood up, slinging his camera bag over his shoulder, and said, "You work homicide long enough you see everything."

Dougherty was thinking Rozovsky looked no older than he was and certainly hadn't been on the job any longer, but then he figured he'd probably started right away taking pictures at murder scenes and working out of Bonsecours Street, so he was more of an insider.

"Have *you* seen anything like this?"

"I've seen a few stabbings."

"The knife left?"

"Saw one last month," Rozovsky said, "but it was in a kitchen, guy stabbed his wife, that's not what you mean is it?"

"No," Dougherty said, "I mean, what do they think this is?"

Rozovsky started back towards his car on St. Catherine. "Do you remember last year, a guy was killed in Parc des Hirondelles?"

"No."

"Montreal North. He was stabbed fifty-five times."

"Maybe I remember something about that," Dougherty said.

"He was in a motorcycle gang, the Popeyes."

They were on the sidewalk now, and Rozovsky had the trunk of his car open. "The guys who killed him were in another gang, the Devil's . . . somethings."

"This has something to do with that? A revenge thing?"

"Don't know," Rozovsky said. "Could be. Or it could have to do with selling drugs. Maybe this guy wasn't supposed to be in this park."

Dougherty said, "Oh okay," thinking that was possible. They'd killed him in a way word would get around, other dealers would hear about it. "Who's supposed to sell here?"

"Who knows." Rozovsky shrugged. "Everybody's getting in on the drug business now." He walked around his car and opened the front door. "Keeping us busy, that's for sure."

CHAPTER
TWENTY

Ruth said, "I wonder if he's CIA?" and Dougherty said, "What do you mean?"

Ruth pointed to the newspaper and said, "'Agency for International Development'; what do you think?"

"I don't know." Dougherty looked at the article. It said an American named Daniel Mitrione had been kidnapped in Uruguay and the Tupamaro Guerrillas had demanded the release of 150 political prisoners. "Does every country have terrorist groups these days?"

"It comes with American imperialism, I think."

Dougherty had a cup of coffee held halfway to his mouth and said, "Do you believe that?"

"I believe they believe it."

Dougherty said, "Yeah, I guess so." They were sitting

at Ruth's kitchen table drinking coffee and eating toast.

"I thought you'd have bagels," Dougherty said.

"I can't find any around here."

"No, you have to go up to St. Viateur or Fairmount."

It was Sunday morning. Dougherty had finished his last night shift a few hours earlier and waited until ten o'clock to call Ruth to tell her he'd been asking around about Sylvie Berubé. Before he could say he hadn't really found out anything useful, Ruth had invited him over for breakfast.

"He had nine kids."

Dougherty said, "Who did?" and Ruth said, "The American killed in Uruguay."

"Well, maybe he was CIA and maybe not, but nine kids, he was sure Catholic."

Ruth got up and took a couple steps to the stove and stopped with her hand on the coffee pot. "Are you?"

"Am I what?"

"Catholic."

Dougherty put the paper down and looked at her. "Oh, I thought for a minute you meant CIA. Yeah, I'm Catholic. Well, my mother is, you know, so I am. My father never converted, he's Protestant, so they couldn't get married in the church — they had to get married behind the altar or something like that. We're all kind of lapsed, I guess you know, we go to mass on Christmas and Easter, that kind of thing." Then he looked back at the paper and said, "Wow, they shot this guy and then left him in the trunk of a car."

Ruth poured them both more coffee. "I guess you've been asked to do that kind of work, though, undercover?"

"No, I haven't."

"I just figured . . ."

Dougherty said, "Figured what?" and Ruth said, "Well, pretty much every student group back home thinks they have members who are really cops, FBI, that kind of thing. Must be the same here."

"I guess so."

"I remember when they had the demonstrations at Columbia."

"Was that after Martin Luther King was killed?"

Ruth put the coffee pot back on the stove. "It started before that. We didn't really get the riots after the assassination in New York like they did in Chicago and Washington and wherever."

"Were you involved in any demonstrations?"

"Why, do you have a file on me?"

"Should I?" Dougherty said, but he was smiling a little when he did.

Ruth said, "It's not funny, you know," and Dougherty said, "I know."

"But no, I wasn't involved in any of the demonstrations. NYU didn't shut down."

"You don't agree with them?"

"I don't like the war in Vietnam, but that's not really what it was about at Columbia, not at first," she said. "Anyway, I was more worried about missing class."

"They don't seem worried about that here," Dougherty said. "They're walking out all the time."

"Some of them."

"Yeah, some of them," Dougherty said. "The ones I see."

"The police don't really see the kids who are going

to class and working hard."

Dougherty said, "No, I guess we don't. Anyway, that's not what I called you about. I talked to someone about Sylvie Berubé."

"What did you find out?"

"I don't think she was a prostitute."

"But you're still not sure?"

"There weren't many people who remembered Sylvie. There weren't many people still there who were working when she was — it's been over a year. There's a big turnover, girls leave all the time."

"And new ones come in."

Dougherty said yeah. He'd surprised himself with how easily he'd gone into the Casa Loma and asked around, how easily he'd walked the Main. How he liked the way people looked at the uniform and were a little scared of him. And then he'd wanted to call up Ruth right away.

"But I did find someone who said she knew her."

"And you believe her?"

"I do, yeah. Woman named Nathalie. It's funny, what she remembered was that Sylvie was shy."

"Shy?"

"The bar, it's a topless joint," Dougherty said, "and Sylvie was a waitress. But she wore pasties."

"Pasties?"

"Yeah, turns out there's a place here in town on Mansfield, Johnny Brown's. He's the pastie king of Canada, has a whole catalogue."

"I don't know anything about that," Ruth said.

"Neither did I, but I got the whole rundown from Nathalie. They also make custom pasties but they're more expensive. The dancers have to wear them but the waitresses don't."

"What?"

"Something to do with stage performing, from burlesque, I guess, but there was never any law about the rest of the staff. So some waitresses wear them and some don't and Sylvie always wore pasties."

Ruth drank a little coffee and then picked up her cigarettes and said, "Well, if Bill saw her nearly naked in a bar he wouldn't have thought she was shy."

"He would have found out if he'd tried to talk to her."

"If she really was shy."

"And if she spoke English."

"What?"

Dougherty said, "English people think every French person in the province speaks English, but it's not true. If Sylvie had only recently moved here from the Gaspé chances are she didn't speak much English."

"But the others did," Ruth said.

"Did they?"

"Marielle Archambeault worked in a store in Place Ville-Marie, she'd need English for that, wouldn't she?"

"In PVM," Dougherty said, "yeah. And the others were English."

"This fits," Ruth said. "It's possible he didn't even speak to Sylvie, he just pulled her into his car. Then as he progressed he spoke to the others."

"Getting more personal."

Dougherty thought for a second he saw Ruth smile a little, but she was looking very serious as she wrote in her notebook.

"The others were sexual deviants."

"What?"

"Yes," Ruth said, still writing, not looking up, "they may have been sex-cult fetish devotees, that would make it easier for Bill to talk to them, before he moved on to someone more . . . innocent."

"Brenda Webber."

Ruth stopped writing and looked up. "Yes."

Dougherty said, "It could be."

"You know what else?" Ruth said. "It could explain the biting, and the lack of biting."

"How?"

"The pasties are glued on, aren't they?"

"I'm not sure. I guess so."

"So if Sylvie had them on at work and there was still glue on her breasts and he tasted it . . . and then by Brenda Webber, who was closer to his ideal, closer to an innocent girl, then he didn't bite her."

"You think Brenda was his ideal girl?"

"A representation of an ideal." She looked at Dougherty then and said, "Well, I'm not sure yet, this is still early stages. But this will certainly be a fascinating interview when you catch him."

Dougherty said, "Yeah."

Ruth stood up and said, "You will catch him," and Dougherty stood up and said, "I hope so."

"Oh, you have to."

Ruth started cleaning up the table and Dougherty was suddenly very tired, being up all night finally catching up. He said, "Okay, well, I've been on nights for a couple of weeks and I just finished a shift a few hours ago so I think I should get some sleep."

Ruth said, "Sure, of course," and walked him to the door.

But Dougherty rode the Métro back downtown, knowing he wasn't going to get any sleep. Not for a long time.

———

Five o'clock in the morning in the parade room at Station Ten, Detective Boisjoli stood in front of a dozen uniformed cops and pointed to a couple of eight-by-ten pictures thumbtacked to the cork board.

"These are the two Americans, consider them armed and dangerous."

Dougherty was standing at the back of the room looking at a copy of the Canada-Wide Alert issued by the RCMP and he didn't see "armed and dangerous" on it anywhere. He saw smaller versions of the two pictures, of David Sylvan Fine and Leo Frederick Burt, and that they were wanted in the bombing of the Army Mathematics Research Center in the Sterling Building on the University of Wisconsin campus.

Boisjoli was saying, "We have information that both of the fugitives are here in Montreal. We have reliable intelligence among the draft-dodger community here."

The Canada-Wide Alert said they may have been seen in Peterborough, Ontario — a lot closer to Toronto than Montreal — but if they were in Canada they could be anywhere.

"They killed one man with the bomb," Boisjoli said.

Beside Dougherty another young cop in uniform said, *"Maudits hippies."*

The Americans in the pictures didn't look like

hippies to Dougherty — they had short hair and deer-in-the-headlight looks on their faces. They looked about twelve years old.

"*Bon*," Boisjoli said, "we'll get them while they're asleep."

"We could go at noon," one of the detectives said, "they'd still be asleep," and the cops laughed on their way out.

Down the hill to St. Henri. A three-storey row house. Dougherty and a couple of other uniforms sent around back through the lane, past the shed to the back door. Wait a few seconds, the sound of the front door being busted open in the early morning silence. Bust open the back door.

"Okay, wakey-wakey, let's go!"

Boisjoli and the other detective followed uniform cops in through the front door. Dougherty stood by the back door and looked down the long hallway, watching the cops stream in the front and bang the walls with nightsticks.

"Everybody up, let's go!"

A bedroom door opened and a naked man stepped out into the hall, saying, "What the hell are you doing?"

He was grabbed right away, arms pulled behind his back, face slammed into the wall.

"Let go of him!" A woman, wrapped in a sheet, coming out of the bedroom was grabbed and shoved against the wall.

A cop pushed past them into the bedroom and said, "*Eille, une autre,*" then pushed another woman into the hall.

Another bedroom and two more people, a man and

a woman, and they were all shoved down the hall into the living room.

Dougherty stayed in the kitchen. It was clean but cluttered. The table was too big for the room and there were too many chairs. Most of the cupboards had no doors and were filled with pasta and rice and big cans of beans and soup like a restaurant would have. There was a pot on the stove so big it covered two burners.

In the living room there was shouting about fugitives and lawyers and rights.

There were the usual posters thumbtacked to the walls — Che and Jimi. The apartment could have been anywhere from London to Paris to New York to Rio. There were local posters, too, announcing meetings of the Company of Young Canadians and the St. Henri Workers' Committee and concerts raising money for the Milton Park Defence Fund with Jesse Winchester at the Back Door. On the front of the fridge was a smaller poster that Dougherty had seen in many apartments he'd been in, it was probably all over the world, too. It was a sunset with words over it: "I do my thing, you do your thing. I am not in this world to live up to your expectations. You are not in this world to live up to mine. You are you and I am I, and if by chance we find each other, it's beautiful."

This time, though, Dougherty noticed one more line on the end that he didn't remember seeing on any of the other posters: "If not, it can't be helped." That didn't sound like these activists — can't be helped — they were always talking about helping someone, changing something.

A cop came out of the bedroom, dropped a pamphlet

on the table, saying, "'*ostie*, every fucking time," and walked back towards the living room.

Dougherty picked up the pamphlet and the words across the front were familiar: "*Stratégie révolutionnaire et rôle d'avant-garde.*" He'd seen it as often as the "I do my thing" poster.

The pamphlet was only ten pages and talked about how a revolution was fought in three stages. The first, radicalization of spontaneous agitation, was the demonstrations, occupations, strikes and bombs, and Dougherty figured Montreal had all of those covered in the past year. The second stage was organizing the masses for armed uprising, and then it said the third stage, the revolution, would be militarily and politically inseparable as in Vietnam.

Dougherty thought, Shit, Vietnam, isn't that what these people are trying to avoid? Other parts of the pamphlet talked about how they needed to be more like the Black Panthers and "prepare themselves for armed combat, for urban guerilla warfare."

The other cop came back into the kitchen, holding a girl by the arm. "They're not here."

For a moment Dougherty thought about saying something about that "reliable intelligence in the draft-dodger community," but it passed and he said, "So what are you doing?"

"We're taking these ones in."

"What for?"

"Boisjoli says he'll think of something on the way."

The cop let go of the girl, and Dougherty realized that meant she was all his. She'd gotten dressed, pulled on some jeans and a blouse, but she was barefoot and her hair was all over her face. "Okay, let's go," Dougherty said.

She looked at him and he realized she was at least his age, maybe even a couple of years older.

She said, "Can I get my boots?" and motioned to where a few pairs of shoes and boots stood in a neat row by the door.

Dougherty said sure, and watched her pick up a pair of work boots, steel-toed like his father wore on the job, and sit down on one of the chairs. When she finished tying the laces she stood up and looked around the kitchen, and Dougherty got the feeling that it was her place, she was in charge of it, though by the way she looked as they were going out the back door, Dougherty thought she might be getting tired of it.

He led her into the lane where his squad car was parked. The sun was up then, the beginning of a hot, humid August day, and Dougherty still had his regular shift to work.

He opened the back door and said, "Watch your head."

"You're not going to slam it into the roof of the car?"

"This is a clean shirt," Dougherty said, "and I don't have any more."

She looked at him like she didn't understand for a moment and then she said, "Oh," and nodded. "A joke?"

"You're older," Dougherty said.

Getting into the back seat she said, "Older than what?"

Dougherty pulled out of the lane slowly. "Do you all live there together in that apartment?"

In the back seat the woman rolled her eyes and looked away, shaking her head and saying, "Yes, it's nothing but drugs and orgies, all day and all night."

"Yeah? Who keeps the kitchen so clean?"

Dougherty was looking in the rear-view mirror, and she was looking out the window.

And then he was thinking how crazy that sounded, orgies all the time, and how it was probably also crazy that the women Bill killed had been sexual deviants. They were just normal women, they could have been anyone.

And Bill probably looked like a normal guy.

He could be anyone.

TWENTY-ONE

It poured Sunday afternoon. Dougherty took Tommy out to Jarry Park, hoping the rain would stop and the Expos could play.

But every once in a while it looked like it might clear up so they stayed in their seats. They sat for almost an hour before the game was postponed to Monday night. Tommy was wearing a jacket and his red, white and blue Expos cap — Dougherty remembered when they'd first introduced the uniform and some reporter held up the hat and said, "Where's the propeller?" — but Dougherty was just getting wet. They were eating hot dogs and Dougherty was drinking a beer.

Tommy said, "They won yesterday, did you see?" and Dougherty said, "No, did you?"

"I heard it on the radio, John Bateman got a couple of hits."

"I hope John Boccabella is playing today," Dougherty said, "I like the way the announcer says his name," and he and Tommy said it at the same time, drawing it way out like the P.A. announcer: "Jooooohnnn Boc-a-BELL-aaaaaaaaaa," and they both laughed.

"Steve Renko pitched a great game."

"Is he your favourite?"

Tommy said, "I don't know." He looked out at the left field bleachers and said, "Last time I sat in Jonesville."

"Did Dad bring you?"

"No. Our hockey team came. Expos lost."

"Who did they play?"

"The Mets."

A hostess came by and offered Dougherty a hat, and he said, "No thanks," and she smiled and said, "If there's anything else you'd like."

"Thanks."

Back in Greenfield Park, their mom said it was too bad the game was rained out but that meant he could stay for dinner, and Dougherty couldn't come up with a good reason not to.

Cheryl didn't show but they were pretty sure she was still in town somewhere. "That last festival," his dad said, "was a disaster."

Dougherty said yeah. The Manseau Festival had been pretty much rained out but even before that not many tickets had been sold and there were rumours the whole thing was just a fraud. Didn't seem like there would be any more Woodstocks.

"And that girl from Ville LaSalle," Dougherty's mother said, shaking her head. Dougherty didn't know what she was talking about. LaSalle was where they'd found Brenda Webber's body but he hadn't heard of any other girls killed there, and his father said, "Murdered in British Columbia."

"Dead a month when they found her," his mother said. "In the woods. Eighteen-year-old."

Dougherty didn't have anything to say to that.

After dinner and after his mother had done the dishes and cleaned the kitchen, Dougherty was ready to leave but his father said, "Do you want a drink?" and Dougherty said okay. He sat at the kitchen table and watched him fill a couple of glasses with ice, then rum and Coke, rum and Pepsi, really.

His dad said it was too bad the game was rained out, "But Tommy had a good time anyway."

"We ate a lot of hot dogs and we went to Orange Julep and had ice cream."

"That's good. He didn't get much of a summer vacation. I think he was bored in New Brunswick."

"But you stopped at Frontier Town on the way back, didn't you?"

"Yeah."

September was only a week away and school would be starting.

"How come Tommy isn't going to a French school, like I did?"

"There's a school two blocks away."

"It's public, it's not even Catholic."

"Your mother's not so insistent anymore," his father said, "about that or the French."

"But he'll need it."

Dougherty's father took a swig of his rum and Pepsi and said, "Now it feels like we're being forced."

That sounded a little more pointed than Dougherty expected from his father, and he said, "It feels like?"

"We just get it all the time, it's all anybody talks about anymore."

"Yeah." Dougherty got that all right. "It's like every conversation is political."

"Like it's the only issue," his father said. "Doesn't matter if it's at work or at the Legion or at the store."

Dougherty was pretty sure his father never went to the Legion, but maybe that was something else that was changing.

Then his father said, "They're talking about a wage freeze, about inflation, everybody's going on strike. And the only thing we talk about is language politics, as if it would be okay if we all lost our jobs as long as we speak the right language."

"I think the idea," Dougherty said, "is that when they get rid of the English bosses everything will be great and we'll all get raises."

"We, *kemosabe*?"

"Everywhere I go I see pictures of Che Guevara and Fidel; it's supposed to be a socialist revolution."

"These idiots aren't Wobblies — nobody's talking about One Big Union. They're not socialists, they're nationalists, they're fascists, they just don't realize it."

"But they're not the politicians."

"Did you hear Lévesque? This kind of thing provokes explosions."

"What? I didn't hear that."

"Talking about the next election. We just had an election and he's already talking about the next one."

"But what's this about explosions?" Dougherty had noticed the stack of newspapers by the garbage cans in the backyard, his father reading the two dailies, the *Gazette* and the *Star,* every day, and now the *Sunday Express,* too. At least there didn't seem to be any *Allo Police* in the stack.

"Because the separatists got twenty percent of the vote but only six seats. Lévesque is supposed to be the level-headed one, and he says some people will be tempted to destroy democratic institutions."

Dougherty thought, Shit, more bombs. He liked René Lévesque with his comb-over and a smoke always in his hand, the way he tried to shrug everything off, but since he'd left the Liberal party and started up the Parti Québécois and made separation the priority, there was a whole gang with him that Dougherty wasn't sure Lévesque could control.

"Well," he said, "it could be worse, we could be back in Ireland. They've got more riots and they say they're on the verge of civil war."

Dougherty's father finished his drink and walked to the counter to make another. Dougherty had barely made a dent in his own.

"It's everywhere," his father said. "Did you see the two FLQ guys in Jordan?"

"Where?"

"Training they say, with Palestinian commandos." He motioned to a pile of magazines on the little table under the telephone on the kitchen wall.

Dougherty picked up the magazine on top of the

pile, *Weekend*, that came with the *Saturday Star* and flipped through to the article his father was talking about. Two men, their faces covered with some kind of scarves, standing in a desert somewhere. Dougherty read the boldface under the pictures: "They say their names are 'Salem' and 'Sélim' and they say they've taken part in 20 FLQ 'incidents' up to 1969, when they slipped out of Quebec."

As he read the article, though, all the talk was about how "we want to orient our military tactics towards selective assassination. For too long the FLQ has been synonymous with bombs and useless violence. We intend to pick our targets so that the people who are responsible will pay." It went on: "We are learning more how to kill than how to mobilize popular movements." It seemed off to Dougherty, it didn't sound like any of the guys they'd arrested. He'd never heard anyone say anything like "orient our tactics" or "mobilize movements," and he could hear Ruth's voice saying something about how all the student groups in the U.S. had been infiltrated by the FBI. He couldn't really imagine any of the RCMP guys he'd met pulling something like this, but anything was possible.

Still, he looked at his father, now back down at the kitchen table and lighting another Player's Plain, and figured that for guys like him it sounded right.

It sounded scary.

"They're just punks," Dougherty said. "They just want to be like the rest of the world."

"And they will be," his father said. "It's easy — just set off some bombs and hijack some planes, assassinate a few people like Martin Luther King and Robert Kennedy."

He downed his drink and stood to make yet another one, this time saying, "You want a nightcap?" and Dougherty said, "Yeah, okay." He didn't really want another drink, but he felt like he should stay and get his father talking about something else. It was true: it was the only topic of conversations these days.

Except, Dougherty thought, when he was with Ruth, when they talked about women being murdered.

These days . . .

When his father returned to the table with fresh drinks, Dougherty said, "You've got to stop reading the papers," and his father said, "Yeah, that'll solve everything."

They'd never talked hockey or much of anything when Dougherty was growing up, and then the arguments started, and now it seemed a little late for small talk. They tried for a few minutes but it was nothing but awkward.

On his way back, Dougherty decided to take the Victoria Bridge instead of the Champlain and the expressway.

He drove through the Point, examining all the parked cars, but the only Lincoln he saw was black and it looked ten years old.

The parking lot behind the Arawana Tavern was empty.

CHAPTER
TWENTY-TWO

"Where we going?"

Dougherty got in behind the wheel and said, "The Hawaiian Lounge."

"On Peel?"

Dougherty pulled the squad car out of the parking lot behind the station house, the red light flashing but no siren, and said, "No, that's the Kon Tiki. Hawaiian's on Stanley."

The other cop, a rookie named Gagnon, a couple years younger than Dougherty, held on and said, "Oh yeah, that the fag bar?"

"No," Dougherty said, "that's Bud's, downstairs."

Gagnon said, "You know them all, eh," and Dougherty said, "Haven't you worked overnights before?" and Gagnon started to say, "Yeah, sure, it's just . . ." but Dougherty cut him off, turning hard onto Dorchester. "The fight's in the back."

They drove fast on Dorchester, and then took a hard left into oncoming traffic and blaring horns and onto Drummond. Dougherty got out of the car, nightstick in his hand, and rushed into the fight, pushing his way through the outer circle, maybe six or eight guys, and grabbing an arm pulling back for a punch.

The guy turned around fast and jabbed at Dougherty, but the nightstick took care of him. Another guy jumped at him, and Dougherty landed another hit but took a punch in the side of the head he didn't see coming and staggered. Then another punch to the back of the head.

Dougherty lunged forward, falling to his knees, but as he did he caught a glimpse of a man on the ground getting up and lunging past him, driving a punch.

On his feet again, Dougherty saw Gagnon get his nightstick across a guy's throat and yank, dropping him to the ground, then going after another guy.

The crowd was scattering then, guys going up and down the lane and disappearing into the dark and, breathless.

Gagnon said, "Do we go after them?" Even the guy he'd choked had gotten up and run.

Dougherty said no and looked at the guy who'd been on the ground and come up swinging. "Hey Mick."

"Finally you get here," the guy said.

They were all catching their breath.

Then Mick said, "I threw them out, two of them, but they came back in this way," pointing to the back door. "The others got into it, too." He kind of smiled and winked at Dougherty.

Dougherty said, "It's not supposed to be fun," and Mick said, "It's not?" Then he motioned to Dougherty and said, "Come on, let's clean that up."

Dougherty touched his own neck and realized there was blood coming from a wound on his head. "It's okay."

"Come on."

Dougherty looked at Gagnon and then motioned to Mick. "This is the manager of this place, you'll get to know him."

Gagnon didn't look too happy about that.

Inside, the band was still playing. Dougherty barely recognized Proud Mary rolling on the river, and then he saw that all four members of the band were women.

He followed Mick around the edge of the club, guys yelling, "Shake 'em, baby," and saw all the band members were topless, nothing but pasties and G-strings.

They put the big finish on "Proud Mary," the girl playing the organ holding one hand up and pumping it and the guys yelling, "Oh yeah, baby," and then they went right into "Sugar, Sugar."

Mick held the door and Dougherty followed him into the dressing room, looking back at Gagnon, who said, "I'll wait here."

"Yeah," Dougherty said, "of course you will."

In the dressing room it wasn't quite so loud, and Mick said, "They're good-looking broads, but they can't fucking play a note."

"The crowd doesn't seem to mind."

Mick dug around in the piles of make-up and clothes

on the table and tossed a small towel to Dougherty, who took a seat on the couch shoved into the corner.

The door opened and a waitress, topless, stuck her head in. "Everything okay?"

Mick said, "Yeah, but we're thirsty. Bring us a couple of drinks."

Dougherty said, "No, I'm fine," but she was already gone and Mick was beside him with a couple of Band-Aids, saying, "Your head really is square, you know."

"I've heard."

All patched up, Dougherty leaned back on the couch and relaxed for the first time since the call had come in. When he'd heard it was the Hawaiian he knew there'd be action, the place being a lot more tough than tropical these days. The downtown nightlife was all moving downscale from what Dougherty could see, no more getting dressed up for the Stork Club, no more big bands.

The waitress was back then with a couple of beer bottles and a couple of shots on her tray. Dougherty took the small glass and downed it and then shuddered a little, and Mick said, "Canadian Club it's not," and knocked his own back.

With the door open, Dougherty could hear the ending of "Sloop John B" building, the line about being so broke and wanting to go home sung with the first real emotion he'd heard from the band.

There wasn't much applause.

Mick said, "They call themselves Eight of a Kind, but it's not true — only two of them really have any tits."

A woman's voice said, "I thought more than a handful was a waste," and the four topless girls were coming into the dressing room, a couple of them grabbing jackets and purses and heading right out, and a couple sitting down and looking at Dougherty, one of them saying, "Our brave boys in blue," giggling.

Another waitress came in with two drinks on her tray, highball glasses, and one of the girls in the band said, "Hey, this isn't tropical — where's the little umbrella?"

The waitress looked at Mick and said, "Claude wants to see you," and left.

Mick looked at Dougherty. "You okay?" Dougherty didn't say anything right away so the girl in the band said, "He looks fine," and then the two of them started singing "He's So Fine," off-key but with a good beat.

Dougherty said, "Yeah, I'm fine," so Mick left, saying, "Let me know if you need anything."

One of the girls put on a shiny jacket but the other one just leaned forward with her elbows on her knees. "Did you like what you heard?"

"I liked the Beach Boys number."

The girl smiled. "Me, too. I wanted to do 'There's a Riot Goin On' but they won't let me."

"I don't know that one."

"Nobody does," she said, "but it's good. I'm Jasmin, I play guitar. This is Kathy, she's drums."

"Eddie Dougherty, constable."

Jasmin leaned forward and shook Dougherty's hand. "Nice to meet you."

No one said anything for few seconds and it started to get awkward. Dougherty said, "This is like that movie," and Jasmin said, "Which one?" and he said, "What do you say to a naked lady?"

Jasmin laughed and Kathy said, "Jaz, put on some clothes."

"She spends all her time back behind the drums, she hasn't gotten used to this yet."

Dougherty said, "Neither have I," and Jasmin laughed too much and said, "I lived in Rochdale in Toronto — I was a dirty-clean hippy. Kathy was a dance teacher."

Kathy was lighting a cigarette and she blew out a stream of smoke. "Ballet."

"And now," Dougherty said, "you're rock 'n' roll stars."

"That's right," Jasmin said and laughed too loudly again. Then she got up and searched the small dressing room until she found her cigarettes on the table. She opened the pack and got one out, pretended to look around for a match, then turned her head a little and looked over her shoulder at Dougherty.

"Have you got a light?"

He laughed a little and stood up, getting out his matches and striking one. Jasmin had the cigarette in her mouth, and she took Dougherty's hand in both of hers and pulled it close. When the smoke was lit, she leaned her head back and exhaled towards the ceiling.

"Well, I guess everything's okay here. I better be getting back to work."

"We have to play one more set," Jasmin said. "Why don't you stick around?"

"I can't leave the city unprotected."

"Maybe you can come back?"

Dougherty said maybe, and nodded a little at Kathy, who was flipping through a magazine. Then he looked at Jasmin and nodded a little, and she looked right back at him.

He walked out, thinking maybe he would come back.

In the lane behind the Hawaiian Club, Dougherty started to get into the squad car but stopped when he saw something in the small parking lot on Drummond.

Gagnon was opening the passenger door, and he looked over the roof and said, "What is it?"

Dougherty closed the car door and walked, and then started to run, as the car he was looking at drove away.

A white Lincoln.

Gagnon was beside him then, and Dougherty said, "Did you see who got into that car?"

"No."

"Did he come out of the Hawaiian?"

"I don't know."

"Shit."

Gagnon said, "What is it?" and Dougherty said, "Come on, we have to go back in."

"The first good thing you say all night."

Back inside the club, Dougherty cut through the crowd, looking for Mick. From the stage Jasmin saw him and waved a drumstick. He made eye contact but kept moving until he found Mick standing by the bar.

"I need to talk to the waitresses."

"Why?"

"I'll do it in the dressing room, send them in."

Dougherty went to the dressing room and a minute later one of the waitresses came in. "What's going on?"

"I'm looking for a guy."

"Bud's is downstairs."

"Did someone try to pick you up tonight?"

She rolled her eyes. "If you're going to arrest them for that we won't have any customers."

"He's a young guy, good-looking, charming."

"In here? No, I don't think so."

Another waitress came in then and asked, "What's going on?" and the first waitress said, "He's looking for a guy who tried to pick you up tonight."

"That's all?"

"A young guy," Dougherty said, "good-looking, just left a few minutes ago."

The first waitress said, "There was a guy talking to Kelly, one of the girls in the band. He left when they went back onstage."

"Which one's Kelly again?"

"The bass player."

Dougherty pushed past the waitresses and stood in the dressing room doorway, looking at four topless woman moving to a slow beat. "The one with the long hair? The bangs?"

"Yeah, her."

"Okay, thanks."

The waitresses went back to work, and Dougherty wanted to go onstage and stop the show and talk to this Kelly right away but he waited.

He paced the small dressing room and waited.

Eight of a Kind ran through a predictable set of pop songs: "Touch Me" was too cute and "These Eyes" was too slow, but "To Sir With Love" was pretty good.

Dougherty looked at the crowd, the men and a few women, and saw mostly serious drinkers, people looking like they were on the downward slide, just like the Hawaiian Lounge.

But he could see a guy like Bill working this room. He'd picked up one of the women working in a jewellery store in Place Ville-Marie, a few blocks away. The two women he'd killed in apartments no more than ten blocks away. He could easily have met them in the Hawaiian, or a place like it, taken them home.

Gagnon came to the dressing room. "We going?"

"No, I have to talk to the band again," and Gagnon said, "Sure you do."

"Just watch the show."

Gagnon returned to the lounge and took a seat near the back door.

A couple more songs and then "Respect" was supposed to be the big finisher, but the crowd wasn't really into it.

Dougherty stepped aside as the band members returned to the dressing room, and then he went straight to Kelly. "You were talking to a guy tonight?"

She said, "What the hell?"

"It's important, I need to know about the guy you were talking to."

Jasmin stepped up. "What's going on?"

"Was his name Bill?"

Kelly was pulling a sweater over her head and she said, "No, it's not Bill."

"Is he coming back?"

"What's it to you?"

Dougherty wanted to shake her. He was balling his hands into fists. "I need to know."

"Yes."

Jasmin said, "What is it?"

The girl who'd been playing the organ said, "Can

you get out? I want to get changed."

Dougherty said okay and looked at Kelly and said, "I want to talk to him."

He stepped out of the dressing room and stood by the door as it closed.

A few minutes later, Jasmin came out dressed in bell-bottom jeans and an old brown leather jacket. "Is everything okay?"

"Yeah, fine."

"Do you want a drink?"

"No."

Jasmin said okay and went to the bar.

Dougherty waited and watched a few people leave, but no one came in.

After a few minutes, Kelly came out of the dressing room wearing a minidress and a long coat and walked past Dougherty towards the bar. She stood with Jasmin and got a drink, another highball without a little umbrella, and Dougherty watched them sipping their drinks and talking. A couple of minutes later a guy came in and Dougherty watched him scan the room until he saw Kelly and Jasmin at the bar and walked straight to them.

Dougherty walked over, too, reaching the bar at the same time. The guy looked like a picture in a catalogue, under thirty, an expensive haircut, leather jacket. Confident, easy smile as he started talking to the girls.

But that changed when he saw Dougherty.

Jasmin said, "So now you want a drink?"

Dougherty looked at the guy. "What's your name?"

"Wayne . . . wait, why do you want to know?"

"Why don't you want to tell me?"

"What's going on?" Jasmin said, and Dougherty kept looking at the guy, Wayne. "Do you drive a Lincoln?"

"No, a Cougar, what's this about?"

"Do you live around here?"

Wayne said, "No." Then he looked at Kelly. "Actually, I just came back to tell you I can't stick around tonight, I have to go."

"Why?"

Wayne said, "Family emergency, sorry," and walked out without looking back.

Dougherty was about to say Wayne was a shitty liar, when Jasmin said, "Well, that was a bad lie."

Kelly looked at Dougherty and said, "Thanks a lot."

"Yeah, you should thank him," Jasmin said.

Kelly stopped, turned around and said, "What?"

"Come on, that guy's married."

"No, he's not."

Jasmin just kept looking at Kelly, then Kelly said, "I don't care," and walked away.

"She doesn't," Jasmin said, "tonight. But tomorrow . . ."

Dougherty said, "Yeah, I guess."

"You're not married, are you?"

"No."

He was thinking about Ruth now, how he'd like to know what she thought of this Wayne, but also how she'd look so out of place in the Hawaiian Lounge. She'd have nothing to say to someone like Jasmin, someone Dougherty found easy to talk to.

"So, do you want a drink?"

Dougherty looked at Jasmin and said, "I better get back to work."

"Okay, but we're here till Saturday."

"Okay."

He walked out, trailed by Gagnon, and this time the parking lot was empty.

CHAPTER
TWENTY-THREE

Dougherty was working a quiet Labour Day, sitting in the Station Ten parade room, getting caught up reading the alerts and old memos from HQ.

A couple of older uniform cops came in and poured themselves stale coffee, one of them was saying something about *"détention illégale de suspects"* and the other one scoffing and saying, *"Maudits juges,"* and Dougherty realized they were still talking about what a judge had said, how he'd called the whole Montreal police force sloppy and dishonest and, like the first cop said, accused them of illegally imprisoning suspects.

The cop said it again on the way out, *"Maudits juges,"* and Dougherty remembered that when the story first broke another judge had said it wasn't the *entire* police force.

He got up to pour himself a cup of coffee and thought about making a fresh pot, and then he saw a *Playboy* magazine on the counter. There was a blonde woman on the cover, wearing a tight blue sweater, a headband and holding up two fingers in a peace sign. Dougherty picked up the magazine and looked over the list of articles: an interview with Peter Fonda, the Abortion Revolution (jeez, another revolution), a "Loving Look at the No-Bra Look" and "Elke Sommer au Naturel." He figured the blonde must be Elke Sommer, but he didn't recognize her.

On the bottom left of the cover was the sell for another article, "*Playboy* Polls the Campuses, a National Survey of Student Attitudes on Today's Major Issues" and Dougherty thought that might actually come in handy with the calls he was getting to McGill and Sir George. It might even help him get a handle on Ruth, though that seemed more doubtful.

Then a man with a French accent said, "This is what we pay you for, reading skin mags?"

It was Carpentier.

"I only read the articles," Dougherty said.

"Really? That Elke Sommer has a great rack."

Dougherty dropped the magazine. "I'll have to take your word for it."

"No coffee?" Carpentier said, "Come on, let's go then."

Dougherty followed him around the corner to the Royal.

As soon as they sat down Carpentier said, "Have you heard what happened to your friends from the Point?"

A waiter was at the table then, and Carpentier ordered a rum and Coke and looked at Dougherty.

Dougherty was going to point out he was on duty and it was ten o'clock in the morning but he said, "Just a beer, a Fifty," and the waiter nodded and left.

Carpentier said, "So, two of the Point boys were killed in Toronto; do you know Stanley Murray and Brian Melvin?"

"I know Allison Melvin. She might be a sister."

"She might be. The two men were killed by the Toronto police, shot while they were in an antique store. They had robbed a bank the day before."

"In Toronto?"

"Yes."

The waiter arrived with their drinks.

"Melvin just got out of jail in May. Do you remember, he shot that constable from Station Four?"

"When was that?"

"A few years ago, maybe five?"

"I wasn't here then."

"Okay, he went in then and just got out," Carpentier said. "So this means there will be changes with the Point boys — opportunities, promotions."

"I guess so."

"It could go well for your friend, what's his name?"

"Buckley."

"They've been running a scam with truckers, they're buying heating oil and reselling it."

"What?"

"It's the same product," Carpentier said, "but the truck fuel has a tax added, twenty-five cents a gallon. The Point boys, not just them, the Italians, too

— they're buying the heating oil for nineteen cents a gallon and selling it to truckers for forty cents and not paying the tax."

"Do the truckers know?"

Carpentier shrugged, "Who cares?" He finished off his drink and looked around for the waiter. "You want another?"

Dougherty had barely touched his beer. "I'm fine."

The waiter took Carpentier's empty glass without saying a word.

"It's a good scam," Carpentier said.

"How do you know about it?"

"There hasn't been much terrorist action," Carpentier said, "but we're still bringing in informants. Life goes on, you know?"

"I know."

The waiter brought Carpentier another drink.

"We can't be on this task force forever; we'll have to get back to work soon. I wanted you to know your friend might be in a better position soon, and if he's in a better position, you're in a better position."

"I haven't talked to him in weeks," Dougherty said.

Carpentier looked surprised. "You should be buying drug from him every week."

"I've been busy."

"We're all busy," Carpentier said.

"What about Bill?"

"Bill who?"

Dougherty stared at Carpentier for a few seconds and then said, "The guy who's killed five women in the last year."

Carpentier shook his head. "His name's not Bill."

"What?"

Another long drink, almost draining the glass. "The girl at the jewellery store, the other one who work there, Susan Bentley, she saw Bill again so she call us and we pick him up but it wasn't him."

"You're sure?"

"Yes, we're sure, we talk to him. It's not him."

"So, who made the date with Marielle?"

Carpentier shrugged. "We don't know. The girls at the store, they see a lot of men, they got them mixed up."

"So you've been working on this?"

"Of course we have."

"Has there been anything else?"

"No. What about you, did you find out anything more about the Lincoln?"

"No."

"Well," Carpentier said, "keep looking. But also, go and talk to your friend in the Point, tell him that you've heard talk about the fuel oil scam and to be careful."

"You want me to warn him?"

"Sure, be his friend. Tell him they're being watched more, the Point Boys. They know it, I'm sure, they're moving up, you know. But let him know."

Dougherty said, "Okay, sure. Be his friend."

Carpentier dropped a few bills on the table. "And don't say anything to the other guys, just keep it to yourself."

"Sure, yeah, of course." Dougherty finished off his beer and stood up himself.

Walking out, Dougherty wondered if Carpentier

agreed with that judge who said the Montreal cops were sloppy and dishonest. Then he wondered why he was so sure Carpentier was being straight up.

Shit. No way to know really.

It wasn't until the weekend that Dougherty got to the Point to talk to Buck-Buck and everybody was talking about the hijackings — four planes in one day, all headed for New York. Three of them ended up in the desert in Jordan, 310 hostages.

Enough to keep Carpentier and the rest of the detectives on the anti-terrorist squad till Christmas, whether anything was happening in Montreal or not.

Danny Buckley wasn't in the Arawana, but a couple of the younger Higgins brothers were. They stared at Dougherty and he stared back. The whole thing had a kind of first-inning feel to it, like they all knew there was a lot more game to be played. Nothing would be decided for a while.

After a minute standing by the door, Dougherty turned and walked out.

He drove up and down Wellington a couple of times and along St. Patrick past the Northern Electric plant, a few thousand people in there making telephones, and he wondered if he might have been one of them if his family hadn't moved out of the Point.

Northern Electric or CN or the Canada Packers plant. One of them, anyway.

Or would he be like Danny Buckley or the Murphy kids or the Higginses, looking for a bigger score?

Dougherty parked his Mustang and walked through

the neighbourhood, making sure not to walk down Coleraine so he wouldn't have to pass the Webber place and maybe see Arlene.

He looked in on Nap's and a couple other places, then stepped into the One and Two on Butler and found Danny Buckley standing at the bar by himself.

Dougherty walked up to him and said, "They get them yet?"

Buckley was looking at the black-and-white TV flickering behind the bar, and he didn't take his eyes off it. "Fuckin' ragheads."

On TV was a scene in some desert in the Middle East, where three of the hijacked planes had been taken. Walter Cronkite was talking but the sound was off.

"The Americans going in?"

"Don't know what they're waiting for."

On the day of the hijackings one plane had landed in London. One of the hijackers was killed and another, a woman, was arrested. Another plane landed in Cairo and when everybody got off one of the hijackers detonated explosives he'd brought on and blew up the empty plane.

Now the whole world was watching the last three planes in the desert and waiting.

Buckley turned to Dougherty and said, "What can I do for you, officer?"

"Or what can I do for you?"

Buckley turned back to look at the TV, and Dougherty said, "There's a lot of talk about the fuel oil scam."

Buckley didn't budge.

"You're being watched a lot more these days."

"Oh yeah?" Buckley said, turning his head slowly to look at Dougherty and then nodding slightly towards the TV. "You're not watching all the terrorists here. They must be watching this, too, getting some ideas."

"Ideas they've got," Dougherty said, "it's balls they don't."

Buckley gave a little shrug, "But they're stupid — that usually makes up for it."

"Maybe."

"So," Buckley said, "you looking for some more hash?"

"Have you got any? That's not screwing up your supply?" Another glance at the TV. And now Dougherty noticed a lot of Jeeps driving away from the planes.

"They're letting some of the hostages go," Buckley said. "They're just keeping the Jews it looks like."

"Figures."

"They think they can do anything, because they always have the Jews to blame."

Dougherty heard something at the door and turned to see a couple of guys coming in, both wearing identical leather jackets. One of the guys made eye contact with Buckley, and then the two guys in leather sat down in a booth against the far wall.

As they were sitting, Dougherty saw the jackets both had big insignias on the backs, some kind of skull and fire in the middle, the word *Devil's* across the top and *Disciples* across the bottom. It took Dougherty a second to realize they were the same gang Rozovsky had mentioned at Atwater Park, the ones in the fight with the guys calling themselves the Popeyes.

It sounded like something out of a movie, Marlon Brando being a tough guy, but Dougherty got the feeling these guys were for real.

Buckley said, "I have to talk to somebody, but go over to the Arawana parking lot around eleven — somebody'll meet you."

Dougherty said okay and started to leave, then he stopped and looked back at Buckley. "You know anybody drives a Lincoln?"

"Like a limo?"

"No, a white Lincoln with a black roof, what do you call it, brougham? I'm looking for the guy driving it."

"You a fag now, Dougherty?" Buckley said. "Looking to get laid?"

Dougherty said, "Fuck you," but then he said, "If you see the Lincoln, let me know," and walked out while Buckley went to meet with the two Devil's Disciples.

Outside there were two motorcycles, Harleys, parked right in front.

It was just after ten, so Dougherty didn't have too much time to kill before he drove to the Arawana and parked behind the one-storey brick building. He got out of the car and leaned against it, smoking a cigarette.

A few guys went into the bar and a few guys came out, but no one looked at Dougherty.

Now a guy was walking towards him, not coming from the bar but from further up Bridge Street. Dougherty didn't recognize him, but he was the kind of guy you could never pick out of a lineup, because he looked like every other twenty-year-old: long hair, scraggly beard, jeans, jean jacket.

The guy said, "You want a dime?" and Dougherty said yeah, and handed him a couple of fives. The guy handed Dougherty the tinfoil ball and walked away.

Dougherty got in his car and started it and sat there for a minute. So this was it now? Buck-Buck already getting too big to do the deals himself, working with biker gangs and moving up in the Point Boys.

Driving out of the Point past the row houses and corner stores and bars and over the bridge across the Lachine Canal, heading up the hill towards downtown, he was thinking maybe Carpentier was right, it could be good for Dougherty's career, getting in on the ground floor with these guys.

Wasn't helping him catch the bastard who killed Brenda Webber and the other women, but that was feeling like old news now.

And that felt wrong.

CHAPTER
TWENTY-FOUR

Ruth said, "You didn't hear about the Women's Conference?" and Dougherty said, "No, why would I?"

"They had to call the cops."

"What?" Dougherty was pretty sure he saw her smile a little.

They were walking across the McGill campus, the big green lawn spotted with small groups of students talking and reading. It was quiet and peaceful, a beautiful Saturday afternoon at the beginning of October, and Dougherty was thinking this was probably his father's idea of college life.

"The conference was divided between French and English, and some women from the French side came in and took over the English side — they grabbed the microphone and it got quite ugly."

"Where was this?"

"Part of the Women in Business Conference at Man and His World," Ruth said. "And that's irony, too."

"What did they want?"

"They were mad at the organizers. One of them was French — one of the organizers I mean, maybe they all were, I'm not sure, they spoke English. Anyway the ones who came in were calling this one a traitor and other things, I didn't really understand. Someone slapped her."

"Someone slapped the organizer?"

"That's when the police were called, but it was calmed down by the time they got there."

"That's the way we like to time it," Dougherty said. "Less for us to do that way."

"Very funny," Ruth said. "They had a point, though, the French women. Their side of the hall was smaller and yet they had a bigger crowd. There was a vote to change rooms but by then no one really wanted to."

"What were you doing there?"

"What do you mean? I'm a woman."

"Yeah, but not in business."

"There were academics, too. One of the speakers was Dr. Marlene Dixon — she's also in the sociology department here."

He said, "Are there a lot of women professors in sociology?"

"There aren't many professors, period, in sociology. It's a small department."

"But you're going to be one?"

Ruth said, "Oh yes. I don't know about here, but somewhere." She looked at Dougherty and said, "Yes, I'm going to have a career. I'm always going to work — does that surprise you?"

Dougherty said, "No. My mother's always worked, at least as much as she could once the kids were in school. She was part-time at the Bell: they call it the May Move when everybody moves and get new phone numbers, and she worked for a couple months every year for that. She worked during the war and then after she and my dad got married she kept working. It's a little different."

"Not as different as you think — a lot of women work."

"I guess so."

"But at women's work."

Dougherty said yeah, and Ruth said, "And police work isn't women's work."

"There are women police officers."

"Yes, but you couldn't have a woman for a boss."

"A boss?"

"At the conference, one of the things they said was female police officers can only rise in rank above other women."

"Yeah, I guess that's true."

"And female constables aren't allowed to carry guns."

306 "Yeah, that's right." Dougherty said. He was going to say that the women were usually used only to deal with female suspects during arrests, when they had to be searched and booked, that kind of thing, but it didn't take a detective to see Ruth wasn't looking at it that way.

She said, "The conference was interesting, though. It was supposed to be about the choices for a woman after graduation — the hostesses at the pavilion are all heading into their last year of school. Did you know all of the managers and assistant managers at the pavilions are men but all of the hostesses are women?"

"No," Dougherty said, "I didn't know that." Man and His World was sort of leftover from Expo 67, and Dougherty didn't really understand what it was about now that the World's Fair was long gone. La Ronde, the amusement park, was still there and there was an aquarium with dolphins and penguins, but the pavilions that had been built by countries from around the world were all — or almost all, he wasn't sure — given other purposes.

"Yes," Ruth said, "so the choices they mentioned were marriage and staying home or a career, or a combination of both. But the audience wasn't all university students — there were a lot of working women," she paused and looked at Dougherty, "like your mother, I guess. So for them the issues are things like daycare and opportunities at work, trying to get promotions or trying to get into men's jobs, where the pay is better."

"Like constables with guns."

"Even sergeants. Could you work for a woman sergeant?"

"Couldn't be much more of a girl than Delisle."

Ruth said, "Very funny."

They were at the Roddick Gates then, on Sherbrooke, and Dougherty said, "Do you want to get a drink?"

Ruth said, "Sure," and Dougherty thought for a second and then said, "We might as well walk to

Crescent from here."

Along the way Ruth told him a little more about the conference and then she told him all about a study she'd just read, how there were a million kids in Canada under fourteen with working mothers and how less than twenty-five percent of them were in proper daycares and how there was so much more to study that by the time they got to Winny's, Sir Winston Churchill's Pub on Crescent Street, Dougherty realized they hadn't talked about the murders or her progression theory or anything like that at all.

And Ruth seemed happy about that, so Dougherty didn't say anything about it.

They sat on the patio at Winny's and watched people go by on Crescent as the sun went down. Saturday night was hopping, as usual.

Later, after a couple of drinks, when they were crossing the street to go to a French restaurant, there was a loud bang and Ruth grabbed Dougherty's arm and he said, "It's just a car, a backfire."

In the restaurant Ruth said, "At least there hasn't been a bomb here in a while," and Dougherty said, "Yeah, that's good."

"Do you think that's over?"

"Who knows? Everybody's still watching the Middle East."

"Those poor people," Ruth said.

"Which ones?"

"All of them."

After the hijackers blew up the three planes in the desert — a British TV crew filmed it and it had been showed about a million times, looking like a movie — the hostages were moved into the city, Amman. Then King Hussein declared martial law and the bombing started.

"They're calling it Black September," Dougherty said.

"It's just awful."

"Well," Dougherty said, "maybe it'll give these guys something to think about; maybe terrorism doesn't look so good now."

"You think so? That's what they're going to think?"

"I don't know. I hope so."

Ruth said, "Yeah, let's hope."

They skipped dessert and Ruth said, "You're too drunk to drive," and hailed a cab. In the backseat she said, "But not *too* drunk," and kissed him and he kissed her back and said, "How drunk are you?"

"Not at all."

And the next morning neither one of them was too hungover, so they stayed in bed and made out again.

Dougherty left after lunch, Ruth kissing him goodbye at the door, still in her robe, the belt undone and his hands reaching in and touching her skin. She finally had to take his wrist and kiss his fingers and say, "I've got work to do."

One more grope, one more kiss, and Dougherty left, thinking he liked this, this could be something really special.

The next morning the British Trade Commissioner was kidnapped from his house a few blocks away from 309 Ruth's office at McGill, and Montreal was on the front pages of newspapers around the world.

And Dougherty got new evidence in the Brenda Webber murder.

PART THREE

CHAPTER
TWENTY-FIVE

Monday morning Dougherty started two weeks of days and was sitting at a desk in Station Ten at eight thirty when Delisle hung up the phone and said, "Dougherty, a call."

"What is it?"

"A domestic, down the hill in St. Henri."

There were two other constables in the station; Turcotte, drinking coffee and reading *Allo Police*, and the rookie, Gagnon, standing by the corkboard looking at the memos, but Dougherty didn't say anything to them, he just stood up and took the note with the address on it from Delisle and headed for the parking lot.

Dougherty was getting into a squad car when Gagnon came running out of the station house, saying,

"Attends, Dog-eh-dee, t'as un autre appel."

"What do you mean, another call?"

Gagnon ran around the car to the passenger side and got in. "There's been a kidnapping at the Greek consulate."

Dougherty was behind the wheel and pulling out onto St. Matthew. "What street?"

"Simpson," Gagnon was staring at a piece of paper in his hand, "between Sherbrooke and Dr. Penfield."

"I know."

"*'ostie*," Gagnon said, "a kidnapping."

Dougherty drove fast, cut across traffic on Sherbrooke and up Simpson past the old Golden Mile mansions that had been turned into consulates and new high-rise apartment buildings. He wasn't surprised there'd been a kidnapping after the attempts on the Israeli and the American embassies, but he wondered, Why the Greeks?

Halfway up the block, two squad cars were stopped at angles blocking the street, and Dougherty pulled up and jumped out, running towards the building, then a cop came out waving him back towards the cars.

"C'est la mauvaise adresse."

"What?"

"Dispatch make a mistake. It's not here — it's Redpath, the crescent."

Dougherty and Gagnon got back in the car and followed the other two further up Simpson, a block on Pine Avenue and then up the winding Redpath Crescent at the base of Mount Royal.

They all stopped in front of an old stone house on the north side.

Dougherty got out of the car but held back as cops rushed up the stone steps to the front door. A couple of detectives were already there talking to two women, looked to be one in her twenties and one in her forties.

Gagnon got out of the car and said, "What should we do?"

"I don't know."

He wanted to say we should go back and find that domestic in St. Henri, and he was wondering how dispatch could make a mistake between the Greek Consulate and this house on Redpath Crescent that didn't look like any kind of consulate.

Then Detective Carpentier came out of the house and walked past Dougherty, motioning for him to follow him across the street to where a man stood by the three-foot-high stone wall in front of a house.

"Did you see a car here a few minutes ago?" Carpentier said.

The man said, "About half an hour ago."

"What kind was it?"

"A taxi."

"Which company?"

"I don't know."

"What colour was it?"

"I'm not sure, blue? Maybe black?"

"What about its sign?"

The man thought for a moment and then said, "Yellow."

Carpentier looked to Dougherty for help. "LaSalle?"

"Yeah, and there's another company that uses yellow," but Dougherty couldn't think which one.

Carpentier looked back at the older man. "Did it go

straight down the hill?"

"No, it was facing that way," he said, pointing towards Mount Royal, "and when the men got in, it pulled a U and then went that way."

"The driver was already in it?"

"I think so — I didn't really notice it until it was moving — there are always taxis on this street."

Carpentier said okay and then turned to Dougherty. "Get his name and information, bring it to me," and he headed back to the house, now swarming with cops.

"So, what's your name?"

"Fred Davidson, I'm the gardener." He gave Dougherty his address in Verdun and the name of his employer on Redpath. Then he said, "Running around like chickens with their heads cut off."

"Yeah," Dougherty said, "that's what we do."

He started back across the street, looking at the house, cops going in and out, everyone a little panicky. He didn't see the older woman or the woman in her twenties.

Gagnon was coming towards him then, motioning to the squad car. "We have to go; they're closing all the bridges."

"What?"

"We got the Victoria."

Dougherty started the car. "And we're looking for a taxi?"

"All they say to me was close the bridge."

"So who is it? What happened?"

"A British guy. Something with the British government, he live there," Gagnon said, motioning back to the house as they turned off Redpath onto Pine, heading for Atwater.

"And he was kidnapped?"

"Yeah, they say three men come into the house with guns; he was getting dressed."

"It's going to be a long day," Dougherty said.

They got to the Victoria Bridge a few minutes later, and Dougherty stopped at Mill Street and parked the squad car across the two lanes. He got out and started waving the approaching cars onto Mill Street.

A couple of cars made the turn, but then one stopped and a man leaned out the window and said, "What's going on?"

"Bridge is closed."

"A bomb?"

Dougherty said, "I don't know," and the guy waved, dismissing him, and drove down Mill.

Gagnon stepped up beside Dougherty. "It's going to get ugly," and Dougherty said, "Yeah, wait till they find out all the bridges are closed."

The Jacques Cartier a few miles east, the Champlain and then the Mercier — all of them had steady lines of traffic crossing all day.

But not today.

"And the tunnel," Gagnon said.

"Yeah, if somebody remembered." The Louis Hippolyte Lafontaine Tunnel in the east end. "And the bridges to Laval," Dougherty said, "and the 2-20 off the west island."

"Should we stop the taxis?"

"Yeah, if we see one with four guys with guns, we'll stop it."

"How long do we stay here?"

"Till they tell us to go somewhere else."

Dougherty leaned against the squad car and crossed his arms over his chest. All the drivers in the cars inching their way around the corner onto Mill Street, under the shadow of the Autostade, glared at him. A few gave him the finger and some swore at him. A couple asked if he knew what was going on.

In the early afternoon, a police motorcycle came along the sidewalk on Bridge Street and pulled up to Dougherty's squad car. The cop took off his goggles and said, *"Okay, ouvrez le pont."*

Dougherty said, "Finally," and started to open the squad car door.

Gagnon came over and said, "Did we get them?"

The motorcycle cop said, "Who?" and Gagnon said, "The kidnappers."

"No, we got a communiqué."

"The manifesto?" Dougherty said.

"I don't know. They phoned in a bomb threat to the radio station, and when the bomb squad got there, it was only an envelope."

Gagnon said, "Where was it?"

"Pavilion Lafontaine, the Université du Québec."

"What do they want?"

Dougherty said, "Get in the car or I'll leave you here," and Gagnon made a face at him, but Dougherty already had the car started and was pulling away.

A guy in one of the cars stuck in traffic yelled, *"Merci, tabarnak,"* out the window as he almost jumped the curb and raced past Dougherty towards the bridge.

Back at Station Ten, Dougherty had to park on de Maisonneuve because there were cop cars all over the

318

place. The station was full of cops, and Dougherty squeezed his way to Delisle at the desk.

"What the hell?"

Delisle came over, shaking his head. "They called in every cop in the city. We're pulling over every taxi and then they get the note and it says to stop all police activities."

"So we stopped?"

"We pulled the uniforms in. We're going out in plainclothes."

"Unbelievable."

Delisle shrugged. "We've had three more bombs called in, all false alarms."

Dougherty looked around the crowded station house at all the cops and didn't recognize anybody — they all looked mostly like guys from the suburbs.

"So, who was it?"

"Who was what?"

"Who was it they kidnapped?"

"Where have you been?" Delisle said.

"Pissing people off at the Victoria Bridge," and for a second he thought he saw Delisle smile.

"You're lucky they didn't run you over. It was some British government guy, something Cross."

One of the cops nearby said, "James Cross, the trade commissioner."

Delisle looked at Dougherty and nodded. "That's him."

"I saw a couple of women at the house."

"The wife and the maid," Delisle said. "The maid has a daughter in the house, too."

"Four men with guns?"

"Three with guns went into the house," Delisle said. "One waited in the cab. He probably had a gun, too."

"So now we're pulling over taxis?"

"It's all we have."

"What happened with that domestic?"

"What domestic?"

"In St. Henri," Dougherty said. "I was headed there this morning before I got sent on this."

Delisle shrugged. "I don't know, nothing, I guess."

"Damn."

"Go get changed," Delisle said. "Start looking for taxis."

Not liking it at all, Dougherty started pushing his way through the crowd towards the locker room.

As he was squeezed between a couple of cops he caught a piece of a sentence, "pull her into his car, but she . . ." and he turned and grabbed the guy by the shirt collar. "Where!"

The cop pulled Dougherty's hands off him. "Hey, watch it!"

Dougherty let go but kept staring at the guy, "What happened? You said a guy tried to pull a girl into his car?"

"What's it to you?"

"It's important," Dougherty said. Everybody was looking at him then. The crowd had parted a little to give them room if they were going to start throwing punches and Dougherty, calmer now, said, "It could be important, where was it?"

"In NDG."

"When?"

"Yesterday."

Sunday. "Did you take the report?"

"There was no report."

It was too crowded in the station house, so Dougherty said, "Come here," and led the way out into the parking lot. There were a lot of cops there, too, but they had more room.

Dougherty said, "Look, I'm sorry. I'm working on something, and it could be connected."

"I don't see how," the cop said. Out in the sunlight Dougherty realized the cop was older than he'd thought, probably in his fifties, and he looked like he could be used in one of those cops-talking-to-kids ads, smiling and being their friend.

"I'd like to check," Dougherty said. "I'd like to talk to the girl — what's her name?"

"I'm not sure."

Dougherty was having trouble keeping calm. "You didn't write it down?"

"I was talking to the mother, she told me about it."

"Okay," Dougherty said, "who's the mother?"

"You don't walk a beat, do you?" the older cop said.

"No." He didn't even know they still had cops walking beats. Now he was realizing that this cop was English and he was thinking the guy would probably just like to be left alone out in NDG till he retired.

"Okay, when you walk a beat you get to know people. Do you know Westhaven Village?"

"No."

"Upper Lachine Road and Elmhurst, by the dairy?"

Dougherty said no.

"All right, there are apartment buildings there. The

mother was on a balcony, we got to chatting. It's what you do when you walk a beat."

"And she told you a guy tried to pull her daughter into a car."

"And the girl got away, yeah."

"The apartment is on Elmhurst?"

"First floor."

Dougherty said, "Okay, thanks."

He pushed his way back through the station, and as he passed the desk Delisle said, "You're not changed," and Dougherty said, "I've got something I need to do," and walked out the front door.

Every cop in the city was working this kidnapping: they wouldn't miss one person.

CHAPTER
TWENTY-SIX

St. James West, what the old beat cop called Upper Lachine Road, was lined with motels thrown up for Expo 67, the Rose Bowl alleys, a lot of small bars, gas stations and garden centres.

Dougherty didn't know the area: his image of Notre Dame de Grâce was stores lining Sherbrooke Street and old brick houses getting bigger and bigger as they blended into neighbouring Westmount. He'd worked a Sunday in the Park festival the year before but nothing happened from a cop's point of view: bands played, kids danced and people sold homemade jewellery and muffins.

But this part of NDG was literally below the tracks — the commuter train from Windsor Station downtown ran a block south of Sherbrooke here — and the houses south of that were duplexes and fourplexes and small apartment buildings.

Now he saw the dairy the old guy mentioned and remembered coming to it as a kid with his father, the two big plaster cows' heads above the window where they bought ice cream cones and bottles of milk. Seeing the area as an adult, Dougherty realized the rows of apartment buildings across the street were probably some kind of housing project.

He turned onto Elmhurst Street and pulled over and parked.

Kids were just getting home from school and the neighbourhood was filling up. Dougherty walked along the sidewalk, looking at the apartment buildings, thinking he should have brought the beat cop with him, had him point out the apartment.

There were hundreds of apartments — it could be any one of them.

No, he remembered, it could only be the first floor. Dougherty walked up and down Elmhurst and at the corner of Trenholme, which was also lined with apartment buildings, and he saw a woman sitting on a balcony on the first floor.

"Hey."

The woman looked down at him, and Dougherty said, "Did you talk to the police about a man trying to pull your daughter into his car?"

"I don't have a daughter."

"Do you know anyone this happened to?"

"No."

Dougherty moved on, thinking it was a lot like

the Point here, another neighbourhood where no one wants to talk to the cops.

And then he realized that it was another low-rent English neighbourhood.

He kept walking and asking people if they knew anything about a girl being pulled into a man's car, and no one knew anything until he talked to a guy who looked like he was walking home from working a shift at the dairy. "Yeah, Karen Barber's girl."

"Where does she live?"

The guy pointed across the street to an apartment building almost on the corner of St. James, and said, "Right there, first floor. On the left."

Dougherty realized the guy meant the apartment to the left of the front doors, the balcony crammed with wooden chairs and a stand for drying clothes.

The lock on the front door was busted so he didn't have to buzz to get let in. He went up the few steps and down the hall to the left and knocked on the first door.

"What now, why don't you . . ." and she stopped as she opened the door and saw Dougherty. "What do you want?"

She was younger than he expected. "Are you Karen Barber?"

"What's it to you?"

"Did a man try to pull your daughter into a car?"

Karen Barber, in jeans, a t-shirt and slippers, looked Dougherty up and down. "I already told Officer Gravenor."

"I'm doing some follow-up."

She had one hand on the door and the other on her hip. "Why?"

"Because it's my job."

Dougherty said, "I'd like to talk to your daughter."

"You got a line on this creep?"

"I'm working on it."

She moved aside from the door a little, and Dougherty stepped into the apartment.

"Nancy'll be home any minute."

They walked past the small kitchen and into the living room. The TV was on, a soap opera, and past that was the balcony looking out on Elmhurst and St. James. The Elmhurst Dairy was across the street.

Now Dougherty was thinking this probably wasn't the same guy, this woman's daughter was probably five or six years old, nothing like Brenda Webber.

Dougherty said, "Did it happen out front here, on the street?"

Karen Barber stepped up beside Dougherty, looking out on the street. "No, it was there, across St. James."

"By the dairy?"

"That's right."

Karen picked up a cigarette that was burning in an ashtray and took a drag. "Do you want a cup of coffee or something?"

Before Dougherty could say no, the apartment door opened and a teenage girl came in and dropped a bag on the floor. Then seeing him she said, "What's he doing here?"

Karen said, "He just came by. He was asking about the man."

The girl went into the kitchen, saying, "I told you, nothing happened."

Dougherty was looking at Karen then, realizing that

the teenage girl was the daughter and that the mother could only have had her when she was a teenager herself.

"I just want to ask you a couple of questions."

The girl came out of the kitchen and walked across the living room to the TV.

"Can you tell me what happened?"

"Didn't she tell you?" Not looking at her mother, the girl changed the channel on the TV, clicking the dial halfway around to a different soap opera. This channel didn't come in nearly as clearly, the screen covered with snow.

"I'd like to hear it from you."

She flopped down on the couch and put her feet up on the edge of the coffee table. "Nothing happened."

"It was Friday night," Karen said, looking at her daughter, "but I didn't find out about it till Sunday."

"There's nothing to find out."

Karen looked at Dougherty and said, "I heard her telling one of her friends on the phone."

"Listening in on my calls."

"You were standing in the kitchen."

"I need a phone in my room."

"You wanna pay for it?"

"Okay," Dougherty said, "I just want to know what happened. And don't tell me nothing." He stepped between the couch and the TV and looked down at Nancy. "Start with where you were."

The girl looked up at him, a little scared, but then she shrugged and said, "I was coming home, on St. James."

"Right across the street?"

"A couple blocks away, on the other side, by the motel."

The mom jumped in with "What were you doing there?" but Dougherty quieted her and said, "Were you by yourself?"

"Yeah."

"And the car slowed down, offered you a ride?"

"I told him I didn't need one."

The mom broke in again, saying, "I told you not to talk to strangers," and the daughter yelled back, "I'm not a baby."

Dougherty held up his hands. "Quiet."

Then he looked at Nancy. "I need to know exactly what happened. Okay, he tried to pull you into the car?"

Now she was looking past him at the TV. The soap opera had a vampire. Dougherty moved to block her view and said, "You got away?"

"He stopped the car," Nancy said, "and he got out but I kept walking."

"Did he offer you anything?"

"Like what?" Karen said.

Dougherty was looking at Nancy, waiting for an answer, and she shook her head no, but he had a feeling he would get a different answer if her mother wasn't here.

"You must have been scared."

"No."

"Was he creepy?"

A shrug. "I guess."

"Did he chase you?"

"When I kept walking he got back in the car and I ran across St. James."

"Through traffic?"

Another shrug. "A little, I guess."

"So he couldn't follow."

She didn't say anything.

"Okay," Dougherty said, "what did the guy look like?"

"I don't know, it was dark."

"Young or old?"

She looked up at Dougherty and said, "Young, I guess."

"Short hair, long hair?"

"Short. He looked like that guy on *Ironside*."

"The guy in the wheelchair?"

She looked at Dougherty like he was an idiot. "The *other* one."

"So . . . clean-cut."

"I guess."

"Did he speak English?"

"Yeah."

"Did he have an accent?"

She shook her head. "No."

"Jesus Murphy," Karen said, "how long were you talking to him?"

Dougherty kept his eyes on Nancy. "What kind of car was it?"

"I don't know."

"Was it big or small?"

"Big, I guess."

"What colour was it?"

"I don't know. White."

"With a black roof?"

"Yeah, that's right."

"Okay, that's good," Dougherty said. "I guess you didn't see the license plate?"

She looked at him and smirked and raised an eyebrow.

He relaxed a little and moved out of the way so Nancy could see the TV.

Karen said, "You know this guy?"

"I'm going to," Dougherty said and made his way out.

He drove straight to Bonsecours Street to find Carpentier and tell him he could now place the same car at two abductions — or one almost-abduction — so excited he'd forgotten all about the kidnapping.

Until he got to headquarters and the place was lit up like Christmas and every cop in the city was there.

CHAPTER
TWENTY-SEVEN

On the third floor, Dougherty tried to get into the homicide office but the place was packed. It looked like every detective on the force was crammed in there — and every one of them seemed to be smoking two cigarettes.

Down the hall he saw Rozovsky by himself in the ident office.

"Did you hear?" Rozovsky said, and Dougherty said, "Something about a kidnapping?"

Rozovsky looked up from the file he was holding. "No, Janis Joplin died. What's this about a kidnapping?"

"Funny," Dougherty said. "And what's-his-name last month."

"Jimi Hendrix. My sister cried."

"Mine, too. Not as much as she did over the other one in court."

"Which one?"

"The one waving his dick around onstage."

"Oh yeah, Jim Morrison. Yeah she cried about that, too, but it doesn't look like he'll get any jail time."

Dougherty said, "Too bad," then he looked at the photos Rozovsky had on the table. "That the ransom note?"

"Hey, hey, we never use the word *ransom*. This is the communiqué."

"But it's the same demands they had written up last time, when they were going after the American?"

"Pretty much, yeah."

Rozovsky spread a few eight-by-ten black-and-white photos across the desk, each one showing a page of the communiqué. "Seven demands. My French isn't great."

Dougherty translated as he read. "Number one: must see to it that repressive police forces do not commit the monstrous error of attempting to jeopardize the success of the operation by conducting searches, investigations, raids, arrests by any other means."

"Of course, can't do our jobs."

"Next: the manifesto has to be published on the front page of every newspaper in Quebec. In case nobody else knows what the problem is, I guess."

"I like number three," Rozovsky said, "releasing the prisoners."

"Like that's going to happen."

"They released that one in London," Rozovsky

said, "who hijacked the plane."

"What?"

"Come on, just last month — three planes blown up in the desert."

"Yeah," Dougherty said, "it was in all the papers," using the line his father always used for World War II.

"So, remember one of the planes landed in London, two hijackers onboard with guns and hand grenades. The guy — he was from Honduras or Nicaragua or something — he was killed on the plane and she was arrested?"

"Yeah, I guess."

"So, she got released last week."

"Well, these guys aren't hijackers," Dougherty said, "Geoffroy put the bomb in Place Victoria."

"And about a hundred more. He's serving a 124-year sentence."

"Most of the rest are in jail for armed robbery."

"Collecting voluntary taxes, they call it."

"All right, then they want a plane to go to Cuba or Algeria — they still haven't made up their minds. They just know they want out of here. The Lapalme boys again, and then here's your voluntary tax, half a million dollars in gold bullion. Then it says, When one recalls the spending caused by the recent visit of the Queen of England, the millions of dollars lost by the Post Office Department because of the stubborn millionaire Kierans, the cost of maintaining Quebec within Confederation, etc. . . . $500,000 is peanuts! Nice of them to point that out."

"They saved the best for last," Rozovsky said. "They want the name and the picture of the informer who gave up the last kidnap attempt."

Dougherty looked up. "I would've liked to see the look on Carpentier's face when he read that."

"Then there's lots more political stuff," Rozovsky said, "and then the instructions."

Dougherty said, "I like this part at the end: 'We feel confident that the imprisoned political patriots will benefit from the experience in Cuba or Algiers and we thank them in advance for the concern which they will express for our Quebec comrades.' So they're getting on the plane whether they want to or not?"

Rozovsky read the last line: "'We shall overcome.'"

"Yeah, on a beach in Cuba with half a million bucks. So what's happening now?"

"You didn't hear?"

"I've been busy."

"They had a press conference, said they received the demands and they're working on it."

"What are they going to do?"

Rozovsky shrugged. "No idea, but I can't see them going along with any of this. They're putting together a list of suspects now: the guys from the last time, the ones arrested up north — they're out on bail."

"And the ones from last winter — they had the same demands and the manifesto. They were going after the Israeli ambassador."

"Everybody's been called in."

Dougherty shook his head, couldn't believe it, but then he wasn't all that surprised, either. "Like we don't have anything else to do."

"And they want the manifesto read on TV."

"Is it the same one they had in the summer?"

"No," Rozovsky said, "I don't think so." He pulled a few more of the eight-by-ten photos from the pile and spread them out on the table. "I think it's longer."

Dougherty said, "Great." Then he scanned the typewritten text in the first photo and read, "'*Le Front de libération du Québec n'est pas le Messie, ni un Robin des bois des temps modernes.*' Okay, so they aren't the Messiah or a modern-day Robin Hood, that's good to know." He read some more and then said, "It is a group of Quebec workers '*qui sont décidés à tout mettre en œuvre,*' who have decided to use every means possible so the people of Quebec '*puisse prendre définitivement en main son destin.*' Take control of their own destiny. By any means necessary. What are they now, Malcolm X?"

"Yeah, that's good," Rozovsky said. "This is Marcel X."

Dougherty skimmed the photos Rozovsky had spread out on the table, saying, "The usual stuff: the FLQ is not an aggressive movement, it's a response to big business and the '*marionnettes des gouvernements fédéral et provincial,*' the puppet governments."

"Yeah," Rozovsky said, "of course."

"'*Le show de la Brinks,*'" Dougherty said, "What's that?"

"Remember, before the election, that bank had a convoy of Brinks trucks move all the money to Toronto."

"Oh yeah, the Royal Bank."

"Royal Trust, I think, and I don't think it was money — it was securities or something."

"Or nothing," Dougherty said, now remembering

the rumour at the time, that the trucks were empty, like the manifesto said, just a show. Then he read some more and translated, "The Lapalme boys get another mention. They really want them hired back."

"Good jobs, working for the post office," Dougherty said. "Federal government jobs."

Rozovsky said, "Right. And Bill 63, I guess they figure it didn't go far enough making French the language of Quebec."

Dougherty was still reading. "Shit, they mention Cotroni by name."

"He's not going to be happy."

"'*Faiseurs d'élections Simard-Cotroni*,'" Dougherty said. "Election fixers. I guess that's Édouard Simard."

"The Premier's father-in-law."

"And the mob — they're covering everybody. Then it's a democracy of the rich and the '*parlementarisme britannique, c'est bien fini*,' and that's it for democracy."

"Parliamentary democracy anyway."

"Yeah, well," Dougherty said. "Like my father says, democracy is a terribly flawed system, it's just the best one we've been able to come up with so far."

"But these guys have something better in mind."

"I'm sure they do." He read some more, saying, "Lots of reasons for the poverty, unemployment and slums, lots of reason for you, '*M. Bergeron de la rue Visitation, Madame Lemay de St-Hyacinthe, M. Tremblay de la rue Panet*,' lots of reasons why you do not feel free in our country of Quebec, why you drown your despair '*dans la bière du chien à Molson*.' Okay, Molson is no Labatt's, but dog beer?"

"They're naming all the names," Rozovsky said.

"Yeah, but Mr. O'Malley of Liverpool street, nobody cares about your poverty," Dougherty said and then read, "'We live in a *société d'esclaves terrorisés*, a society of terrorized slaves' — a little extreme — '*terrorisés par les grands patrons: Steinberg, Clark, Bronfman, Smith, Neaple, Timmins, Geoffrion, J.L. Lévesque, Hershorn, Thompson, Nesbitt, Desmarais, Kierans.*'"

"Making it personal," Rozovsky said, "not a bad idea."

"Yeah, Trudeau '*la tapette*,' always calling that guy a fag."

"Barbra Streisand's just a beard."

Dougherty read some more. "Terrorized by the church gets a mention, of course, Household Finance Corp., Eaton's, Simpsons, Morgan's, Steinberg's — didn't they mention Steinberg's already?"

"Can't mention the Jews enough," Rozovsky said. "And what's that, terrorized by science?"

"By the closed circles of the universities and their monkey-bosses." Dougherty shook his head, thinking how much his father had wanted him to go to one of those universities. "Robert Shaw is only the assistant monkey — he's the McGill guy, right?"

"Vice-principal. He was the one they went after in that McGill-Français stuff."

Dougherty said, "Oh yeah, there was a big protest. I wasn't on duty for that one."

"And the cops are bad, too," Rozovsky said, reading the next page. "Arms of the system?"

"Strong-arms. They should understand these reasons

— they should have been able to see that we live in a terrorized society because, without their force, without their violence, everything fell apart on October 7."

"I like the way the cops are the bad guys," Rozovsky said, "but also without us the place will blow up into anarchy."

"A one-day wildcat," Dougherty said, "and no one will ever forget it." Then he read some more. "'*Le jour s'en vient où tous les Westmount du Québec disparaîtront de la carte.*' All the Westmounts of Quebec will disappear from the map.'"

"Big talk."

"And the usual ending," Dougherty said, dropping the photo, "'*Vive la révolution Québécoise! Vive le Front de libération du Québec!*'"

Rozovsky said, "It's just the usual half-baked Marxist stuff you get on every campus in the world these days with some local names thrown in."

Dougherty peered down the hall. The homicide office was still full of men and smoke. "I got a good lead on the car."

"The taxi?"

"No, the murdered women."

"What did you get?"

"The guy tried to grab another girl, in NDG, out by a motel on St. James. She identified the car, it's definitely a Lincoln."

"Licence number?"

Dougherty looked at Rozovsky, smirked and raised an eyebrow. "But Carpentier said because it had only been linked to one of the murders, Brenda Webber in the Point, he wanted to be sure it connected to the others."

338

"But this wasn't a murder."

"No, but Ruth said there'd be more."

"Your girlfriend?"

"This means she's right. There are going to be more — the guy is still out there trying."

Rozovsky said, "Everybody's looking for the taxi."

"They can look for Lincolns at the same time."

"You think so?"

"Sure."

Rozovsky gave him a look, and Dougherty knew that wasn't going to happen. "God dammit." He paced the office. "Is Carpentier in there?"

"I think so."

Dougherty walked out of the ident office and down the hall. He pushed his way into the homicide office and saw Detective Carpentier in a far corner with a few other senior detectives and made his way through.

"Can I talk to you?"

"Now?"

"Yes, now."

"Okay."

Dougherty was nervous — the other detectives around Carpentier were looking at him. He said, "I talked to a girl today. A man tried to abduct her."

"Tried?"

"She fought him off, got away."

"The same car?"

"Same car."

"What was it, a Cadillac?"

"'65 or '66 Lincoln."

"Where?"

"NDG, St. James Street, past Cavendish."

"All those motels?"

"Yeah, right there."

Carpentier considered it and then said, "Maybe he's from out of town."

Dougherty hadn't thought of that. "You think he'd try and grab a girl right in front of his motel?"

Carpentier shrugged, "I have no idea, just a thought."

A detective pushed his way past Dougherty and handed Carpentier a piece of paper. Carpentier read in silence for a moment, then said, "Maybe you should see if someone driving a car like that was staying in one of the motels?"

"There are dozens of motels along that strip."

Carpentier looked up at Dougherty. "Yes, so?"

"Well, you want me to check them all myself?"

Carpentier handed the paper back to the other detective and nodded his approval for whatever was written there. "Yes. We've got a list of people we're putting under surveillance tonight. With any luck we will end this thing tomorrow."

"And in the meantime?"

Carpentier shook his head. "Hope the next one can fight him off, too."

CHAPTER
TWENTY-EIGHT

It was after nine that evening when Dougherty left Bonsecours Street and headed west out of Old Montreal. He took the Bonaventure Expressway and then the 15 north, heading towards the Décarie, through the Turcotte Exchange. All these brand-new expressways, two and three levels, built just in time for Expo 67, and Dougherty wondered how the tourists had managed — the whole thing looking like spilled spaghetti.

He took the Sherbrooke Street exit and then doubled back a little to Upper Lachine — still Upper Lachine at this end before it joined up with St. Jacques — and there were a couple of motels right there, the Aubin and Town Squire Motel.

Dougherty pulled up in front of the office of the Town Squire and went inside. There was a man, probably sixty years old, sitting behind the desk, reading a paperback, and he didn't look up until Dougherty was right in front of him. All he said was, "All night?"

"What?"

"Do you want the room for the whole night or do you have someone in the car?" He sat up a little and leaned past Dougherty, spotted the squad car and said, "Could you park that around back?"

"I don't need a room," Dougherty said, "I need some information."

The man shrugged.

"I need to know if someone driving a Lincoln was registered here over the weekend."

"I don't know — I don't work weekends."

"Can you check?"

The man stood up slowly and opened up a big ledger on the desk. "All weekend?"

"Friday night, start with that."

A TV was mounted in the corner of the office and the news was on, scenes of big cars pulling up in front of the National Assembly in Quebec City.

"They better not give those punks anything they're asking for," said the man.

Dougherty said, "No, I hope not."

"Nothing," the man said closing the ledger book. "I got Chevys, I got Fords, but no Lincolns."

Dougherty wanted to say "Are you sure?" and he considered making the guy look again and look over Saturday and Thursday, but he had a lot more motels to cover. "If you remember one," he said, "or the weekend guy remembers, call Station Ten and tell them, okay?"

The man behind the desk said sure, but Dougherty knew this was a lost cause.

He got nothing from the Motel Aubin, the Nittolo Garden Motel, the West End Motel or the Laval.

Past the Elmhurst Dairy, St. Jacques Street split in two and Dougherty followed the Montreal-Toronto road and pulled into the Motel Raphaël parking. The Motel Raphaël was a big place built on a slight hill, so there were two rows of rooms with parking in front of each row. There was a pool in front and the office and restaurant were in a separate building. It wasn't one of the motels thrown up fast for Expo — the Raphaël had been around a long time.

The woman at the front desk looked to be in her forties, with a lot of make-up, her hair in a huge bun and cat-eye glasses. "Hello, officer. I don't recall a request to the men in blue."

"No," Dougherty said, "I've got some questions for you. I'm looking for a car."

"A taxi, right?"

It took Dougherty a second to realize what she meant, and he said, "No, it's not about that."

"I thought every officer in the city was working on that."

"Not every one."

The woman raised her heavily painted eyebrows and said, "Well, I sure hope they catch those guys. Imagine, a kidnapping right in broad daylight in Montreal!"

"Yeah," Dougherty said, "amazing."

"It's not like this is Beirut or South America or some dictatorship or communist country."

"No, ma'am."

She looked a little peeved at being called ma'am. "Son, what car are you looking for?"

"1965 or '66 Lincoln that may have been here Friday night."

"Well, I don't work Fridays or Saturdays, but I can check."

She picked up a big ledger, almost exactly the same as the other four or five Dougherty had seen in the last hour, and he was expecting the same no-Lincoln response when this woman said, "Oh yes, here it is. Actually it was me who checked them in on Thursday."

"Driving a Lincoln?"

"I didn't see the car myself," the woman said, "but it's in the register as a Lincoln."

"You sure?"

"1966."

Dougherty tried to keep his voice calm. "Have you got the licence number?"

"Yes, I do."

"That's great," Dougherty said, rising up on his toes and balling his hands into fists. "Who's it registered to?"

"It's a Mrs. Burke, of Toronto."

"Mrs. Burke? Are you sure?"

"To be honest, I don't think she really was *Mrs.* Burke and I don't think the other *Mrs.* Burke was really her sister-in-law."

"It was two women?"

"Oh yes, and they were very much together."

"Okay," Dougherty said, "can you write down the name and contact information you have there, phone number and so on?"

The woman got out a pen and a postcard showing a colour picture of the Motel Raphaël. She turned it over and wrote on the back, saying, "May I ask what this is about?"

"You can ask," Dougherty said, taking the postcard from her, "but I can't tell you."

The woman looked just as annoyed as she did excited.

Dougherty drove back along St. Jacques, past the Husband Transport yard full of trucks, past the forty-foot-tall sign of a man holding a muffler, past the Bon Voyage Taverne and the Donut King. He got nothing from the night clerks at the Gem or the Calibri Motels.

It was a little after midnight, but the A&W drive-in next to the Rose Bowl was open. Dougherty used the radio attached to the pole to order a cheeseburger and a cup of coffee.

There weren't many cars on St. Jacques — a couple of trucks rumbled past and then Dougherty saw a taxi pull into the parking lot of the Nittolo Garden Motel across the street. He watched a couple of guys get out. The cab wasn't black, it was blue, but the light on top was yellow, and Dougherty remembered the other company that used yellow signs was Hemlock, out of Verdun.

A girl came out of the restaurant and walked to the squad car. Dougherty rolled the window halfway down, and she rested the tray on it and said, "Hey Officer."

Dougherty said hi, and then as she was walking away he called to her back. "Can I ask you something?"

She stopped and only turned halfway around and smiled at him. Dougherty realized he was supposed to be looking at her ass in her hot pants uniform, which he hadn't been. He really was tired. He said, "Has there been a guy in a Lincoln here recently?"

"A what?"

"A car, a Lincoln, a big square car, white with a black roof?"

"Do you know how many cars I see?" she said, starting to giggle. "It's a drive-in."

"Right, thanks."

Now she was really laughing and walking back to the restaurant, and Dougherty was thinking, Bullshit.

He ate the cheeseburger, the Papa Burger they called it, and drank the coffee.

It wasn't a bad idea Carpentier had. Maybe the guy in the Lincoln — not Bill — was from out of town, staying in one of the motels here. Maybe he came into Montreal on business every once in a while and raped and murdered a woman while he was here. Maybe he was from Toronto. Maybe he was from New York and he stayed in a motel on the South Shore.

Maybe it was all bullshit. Maybe not.

As he was putting the hamburger wrapper back on the plastic tray attached to the car window, Dougherty glanced again at the two guys who'd gotten out of the taxi, and he realized one of them was Danny Buckley and the other was one of the Higgins brothers, and now there was a third guy with them.

A car pulled up and Buck-Buck, Higgins and the other guy all got in the back, and the car pulled out again, fast.

As it drove by, Dougherty saw the guy in the passenger seat but didn't recognize him.

Bullshit, just bullshit.

CHAPTER
TWENTY-NINE

Tuesday morning at seven thirty, Dougherty walked into Station Ten, and Delisle told him to head over to Redpath Crescent.

"Why? You think they're going to kidnap the maid now?"

"We need to show a police presence. Get over there and relieve the guys."

"You had guys standing in front of the house all night?"

"And you're going to stand there all day."

"I thought they said if their demands weren't met by eight thirty that would be it."

"Yeah, well, the demands have been rejected. 'Wholly unreasonable,' they say."

"Who's they? What will happen to Cross?"

Delisle shrugged. "The government has asked for a negotiator to be named."

Detective Boisjoli arrived then, saying, *"Les maudits flics du CN, tabarnak."*

Dougherty said, *"Qu'est-ce qui s'est passé?"*

"None of your business what happened," Delisle said. "Get over to Redpath Crescent."

Boisjoli said, "The CN got rob last night, hijack, two trucks."

"Where, Turcotte yards?"

"Yeah, they took two truck full of cigarettes, three hundred grand they say it's worth. In and out in five minute, they take the two truck and they steal two car."

"What time?"

"Middle of the night."

"How many were there?"

"Why?" Boisjoli said. "You know something?"

"How many?"

"Five, wearing mask, they handcuff a guard and four employee. They know exactly what they do."

"God dammit," Dougherty said, "it's the Point Boys."

Delisle said, "This isn't yours, Dougherty," but Boisjoli was already in his face, saying, "How do you know?"

348

"I saw them last night; I was at the A&W on St. Jacques. Five of them met up at Nittolo's and left in one car."

"Who did you see?"

"The only ones I recognized were Danny Buckley and one of the younger Higgins, not sure which one."

Boisjoli said, "I don't know this Buckley. The CN cops are in the way, of course — they know it was inside job. Could be these Point Boys, *câlisse*."

Dougherty asked Delisle, "Do you want me to find Buckley?"

"No, Dougherty, you go to Redpath Crescent right goddamned now."

Boisjoli said, "I take from here — if I need you, I know where to find you," and he was out the door.

Redpath Crescent was lined with cars, mostly reporters by the looks of the sandwich wrappers and Coke bottles and paper coffee cups piled up on the dashboards and seats, and Dougherty had to park the squad car a few houses down from the Cross place.

There were about a dozen uniform cops in front of the house, a couple by the door and the rest on the lawn and the sidewalk. Detectives were going in and out.

Dougherty found Mancini and another constable he didn't know standing at the curb. "You guys been here all night?"

"Since yesterday afternoon."

"Okay, well, beat it. But talk to Delisle. If this is still going on tonight you'll probably be back."

"It won't be," Mancini said. "We're out picking up guys now."

"That's not what it says in the paper," Dougherty said, motioning to the headline on the paper clearly visible on the back seat of a car parked half on the sidewalk and half on the street: "Police stop hunt, fear man's safety."

"Yeah," Mancini said, "because the kidnappers

asked us to. Says we don't want to make them jittery."

"You think they'll believe it?"

"You think they believe anything they read in the paper?"

"They must," Dougherty said, "it's what got us into this mess."

Then the car door opened and a man got out and stretched, looking like he'd slept all night in the car. He said, "I wrote that article."

Mancini nodded at the other constable and said, *"Viens avec moi,"* and they walked back down Redpath. Dougherty called after them, "Talk to Delisle and come back tonight."

"You're English," the reporter said.

"So are you."

The guy laughed. "I guess I am."

Dougherty squinted at the byline on the story and said, "Keith Logan."

"Right. I also wrote the one about how Cross needs his medication." He waved the paper around. "Do you have any idea how to spell Serpasil-apresoline?"

"No, but it's for high blood pressure," Dougherty said. "My father takes it."

"Everybody's on this," Logan said. "Wiltshire had to call embassies. The Cubans and the Algerians both said they have no connection to or knowledge of the FLQ."

350

Dougherty said, "I guess they do now."

"They're a little late. Did you know this was the Year of the Kidnapping?"

"No."

"Neither did I, but we're all over it now." He flipped

a few pages and read, "Nineteen-seventy — year of the terrorist kidnapping." He stopped and looked at Dougherty. "We're not supposed to call them terrorists here — though, we call them Felqists."

"We don't call them freedom fighters?"

Logan almost smiled, but then deadpanned, "Not yet. So, in the last year there have been twelve kidnappings. Well, there've probably been a lot more but they were local. These are the twelve 'diplomats and foreign citizens,' as we say."

Dougherty was reading over Logan's shoulder now. "Are they all South American?"

"Yeah," said Logan. Then he laughed, "Oh, that's in poor taste."

"What?"

"Look at this ad, 'She used to be a hippie.' Look at the drawing."

"'But then she got hips,'" Dougherty read from the ad for the Stauffer Figure Salon on the West Island.

"Who does the hippie look like?"

"Like they all do," Dougherty said, "a chick in a flowered dress with a guitar."

"That's right," Logan said, "like Janis Joplin. The recently deceased Janis Joplin."

"Oh right."

"My paper, jeez. I'm surprised they didn't run this ad yesterday next to the story about Joplin dropping dead. 351 Anyway, yeah, twelve kidnappings since last September. In most cases they traded them for political prisoners and let the kidnappers go to Cuba or Algeria."

"See? These guys have been reading the papers."

Before Logan could say anything, a man in an

expensive suit walked up and pointed at Dougherty. "Officer, why aren't you clearing the street?"

Dougherty said, "Good morning."

"Don't give me that attitude, young man. These cars have been double-parked up and down this street all night, these : . . . reporters have been walking on the lawns, standing around all day, leaving garbage — it's got to stop."

Dougherty said, "It's a public street," and the man leaned in closer and said, "What's your name, Officer?"

Logan pulled a notebook and a pen out of his pocket. "What's yours?"

The man ignored Logan and glared at Dougherty. "I'm calling your sergeant."

Dougherty shrugged and said okay.

The man walked away, and Logan said, "That was fun, we should hang out more."

Dougherty said, "Yeah, I'd like that."

Logan laughed. "Sarcastic bastard."

"Hey, any idea who that is?" Dougherty pointed to a woman in her early twenties being taken into the house by a detective.

"I think it's the daughter," Logan said, "Susan."

"Susan Cross?"

"No, she's married." Then Logan smiled. "And a little out of your league."

"I thought the daughter was a little kid."

"No, that's the maid's kid."

"She still here?"

"The kid or the maid? The maid probably is, house needs to be cleaned even more now with all you cops walking all over it."

"The maid had the gun shoved in her face. You think they're making her work?"

"You can be sarcastic," Logan said, "and yet you can't recognize it."

"You know, they tell us in training not to talk to reporters."

Logan said, "Do you know when the last kidnapping was in Montreal?"

"I didn't know there was ever a kidnapping in Montreal."

"Twelve years ago. Two-year-old kid, one of the Reitmans, was kidnapped by the maid."

"You think this maid is in on it?"

Logan shrugged. "No idea. But the Reitman kidnapping was kept out of the news, wasn't even in the papers, and the baby was abandoned in Ottawa. The maid was arrested in Toronto."

"These guys," Dougherty said, "will be arrested here in Montreal."

"Yeah, and sent to Cuba."

"No way. They're not going anywhere."

"Hey," Logan said, "who's that?"

Dougherty looked at the front door of the house and saw a couple of detectives walking out in a hurry. "Social Security squad."

"I guess that's better than the Night Patrol."

"Don't worry," Dougherty said, "the Night Patrol guys'll be talking to informers."

"Yeah, talking."

"Sarcasm?"

"Maybe it's irony this time. I'm never sure."

"What's that one?" Dougherty pointed to the

newspaper and Logan said, "Seems pretty clear: 'Lull reported in Medicare controversy.'"

"So the doctors aren't going on strike?"

"When it's doctors we don't say strike." Logan scanned the article and read, "'20 to 30 percent of the specialists have withdrawn services.'"

"That's a lull?"

"It's not all of them."

"Not yet."

Dougherty looked up and down Redpath Crescent, all the cops and reporters in front of all the big stone mansions, everyone too late to do anything.

And Logan said, "All right, I better get back to work." He climbed into his car and started the engine. He looked back at Dougherty and said, "Anything else going on?"

"Nothing." Dougherty shook his head and said, "Not a thing."

CHAPTER
THIRTY

When Dougherty and the rest of the day shift got relieved, just after six, he walked down the hill to the McGill campus and found Ruth in her office. He knocked on the slightly open door. "I just happened to be in the neighbourhood."

She smiled, happy to see him, then looked serious. "Were you . . . at the house?"

"All day."

"Those poor people." She picked up a cigarette that was burning in a big glass ashtray on her desk. "How are they doing?"

Dougherty stepped into the office. "Okay, I guess. Another couple came from the British embassy in Ottawa. I think they knew the Cross family from before."

"That's good."

"Yeah. Anyway," Dougherty said, "you were right."

"I was?"

"He tried to grab another girl."

It took her a second to make the connection, which surprised Dougherty a little, but then she said, "Dammit. I knew it, dammit." She leaned forward and stubbed out the cigarette, mashing it long after it was out. "Is she all right? Did you see her?"

"Yeah, I talked to her. She says she fought him off and got away."

Ruth pushed papers aside on her desk. "He's going to try again."

"I know."

"It's the progression. Damn. I knew it."

"Your theory."

Ruth said quietly, almost to herself, "Not like anyone took it seriously," and Dougherty said, "What?"

"Nothing, never mind." She looked at him and said, "He's going to try again."

"I believe you."

She looked at him and nodded a little. There was a lot going on here that Dougherty had no idea about, he could tell that, but he knew now wasn't the time to try to get into it.

Then Ruth said, "Why are they doing this?"

Dougherty said, "Doing what?" He was startled by how angry she looked but in a flash it was gone. Then her face darkened and she shook her head.

"All these bombs and demonstrations and riots and now . . . this *kidnapping* . . . everyone so scared — why are they doing it?" She was the most vulnerable

Dougherty'd ever seen her, and he wanted to reassure her somehow, but all he could do was try to make a joke.

"It's the in thing," he said. "Everybody's doing it."

She shook her head. "What will you do now?"

"Keep looking."

"Where?"

"Everywhere. All I've got is the car; I'm looking for that."

"Needle in a haystack."

Dougherty said yeah, and Ruth picked up a stack of files but then just slammed them back down on the desk, and Dougherty said, "Whoa."

"Look at all this, look at this research we're doing — all these interviews, all this evidence." She opened a file and held up a picture, a woman's dead body, a girl's really. "What good is it?"

"What?"

"All this and we don't know anything." She turned the picture around and looked. "Except that he's going to do it again."

Dougherty said, "And we're going to catch him."

Ruth put the picture back in the file and nodded. "I hope it's soon."

"Me too."

He went home and changed into street clothes, got into his own car — no destination, no plan, he just drove around.

He joined the expressway at Guy, thinking this was probably where the guy in the Lincoln got on after he killed Shirley Audette and Jean Way, and instinctively headed west.

Probably what the murderer had done.

He passed the Ville St. Pierre exit that would have taken him into LaSalle, where Brenda Webber's body had been left, and realized that was also likely where the guy got onto the expressway after trying to grab Nancy Barber in NDG.

Dougherty drove past the exit for the Mercier Bridge. He wasn't thinking, really, he was just driving, feeling the road going by and his hands on the wheel. He liked driving, always had, and he'd never thought about why. Now he was thinking it was almost hypnotic — the power of the car, the constant forward motion. He could drive all night.

And he more or less did.

He drove out to Dorval and around the interchange, the traffic circle, and headed back into town. The West Island suburbs were sleepy, street after street of red brick houses filled with office workers from downtown, their wives and kids all tucked in for the night.

Back through downtown, into the Ville-Marie Tunnel and coming out a block or two from where Sylvie Berubé's body was found. Another bridge, the Jacques Cartier, and Dougherty didn't take that one, either. He had no idea why, but felt he should stay on the island of Montreal.

Stay on the expressways.

It was almost three in the morning when he finally headed home. A few hours later he was back standing in front of the house on Redpath Crescent.

It was Wednesday now, and the federal Minister of

External Affairs, Mitchell Sharpe, had announced that the government had rejected the kidnappers' demands and asked that a negotiator be named. Meanwhile, the CAT Squad picked up twenty-seven people and the doctors went out on strike.

Dougherty spent ten hours standing in front of the house on Redpath Crescent, then got back on the roads and drove all night.

Thursday night the manifesto was read on French and English TV.

And Dougherty spent another night driving.

Friday, after he was relieved at six, Dougherty went to Bonsecours Street to talk to Detective Carpentier. He found him in the homicide office with a few other detectives on the CAT Squad.

"You got your car," Dougherty said, and Carpentier said, "No, we got a stolen taxi, but it's not the one."

"But you have suspects."

Carpentier said, "Of course. It's the same ones we got last March when they were going to kidnap the Israeli ambassador."

Dougherty was standing in front of Carpentier's desk, and he was the only one in the room wearing a uniform. The other dozen men in the room were detectives working the phones. But for once Dougherty didn't feel intimidated in the homicide office. "They're out on bail?"

"That's right. Mrs. Cross has identified a photo, Jacques Lanctôt."

"So you'll get him soon?"

"We're looking. What about your car?"

"I've got nothing."

"But you're sure it's him?"

"Yes," Dougherty said. "And so are you."

Carpentier nodded. "All right, we should have more men soon."

Dougherty said, "Good," and left the office.

He saw Rozovsky by the elevator, slinging a couple of camera bags over his shoulder. "Going on a call?"

"It's not all fun and games," Rozovsky said. "Sometimes there's real work. Tonight's the Bunny of the Year contest at the Playboy Club."

"And you're taking pictures?"

"No, I'm . . . never mind, that's too easy. Are you off duty? Do you want to come along?"

Dougherty said no, but then he thought maybe that was the kind of event the murderer might like, maybe he'd moved along in his progression from the Casa Loma to the Playboy Club. "Actually, yeah, I will."

The building still had ghost images of the graffiti on the walls — "Castrate Hugh Hefner," and "This Building Exploits Women" — from the protest back in the summer, but it was nearly completely faded now.

It was set up like a beauty pageant, with judges — a couple of newspaper reporters and a radio DJ — and the girls in their bunny uniforms with the cottontails. There was a talent contest, and they were all asked questions that were all to be sophisticated and sexy set-ups for the girls, but almost all got drowned out by the couple hundred rowdy guys in the place.

And any number of those couple hundred guys could have passed as the cop sidekick on *Ironside*, as Nancy Barber had described the guy in the Lincoln.

In the end Lorna Scoville from Sudbury, now a

McGill student (something the emcee made sound dirty), beat out Roxanne "Rocky" Rozon from Montreal to win Canadian Bunny of the Year. Her prize was a snowmobile and a trip to Chicago to compete for International Bunny of the Year.

Saturday, the Quebec Justice Minister, Pierre Laporte, was kidnapped from the front lawn of his house in St. Lambert on the South Shore, a couple of miles from Dougherty's parents' house in Greenfield Park, where he went for Thanksgiving dinner on Sunday.

CHAPTER
THIRTY-ONE

Thanksgiving.

"Why do you have to work tomorrow?" The first thing Dougherty's mother said when he walked into the kitchen from the yard.

"What's the big deal? We have the turkey today, and you don't have to cook tomorrow."

"Don't have to?" She gave him a quick kiss on the cheek and turned back to the stove.

"Where's Dad?"

"In the basement; he says he's working."

Dougherty went downstairs and found his father in the rec room with the furniture pushed against one wall and a pile of lumber against the other. He said, "Your mother wants it carpeted down here."

"Why?"

"She wants to move the TV down here."

Dougherty knew enough not to bother asking why, neither of them would ever be able to figure that out. They could only work on how.

"So what's with the wood?"

"We'll have to raise up the floor a half inch or so."

"Why can't you put the carpet down on these," Dougherty said, tapping his foot on the black and white tiles he and his father had put down directly over the concrete floor a few years earlier.

"That's what your mother suggested, but it would be too damp."

"If you say so."

Tommy came downstairs then and said, "Ed-die," when he saw his big brother.

"You helping?"

"Yeah." Tommy handed his dad a pencil and said, "Sharpened."

They worked together for a couple of hours, putting down strapping and then plywood on half the basement, then moved the furniture onto that and started the other side. About an hour in, Dougherty's dad said, "Do you want a beer? There's some in the fridge," and Tommy said, "I'll get it," and ran up the stairs.

A little while later they heard Cheryl come in, and Dougherty and his dad stopped what they were doing and stood, waiting, Dougherty with a hammer in his hand and his father with a saw, but they didn't hear any fighting. After a minute they heard voices, then footsteps and drawers opening and the table being set, and Dougherty even thought he heard someone laughing at one point.

When they sat down for dinner, Dougherty's father said, "Well, it's good to have everyone together for Thanksgiving."

"And no politics," his mother said.

So Tommy told them the Boston Bruins were going to win the Stanley Cup, and Dougherty told him, "The season just started," and Tommy said, "Yeah, but they have Bobby Orr."

"So, the Canadiens aren't going to win it?"

Tommy said nope.

Dougherty looked at his sister and said, "So, Cheryl, how's CEGEP?"

He half expected her to get mad and yell at him, maybe he even wanted that, the peaceful dinner not what he'd expected at all, but instead she said, "It's okay. It's really just more high school, but they don't take attendance."

"So, do you bother to go to class?"

She looked at him, more exasperated than upset. "Yes, I go to class." There was even a little smile.

They finished the turkey and cleared the table and had pumpkin pie and whipped cream for dessert. Dougherty volunteered to wash the dishes if Cheryl would dry, the way they had when he'd lived at home. To his surprise she said sure.

364 Later that night Dougherty and his father sat at the kitchen table in the quiet house and shared a couple of drinks and some small talk.

Dougherty felt good when he left. But he didn't go straight home.

He drove through Greenfield Park and into St. Lambert. It was barely out of his way and he cruised through the newer part of the suburb — post-war bungalows and split-levels, nice houses, more expensive than the semi-detatched his parents had bought in the Park, maybe something his father's boss might live in, but not a company vice-president or anything like that.

He turned onto Robitaille Street. It was deserted. Cars in driveways and TV light flickering in living room windows.

Nothing to show that a man had been kidnapped here the day before.

It didn't look anything like Redpath Crescent at the foot of Mount Royal, lined with old stone houses — mansions — and now also with police.

There was a single cop car in front of 725, a guy in the driver's seat and another in the passenger seat. They both stared at Dougherty as he drove by but didn't move.

The house was about twenty feet back from the street. There was a driveway beside a neatly trimmed front lawn. The lawn where a kid threw a football to his uncle and a car pulled up and men got out. Men who shoved a gun in a man's face, then forced him into the car and drove away.

Men forcing people into cars. Politicians. Women. Girls.

It was a fucking epidemic.

Dougherty sped up, turned the corner and didn't look back.

The next morning he was in Station Ten at seven thirty along with every other cop on the day and night shift. Delisle got them all together in the parade room and told them Captain Perreault would be talking to them. A few minutes later, the captain came out of his office. It was the first time Dougherty had ever seen a captain address the troops, and by the looks of the older cops in the station house he had a feeling it was the first time for most of them, too.

Captain Perreault started by saying, in French, "As you know, all vacations have been cancelled. Every officer of the Montreal police is working double shifts. These kidnappings are not our number one priority, they are our *only* priority."

He paused and looked around the room, and there was enough grumbling for Dougherty to know he wasn't the only one who could think of a few other priorities.

"Every man on every police force in the province — the QPP, the RCMP, *every* police force — is working this." He paused again and the grumbling died down and no one said anything. "Now, this is a very difficult situation, we all know this. The lives of two men, two very important men, are at stake. As you know, the kidnappers have demanded that all police action be stopped. Of course, we're not doing that, but we are using the utmost discretion." Another pause, another slow look around the room. More tension, every cop in the place feeling it.

Detective Boisjoli said, *"Tabarnak, Denis, c'est fou,"* and Dougherty was thinking, Yeah, that's for sure, but "crazy" might not be the word I'd use.

Perreault said, "Kid gloves. We don't want to make them . . ." and he paused again before settling on, "nervous. No one is to attempt individual action. No unpremeditated moves by individuals or partners. If anyone finds a strong lead as to the whereabouts to either of the hostages, bring that information back here."

Everyone in the room knew how ridiculous this all was but no one said anything. They could all tell Captain Perreault was just reading something he'd been sent from higher up. It was likely every captain in every station in the city was reading the same thing.

"If and when there are solid leads," Perreault said, "contigency plans will be put in motion, the first goal of which is to free these two men safely." Another pause, another look around the room. "After that the guilty parties will be taken, but only then."

Someone said, "Taken down," and someone else said, "All the way down."

Captain Perreault looked at Sergeant Delisle and said, *"Bien, au travail."*

Deslisle said, "You heard the man — let's get to work."

Cops started filing out of the station and Dougherty stepped up to Delisle, but before he could say anything, the sergeant said, "You're back on Redpath."

"What for?"

"That's your job. We're now covering every consulate, every diplomat, every judge, every minister in the government. We're swamped — we have far more to cover than we have men."

Dougherty said, "Why don't they hire their own security, get Pinkertons or Burns or something?"

"They have, they're swamped, too."

"And you want me standing around on the street?"

"It's important for the Cross family to see the police," Delisle said. "And for the reporters. Go."

"Look," Dougherty said, "there are other things we need to do."

"Dog-eh-dee, you just do your job, okay?"

And right now Dougherty's job was to stand in front of the house on Redpath Crescent and do nothing.

The only thing that happened all day was in the early afternoon when a cop on a horse came down from Mount Royal and clopped along Redpath. The Cross daughter came out of the house with the maid and they fed the horse some apples. It was probably the first time the daughter — and the maid — had smiled since this whole thing started for them a week ago.

Then it was back to standing around and doing nothing.

The reporter, Logan, came by in the afternoon, and Dougherty asked if there was anything else going on in the world.

"A plane was hijacked in Iran and taken to Bagdad. They're demanding the release of twenty-one political prisoners."

"Only twenty-one," Doughetry said, "we can beat that. Anything else?"

Logan took a pack of cigarettes out of his sports coat, Export A's, and held it out to Dougherty, who took one. "We're recognizing Red China, so Chinese Taiwan is closing its embassy in Ottawa."

"That's one we don't have to cover."

Logan said, "Very funny." Then he motioned towards the house. "Anything going on here?"

Dougherty told him about the horse, and Logan said he might be able to use that. "Human interest. I heard Mrs. Cross identified a picture — you know anything about that?"

"From the last time they tried to kidnap someone,

the American."

"That's the cab driver?"

Dougherty said, "I think so."

"Master criminals."

"They've got us jumping through hoops."

"Yeah," Logan said, "but you're all jumping through the same hoop."

"I read the papers," Dougherty said, "you're jumping through it, too."

Before Logan could say anything, a dark sedan pulled up in front of the house and two men in overcoats jumped out and rushed past Dougherty and into the house.

Logan said, "Inspector Roland Jodin, intelligence squad, organized crime, undercover operations," and Dougherty said, "We call it the Social Security Squad. And he's Chief-Inspector."

"I'll be sure and mention that." Logan was writing in his notebook.

"He's been running the CAT Squad for months."

"I know," Logan said. "What do you think's going on?"

"I think if you want to know what's going on, standing next to me is the last place you should be."

Logan didn't smile, but Dougherty could tell he appreciated the joke.

About half an hour later, Jodin and the other detective came out of the house, got back in their car and drove away.

Then Gagnon came out and lit a cigarette and Dougherty said to him, *"C'est quoi?"*

"They got another note."

Logan said, "Another communiqué?"

Gagnon shook his head. "No, from Cross. Handwritten."

"What did it say?"

"Not much. Said he listened to Bourassa's three-minute speech on the radio and that he was well."

"That's it?"

"Then there was the usual stuff probably dictated by the kidnappers, you know, how he's sure they will keep their word and release him once all the political prisoners get to Cuba or Algeria or wherever. Then he says, 'Thank you for saving my life and that of Mr. Laporte.' That's it."

Logan was looking at the house and said, "Shit, they must be going crazy in there."

And Dougherty was thinking, Shit, I'm going crazy out here, standing around doing nothing.

Gagnon said, "Maybe the negotiator will get something."

"What negotiator?"

"The government named a negotiator," Logan said, "some lawyer namd Demers."

"Who's he supposed to negotiate with?"

"The FLQ lawyer, Lemieux."

"Didn't he get arrested?"

"Don't they tell you anything?" Logan said and held up his hand. "Of course not, what am I thinking. Yeah, Lemieux was arrested but Demers is meeting with him in his jail cell."

Dougherty said, "Shit. That sounds like a publicity stunt."

"Everything they do is a publicity stunt."

Dougherty looked at the house. "Tell that to them."

THIRTY-TWO

"Well, he's fucking right, they are bandits."

"Every one of them. They can't be seriously thinking of letting them out of jail."

"Sending them to Cuba."

"Or Algeria, they'll just come right back, start robbing banks again."

Dougherty was leaning against Delisle's desk and staying out of the conversation — all these cops talking about Pierre Trudeau's speech. Not really a speech, he'd been walking into the Parliament Buildings and a bunch of reporters started yelling questions at him, so Trudeau, being Trudeau, stopped to talk to them. Prime Minister of the country, two men kidnapped and he was toying with reporters.

Some of it had been on TV but Dougherty hadn't seen it, so he'd read the story in the paper, the headline, "An angry Trudeau is interviewed: 'Weak-kneed bleeding hearts hit.'" But it wasn't really an interview, either. One of the reporters had said something about all these "men with guns around here," and Trudeau took over, saying, "What's your worry?" and "Have they pushed you around?" and the reporter said, "They've pushed around friends of mine," and Trudeau said, "Yeah? What were your friends doing?" He was still smiling then, playing with the reporters, but then he was the one who got serious first.

Some combat troops had been called out to Ottawa to show the flag around Parliament; that's what the reporter said he was worried about. But he didn't have much of an answer when Trudeau asked him what his position was, would he give in to blackmail? And it just got worse after that, Trudeau easily backing the guy into a corner and the guy saying, "Well, I don't know."

Then Trudeau told reporters they shouldn't use the term "political prisoners." "They've been tried before the courts and condemned to prison terms, you should stop calling them political prisoners. They're outlaws, they're criminal prisoners."

Dougherty was looking over at all the cops in the room, thinking there probably wasn't a single one of them who'd supported Trudeau before, but they sure agreed with him now. And they agreed with him when he said we had to get rid of people who are trying to run the government by kidnapping and blackmail.

A reporter finally asked Trudeau how far he would go, and the prime minister said, "Just watch me," and then he said it again, that it was only weak-kneed bleeding hearts who were afraid to take these measures.

Delisle was talking then, trying to get everyone's attention, but no one listened until he said "a fingerprint on the communiqué from Laporte's kidnappers," and then they all looked up. "A guy name Paul Rose. We know him."

There was a lot of grumbling in the room then, and Delisle held up his hands and said, "You'll all be picking people up today — the detectives have the assignments."

One of the older uniform cops said, "Hey Delisle, is the army coming here?"

"No. The federal government can't send in the army. Bourassa has to ask for it."

"Come on, he does what he's told. Have we asked for it?"

"No."

The meeting was already breaking up into smaller groups, a half-dozen detectives taking three or four uniforms each.

Boisjoli waved Dougherty over and said, "Come with me."

"I'm up at Redpath," Dougherty said. "A squirrel might run on the lawn."

"The night shift is staying," the detective said. "They can sleep in their cars in the day as easily as in the night. We're going to St. Henri, come on."

"Back to St. Henri?" Dougherty said, and Boisjoli said, "That's right."

"Now we can get rid of all these commies."

They spent the morning rousting people out of bed

in row houses in St. Henri. The first time one of the long-haired guys called him a "jack-booted thug," Dougherty said, "I'm wearing shoes," but after a while he was starting to feel the part and not liking it very much.

After lunch Boisjoli told him they got a call and they drove fast to Place Bonaventure and met the bomb squad, Vachon and Meloche.

Vachon said, "The call said it was here. It didn't say if it was in the hotel or the mall or the exhibition place. It could be anywhere."

Boisjoli said, "Another communiqué?" and Meloche said, "Maybe, but it could also be a bomb, be careful."

"This is crazy," one of the cops said, and Vachon said, "Yes, of course it is."

They split up and searched.

Half an hour later, Vachon found it in a garbage can in the hotel lobby. By the time Dougherty got there he saw a few reporters were there, too, and he stepped up to Logan and said, "You got here fast."

"We got here before you did." He motioned to one of the other reporters and told him, "He found it."

Dougherty helped move the hotel staff and other people out of the lobby, and then stood by the door with the other cops and some reporters.

They watched Vachon, by himself in the lobby, take the blue Expo 67 flight bag out of the garbage can and slowly pull the zipper. When he reached in and pulled out an alarm clock and said, "No bomb," Dougherty could feel everyone in the place let out breath.

"It doesn't look like a communiqué," Vachon said. He held up a white envelope.

The senior guy at the scene, Boisjoli, said, "Give it here," and he opened it. It was a single typewritten page in English. Boisjoli said, "It's for the FLQ lawyer. It says: 'To Robert Lemieux, a real dirty bastard.'"

Some of the cops laughed, but Dougherty looked at Logan and saw the reporter writing in his notebook. "This isn't going to be good," he said, and Logan said, "But it's going to be good for the paper."

Boisjoli read some more, a little about how Lemieux worked for dirty anarchists and accepted stolen money for his fees, and then he read, "If anything happens to Mr. Cross, we shall come and slaughter you and yours. If any prisoner is released and leaves the country, we will kill members of their family. This is no joke."

"*Siboire.*"

"It's signed 'The Canadian Vigilantes,'" Boisjoli said.

"It's bullshit."

"Well," Boisjoli said, "we should warn Lemieux anyway."

As people were filing out, Dougherty looked at Logan. "Are you going to report this?"

"It's news."

"But it's probably bullshit."

Logan said, "It's interesting they didn't mention Laporte."

"Why?"

"I'm not sure. Maybe they're Irish. Did you know Cross is Irish?"

Dougherty said, "But he's the British Trade Commissioner."

"Yeah, but he's from Belfast, Irish Protestant."

375

"So? This is still bullshit."

"Haven't you been following the news in Ireland? They're killing people every day — they make these FLQ guys look like amateurs. They could be here, or they could have family here."

"We've never heard anything about that."

"Maybe you're hearing it now. Anyway," Logan said, "this'll probably get buried on page six, there's so many other stories."

"And they're all bullshit," Dougherty said.

Logan flipped through his notebook. "The result of terrorism is that people are ready after a time for any police madness to restore peace." Then he looked at Dougherty and asked, "That what you're doing?"

"You want a comment from me?"

"How about this?" He looked back at the notebook. "In Germany in 1932 extremists claiming to act for the workers led the country towards anarchy and that brought Hitler."

"Who said that?"

Logan was walking away then, saying, "They all want to be Che but they all end up being Stalin."

Dougherty followed him through the lobby and went back to work thinking, Commies and Hitler, right here in Montreal.

And now the Irish, was it possible? Like Dougherty, 376 the Higgins brothers and Danny Buckley and most of the other guys in the Point were Irish, but could any of them be connected to anybody in Ireland?

Then Dougherty realized, Sure, why not?

This was as bad as it could get. And then on Saturday it got a lot worse.

CHAPTER
THIRTY-THREE

The Paul Sauvé Arena was packed, three thousand people all chanting, "F-L-Q! F-L-Q!"

Dougherty stood by one of the back doors with a few other cops, keeping the peace.

The speeches went on for hours, all the bigwigs onstage fired up. It was like a tent revival meeting.

The lawyer, Robert Lemieux, out of jail now and not looking too worried about the Irish, gave a rousing speech, real fire and brimstone, and then one of the union leaders, Michel Chartrand, gave a speech and the crowd chanted, *"Le Québec aux Québécois! Le Québec aux Québécois! Le Québec aux Québécois!"*

One of the cops said to Dougherty, "So, when we get our police union, you don't get to join, Dog-eh-dee," and he laughed. Another cop said, "No, Dog-eh-dee is half French, half of him gets to join," then the other cop said, "What about Mancini, he's Italian," and they looked at the young cop and then motioned "out" with their thumbs. "You gotta go, kid."

One of the older cops said, *"Ce n'est pas drôle,"* and Dougherty agreed it wasn't funny, but knew better than to get into it.

The speeches went on for another couple of hours, all of them demanding that the government release the "political prisoners" and one of them calling the kidnappings a huge victory, no matter the outcome, because they meant the beginning of popular power.

"And the end of us."

Dougherty looked at the older cop. "Come on, even in the communist paradise they need cops, don't they?"

"I don't know what the fuck is going on. All the students went on strike today, did you hear? All the universities and the colleges, shut down." The older cop was looking lost.

Dougherty said, "They're just kids; they like the excitement."

"Ce n'est pas un jeu."

"I know," Dougherty said, "it's not a game."

The rally finally ended with more chanting: *"Le Québec aux Québécois!"*

When Dougherty got to Station Ten at six thirty the next morning Detective Boisjoli was already there and called him over to his desk. He started in right away. "This Buckley in the Point — how well you know him?"

"I know him okay. What's going on?"

"Looks like you were right — he's one of the guys hijacked the truck, the cigarettes."

"You got him?"

"We got a guy owns a bar, says he bought some of the smokes."

"From Buckley?"

"Maybe, he won't say." Boisjoli shrugged and picked up a pack of cigarettes from his desk and got one out. "We were talking to him about the people in his bar, the connections to this other thing," and he lit his cigarette and waved the match around and Dougherty realized he meant the kidnappings. "And he offered up the smokes."

"We're going to pick these guys up?"

Boisjoli shook his head. "This guy won't identify anybody. But look, it's a lot of smokes — they got to be keeping them somewhere. Maybe you can find out where."

"Me?"

Boisjoli looked around the room and then at Dougherty and shrugged.

Dougherty said, "Okay," and he was thinking of ways he could do it, running into Buck-Buck, buying more hash, asking about cigarettes, just working it into the conversation.

"If you can, you can," Boisjoli said. Then he put the cigarette in the corner of his mouth and went back to the papers on his desk. "If not, don't worry about it."

"Sure, I'll do it."

Then Sergeant Delisle said, "Dougherty, take Gagnon and get down to HQ. They need more bodies."

"When you get a chance," Boisjoli said.

On the drive down the hill to Old Montreal, Gagnon said, "Bourassa made another offer. Calls this one the final offer."

"What is it?"

"He says they will speed up parole for five of the prisoners."

"He call them political prisoners?"

"I don't know. And he said safe passage to the country of their choice for the kidnappers."

Dougherty said, *"Tabarnak,"* and Gagnon said, "I know. He says they have six hours."

They spent the morning taking prisoners from the cells in the basement to the interrogation rooms on the third floor and back.

Then when Dougherty came back from lunch, a couple of steamed hot dogs and fries, the desk sergeant said, "Get over to the Nelson — you know it?"

The hotel was only a couple of blocks away and when he got there Dougherty saw a crowd had spilled out onto the cobblestone street of Place Jacques Cartier, yelling and waving fists in the air.

Dougherty joined in with the other cops pushing people back, grabbing them and tossing them aside until a couple of cops made their way out with a man walking between them. The mob was shouting at the guy the cops were dragging out, and Dougherty and a few other uniforms got between them and the crowd. They took the guy up the street towards St. James and the crowd stayed where it was. When they were a block away the guy said, "Bloody hell," and he was smiling.

"What happened?" Dougherty said.

One of the cops said, "Lemieux quit."

They were walking back towards police HQ on Bonsecours Street.

"Who quit?"

"The FLQ lawyer."

Dougherty remembered him then from the night before at the Paul Sauvé. Then he looked at the guy they'd pulled out of the crowd and said, "What's your story?"

The guy was still smiling. "I asked him to give a statement in English. I'm with Reuters."

"So what happened?"

The guy had a British accent. "They didn't like that, mate."

Back at HQ, the Reuters guy said, "Well, now I've got a story," and went off to write it.

Dougherty spent the rest of the day taking guys back and forth from the cells to the third floor until he got relieved a little after eleven. He went home and changed, then drove down the hill to the Point.

He parked his Mustang in the lot behind the Arawana Tavern and was on his way in when he saw the Lincoln cruise by on Wellington.

Fuck.

He ran back, jumped in his Mustang and sprayed gravel onto Bridge Street and around the corner.

There was no goddamned way this could be a coincidence. Again.

Dougherty cruised to the intersection, but he couldn't see the car. It had either turned right and headed over the Victoria Bridge or gone straight, through the Wellington Tunnel towards downtown.

Fuck.

He floored it into the tunnel.

Out the other end, the street was deserted.

It was possible the Lincoln got that far ahead of him, but it didn't seem likely.

He jumped the median and went back through the tunnel. It had one lane of traffic in each direction and a couple of streetcar tracks down the middle that weren't used anymore.

Out the other side, he ran the red light, screeching around the corner and racing towards the bridge, but when he bumped onto the metal slats of the roadway he could see all the way to the South Shore and there was no Lincoln. No cars at all.

Dougherty had to drive all the way across the bridge then and turn around in St. Lambert, and he was still shaking when he got back onto the pavement. As he drove up Bridge Street past the Autostade he realized the Lincoln could have taken Mill Street. He'd lost it before he'd even gotten into his own car.

But that had to be it. A white Lincoln with a black roof.

It must have some connection with the Point.

Dougherty decided then to spend every off-duty minute he could in the neighbourhood until he saw the car again.

Driving up the hill towards his apartment, Dougherty heard the news on the radio that Bourassa had formally requested emergency powers, and there was the prime minister's voice saying, "The government is acting to make clear to kidnappers, revolutionaries and assassins that, in this country, laws are made and changed by the elected representatives of all

Canadians — not by a handful of self-selected dictators. Those who gain power by terror, rule by terror. The government is acting, therefore, to protect your life and liberty."

The War Measures Act was invoked.

At dawn the next day, Hercules aircraft started landing at St. Hubert air force base and long lines of camouflage-green trucks started crossing the bridges into Montreal.

Then Pierre Laporte was murdered, his body left in the trunk of a car a few miles from his home.

PART FOUR

THIRTY-FOUR

When Dougherty heard that Laporte had been strangled, he thought, Were his nipples bitten off, too?, but
he knew he was the only one in the room thinking of
other murders.

Sunday morning, October 18.

The tabloids, the *Journal de Montréal* and the
Sunday Express, both had half their front pages taken
up with headlines: "*Le cadavre de Pierre Laporte
retrouvé,*" and "Laporte killed," the other half featur-
ing the same photo of the opened car trunk and the
body inside.

Captain Perreault was standing in front of the cops
of Station Ten, saying that with the army in town, all
the cops were being pulled off emergency duties — and

then he said, "babysitting," in English — and put back on proper police work. "We now have the power to arrest whoever we want, whenever we want. We will be taking all of the suspects to Parthenais jail and keeping them there as long as we need to."

A detective said, "No warrants?" and Perreault said, "No, no warrants needed."

Dougherty was looking at the other cops, no one smiling, no one joking around, no gung-ho comments, nothing like the charged-up dressing room before heading out onto the ice feel it usually was before nightclub raids or strapping on the riot gear.

And Perreault didn't finish with any kind of rousing go get-'em, boys. He just nodded towards Detective Boisjoli and said, "Claude."

"Okay, men, we have identified two more." He pointed at the mug shots thumbtacked to the bulletin board. "Marc Charbonneau and Paul Rose."

Dougherty was a little surprised to see both men had short hair, although they both did have beards.

"Charbonneau is a cabbie and Rose is a teacher," Boisjoli said. "Also, Rose has a cataract on his left eye."

Dougherty had moved closer to the mug shots and was looking at the others on the board, most of them the usual petty crooks and pimps they were always looking for downtown. He did notice a couple of new ones wanted for selling drugs, and then he saw that the alert from the RCMP with the updated FBI Most Wanted List now included two women, Susan Edith Saxe and Katherine Ann Power, both students at Brandeis University, wanted for the killing of a Boston cop during a bank robbery.

"Yeah, we can look for them, too."

Gagnon was standing beside him, and Dougherty said, "Don't you think we'll be busy?"

"Yeah, picking up radicals. He says we can pick up draft dodgers now," he said, motioning to Boisjoli, who was talking to a couple of uniform cops. Then Gagnon looked at the FBI list and said, "They might be with the draft dodgers. Come on."

They spent the day busting into apartments and dragging people out.

Five hundred and twenty-six people in 319 raids. Every cop in the city working double shifts. But they didn't get Charbonneau or Rose, and no one they did get was talking or seemed to know anything.

It was after midnight when Dougherty finally got off duty, and he went straight home and changed and drove down to the Point to look for the Lincoln. He drove around for a couple of hours and parked on a few side streets, watching what little traffic there was. He had the radio on and heard a lot of talk about how they should be rounding up everybody who ever said the words Front de Libération du Quebec, and when they found the ones who killed Laporte they should put them up against a wall and shoot them.

One of the radio stations also read out Pierre Trudeau's address to the House of Commons. It was one time when the slow, solemn voice of the news guy was probably close to the way Trudeau sounded: "With this deed the FLQ has sewn the seeds of its own destruction. It has revealed that it has no mandate but terror, no policies but violence and no solutions but murder. It is alien to all that is Canadian. It will not survive. Those men with hatred in their hearts thought they could divide us in tragedy, but they bring us together today in a same will. For the only passion that must drive us now is the passion for justice. Through justice we will get rid of the perversion of terrorism. Through justice we will find peace and freedom."

Dougherty listened to the whole thing, unconvinced. He'd spent the day shoving people into police cars, not telling their families where they were going or when they could ever see them again, people screaming at him, calling him fascist pig. Didn't seem like the kind of thing that was going to bring people together.

And he didn't spot the Lincoln.

On Tuesday the whole province shut down for the funeral of Pierre Laporte. And then it was back to business. The army in the streets and double shifts for every cop. More people rounded up, more leads, thousands of tips phoned in, no sign of the Laporte kidnappers and no sign of James Cross.

The first Monday in November the governments of Canada and Quebec announced they were joining together to offer a $150,000 reward for information leading to the arrest of the kidnappers.

Dougherty was in Station Ten when the phone started ringing off the hook, and after taking a few calls Delisle just let it ring. He looked at Dougherty and said, "Do you know where Cross is? He's in the new residence at Université de Québec. No, wait, he's already in Cuba. No, he's in New York, being guarded by Black Panthers. God dammit."

The bigger news that day for cops was that Ottawa had replaced the War Measures Act with something called the Public Order Temporary Measures Act. It made being a member of the FLQ or helping the kidnappers in any way punishable by five years in jail, but it allowed people who were arrested to have access to their lawyer and said they could only be held for three days. The new act also had an expiry date of April 30, 1971.

"So," Delisle said, putting down the memo he'd been sent. "We got a lot of guys to round up before this takes effect."

Dougherty said, "Tonight."

"Yeah, come back after your shift on Redpath."

"I thought the army was handling that?"

"Not Redpath," Delisle said. "Mrs. Cross doesn't want the army in the street, just a couple of cops, regular uniforms."

Dougherty said okay, and Delisle said, "And try not to stand out."

Right, Dougherty thought, try to look like a security guard.

"And come back here when you get relieved."

Dougherty stood around all day on Redpath Crescent and nothing happened, not even a horse eating an apple. When he was finally relieved at close to seven, Dougherty grabbed a quick smoked-meat at Ben's on his way back to Station Ten.

The place filled up through the evening as the raiding teams were put together. Delisle had a list of nightclubs they were going to hit and handed out assignments, saying, "We're handling the downtown clubs: Danny's Villa, the Boiler Room, Winston Churchill and the Whiskey à Go-Go." He looked up from his list, "Hey Dog-eh-dee, you want to take the One and Two in the Point?"

"Not if I don't have to," and then he said, "Okay, yeah, I will."

"Okay, and some of you guys are helping out in the west end: we got the Big Ben Pub on Côte des Neiges, the Little Old Pub, Blue Top Lounge on St. James, a few more — see the detectives." He did a little spin in the middle of the room before stepping behind his desk.

Dougherty met up with the cops at Station Nine in the Point and the detective in charge, Kennedy, spoke English to them. "The place is a little different than last time: there are some bikers hanging out there now as well as the usual thugs. This is going to be fun."

They hit the One and Two just after midnight, going in the front and back doors at the same time.

Kennedy yelled, "Nobody move!" but the place was already going crazy, people taking off in every direction. There were a couple of bikers who wanted to fight and a few other guys who wanted to fight and plenty of cops to make it happen.

Dougherty saw Danny Buckley heading for the bathroom and slammed him into the wall, pressing the nightstick across his neck and shoving as hard as he could. Buck-Buck went down, grabbing Dougherty, and the two rolled around on the floor, swinging fists and even landing a few punches. Buck-Buck managed to get up and half-crawl, half-run out the back door, but Dougherty caught him in the lane and bodychecked him into the brick wall and got in a good shot with the nightstick across the back of his head. Buck-Buck went down covered in blood.

"Fuck you, Eddie."

People were spilling out of the bar and cops were chasing them.

Buckley crawled to the garbage cans, and Dougherty said, "How much you got on you, Buck-Buck?"

"Fuck you."

"They want you for the cigarettes, too, the truck hijacking."

"Eat shit."

The lane was quiet then, the bar empty except for the handcuffed bikers, the bartender and a few other people the cops would be taking back to Station Twelve.

"If there was a Higgins in there we'd take him," Dougherty said, "but you'll do."

Buckley made a move and Dougherty stepped on his hand, driving his boot down hard. He heard bones break. "Is it just hash?"

"Fuck you."

"You know the fun part," Dougherty said. "We get to keep you locked up as long as we want."

"Let me go."

"You're going away for a long time, Buck-Buck, grown-up fucking prison now. How's your French? You're gonna need it inside."

"Fuck you."

Dougherty leaned down and grabbed a handful of hair. "No, say fuck me — that's what they're gonna make you say."

Buckley squirmed and Dougherty let go of the hair and stood up, the heel of his boot still on Buck-Buck's hand. "And everybody's gonna know you talked, Buck-Buck, everybody we pick up now."

"I'm not saying shit."

"That doesn't matter, you know that. You go in tonight and everybody we pick up, every fucking Higgins brother we get is going to think you gave him up."

Buck-Buck rolled over a little and looked up at Dougherty. "I know who's driving the car you're looking for, the Lincoln."

Dougherty grabbed him, picked him up by the throat, slammed him into the wall.

"Who?"

"I don't know his name."

Now Dougherty had two hands on Buck-Buck's throat, squeezing as hard as he could. "He killed Brenda Webber."

Choking, barely getting words out, "M-maybe."

Squeezing harder.

"Who is it?"

"G-guy w-works for F-Frank."

Harder.

"What's his name?"

"I-I don't know. C-Craig, I think."

Dougherty punched him in the face. "How do you know?"

"He w-works for a custom b-broker. F-Frank uses h-him sometimes for p-paperwork."

"That's all you know?"

"Yeah."

Dougherty hit him again and let go of his neck and Buck-Buck fell to his knees, gulping air.

Dougherty said, "He fucking killed Brenda Webber."

"Maybe."

Dougherty kicked him in the stomach, knocking him over. "You're fucking scum."

Buck-Buck didn't even look back, just crawled off, staggered to his feet and ran.

By the end of the night the cops had hit thirty bars and arrested nine guys with outstanding warrants. They also got a lot of hash, marijuana and even heroin, plus guns, hoods, handcuffs, 16 mm porno movies and some illegal hockey lottery tickets.

And Dougherty had something to tell Carpentier.

CHAPTER
THIRTY-FIVE

The next day a picture of James Cross sitting on a wooden crate full of dynamite was delivered to the *Québec-Presse* newspaper and ran on the front page of newspapers around the world.

Dougherty got to Station Ten first thing in the morning and told Delisle he was going to find Detective Carpentier, but Delisle said, "No, you're not — you're going to Redpath Crescent."

"I need to talk to the detective."

"He's busy, Dougherty — all the detectives are busy."

"This is important."

"Tell it to me."

"I have a lead on a murder," Dougherty said.

"Oh, for Christ's sake, you're a constable. Go with

Gagnon, he's going to drop you off."

"I'm not taking a car?"

"All the cars are in use. You don't need one standing around."

"I don't need to be standing around."

"Go, Dougherty, right now."

So Dougherty spent another morning standing in front of the house on Redpath, but in the early afternoon the reporter, Logan, came by and Dougherty asked him if he was going back to the *Gazette* office.

"Why, you got a story?"

"I got nothing," Dougherty said. "But I could use a ride."

"You don't have a car?"

Dougherty shook his head. "They're all out picking people up; we just stand here."

"So don't you have to stay?"

Dougherty pointed to the other cop in front of the house, a beat cop close to retirement. "Don't you think he can handle anything that happens?"

In the car Logan said, "This isn't personal time, is it?" and Dougherty said, "I told you, it's nothing."

"I don't believe you."

They were heading down Beaver Hall Hill, and Dougherty told him, "I can get out at the bottom here, Victoria Square."

"How about this," Logan said, "when whatever it is you're working on happens, you tell me first?"

"There's nothing to tell."

"I've seen plenty of cops sneaking off to get laid," Logan said. "And they don't have that look on their faces." He was pointing at Dougherty, his business card between his fingers. "Call me."

Dougherty slammed the car door and walked down McGill Street towards the customs building. Past Victoria Square he crossed Craig Street and thought for a second that Buck-Buck had been shitting him. Then he remembered the real fear in his eyes. Buck-Buck was afraid of him, and Dougherty liked how it felt and wanted to feel it some more.

McGill Street, the western edge of Old Montreal, was lined with office buildings. Most of the offices were filled with custom brokers and importers, businesses that needed to be close to the port. A couple of blocks farther west were a few parking lots, probably for a couple thousand cars.

Dougherty spent an hour walking through the lots and then up and down the side streets in the area and found two white Lincolns. They were both pretty well-kept cars. He wrote down the licence plate numbers.

Then he walked to the customs building, a big old stone fortress on Place D'Youville. Dougherty watched people going in and out of the big front doors, a sign beside each one — *Douanes* on the left and *Customs* on the right. Lots of young men who could be Craig, probably runners for the brokers and importers, clearing things through customs. It seemed the Higgins Brothers were moving up from just losing the odd crate coming off a ship and doing some importing themselves.

Walking back up McGill Street, Dougherty stopped at the parking garage and looked for the attendant. The garage was about six storeys high and had an elevator that moved the cars up and down and made a hell of a noise.

After a couple of minutes, an old guy came out of the darkness of the garage, wiping his hands on his shirt, and said, "Keys," holding out his hand.

"No, I didn't park here," Dougherty said. "I'm looking for a car."

"Your car?"

"No, I'm looking for a Lincoln, you got one?"

"This isn't a dealership, kid."

"A white one, '65 or '66."

The guy said, "Yeah, maybe."

Dougherty said, "Show me."

"I can't do that."

"Yeah, sure you can — come on." Dougherty shoved the guy forward a little and the guy resisted for a second, then turned and took a few steps to the elevator controls. Then he motioned to the steel platform and said, "Okay."

Dougherty stepped on the platform and lost his balance when it jerked and lunged for a few feet until it got going and the ride smoothed out. When stopped at the sixth floor, Dougherty stepped off the platform and searched up and down the rows of cars until he found the Lincoln. Close up he realized it wasn't white, it was light blue, but the Brougham hard top was black so he wrote down the licence number anyway and went back to the elevator. He had to shout down a few times before the old guy started it up and brought him back down to street level.

Dougherty said, "Thanks," and the old guy said, "Don't mention it."

A few blocks east and Dougherty was at police HQ on Bonsecours Street. He went straight to the ident office, where he found Rozovsky separating a pile of photos into three stacks.

"I've got three licence numbers I have to look up."

Rozovsky looked up and was about to say something but stopped. "Give them here." He took the notebook page from Dougherty. "It'll take about half an hour."

"I'll wait."

Closer to an hour later, Rozovsky was back and handed the paper to Dougherty saying, "This your Lincoln?"

"Maybe." Three names and addresses. Dougherty said, "No Craig."

"Nope. You got Rejean Roberge, Anne Connelly and Jacques Filippi."

"Outremont, Dorval and Châteauguay."

"Where did you find these licence plate numbers?"

"Near the customs building. Do you know where Carpentier is now?"

"Probably Parthenais," Rozovsky said. "Interviewing people."

"How many are there now?"

"I don't know, hundreds. They're letting some go but they're picking up more all the time."

"I guess I'll have to check these out myself."

As he was walking out, he heard Rozovsky say, "Now you're getting the hang of it."

It was close to six now, so Dougherty took the Métro back to Guy and walked past Station Ten to his apartment. He changed and got into his Mustang and sat there for a moment, looking at the addresses Rozovsky had written down for him. Both Dorval and

Châteauguay would mean taking the expressway and that seemed the most likely. He drove down Guy and took the on-ramp to the 2-20 and headed west.

He sat in traffic and inched his way across the Mercier Bridge. After half an hour driving around Châteauguay, he found the address and ten minutes later the Lincoln pulled into the driveway and a middle-aged guy with a moustache got out and entered the house.

Dougherty got out of his car and walked by the house. It looked like *Leave It to Beaver*; Mom, Dad and the kids in a split-level bungalow in the suburbs.

This guy didn't look anything like the young cop from *Ironside*.

Dougherty walked around the block, then got back in his car. He was thinking it was possible Nancy Barber in NDG was wrong, that the guy who tried to pull her into the car was older. And had a moustache. And was wearing glasses.

It could be this guy. He could be a customs clerk, that's for sure.

But it was hard to imagine him working for the Higgins brothers.

Dougherty put him down as a maybe, drove back across the Mercier Bridge and kept going west to Dorval.

This house was a little more upscale than the one in Châteauguay; older, pre-war probably, bigger and set back on a bigger lot with a few mature trees. There was a separate garage at the end of the driveway behind the house and the whole place looked empty. To Dougherty it didn't look very lived-in: it looked more like the house of someone who was retired.

He parked a few houses down the street and walked back and up the driveway. He tried to look into the garage but the windows were covered. Up close, though, the garage wasn't big enough for a Lincoln anyway, so he headed back to his Mustang and waited for a while.

The street was dark. There were no streetlights or sidewalks and almost no people. A guy passed, walking a dog and a couple of cars pulled into driveways. Around nine some teenagers walked by and stared at Dougherty but kept going. He listened to the radio, CKGM playing all the hits, and he waited.

A little after ten, Dougherty drove the few blocks to Lakeshore Boulevard and found a restaurant and had a hamburger and a beer and then returned to the house and waited.

Just after midnight, the Lincoln pulled into the driveway and a guy in his mid-twenties got out, unlocked the side door of the house and went inside.

Dougherty sat bolt upright. He wanted to jump out and run to the house, bust in the door and drag the guy out. But he didn't move. He sat and watched as lights came on in the house, in the kitchen first and then the living room, and then the light of a TV.

A half hour later, the TV was turned off, the lights downstairs went out and a light came on upstairs. Dougherty watched and waited a few more minutes until those lights went out, too, and the house was dark.

He sat for a few more minutes, thinking this Lincoln may have been registered to Anne Connelly but the guy driving it and living in this house could sure be the guy they'd mistakenly called Bill for almost a year.

CHAPTER
THIRTY-SIX

"It's not really evidence," Carpentier said.

"But it's not nothing."

They were standing in the parking lot behind the courthouse. The building was packed, the arraignments of the most famous people who'd been picked up were starting — the lawyer, Lemieux; the labour leader, Chartrand; and even a writer, Pierre Vallières.

Carpentier took a drag on his cigarette. "No, it's not nothing, but under normal circumstances we would need a lot more."

"But these aren't normal circumstances," Dougherty said.

"No."

A dozen reporters and photographers rushed out

of the building towards a car that was pulling into the parking lot and swarmed it before the driver and his passenger could even get the doors open. Cops moved in then, pulling people away from the car, and there was a lot of shouting and shoving.

Dougherty said, "I started calling custom brokers first thing this morning. Craig Connelly works a few blocks from here. We can bring him in, talk to him."

"You don't think it's a little crowded?" Carpentier looked at the mob entering through the back door of the courthouse. "From here to Bonsecours Street and back, it's going to be like this all day."

"We can take him to Station Ten."

Carpentier thought for a second and then said, "Aren't you supposed to be on Redpath Crescent?"

"Mrs. Cross and her daughter are going to Switzerland, staying with family friends there."

"I can't believe this is still going on."

"Yeah, me, too."

After a moment, Carpentier dropped his cigarette on the ground and stepped on it. "Okay, let's go talk to this guy."

A few minutes later, they were parked in front of a ten-storey office building on McGill Street. Carpentier and Dougherty entered the building. There was a restaurant to their right and a bank on the left. Straight ahead in the small lobby was a wide staircase and beside that a couple of elevators.

"It's only the fourth floor," Dougherty said, starting up the stairs, but the elevator door was already opening.

"I'll meet you."

Dougherty got to the fourth floor at the same time as the elevator. Both men had turned the wrong way and stopped at a door marked *F.B. Allen — Importers-Exporters*.

The rest of the office doors on the fourth floor were custom brokers and shipping companies. At the far end of the hall, Carpentier opened a door marked *Garvey-McDonald — Freight Forwarders, Marine Insurance, Charter Brokers* and stepped into the office.

A young woman sitting behind a receptionist desk looked up, a little startled at Dougherty's uniform. "May I help you?"

"Yes, we'd like to talk to someone who works here," Carpentier said, "a Mr. Craig Connelly."

The receptionist said, "I'm sorry, he's not in right now," and then looked past the cops and said, "Oh, here he is now. Craig, these men want to talk to you."

Dougherty turned and saw the guy he'd seen the night before in Dorval.

The guy turned and ran.

Dougherty was after him, charging down the hall, and as he took the corner towards the stairs he ran into a woman coming out of F.B. Allen and knocked her over. The package she was carrying hit the floor and thousands of colourful beads bounced everywhere.

She said, "Oh my god," and Dougherty said, "Sorry," as he ran down the stairs.

On McGill Street he saw Connelly already a block away, pushing his way past people on the sidewalk.

Dougherty held up his hand and ran into the street, keeping his eyes on Connelly as he crossed St. Paul and kept going.

Carpentier was behind them in the car, coming up McGill fast, but Connelly ran into the Métro station entrance on the edge of Victoria Square.

At the bottom of the escalator, Dougherty saw Connelly disappear around the corner of the long, winding hallway and he kept running as fast as he could. He jumped a turnstile and ran down the stairs towards the tracks. Dougherty lunged and tackled him just as a train came speeding into the station on its rubber wheels.

Connelly struggled to get away and said, "No, let me jump," but Dougherty held him down, rolled him onto his stomach and got a knee into the small of his back. Connelly continued to struggle. "Why don't you just kill me now?"

The handcuffs locked around Connelly's wrists, and Dougherty stood up, still panting. "Come on."

"I want to die."

Dougherty bent down and grabbed Connelly by the elbows, stuck out behind his back like chicken wings, and said, "Get up, come on."

People were gathering around them then, and now Dougherty wasn't feeling at all like he'd expected to. He said it again, "Get up," and pulled a limp Connelly to his feet.

The crowd was closing in, and Dougherty said, "Okay, move aside. Give us some room, come on," and pushed the man towards the stairs.

As they walked, and as the crowd stared them down, Dougherty could feel Connelly rising up, muscles tensing, his whole body changing as they pushed through the crowd. By the time they were ascending the stairs, Connelly was practically snarling, his head snapping from side to side and saying, "What are you looking at?" He hissed at the ticket-taker in his booth as Dougherty shoved him through the turnstile and by the time they got out onto Victoria Square he was saying, "I'm telling you, you got the wrong guy."

And Dougherty was thinking, This is more like it.

Carpentier was waiting by the entrance to the Métro station.

"Good work."

"Thanks." Dougherty shoved Connelly into the back seat of the patrol car Carpentier had called to the scene. "I'll go with him?"

Carpentier said, "Yes, Bonsecours Street. I'll meet you there."

The madhouse at police HQ was still raging, with people being moved from the cells to the courthouse and back. Dougherty took Connelly up to the third floor and put him in an interrogation room.

Connelly said, "I don't know what you think is going on, but I didn't do anything."

Dougherty looked at him. "No? Then why did you want me to let you jump in front of the train?"

Connelly shook his head like he felt sorry for Dougherty and said, "I don't know what you're talking about. Anyway, I guess I better call a lawyer."

"Haven't you heard of the War Measures Act?" Dougherty said, "You don't get a lawyer."

For a second Connelly looked scared, but then he smiled a little. "We'll get this straightened out. It's a mistake, you'll see."

"Sure."

Dougherty stepped out into the hall and closed the door and saw Carpentier coming towards him, carrying some thick file folders. Another man was with Carpentier. He was in his late fifties, looking like he just came from the barber, and maybe the tailor with that brand new suit and tie.

Carpentier said, *"Voici le constable dont je vous ai parlé."* Then he looked at Dougherty. "Dougherty, this is Detective-Lieutenant Desjardins."

Desjardins had his hand out, and Dougherty shook it, saying, "Sir."

"Detective Carpentier said you did good work, Constable."

"Thank you, sir."

Desjardins gave a small nod, and then turned to Carpentier. "Okay, let's see what he says," he said, then went in to interrogate Connelly.

Carpentier pulled Dougherty away from the door and leaned in closer, saying, "Stick around. We'll talk in a while."

"Yes, sir."

Carpentier went into the interrogation room as well and the door closed.

The hallway was quiet, and Dougherty fought the urge to jump into the air and shout and punch a wall in celebration. He got himself under control and went in to the ident office to use the telephone. He dialled from memory.

When Ruth answered, Dougherty said, "We got him."

She started to say, who — then stopped and said, "Oh my god."

"Desjardins and Carpentier are questioning him now."

"You're sure? Oh shit, Eddie, this is fantastic."

"Yeah."

"You got him."

"Yeah," Dougherty said. "We did."

There was a pause. Dougherty didn't know what else to say, and he didn't know what he was expecting from Ruth. Finally, he said, "I guess you'll want to interview him, too?"

"Yes, I guess so."

"All right, well, I don't know how long they'll be. I'll call you later."

Ruth said, "Okay," and hung up.

Dougherty put the receiver back in its cradle and looked around for a chair.

Rozovsky said, "Did you hear we got him?"

"You're telling me?"

Rozovsky was stopped in the doorway. "An apartment on Queen Mary Road, traced a phone number from a piece of scrap paper in the Armstrong Street house. Only one guy, but he'll lead us to the rest."

"What are you talking about?"

"The Laporte kidnappers. We got one. What are you talking about?"

"The guy we were calling Bill. His name's Connelly."

Rozovsky stared at Dougherty. "Shit, you got him?"

"We got him."

"Five women he killed?"

"That's right."

"And you got him."

"Yeah."

A couple of hours later, Desjardins and Carpentier came out of the interrogation room and Carpentier said, "*Bon*, let's get drunk," and Dougherty went with the rest of the homicide squad to the bar across the street. They made their way through most of the bars in Old Montreal until the sun came up, and Dougerty went home and put on a clean dress uniform and drove Carpentier and Desjardins to Coleraine Street in the Point. He was amazed how the two men looked as if they'd each had a full night's sleep and figured it must be some detective trick. Or experience.

Arlene Webber opened the door to her parents' house and looked past the detectives to Dougherty and said, "You got him?"

Dougherty nodded and Arlene Webber said, "Good."

She didn't start crying until her mother came to the door, asking who it was, and then they were both crying.

When Joe Webber came to the door, Carpentier said, "May we come in?" and he and Desjardins walked back to the kitchen with the Webbers.

Dougherty waited outside on the stoop. He looked up and down the street, all the row houses quiet this early on Saturday morning, the whole Point St. Charles quiet.

Half an hour later, Desjardins and Carpentier came out of the house, and Dougherty drove them back downtown. After that it was like no one else in the world noticed. The rest of the city, the country, was still waiting for any little detail about the kidnapping, for any news about James Cross, praying he was still alive. And waiting for news about the manhunt for the men who had killed Pierre Laporte.

Dougherty didn't hear from Ruth until Thursday, when she phoned him and said, "He didn't do it."

"What?"

"Connelly. He didn't kill Marielle Archambeault, Shirley Audette or Jean Way."

"What are you talking about?"

"His teeth don't match."

CHAPTER
THIRTY-SEVEN

Dougherty said, "What about Sylvie Berubé and Brenda Webber?"

"It looks like just Brenda Webber."

"I was told the detectives found evidence at his house, his mother's house."

Ruth looked around the restaurant. They were at Ben's, sitting at a table by the big windows looking out on de Maisonneuve, and she lowered her voice a little and said, "Yes, they found clothes, underwear that belonged to Brenda."

"So, what is this, the teeth don't match?"

"The bite marks he left on the three women, the three downtown — they don't match Connolly's teeth."

"And that's it?"

Ruth shrugged. "No, there are other things. He was in Florida visiting his mother when Jean Way was killed."

"Shit." Dougherty finished his sandwich. "Only one. This must really screw up your progression theory?"

"I don't care about that. You think that's what this is about?"

Dougherty said, "No." He didn't know what it was about. He'd tried to call Ruth a few times since the arrest but she never answered at home or in her office. She hadn't even wanted to meet for lunch. She'd called to tell him that Connelly hadn't killed the other women, and then she'd told him she was moving to Toronto.

Now he said, "So what's going on?"

She pushed her plate away, one bite out of the sandwhich, and picked up the coffee cup. "Dr. Pendleton was excited. He was happy."

"The whole homicide squad celebrated for days."

"I'd already started doing other work. Remember I told you about Women's Studies?"

"At Sir George?"

"Yes, and now U of T is starting a program. I think I can do more good there."

"But you did good here."

She put the cup down and it clattered on the saucer. "I can't do it. I can't spend every day with death. I can't make a career out of it."

"But you're doing good. You knew he'd go after another woman — you kept the investigation going."

"You think anyone listened to me?" Then, before

413

Dougherty could say anything she said, "Don't worry, Pendleton is happy to keep working on it."

He noticed it was the first time she hadn't used "Dr." He said, "You've been thinking about this for a while?"

She said yes. She drank a little coffee, really just stalling before she said, "It's been a while. I didn't say anything — I wasn't sure."

"Sure, I get it." He didn't really, but he was starting to understand the reason he could never get a handle on Ruth was because she didn't have one on herself.

She said, "This doesn't have anything to do with you, Eddie."

"If you say so."

A couple of Jeeps and army trucks drove by on de Maisonneuve, followed by a city bus and a steady stream of cars. People were out walking. It was overcast and cold but there was no snow.

Finally Ruth said, "I guess you better be getting back to work."

Dougherty said, "Yeah, I guess."

On the sidewalk Ruth said, "Well, goodbye," and held out her hand. Dougherty shook it and then he watched her climb the hill towards McGill.

———

James Cross was released by his kidnappers on December 3.

A week earlier the police had finally found the hiding place, a house on Rue des Récollets, in the north end of Montreal. He'd been there the whole sixty days, taken straight there from his home on Redpath

Crescent. Never left the island of Montreal.

The house was put under surveillance and after watching it for days and deciding that storming the place would only end with the deaths of Cross and the kidnappers, negotiations began and it was agreed that in return for the safe release of Cross four kidnappers would be given safe passage to Cuba.

Dougherty stood in the parade room of Station Ten and watched it live on TV with a few other cops. Just before two o'clock in the afternoon, a grey Chrysler drove out of the garage and was escorted by dozens of motorcycle cops and police cars across Montreal and onto Île-Ste-Hélène, where Expo 67 had been, and which had been declared temporarily Cuban territory.

Delisle said, "Fucking cunt, I don't believe it."

The rest of the cops in the room couldn't believe it, either.

A little while later, a helicopter took off and flew to Dorval airport.

The cops muttered and grumbled, but by then no one was really surprised, and it played out the way it was supposed to. Four kidnappers were joined by a few others — one man's wife, another couple and a young boy — and they boarded a Canadian Armed Forces Yukon transport plane.

"There they fucking go."

The plane took off just before seven and flew directly to Havana.

415

A couple of days after Christmas, the three men who had kidnapped Pierre Laporte and were still at large were arrested in a farmhouse south of Montreal. The most embarrassing thing about it for the police was that all three men had been hiding behind a false wall in the closet in the apartment on Queen Mary Boulevard back in November when the place was raided and the fourth member of their cell was arrested.

At the end of May, Dougherty was sitting in Station Ten, filling out a report about a traffic accident between a bus and a taxi on Atwater Street when Detective Carpentier walked in.

"Hey Doe-er-tee, how you doing?"

"Good, Detective, you?"

"I thought you would be interested, the vampire killer, the man who bites the women breasts?"

"Yeah."

"He kill another woman in Calgary, and they got him."

Dougherty said, "You sure?"

Carpentier was still standing in the doorway. "Not yet, but it look like it. He rape and kill a woman and bite her breast. When they got him they found he lived here before he moved to Calgary, so they called. We're going out west to talk to him."

"That's good."

"Yeah."

"How did they catch him in the end?"

Carpentier shrugged a little and said, "His car. Somebody recognize the make."

Dougherty said, "Shit."

"Yeah, well, I just want to say, good work."

Dougherty said, "Thanks."

"You should take the detective exam as soon as you can."

After Carpentier left, Dougherty thought about

phoning Ruth in Toronto but decided not to. He could understand why she didn't want to spend her life dealing with murder and death.

He looked around Station Ten and decided that he liked being a cop.

AUTHOR'S NOTE

Many of the events in *Black Rock* really happened. Between 1968 and 1970 (the so-called "third wave" of terrorist activity in Quebec) over two hundred bombs were placed in and around Montreal and Robert Côté and his team dismantled almost all of them, including one in Eaton's (as it was known then) department store and one containing 150 pounds of dynamite in a Volkswagen in Old Montreal. But some bombs exploded. A bomb went off at the Montreal Stock Exchange, five bombs exploded in Westmount in one night, a bomb did destroy part of Mayor Drapcau's home, bombs went off at McGill University and City Hall and federal government buildings. Jeanne d'Arc Saint-Germain was killed by a bomb that exploded in a Defence Department building in Ottawa. And a man reputed to be a member of organized crime was killed when his car exploded on an expressway (the Metropolitan, not the Bonaventure). Every bomb in *Black Rock* is based on an actual bomb.

James Cross was kidnapped and Pierre Laporte was kidnapped and murdered. Shirley Audette, Marielle Archambeault and Jean Way were all murdered in Montreal by the same man, Wayne Boden, who was arrested in May 1971 in Calgary after killing another woman, Elizabeth Anne Porteous. It was the first time in Canadian history that forensic odontological evidence was used. Boden was not referred to at the time as a serial killer as that phrase was not then widely used.

At the time, the Montreal police also believed that Boden was guilty of murdering Norma Vaillancourt but he denied it, and in 1994 another man was convicted of that murder. Many Montreal police officers were assigned to the Combined Anti-Terrorist Squad along with officers from the Quebec Provincial Police and the RCMP during 1970.

In 1975 a teenager, Sharon Prior, was abducted in Point St. Charles and murdered. This case remains unsolved.

Two FLQ cells were arrested in 1970 in possession of dynamite, guns and press releases stating that they had kidnapped Moshe Golan, the Israeli Commercial Consul, and Harrison Burgess, the U.S. Consul General. The CN rail yards were robbed and nightclubs were raided during the October Crisis. Medicare was introduced in Quebec and the doctors threatened to strike and the specialists did withhold their services.

Many hospitals were only able to offer emergency care.

The topless rock band Eight of a Kind performed at the Hawaiian Lounge, and the Playboy Club in Montreal held its "Bunny of the Year" contest in October 1970. Police were called to the Women in Business Conference at Man and His World.

With more than a dozen abductions, 1970 was the "Year of the Kidnapping" around the world. In many cases prisoners were released and the kidnappers were allowed to go to Algeria or Cuba. In Uruguay, an American, Daniel Mitrione (who was working for the American "Agency for International Development," advising the Uruguayan government on police and internal security) was kidnapped and murdered.

The Black Rock is a real monument and the story it tells of the six thousand Irish immigrants who died on the ships, or in the sheds in Montreal, is true. My parents bought a red brick duplex in Greenfield Park and I read the Montreal *Gazette* after I delivered the papers. I also delivered the *Sunday Express,* including the edition with the picture of Pierre Laporte's body in the trunk of the car on the front page. I was eleven years old.

Of course, *Black Rock* is a novel and many of the events and characters in the book are entirely fictional. Any mistakes in the research are entirely mine. I'd like to thank everyone who helped in the writing of this book.

My sister Susan Bentley, my cousin Linda McFetridge, my brother Robert McFetridge (who joined the police in 1968, but the RCMP rather than the Montreal police), Robert Côté, Harold Rosenberg (and the

Montreal Police Museum), Barbara McIlwaine (who didn't frequent every bar in the Point, but knew most of their names), Randy McIlwaine, Roy Berger, Michel Basilières, Jacques Filippi, Peter Rozovsky, Keith Logan, Kristian Gravenor (his Coolopolis website is a great resource on Montreal), Kevin Burton Smith and everyone at ECW Press: Jack David, Kevin Connolly, Michael Holmes, Jen Knoch, Crissy Calhoun, Erin Creasey, David Caron and Jenna Illies.

And, of course, my wife, Laurie Reid.